CRIMSON FRIDAY

The gossips of Merristone have been having a field day since the reclusive Mrs. Moran moved to town with her near-deaf maid, Hannah Wilson. Mrs. Moran is seen every day covered in bright flowing gowns and walking her two cats. All everyone knows is that she used to be a famous harpist but she and her maid keep strictly to themselves. So Jane and Alan—renovating the house next to hers, and soon to be neighbors—are completely taken by surprise when Mrs. Moran invites them to tea.

Later that evening, Jane, Al and a few family members drive over to their new house—still under construction—to look at the blueprints. And to everyone's horror, they find Hannah at the foot of the cellar ladder, her head bashed in. Even more mysterious, someone has stolen their car keys so they can't go for the police. Now everyone is scrambling around trying to find a phone, and that's when they realize that the neighboring Mrs. Moran has completely disappeared. Could she have murdered her maid? Or is she a victim of the same killer?

**Dorothy Cameron Disney Bibliography
(1903-1992)**

Novels:
Death in the Back Seat (1936)
Strawstack (1939; reprinted as *The Strawstack Murders*, 1944)
The Golden Swan Murder (1939)
The Balcony (1940)
Thirty Days Hath September (1942; with George Sessions Perry)
Crimson Friday (1943)
The 17th Letter (1945)
Explosion (1948)
The Hangman's Tree (1949)

Short Story:
The Usual Three (*Cosmopolitan*, August 1939)

Crimson Friday

Dorothy Cameron Disney

Introduction by Curtis Evans

Stark House Press • Eureka California

CRIMSON FRIDAY

Published by Stark House Press
1315 H Street
Eureka, CA 95501, USA
griffinskye3@sbcglobal.net
www.starkhousepress.com

CRIMSON FRIDAY
Originally published by Random House, New York, and copyright © 1943
by Dorothy Cameron Disney. Reprinted in paperback by Dell Books,
New York, 1946. Magazine version published by *Woman's Home Companion*,
1942-1943.

"The Story Had Everything" © 2025 by Curtis Evans

ISBN: 979-8-88601-146-3

Text design by Mark Shepard, shepgraphics.com
Cover design by Jeff Vorzimmer, ¡caliente!design, Austin, Texas
Proofreading by Bill Kelly

First Stark House Press Edition: June 2025

"The Story Had Everything":
Dorothy Cameron Disney's Crimson Friday

by Curtis Evans

Although she never actually set one of her nine mystery novels in her native state, Dorothy Cameron Disney was born on Friday the thirteenth, November 1903 in Atoka, Oklahoma (then Indian Territory). The future crime author, who moved with her family from Atoka to Muscogee, Oklahoma when she was a child, was one of three children of Loren G. Disney and his wife Nettie Vansant. Loren G. Disney, known in Oklahoma as "Hell-roaring Disney" (his daughter Dorothy attested to the accuracy of this appellation), was a boisterous Oklahoma attorney, oil company promoter, "Rough Rider" in the Spanish-American War and noted player in progressive Republican politics, while Nettie was the daughter of a farmer from Topeka, Kansas and granddaughter of a blacksmith from Libertytown, Maryland. Loren, the natural son of an unwed mother from Alabama, had been adopted by Alfred Adolphus and Clara Arabelle Disney, the couple having concluded after five years of barren marriage that they were not going to be able to produce any children on their own. Instead, however, Clara gave birth to a boy one year after Loren's adoption, with four more children rapidly following in his wake. Bitterly Loren always felt that his adoptive parents—who never troubled to give him a full middle name, settling for an economical initial—were far more partial to their own blood children, deeming him an unfortunate miscalculation. This sort of unspoken inter-family cruelty and emotional deception had a way of making its way into the mystery novels of Loren's daughter Dorothy.

Dorothy Disney, along with her brothers Loren, Jr. and Stanley, grew up in happier circumstances. After graduating from Central High School in Muscogee in 1920 at the age of sixteen, the boldly outgoing Dorothy spent one year at Washburn College in Topeka, where she worked on the college newspaper, the *Washburn Review*. Then in 1923 she moved to Washington, D. C. to work as a clerk in the Justice Department's formidably titled Office of Alien Property Custodian. For three years she labored there while also attending classes in history, literature and theater at George Washington University under the distinguished and rather pretentiously handled professors Robert Whitney Bolwell, Elmer Louis Kayser and Dewitt Clinton Croissant (!); yet she never graduated from the college. Her son later stated that this was on account of her adamant refusal to enroll in any science classes. Dorothy later drolly recalled that she managed to pile up ninety-six hours in college English classes and zero in science and math. So much for the vaunted core curricula!

Six years after she left Washburn, an article in the *Review* vividly recalled Dorothy from her single, freshman year as a fearless, "most individualistic girl" of great talent but mercurial temperament. "There was one thing she could do and that was write," the article declared. "When it came to hunting up news she took her place as a man, and asked no odds because she wore dresses. And when she turned in the copy it was readable. Dorothy was active in politics, and particularly did she endeavor to help one of her girlfriends get selected to the place of editor of the *Review*. Dorothy alone almost carried the law school, but her friend lost the race. The next year she was not in Washburn."

It was in Washington that Dorothy first encountered native Iowa newspaperman Milton Angus MacKaye. A couple of years older than Dorothy, "Mac," as he was inevitably nicknamed, was then a staff writer with the *Washington Daily News*. His parents, Methodist minister Donald McKay and his wife Mary, were native Nova Scotians of Scots descent. Like a version of a rom-com "meet cute" scene in a Hallmark Christmas film, Dorothy and Mac had an acrimonious initial dustup, when as a judge in a newspaper competition Mac awarded Dorothy second prize. Dorothy, who stoutly insisted that she had deserved first place, indignantly refused friends' well-meant urging for her actually to meet her nemesis in person.

The same year Mac moved to New York City to take a position with the *New York Evening Post*. Dorothy herself relocated to New York 1926, settling among the Bohemians in Greenwich Village. In the Big Apple she attended classes at Barnard College and Columbia University and held a bewildering succession of jobs: "a stenographer in three New York publishing houses, a movie extra, a night-club hostess, an advertising copy writer, a companion to elderly women [and] a receptionist to a salesman of fraudulent stocks."

When Dorothy finally met Mac in person in New York, the pair, again like a couple in a rom-com film, decidedly hit it off. Together they compiled a party game book of word puzzles that had become a rage among the city's highbrow set. Drolly they entitled the book *Guggenheim*, ostensibly in (dis)honor of the city's reputed worst player of the game. The forward to *Guggenheim* was written by future Hollywood film director and producer Nunnally Johnson, then a colleague of MacKaye's at the *Post*. The book sold some two thousand copies in New York in its first week of publication in April 1927. Five months later twenty-three-year-old Dorothy wed Mack in Manhattan. A photo of Dorothy that appeared at the time in newspapers shows a pretty dark-eyed, cloche-hatted woman bearing a certain resemblance to a then-young contemporary writer, Eudora Welty.

The next year Mac, possibly reflecting Dorothy's influence, with Doubleday, Doran published the true crime book *Dramatic Crimes of 1927*, a complimentary annual offering to members of the publisher's newly launched Crime Club crime fiction imprint. Under an alias Dorothy herself began submitting fiction to magazines in 1929. Like her younger brothers Loren, Jr. and Stanley, she had long wanted to write, though belying her bravado had lacked confidence in her abilities. Many years later she credited her husband with much of her later success, modestly telling a newspaper interviewer of Mac in 1951: "He is my most severe critic, a wonderful editor, and he actually taught me how to spell."

During the 1930s the couple independently achieved popular success as magazine writers, Dorothy making a special home for her work under her own name at *Ladies Home Journal* and *Woman's Home Companion*, Mac at the *New Yorker*. Both authors also wrote for the high-profile *Saturday Evening Post*, where Mac produced a succession of lauded profiles of prominent people in politics. First Lady Eleanor Roosevelt once told him that he had written the best article she had read about her husband Franklin's presidential administration.

For several years in the Thirties Dorothy and Mac lived in the West Village with her handsome younger brother Loren G. Disney, Jr., or "Bud" as he was familiarly known, at a turn-of-the-century apartment building on 36 Charles Street. In New York in 1934 Dorothy, now thirty, bore her and Mac's only child, William Ross MacKaye. Her first novel, a mystery set in smalltown coastal Connecticut entitled *Death in the Back Seat*, came along two years later in 1936 and was received with rapturous applause by reviewers. That same year Bud, a writer with the *New York City News*, wed Mignon "Mike" Bushel, a Smith graduate and features writer with the *New York American*. The couple divorced within but a few years, with Bud becoming nothing more than a footnote and punchline in Mike's life. (He was no relation to Walt, she told her future sons.) Like Dorothy and Mac, Mike went on to enjoy a successful literary career culminating in several collections of prize aphorisms known as *The Neurotic's Notebooks*.

Meanwhile, the altogether more amicably wed Dorothy and Mac, with two successful careers now well-launched, having resolved to leave New York apartment life behind them, purchased two houses, their main neo-Georgian residence in Washington, D.C., and a summer home complete with working farm near the coastal Connecticut town of Guildford, a community which has been dubbed "the most charming place in Connecticut." In DC Billy MacKaye, or Bill as he was called when he was older, attended prestigious Sidwell Friends School while his parents kept up their steady flows of lucrative wordage. For four months of the year in Connecticut Dorothy diligently would rise every day at five a.m., pour herself a big cup of coffee and get to work in her latest novel with her pencil and tablet, leaving after three hours of work a mixture of shorthand and longhand scribblings for her secretary to decipher. In 1948, when Bill was fourteen, she freely admitted to neglecting her house "terribly" during those times: "I am not one of those who can run a house beautifully and write three hours a day."

Yet perhaps the give-and-take, with writing doing most of the taking, had become too much of a strain. Beginning with *Death in the Back Seat* in 1936, Dorothy over the next thirteen years published nine mystery novels, three of them set in Connecticut (*Seat, Thirty Days Hath September* and *Crimson Friday*), one in Washington, D. C. (*Explosion*), two in Maryland (*Strawstack* and *The Balcony*), one in Los Angeles (*The Golden Swan Murder*), one in Charleston (*The Hangman's Tree*), and one in Boston and Halifax (*The 17th Letter*). Four years after her final mystery appeared in 1949, Dorothy launched an advice column in *Ladies Home Journal* entitled "Can This Marriage Be Saved?" Helming it for more than three decades from the age of forty-nine into her early eighties, Dorothy became famed throughout the country for her marriage advice, based on the files of real-life couples counselling sessions. A few years after Mack died in 1979 at his and Dorothy's third home, their winter residence in Florida, Dorothy retired from the column, finally passing away in 1992 at the age of eighty-eight. Her ashes along with Mack's were interred next to a glacial rock under a maple tree which her mother Nettie had planted at the house in Guildford in 1950.

For years other, younger women, like syndicated columnist and author Suzanne Britt Jordan, wrote of their fond memories of Dorothy's marriage column, which they had read devotedly. Jordan remembered how as a pre-teen and teenager "I used to get myself a Coke, sling my leg over the arm of the wing chair in the living room and read Dorothy Cameron Disney's "Can This Marriage Be Saved?"—my favorite feature in my mother's *Ladies Home Journal*…. Usually the ending was not completely happy for either side [man or wife] …. the situation was not perfect, and nobody ever lived happily ever after. I loved those realistic endings."

Dorothy's *New York Times* obituary, which was carried all around the country, did not even mention her long-ago mystery writing, focusing instead on the social significance of her long-running marriage column. Dorothy and Mac themselves seem to have enjoyed uncommonly happy endings in their own marriage, as did their son, a newspaperman like his father and pillar of his progressive DC church who passed away in 2023 at the age of eighty-nine—all of which suggests that when it came to marriage advice Dorothy well knew of what she wrote. If anyone ever had it all, enjoying both professional success and a happy home life, it would seem to have been Dorothy Cameron Disney. Still, let us not forget the author's mystery fiction, where the endings, to be sure, were usually happy too—though not without tension, tears and considerable travail along the way.

□ □ □

By morning Merristone was to be famous. A missing harpist, dressed head to tow in crimson, her murdered servant found in the cellar of an unfinished house belonging to "a prominent young advertising executive"—the story had everything.

Crimson Friday, Dorothy Cameron Disney's sixth mystery novel, was published in June 1943 after the appearance of her hugely successful original quartet of criminous tales, *Death in the Back Seat, Strawstack, The Golden Swan Murder* and *The Balcony*, and *Thirty Days Hath September*, a collaboration with respected mainstream author George Sessions Perry. Like her previous works *Crimson Friday* was enthusiastically welcomed by newspaper reviewers. Some of the titles of the reviews betray their laudatory nature: "It's Hard to Stop Reading This Mystery" (Drexel Drake, *Chicago Tribune*), "Good Mystery" (J. L. Greenspan, *Brooklyn Citizen*), "The Mystery Was Just Too Good!" (T. F., *Akron Beacon Journal*).

T. F. avowed that the new novel was "the best mystery story" from the half-finished year and had left the baffled reviewer "in a rage at the way she carefully kept our mind away from the murderer." Greenspan agreed that the novel succeeded admirably as a fair play mystery story, but also added that "even if there were no murder in it at all, it would easily rest upon its merits of character and atmosphere as a sophisticated and ironical novel." Drexel Drake appreciatively noted the "steadily mounting apprehension" which the story induced in the transfixed reader, concluding that *Crimson Friday* was "[a]n immensely successful job of mystery writing and a brilliantly original story of murder."

More than one reviewer compared the novel's author to America's great mistress of mystery Mary Roberts Rinehart, and for good reason. Like Rinehart herself, Dorothy Disney was an adept at atmospheric plotting, what Rinehart herself called the technique of the "buried story." As Rinehart explained it, there were two carefully wrought story lines in her mystery novels, the visible, surface, seemingly placid one and the deadly, submerged, or buried, story, which only pops up occasionally, often in the form of some prelude to violent incident, like the periscope of a preying German U-Boat. Set in January 1941 as war raged in Europe and would soon engulf the United States, *Crimson Friday* is packed with mysterious, foreboding happenstance.

The novel concerns a nice young married couple rather like Dorothy and Mac: narrator Janey Blake and her New York advertising executive husband Al, who as their new residence are restoring—rather in the manner of the nice couple in the 1940 stage comedy *George Washington Slept Here* (filmed in 1942)—an old colonial home in Al's native Connecticut hometown of Merristone. Here also reside Al's elder brother Selby and Selby's wife Ruth; Ruth's widowed architect father Belton Weaver; and Al's and Selby's peppery aunt Mildred Havens and her daughter Sarah, a "spinster" of thirty (!)—though thirty-seven-year-old bachelor Frank Phipps, Al's self-made senior partner, has evinced some interest in her, in spite of her "advanced" age.

Into staid Merristone has come an exotic, alien presence: one Mrs. V. Moran, a reclusive, retired concert harpist who eccentrically dresses in brightly colored veils and dresses—a different color for each day—

when she takes her two pet cats for walks. No one has actually ever been invited into the home of Mrs. Moran, who is attended only by her forbidding, hard-of-hearing maid, Hannah Wilson, and town gossips are simply agog with curiosity. Soon the gossips—and everyone else in the town—find that there is more mystery to derive from the odd doings of this weird couple than they ever imagined! When Hannah is found viciously battered to death in the cellar of Janey's and Alan's house with Mrs. Moran vanished seemingly without a trace, official suspicion initially alights on the mysterious missing harpist; but as crazy, sinister happenings pile up and up and up, it starts to seem in this masterly mystery concoction that culpability might lie within Janey's and Alan's own intimate circle of family and friends.

With the appearance of *Crimson Friday*, Dorothy Cameron Disney had published six mystery novels in seven years. Arguably the novel was one of the high achievements of Mary Roberts Rinehart's genteel domestic anxiety mystery school, which was finally beginning, after many years, to close down, transforming into the more democratic, postwar, mid-century novel of domestic psychological suspense. Dorothy Disney herself would publish only three more mystery novels: *The 17th Letter*, a tale of World War Two espionage reprinted last year by Stark House; *Explosion*, a deliberately drab though penetrating social realism mystery; and *The Hangman's Tree*, a postwar attempt to return to the old classic form, though it was not a patch on *Crimson Friday*.

—March 2025
Memphis, Tennessee

....

Curtis Evans received a PhD in American history in 1998. He is the author of *Masters of the "Humdrum" Mystery: Cecil John Charles Street, Freeman Wills Crofts, Alfred Walter Stewart and British Detective Fiction, 1920-1961* (2012), *Clues and Corpses: The Detective Fiction and Mystery Criticism of Todd Downing* (2013), *The Spectrum of English Murder: The Detective Fiction of Henry Lancelot Aubrey-Fletcher and G. D. H. and Margaret Cole* (2015) and editor of the Edgar nominated *Murder in the Closet: Essays on Queer Clues in Crime Fiction Before Stonewall* (2017). He writes about vintage crime fiction at his blog The Passing Tramp and at Crimereads.

Crimson Friday

Dorothy Cameron Disney

Chapter One:
THE ENIGMA OF A WOMAN

Long before Al and I first laid eyes on her, we referred to Mrs. V. Moran as the Merristone Enigma. After a residence of a year, the village had been unable to discover so much as Mrs. Moran's first name. The provocative initial on her mailbox remained unsolved. In a place like Merristone, in a place where both Harriet Strings and Al's Aunt Mildred resided, that amounted to a miracle.

Mrs. Moran occupied a furnished house, rented from the local bank. It was reported that she'd paid a full year's rent in advance, thus obviating references, and that she'd brought with her an elderly maid as close-mouthed as herself. It was known that the stranger owned two alley cats and that she walked them on a double leash like well-trained dogs—an eccentricity calculated to arouse curiosity anywhere. I was anxious to see this spectacle myself, and whenever Al and I were on Copston Road, which was frequently, I kept out a weather eye. Her house was located on that winding country lane, a wide field away from where we ourselves were building. I was well aware that Mrs. Moran walked only on Copston Road. At least twenty people told me.

In the period of a year Mrs. Moran had not once appeared in the shopping section. She wasn't seen at the movies, in the little steepled church, at the bank, or at the bingo games held on Wednesday nights. Extremely odd, the village felt, and remarked with monotonous regularity. No one called on her either, they complained.

The Moran house was cloaked with heavy draperies, and the draperies were always carefully drawn. Occasionally, working around the premises, Al and I glimpsed the lantern-jawed, bespectacled maid, who had been such a trial to village gossips. Hannah would give us a cold, uninviting stare and grimly continue burning trash or hauling garbage to the dump. I didn't wonder she had baffled the craftiest investigators.

It was public knowledge that Hannah climbed into a battered car every morning at 9:30 and drove downtown to do the marketing and necessary errands. Many had arranged their own plans accordingly— but all in vain. Hannah was equipped with a conspicuous earphone. The earphone had defeated Merristone. The maid either didn't hear "tactful" inquiries about her mistress, or didn't choose to hear them.

Cold, blank eyes, screened by the thick spectacles, looked straight through the most determined interrogator. The village had been tantalized to learn that Mrs. Moran spent twice as much on groceries as the ordinary family, but most people would have preferred to hear the exact amount and source of her income. What they particularly longed to know was where Mrs. Moran and Hannah had come from, and why they had settled in Merristone. What did the maid and mistress talk about during the long winter evenings? Why did they never drive downtown together? No one could find out.

It was Frank Phipps, my husband's partner, who insisted the Merristone Enigma had mastered the whole technique of modern advertising. With a minimum of effort, she aroused interest and maintained it. The less the villagers learned about Mrs. Moran and her forbidding Hannah, the more they craved to know.

Our own affairs—Al's and mine—were an open book, of course. Everybody knew why we had come to Merristone, or, in Al's case, returned. The Phipps-Blake Advertising Agency was located in New York. It would have been much more sensible for us to remain comfortably in our town apartment, within walking distance of the office. Frank remarked on this more than once.

Merristone was some miles beyond the usual commuting distance, but it was my husband's boyhood home. All his family that mattered, with the notable exception of his Cousin Sarah, still resided there. Sarah, of course, was like Al's own sister. He and his older brother had been orphaned early, and had grown up with their cousin under Aunt Mildred's alert and watchful eye. Al and Selby had been her boys since they were toddlers, and hers alone. No Uncle Ned figured in the picture; as Aunt Mildred euphemistically put it: "Ned Havens is dead to the Blakes." By this she meant that five short years of marriage had been the limit of the outsider's endurance. I myself had certain initial misgivings about moving from the city into the close-knit family community of Merristone.

However, when Al's brother found us a perfect old New England house—perfect, that is, if we remodeled from top to bottom—we bought it. I suppose Selby was fascinated by the modesty of the original price, but then so were Al and I.

All my doubts vanished when I first saw the house, along with my good common sense.

In our innocence, Al and I expected our dream cottage to grow a new wing and acquire a bathroom as painlessly as an expanding flower, and even to cost less than we had planned. The village chuckled happily over that. Everybody knew the instant we applied for a second mortgage. It would have been surprising if they hadn't.

We were living with Aunt Mildred, during the frenetic period of remodeling, and I should make clear at once that Al's Aunt Mildred both collected information and dispensed it. Sarah had moved into New York long before we bought our cottage, "to get away from Mama's consuming interest in my activities," and she'd once complained to me, in all seriousness, that her mother wouldn't even let her brush her teeth in privacy, or entertain a beau until the neighbors had been properly advised. I know that Cousin Sarah viewed our living arrangements with keen foreboding.

"You'd better stay in town until your own place is ready. Mama's the oddest mixture. She'll work her fingers to the bone to make you comfortable, and work her tongue twice as hard to wreck your privacy." Sarah's warning had turned out to be correct. Aunt Mildred cooked us wonderful meals, mended my stockings and Al's shirts, but also kept a sharp eye on our mail and a keener eye on all our telephone calls. At least twice a day, she and Harriet Strings got on the wire and briskly traded local news bulletins.

In consequence the village kept in close and constant touch with our affairs, particularly concerning our difficulties with the remodeling venture. Complete outsiders had many an evening's entertainment relating tales of the Homeric battles between our architect and our builder. From the beginning Mr. Thirkle and Belton Weaver used our precious cottage to carry on an unceasing war—one of those wars immediately understood by anyone who has modernized an ancient house with the assistance of an architect and a builder who agree on nothing.

Belton Weaver, our architect, was vaguely in the family—a fact which considerably increased the delicacy of Al's position and mine. Selby was married to Belton's only daughter. Actually it was mostly because of Ruth and Selby that I had been willing to give up our New York apartment and locate in the country. I adored them both, and, as Al had observed in answer to Frank's loud laments, "My brother Selby is a left-handed Thoreau. Being convinced that all of life is contained in Merristone, he likes to stay there." Certainly Selby had seldom been induced to visit us in the city. With perfect content my brother-in-law at the age of 29 conducted a small insurance business on the village square, spent leisurely hours with the most unlikely prospect, and ignored the fact that he could have done much better elsewhere. Money wasn't everything, he said. Sarah's and Al's enthusiasm for New York baffled him.

"What's New York got that Merristone hasn't?"

"It hasn't got Aunt Mildred," I said meekly.

Selby had to laugh at that. But he wasn't at all amused by our chronic worries over our building project. Because he'd chosen the cottage, and was Selby, he felt responsible. Besides, Belton Weaver was his father-in-law.

Belton probably knew more about old New England houses—and our cottage was built in 1790—than anybody in New England. To be strictly frank, however, I often wondered whether Belton didn't know a shade too much about the 17th and 18th centuries and too little about what fine old floors and handmade hardware cost. When a hand-wrought hinge or lovely piece of oak caught his eye, it seldom occurred to Belton to inquire into the price. Mr. Thirkle was his direct antithesis. Where Belton favored beauty and authenticity, our sad-eyed builder stubbornly favored practicality and thrift, and, on most occasions—doubtful taste. Trouble ensued every time the two men met.

"Catching Jane and me squarely in the middle," Al once said, in his sister-in-law's hearing.

Ruth loved her father, but she understood him. "Take care you stay in the middle. Dad's wonderful on design, but somewhat hazy on modern conveniences. And cost sheets baffle him."

"Don't we know!" groaned Al, and added philosophically, "Once you get used to it, they tell me bankruptcy's not so bad. Last month's bill certainly brought it closer."

I saw Selby's thin, fine-drawn face darken. It was a clear fall day, and we were sitting outside on Aunt Mildred's steps. As I recall, Selby was leaning on his cherished blackthorn stick. He dug up a piece of dried, dead turf and carefully replaced it. Suddenly I realized that my brother-in-law had taken Al's lamentations about our financial situation seriously.

"Maybe I can help," he said slowly. "That is, if you badly need it, and let me have a little time."

Al flushed. He'd been half clowning; we really had sufficient cash to see the cottage through, and every one of us knew that Selby was in no position to give anybody financial help.

Ruth sent me a quick proud look to prove that she for one believed in the validity of the offer.

"You can give Al your stick when you get tired of it," I said, feebly attempting to recapture the tone of badinage. "He claimed this morning it would be just the thing to beat me properly."

It wasn't very good, but good enough to get a laugh. Selby's stick had been his great-grandfather's, and he'd inherited it because he was the oldest Blake. It was a handsome stick but cumbersome to carry, and Selby valued it out of all proportion to its intrinsic worth.

"He'd rather give you me," said Ruth. She leaned her fair head against his knee, and her blue eyes brightened as she straightened up to ask, "Is Sarah coming up this weekend?"

I nodded.

"Frank bringing her?"

Again I nodded, and we forgot the men as we exchanged a feminine, conspiratorial glance. Frank Phipps despised the country and old New England houses, but he'd brought Sarah to Merristone three weekends running now. Ruth and I had secret romantic hopes for Frank and Sarah. Frank Phipps might be my husband's partner and devoted friend, but I'd been happy to deprive him of the comforts of our town apartment, of those long, lazy evenings when he'd sat and talked about himself and the horrors of domesticity.

"What are you two giggling over?" Al inquired.

"We're planning the weekend."

"Sarah's birthday falls on Saturday," Ruth said suddenly. "We'll have to keep Aunt Mildred from whipping up a cake, and trotting out the candles."

"That defeats me," said Al, and he and Selby looked at each other in masculine bewilderment. "Why deprive poor Sarah of a celebration?"

Ruth did not reply. But we two knew the answer. Suddenly, with a little shock, it had struck us both that on Saturday Sarah would be 30—six years older than Ruth, five years older than myself. Of course Frank was 37, but age doesn't matter with a man. Sarah had been Frank's favorite girl, and no more than that, for three long years. "Lots of women marry late," Ruth remarked.

"What women?" asked Selby, hopelessly confused. "What women are you talking about?"

"Women in general," Ruth replied with dignity. "Women and men, too. Those that marry late."

Al gave me a rather thoughtful look, as we followed them to their car. Today, months afterward, I can distinctly recall the four of us crossing the yard in the autumn sunlight. Probably because it was one of the last times Ruth and I linked arms, put our heads together and giggled over small happy things like planning to marry Sarah off to an unsuspecting bachelor.

In a sense, it seems to me that Sarah's birthday marked the beginning of our tragedies.

The murder did not occur until some weeks later, but it was on Sarah's birthday—November 3rd—that I first saw Mrs. V. Moran.

Chapter Two:
ALL THE COLORS OF THE RAINBOW

Fall is a variable, uncertain season in Merristone. November 3rd was a wind-whipped, disagreeable day, gray as steel. Ruth and Selby had promised to drop by in the afternoon for cocktails in Sarah's honor. As I recall I spent the morning preparing canapes, while Aunt Mildred occupied herself with the construction of an enormous birthday cake. Naturally I'd lost that particular argument. Frank and Sarah arrived from the city in time for luncheon and the cake.

Sarah looked tired and worn at the festive table, and only pretended to gaiety. She was tall and handsome, with the dark vivid coloring of the Blakes, and I often wished that she would let me choose her clothes. For a car trip of 40 miles, Al's cousin generally got into a rig that would have carried her safely through the heart of Africa: brogues, a heavy skirt and flannel shirt that required no pressing ever. An expert chemist by profession, Sarah didn't seem to realize she didn't need to dress the part. Frank and Al had both been working hard that week— November was always their busiest month—and Frank looked tired himself. Like most apartment dwellers, he preferred the country in the summertime, though he made brave efforts to pretend that he'd enjoyed the drive and wouldn't have stayed in town for anything. Everybody present, except possibly Aunt Mildred, knew how reluctantly he'd torn himself away from the joys of his piled-up desk.

Luncheon was an ordeal, and sticks in my memory because of the foolish lighted cake and Aunt Mildred's determined conversational excursions into everybody's privacy, particularly her daughter's. Directly afterward Sarah went upstairs, and did not come down. Aunt Mildred gazed toward the stairs for fifteen minutes, and then, the light of conviction in her eye, she rose. "Something's wrong with Sarah. Surely you noticed, Mr. Phipps? She hardly touched her food."

"You sit down," I said hastily. "We're walking to the building site, aren't we, Al? It's a good afternoon for a walk, and we'll be back in time for Ruth and Selby. I'll get Sarah."

A moment later I was rapping at her door. Sarah's voice was muffled. "Please go away, Mother. I've got a headache."

"It's me. Janey. Do let me in, dear. We thought we'd walk to the cottage.

You haven't been there lately."

Sarah's step was slow, reluctant, but she admitted me. Her eyes were red.

"Come on down, Sarah," I said, pretending not to notice. "We need you."

"Frank doesn't."

"Of course he does!" And then I had to add, "What is it, dear? Did you quarrel on the way up?"

"We didn't quarrel. We never quarrel. Sometimes I almost wish we would. But for forty miles Frank talked steadily about his work and—"

"His work is important to him, dear," I said slowly.

It wasn't my concern, but it did seem to me that the Phipps-Blake agency loomed disproportionately large in Frank's mind; that like many self-made men he was inclined to use his business as a substitute for a warm and satisfying personal life. He deserved something better, and so did Sarah. Or such was my opinion.

Suddenly, in clumsy haste, Sarah moved toward the dresser. "You haven't seen Frank's present, Janey. What do you think of it?"

With that, she exhibited a gold and chip diamond vanity case. The bauble was exquisite; Frank had studied long and hard before he selected the shape, the size, the delicate monogram. It was a perfect gift for a man's favorite girl, lovely, expensive—completely noncommittal.

"Look, darling," I said carefully. "Frank hasn't wit enough to know what he really wants. He talks and acts like all bachelors. You have to—to wake him up."

"I don't know how," Sarah said. Her eyes filled with tears, as she laid down the lovely vanity case. She tried to blink the tears away. "I'm just like Mother, Janey. She managed to get married, but that was finished with before I was six years old. We're born old maids, both of us. I wish you'd tell me why. What's wrong with me?"

I stared at her helplessly. Sarah knew lots of things, but nothing useful to an unmarried woman who'd just left behind her hardworking, unexciting twenties. What she needed was coquetry and mystery, and a much larger share of plain female vanity.

"Except for Selby and Alan," she went on drearily, "men baffle me. Even my own cousins sometimes do, though I grew up with them. I—I try to be a friend to Frank."

Part of her difficulty lay right there. After we moved out from town, Frank, who had his own moments of loneliness, had begun to depend on Sarah, but I felt sure she'd let him know immediately that she was always available in her apartment, waiting patiently at the telephone. I opened my mouth to give a little lecture, as Al started shouting from the stairs.

I ran into our room, and seized my brightest lipstick. Two minutes' work with lipstick and powder brought out the gypsy look that made Sarah exciting and attractive. I made her take off her shell-rimmed spectacles, change into a pair of my favorite slacks and discard the brogues for wedgies. Frank's face lit with pleasure and surprise when we appeared.

"So that explains the delay. Tricky get-up, Sarah. Did Janey suggest it?"

"Certainly not," I said.

Sarah looked confounded. "Why, Janey, of course you did! All these clothes are yours, except my underwear. And I really need my glasses."

"A marked improvement, anyhow," said Frank, as he ruffled Sarah's short-cropped hair, and sent me a look of quiet understanding.

I've forgotten most of the details of the stroll to the cottage, and our inspection of the new wing which was tediously rising from a mound of ugly, prodigiously expensive fill. I believe I'd hoped to impress Frank with the forthcoming beauties of our home and the solid satisfaction of settling down—a vain hope indeed. The cottage, all litter and confusion, was at its worst. Driven by Mr. Thirkle, several workmen were hammering briskly, apparently accomplishing nothing. The sunless, dirty-colored day, the sodden fields around, didn't help the picture.

I must say Frank did his best, and valiantly professed to find virtues in the house. He stumbled through the debris of the new dining room, peered admiringly at several dismantled fireplaces, gravely inspected the space that was to be a bathroom, and insisted everything was charming.

"I mean it, children, really. Here and now," he said, "Sarah and I enter our claim to your guest rooms. Don't we, Sally? You two may have to take us city dwellers in as permanent guests, if taxes get much worse."

And then he smiled twinkingly at Sarah. I know he only meant to be helpful, but I was annoyed. The guest rooms hadn't even walls as yet.

"Why don't you city dwellers buy yourselves?" I said tartly. "I'll guarantee to find a house big enough for two. It's high time—"

I stopped right there, but Sarah had gone a furious red and Al's outraged glance indicated we would have a discussion later. Nothing irked him more than to have me meddle in his partner's private life. Because Frank had founded the firm and asked him to join it, Al stood a little in awe of the senior partner—a thing I never did. As we left the cottage Frank hung back to speak to me. He didn't seem annoyed. On the contrary.

"Sometimes, Janey dear," he said, "you're awfully wise for a gal of tender years. You're sweet and lucky people, you and Al. Luckier than you know. Your home, your family—stick to them, lady. Living around the way I do in apartments and hotels—well, it isn't always pleasant."

It entered my head that he could change his arrangements any moment that he chose, but I kept discreetly silent. He gave me a sidewise glance.

"Really, Jane, I'm serious for once. Maybe I'm feeling envious. No one, and this is God's own truth, ever cared for me."

"Sarah does," I said snappishly.

"Sarah?"

"Exactly."

"I'm not good enough for Sarah. Not half good enough. And that's true, too."

Well, I was not impressed. I'd heard that kind of talk before from bachelors, shying off from the responsibilities of marriage. If Frank had any important faults, Al and I would have been aware of them. If he were referring to his lack of family and background, Sarah certainly had enough for two. Before I had a chance to express my sentiments, he left me quickly, and strode on to catch up with Sarah. I recall the incident in such detail, because it was almost immediately afterward that we encountered Mrs. V. Moran. We were hurrying home along Copston Road when we met her.

Sarah spied her first. She took a backward step. "Good heavens! Who's that?"

"It's the mysterious Mrs. Moran in person," Al said, looking a little startled himself. The stranger was visible from a considerable distance and walking slowly toward us. "Meet our next-door neighbor, Frank. It's a pity Aunt Mildred isn't with us."

Mrs. Moran was in green from head to foot. Her gown was vaguely Grecian, vaguely Turkish, a floating, diaphanous affair of a type and cut fashionable among "artistic" circles during the Isadora Duncan era. A veil, as green as the dress and almost as unsuitable for country wear, was wound turban-wise around a mop of dyed black hair. Another veil, splashed with tremendous green spots, revealed a thickly powdered, painted face, and huge dark eyes.

She had her two cats in tow—one black and the other white. They wore red-leather collars, and they solemnly preceded their mistress on a crimson leash. I no longer wondered that Merristone was fascinated. Teetering on four-inch heels along a country road, accompanied by the plump and patient cats, Mrs. Moran was definitely a sensation.

"In that rig," said Frank in an astounded whisper, "your neighbor would stop Broadway traffic. She's certainly wasted here."

"Be quiet. She'll hear you."

But Mrs. Moran seemed to be oblivious of the effect she was creating. The dark eyes regarded us through the spotted veil, the cats tugged on their leash, and without a word she passed by. I restrained myself until she was safely out of earshot, and then I clutched Al's arm.

"I believe she's foreign. French or something."

"She was covered up with paint, if that's what you mean," said Al judiciously. "And her hair was dyed. You sound a bit like Harriet, my love. How did the Merristone Enigma strike you, Frank?"

Frank had paused to look back. The merriment faded from his eyes. "To tell the truth," he said uncomfortably, "I've changed my mind. It strikes me the dame isn't very funny. Is she, Janey?"

I turned, too, and saw that Mrs. Moran had also turned. Indeed, she had paused, and was staring rather wistfully after us. In the empty, twilit landscape she looked fantastic and absurd, but not very young or confident or happy. Instinctively I raised my hand to wave. She hesitated, looked me straight in the eye, turned on her heel and was gone. I was somewhat taken aback.

Al was distinctly annoyed. "I do wish you'd be less impulsive, Janey. You let yourself in for that."

I said slowly, "I believe she wanted to wave back."

"Nonsense! You and Frank should consult an oculist. Maybe I'm a hard-hearted wretch, but I can still see well enough to recognize an obvious phony. And to identify an outright cut. She's as disagreeable and unfriendly as that maid of hers. Those women make me sore."

"On third thought," said Frank, "I believe you're right. Suppose we make up a small committee to send your neighbors back where they came from."

Al grinned reluctantly. Any slight to me, fancied or otherwise, always made him furious.

"Don't you ever speak to the maid?" asked Sarah. "I should think it might be awkward, passing every day. Mother said you'd seen her often."

"Never," Al replied with renewed energy. "Hannah looks straight through us, and we look straight through her. Or Janey does. I avert my eyes. One look at Hannah hanging out the wash can spoil my week."

"It seems odd to me," said Sarah thoughtfully.

"What seems odd, for heaven's sake?"

"If Mrs. Moran really wants to avoid attention, why does she dress like that and walk out in public with those cats?"

I thought that was pretty smart of Sarah. The minute we reached home, where we found Ruth and Selby awaiting us at the cocktail shaker, I brought up the encounter on Copston Road. Belton had dropped in too; we'd missed him at the building site. Aunt Mildred immediately forgot that she wasn't especially fond of Selby's father-in-law and disapproved in principle of martinis. She became bright-eyed and alert.

"You say she had on the green? You should see her other clothes! Outlandish, that's the word for them. According to Harriet, Mrs. Moran wears every color of the rainbow. Purple, orange, yellow—even to the hats and shoes. She doesn't mix the colors either, like any Christian woman."

I choked on my canape. Harriet was well qualified to disseminate the details of Mrs. Moran's surprising wardrobe. The Strings' house was also on Copston Road, and the moment her husband left for work Harriet rushed to the window and stood patient watch. It was reliably reported that she didn't even wash her breakfast dishes until she saw Mrs. Moran safely past on her daily constitutional.

"It's ridiculous," Aunt Mildred said, and bit fretfully into a hard-boiled egg. "Ridiculous. Do you realize Mrs. Moran has been here a full year now, and actually no one knows why she came or where she came from?"

"I believe you've mentioned it before. Once or maybe twice," Al said dryly, but she didn't hear him. Eyes narrowed, she was staring into space.

"Where there's smoke there's fire. That woman's so secretive, she must be hiding something. And the maid's helping her. Mark my words, there's something wrong about that pair."

"What, for instance?"

"Something. I can feel it in my bones, Alan. My bones don't lie to me."

A lengthy discussion followed, in which Aunt Mildred carried the major burden. She postulated a dozen theories completely absurd, most of them born of her own grievance. Aunt Mildred's bones always reacted unfavorably to other people's reticences. I listened with only half an ear, though I was amused by Belton's unsuccessful efforts to turn the conversation to architecture. He and Aunt Mildred were always at cross-purposes, like two trains going in opposite directions. Aunt Mildred stuck stubbornly to Mrs. V. Moran, and as usual she carried the day.

I noticed that Selby was taking no part in the talk, and l leaned over to him. "Bored?"

"Not exactly. I just wish Aunt Mildred would stop." His stick was tilted against his chair. In a familiar gesture his long, slender hand reached out to finger the satiny wood. "I don't know, Janey, but suddenly I had a rather odd idea. About all this talk—and about curiosity."

I waited.

"I was thinking," said Selby slowly, "that sometimes hidden things are better left alone.... You never met great-grandfather Blake, did you?"

Since great-grandfather Blake had died when Al was only two and I was reposing in an Ohio cradle, I judged the question to be rhetorical. I looked at my brother-in-law in surprise. For some reason, Selby had suddenly assumed the queer, apprehensive expression of those who claim, only half-humorously, that someone is walking over their grave. I expected him to smile and shrug, as people will at such times.

Instead he said, "The old gentleman was a great storyteller. I was remembering the day he told me about Pandora's box."

I was familiar with the childhood tale of the little girl who opened a forbidden box and unloosed a flood of furies on the world. I started to laugh, and then I didn't.

"Curiosity has a special malice all its own, Janey," Selby said. "I truly believe that. Curiosity has a spiteful way of turning back on the curious. Hidden things are better left alone."

There was a sudden silence. I could have sworn that Selby's queer discomfort had spread until it included all of us. It seemed to me that Ruth went a little pale. Belton frowned, and reached out to touch his daughter's hand. Frank slowly set down his cocktail glass, and looked at Sarah. They felt it, too—the inexplicable, the heavy sense of apprehensiveness, almost of waiting, that gripped the room, as though a distant storm was drawing nearer. Al stopped in the middle of a sentence. Even Aunt Mildred was hushed. Then she got up noisily to fetch a fresh supply of sandwiches, and at the same time managed to knock over Selby's cane. The heavy metal head struck and chipped one of her pressed-glass plates. In the ensuing effort to fix responsibility—

Aunt Mildred held herself quite blameless—the moment passed.

I told myself it had not existed. Mrs. Moran was a total stranger. What did she have to do with us? If Mrs. Moran had a secret, she could keep it. The key to her forbidden box was in safe hands.

It was on January 17th that she invited Al and me to tea.

Chapter Three:
THE FORCE OF CURIOSITY

Before the 17th of January, we passed Mrs. Moran many times on Copston Road—so many times indeed that we should have become used to her. Clad in her fantastic garb, accompanied by her cats, our future neighbor became an almost familiar figure, but I never saw her without a shock of surprise, or grew accustomed to the floating veils, the dizzying succession of rainbow hues. Mrs. Moran stuck to a single style and a single garish color for each appearance, until I wondered whether there wasn't a puzzling consistency in the outrageous wardrobe.

We never spoke. Sometimes though, in spite of Al, I'd catch her eye and nod. From the beginning I felt sure she hadn't meant to cut me, and I was right. She'd hesitantly nod back, and then hurry past on her solitary winter walk. I wondered that she never took her maid along, and wondered, too, about the rumors that ran through the village. People whispered that a curious relationship existed between maid and mistress, that Hannah was no ordinary servant. Some came out flatly with the opinion that the pair hated one another. Why, in that case, they stayed together was left to one's imagination.

For the most part, I must admit my thoughts and energies were spent upon our cottage. We'd optimistically expected to be in possession by Christmas, but at Christmas time we were being introduced to the long-drawn-out process for some reason called "inside finishing." From our experiences "inside finishing" is just another beginning. After the holidays, Al, in desperation, arranged with Frank for a six weeks' leave of absence from the firm. By staying on the spot he fancied he could hasten proceedings, and arbitrate the endless disputes. We put in every afternoon at the building site.

January 17th started badly. In the first place Belton and Mr. Thirkle telephoned before eight o'clock, each to complain about the other. Their immediate difference concerned the stairway, and both men wanted a definite and entirely opposite decision before five o'clock.

In the second place, Aunt Mildred woke with a mild attack of her neuralgia and a recollection that Sarah and Frank were coming for the weekend. It was an extremely awkward day, she remarked, for her to be forced to take to bed. We both clearly understood she wouldn't stay in bed. Torture couldn't have held her there, when the downstairs floor was filled with people and excitement.

She followed me into the kitchen and sat down to nurse her jaw, while I started breakfast. Presently she dropped her complaints to observe that milk was every bit as good in scrambled eggs as cream, and much more economical. Plain tap water, she added, would serve the purpose almost as well. A wonderful cook herself, Aunt Mildred sometimes had those spasms of economy when I was at the helm. To please her I compromised with milk. When I carried the eggs to the stove, I found she'd thoughtfully turned off the gas.

By early afternoon Aunt Mildred's jaw had improved, and she was able to annoy me by asking innocently what we'd decided to do about the stairway.

"Nothing as yet," I said. "Mr. Thirkle wants us to choose a little number from a builders' catalogue, and Belton prefers something more artistic. I do myself."

"Oh, God, the stairway!" said Al. "I remember the good old days when I used to think stairs were what you went up and down on. Merely that and nothing more."

"You've got to select them first," I said unsympathetically. "What did you think of Belton's detail drawing? Remind me to take my blueprints to the cottage, in case we do want changes. Personally I like Belton's staircase as it stands."

"Looks expensive," Al said cautiously.

"Probably inlaid with diamonds, if Belton gets his way," Aunt Mildred commented helpfully. "More of that old wormy wood, no doubt, that you're putting in everywhere. If I'd known people were as crazy as they are, I'd never in this world have traded my old floors here for new. I'd have torn them up myself, and held an auction."

It was a frequent regret of hers. Al didn't smile as he usually did.

"I was talking to Mr. Thirkle," continued Aunt Mildred in her cheery vein, "and he was sick, sick about the expense. You'd better listen to some of his ideas. Might not be so pretty, but Mr. Thirkle's got some sense of money. That cottage will have you in the poorhouse yet."

We were sitting in Aunt Mildred's dining room, with the brand-new parquet floors and the machine-made carpet. Hung over the fireplace was the hideous, real oil portrait of Uncle Ned that at once convinced most observers he'd been dead for years. Uncle Ned had vanished from Merristone at least two decades before I appeared on the scene, but sometimes I felt very close to him and understood precisely why the mustachioed gentleman had made different plans in life. This was such an occasion.

Al gloomily pushed back his chair. "Before we go off to battle, Jane, did you remember to tell Aunt Mildred that we've invited Ruth and Selby to supper? Belton, too."

I hadn't remembered, but Aunt Mildred, who'd spent the morning hovering in the vicinity of the telephone, was suspiciously unsurprised. She brightened. Belton was no enthusiasm of hers, but she loved a party. She hesitated, said suddenly, "Look, children! I'd like to buy the steak."

For some absurd reason that touched me. It was so wholly in character. I leaned over and dropped a kiss on the top of her iron-gray head. "Certainly not! They're our guests, and so are you. And I hope you wear your blue. It does so much for your eyes."

Aunt Mildred colored. Her skin was lined but very fine, and for a moment she looked confused and shy, almost young. Gestures of affection came hard to her. She patted my hand in her stiff and funny way.

"You're a good girl, Jane, and you've been a good wife to Alan. Have your house the way you want it. Pay no mind to me. Alan never had a red cent till he met you, no matter how I jawed at him. I guess you know what you're doing."

"Hear, hear!" cried Al, enormously relieved.

Shortly afterward, we started toward the building site and my spirits lifted. For one thing, I knew Al was pleased with me. I could tell it by the way he held my mittened hand and matched his step to mine, as we strode along Copston Road. We always walked the two miles from Aunt Mildred's to the cottage, but that day we went at a breakneck pace. It was extremely cold.

"You're a nice wife, Janey," Al said. "Sometimes I'm awfully glad I've got you."

"Silly," I said, and stood on tiptoe. Al stooped down and planted a chilly kiss upon my ear.

Simultaneously we heard a violent rapping on a window pane. Without realizing it, we had paused in the middle of the road directly opposite the Strings'. Stationed at her usual watching post, Harriet had watched us play our little scene with great delight. She seized up an Afghan, flung it around her scrawny shoulders, and an instant later appeared on her porch.

"You two looked so sweet," she twittered. "Like honeymooners. It's been three years, hasn't it? And such a cold day, too. I must tell Tully when he comes home tonight. My dear husband's so undemonstrative. How's Mildred's neuralgia?"

"Better," I said briefly.

"Now don't go rushing off. I haven't seen a soul all afternoon." With that introduction, blandly oblivious of Al's impatience and the freezing air, she launched into her favorite topic—viz., Mrs. V. Moran. A pleased gleam came into her eye. "You might mention it to Mildred," she began impressively. "Evidently our neighbor up the road is musical. Mrs. Moran, I mean. She's bought herself a piano. I had it straight from my egg man."

Al didn't look impressed; he only looked confused.

"The egg man is the express agent's brother," Harriet explained, between the chattering of her teeth. "The crate arrived from New York yesterday on the late evening train. An upright, the egg man said. He saw the crate at the station."

I was looking straight at Harriet, and I had an impression that she was about to add something more. She hesitated—a rare thing with her.

At that point Al broke in with a sudden explosive chuckle. "Mrs. Moran may be musical," he said, "but your egg man and his brother aren't. As it happens I saw the crate myself. It isn't a piano, Harriet. It's a concert harp."

"A harp!" cried Harriet.

Al was already striding up the bleak and frozen road. I overtook him.

"You made that up," I said.

"As a matter of fact, I didn't. I picked up our papers at the station this morning. I'd simply forgotten the three-sided crate, and the express agent's pother. It's all quite true. Mrs. V. Moran is musical, and she's bought herself a harp, and what of it, say I."

"But what would she want with a *harp?*"

"Maybe she means to play it," Al suggested.

He didn't even glance up as we neared the small frame house where Mrs. Moran had lived in absolute seclusion for a period of sixteen months. Snow was long overdue, and without the white protective cover the house looked shrunken and ugly against the winter landscape. The curtained windows were cold, unfriendly—secretive.

A plume of smoke ascended from the chimney, rose almost vertically in the chill, unstirring air. Otherwise the dwelling had an air of complete desertion. Then, in the barren backyard, I glimpsed the maid's scarecrow figure. Around the house Hannah evidently was obliged to wear frilly, musical-comedy uniforms of taffeta and organdy, but when she stepped outside she covered up her shame with a heavy overcoat cut like Al's. She wore shoes as large and clumsy as his, and a man's hat was jammed unbecomingly upon straggling locks of thin gray hair. She was hanging out clothes that were frozen stiff before they reached the line.

Naturally we did not intend to speak. I couldn't believe my ears when someone called our name, or my eyes, when I saw Hannah drop her basket and start loping toward as. She reached the road.

"Why, why, hello," I said.

Hannah didn't respond to that, nor did she smile. Her pale, thin lips opened, and in the flat, uninflected tones of the deaf she spoke. "Mrs. Moran wants you for tea," said Hannah.

Al and I were speechless.

"Do you mean now?" Al finally inquired. I perceived that he was meditating the form of his refusal.

Hannah seemed to be at a momentary loss. She glanced toward the house, as though to ask for guidance, and I fancied that I glimpsed a quivering curtain. I wondered whether Mrs. Moran, concealed behind heavy draperies, was watching the colloquy.

"Of course she doesn't mean now," I said quickly. "It's barely three o'clock."

Hannah was a trifle mollified. "The madam wants you, I guess, when you walk back," she said, and attempted unsuccessfully to make the trying voice a little gracious. "She usually drinks her tea around five o'clock."

Before Al could intervene, I said in a hurry, "We may be too late today. Otherwise we'll be delighted. May we leave our acceptance indefinite?"

"I guess you can," Hannah said, and stalked back to the clothesline.

Al was considerably put out with me.

"Why'd you leave the thing indefinite?" he demanded. "With the crowd coming for dinner, too. You must be mad. Why didn't you just say 'no'? Like this—No!"

"Be reasonable, Al," I said. "Aunt Mildred would never forgive us if we passed up the opportunity."

"You mean you wouldn't," he said. And then he grinned. "Seriously, Jane, suppose we skip the tea and crumpets. We won't have time. Besides, I don't like the idea. That woman's got no reason to invite us to tea."

I couldn't think of any reason either. But I wanted very much to go.

I had forgotten all about Pandora's box.

Chapter Four:
WILLY-NILLY GUESTS

Directly we reached the building site, Mrs. V. Moran passed from my thoughts. Or maybe I should say more correctly, that I tucked her surprising invitation into another portion of my mind.

As we approached our future residence, I surrendered to the usual thrill of possessive pride. Before people started arguing, at least once every day, I loved our house. Al and I paused and smiled and marveled. Everything we saw we owned. No city dweller was as rich. Hand in hand, we stepped into the trampled, corrugated yard, crowded past the workmen's trucks, climbed the steep, ugly mound of earth that supported the new dining room and kitchen. Both rooms had been freshly plastered since the day before. We peeped approvingly inside. It was then that Belton discovered us.

A moment later the architect met us at the door. Belton was a big, broad-shouldered man, handsome and successful-looking. Round as a plate beneath a ruff of snow-white hair, his large, pink face wore a confident, charming smile. Ruth had a smile like his. Otherwise father and daughter didn't look at all alike. My sister-in-law was very small.

From the basement and the attic came the thump of hammers, the shrill continuous buzzing of an electric saw. The space beyond the door which was to be our foyer had begun to bear some slight resemblance to a room. The wails were in and the various doors, although stacks of lumber were piled everywhere and an oblong opening cut the floor. A ladder led from the opening to the second floor, another ladder dropped to the cellar, below. The opening and the ladders would remain, as I well knew, until we decided on the stairs.

"I'm sorry I can't offer you a chair, Janey, dear. Unless you'd like a sawhorse," said Belton, welcoming us as though he headed a receiving line. He spied the blueprints underneath my arm. His eyes lit expectantly. "I see you've been studying my stairway. Lovely, isn't it? Simple and yet distinctive. Fits your kind of living, and is perfect for your house."

Al cleared his throat. The trouble had begun.

Belton stepped back and gestured toward the ascending ladder. He traced an enthusiastic outline in the empty air. "Can't you see my stairway rising there? It's good enough to key your whole interior, if I say so myself. The artisan who built this cottage in 1790 thought in just those terms. I hope you observed the baluster detail, and the way the nosing on the treads ties in." He reached for the blueprints.

A small dry cough interrupted us. Mr. Thirkle, hammer in hand, climbed up the ladder from the cellar, "Did you explain about the costs?" he inquired.

Belton started slightly. "The costs?"

"Those stairs," remarked Mr. Thirkle unemotionally, "will take twice as long to build as an ordinary flight, and cost maybe five times as much."

"They'll be five times as beautiful," Belton replied with energy.

Mr. Thirkle was unmoved. His long lean finger stabbed the blueprints. "You call for special millwork throughout, Mr. Weaver. Now special millwork's nice, but we both know stock is cheaper and very few indeed can tell the difference. If you want my opinion—"

It was plain that Belton did not. Mr. Thirkle gave his opinion nevertheless, and at considerable length. He produced a sketch of a stairway in a builder's catalogue which he insisted closely resembled Belton's design. The resemblance was slight, but Mr. Thirkle's stairs did possess the undoubted virtue of economy. Al and I looked at one another.

"Well," said Belton coldly, "I won't defend my work. Do you want my stairway? Or do you prefer to spoil your house with Mr. Thirkle's trash?"

"Trash?" echoed Mr. Thirkle, at once amused. "Trash, Mr. Weaver? I've been in the building business thirty years. Them stairs of mine will last a lifetime."

"God forbid," said Belton.

Two pairs of set, determined eyes were turned in our direction. Al promptly wilted. I tried to say something that would please everybody.

"Can't we compromise? I like Belton's stairway and so does Al—we think it's swell, but it is expensive. Can't we use the cheaper materials where they won't show? After all, when I put down the carpet—"

"Carpet!" cried Belton. "Do you intend to cover up my stairway with carpeting? Do you mean that, Jane?"

"We own a stairway runner," I said meekly.

"Burn it." Belton said. "Burn the carpet, or forget about my stairs. And if you take Thirkle's stairs, you needn't pin your faith on a length of carpet. No carpet can rectify an architectural monstrosity."

He shook his fist under Mr. Thirkle's nose, and stalked off into the dining room. I knew that he was hurt and disappointed about his stairway, and I went after him. Belton might be reckless and extravagant, but he was also extravagant and openhanded with himself and his own undoubted talents. It had been impossible for us to compel him to accept any fee for our job. Al and I, he said, were in the family. I found Belton staring moodily out a window.

"I do like your stairs," I said. "It's just that money—"

"I know, Jane," he said. "I know that money matters, though my own daughter won't believe it. I suppose the trouble is I hate to think of you and Al with shoddy stuff. You aren't shoddy people. It's difficult to explain—"

Anything less than perfect in our cottage would not be good enough for Belton. That was the simple truth. Most of Merristone thought he was queer and crazy, because he lived in a world where honest workmanship and solid, honest materials meant so much. Belton Weaver cared about the things that to most people didn't show, because to his special eye the counterfeit was always glaringly apparent, as was what he called the "withering touch of the machine."

"I'm an absurd old man," Belton said. "We can't turn back the clock. We can't live in the eighteenth century when good taste was the universal possession of the common man. I know that. But when I think in terms of New England houses my head stops working and I start drawing with my heart...."

"You've drawn the stairs we mean to have," I said, and then, before we grew too sentimental, I spread out my blueprints on the white-daubed plastering table. "Now if you have any ideas about the lighting—"

Belton laughed. "The machine age with a vengeance. If I had my way, I'd give you whale oil and candles. And you'd look a damn sight prettier to your husband."

We were bent companionably over the blueprints when a car horn sounded on the road. We glanced in that direction simultaneously. From the corner of my eye I thought I caught an odd expression on Belton's face. I daresay I looked odd myself.

A battered roadster was pulled up just at our completely obstructed drive. In the car, stiff and upright as a poker, sat Hannah. Through the uncurtained window, she fixed a blank, unwinking gaze on me. Then she waved and beckoned.

"What's that woman want?" Belton asked sharply.

I had no idea myself. Puzzled, I stepped outside and picked my way toward the car.

"What is it, Hannah? Is the tea called off?"

"I was to stop and inquire. Are you coming or ain't you?"

I hesitated. Al had made plain his desire to have no dealings with Mrs. Moran, and for that matter I didn't care for Hannah's peremptory manner. She had let me walk across the yard, and hadn't budged herself.

"If you ain't," she said, "there's no need for me to buy a cake and flowers."

"Don't bake a cake just for us," I said quickly. "I'm afraid it's too late this afternoon. We're having dinner guests."

"Hey?" She cupped her hand behind her ear. The seamed, lined face crowned with the wisps of iron-gray hair advanced through the lowered window of the car. I observed that she was without her earphone. She wore earmuffs instead. "But you ain't asked for dinner. Dinner wasn't mentioned. It's tea. Tea at five o'clock."

"It's us," I shouted, and felt extremely foolish. "We're having the dinner guests, and so—"

"You! Oh, I see. What time's your dinner at?"

"Why—why—at seven, I suppose."

"That's lots of time. It ain't four yet. I'll buy the cake. You be there at five o'clock. The madam's expecting you." Hannah started up the car.

"Wait!" I screamed. "We can't come. It's impossible. I've just recalled. We have to go to town ourselves. I forgot some things this morning."

She halted. Again the hand was cupped behind the ear. "What's that?"

I felt desperate. Hannah was a menace to the public without her earphone. I raised my voice to a high-pitched shriek. "Shopping. We've got to shop. We're almost out of butter, and I need peaches for my dessert."

The eyes behind the ugly, steel-rimmed spectacles showed sudden comprehension. Hannah's face contorted in an almost sunny smile as she whipped out a grocery list and a pencil stub. "Butter—peaches. All right, I'll get the stuff for you when I buy my cake. Ain't no trouble. You can pay me later. Mind now, you be at the house at five o'clock."

With that she drove away. I stared blankly after the disappearing car. To save my life I couldn't decide whether Hannah really hadn't heard me, or whether she had simply made up her mind to enforce an acceptance on us.

Chapter Five:
THE HARPIST

I tried to explain the grocery incident to Al as we left the cottage. He was exasperated and suspicious. "I think you rigged it so we'd have to stop."

"Truly, Al, I didn't. Hannah was the determined one. I almost thought she deliberately misunderstood me. She was terribly anxious to get us to the house. You should have heard—"

As usual we set off casually in the center of the road, like country people in a country neighborhood. The temperature had risen slightly, and the pearly, almost luminous texture of the sky suggested that snow was in the offing. Suddenly, when we were only a few yards beyond the cottage, a car horn shrilled behind us. A little grudgingly I moved toward the ditch. Al seized my hand, and jerked me from the road in a hurry.

The car rushed by. Dirt and frozen clods flew in all directions. At the wheel of the car sat Hannah. Groceries were piled around her, a bunch of greenhouse flowers sagged against the window; a large, three-cornered crate was jammed into the open rumble seat.

Al shouted. The car sped on and by. The distance to the Moran house was short, but anybody with common courtesy would have paused to ask if we desired a lift. Hannah hadn't even looked at us.

"You've made your point," Al said ironically. He wiped his face, and handed me his handkerchief. "Hannah is obviously pining for our company."

"She might not have recognized us," I said, though I was positive Hannah had. "And the car was awfully crowded. What do you suppose that was in back? The harp?"

"Indubitably. Console yourself, Janey, with a husband willing to protect you from the horrors of salon music. We'll have to skip the party. And get along tonight without dessert and butter."

I did not protest. Some of my own interest in the tea party had evaporated. We went past the Moran house in silence, and walked perhaps a quarter of a mile in the direction of home. Then to my surprise Al abruptly turned around. I raised an eyebrow. He smiled sheepishly.

"Don't tell anybody, Janey. But I find I've got a certain amount of curiosity myself. Enough to gamble with the harp and Hannah, too. Step on it, dear. If we're going back we've really got to hurry."

Ten minutes later we were again approaching the curtained dwelling and mounting the little porch. Al reached for the bell, and then briefly stayed his hand. Small panes of glass, set in around the door, revealed various bisected angles of a living room dimly lit by wavering candles— a crowded place, cluttered, twinkling and over-furnished. An enormous samovar rose from a loaded tea table pulled up before a smoldering fire. A what-not burst with knickknacks, confused and unidentifiable; footstools and ottomans were strewn like confetti; statuary on marble bases sprouted in the flickering gloom.

Clad in brilliant crimson, like an aging, tawdry Diana in an auction room, Mrs. V. Moran quite obviously awaited us. A tall candelabrum was placed behind her. She sat at the concert harp. The shadows of the strings fell across her painted face and her long thin neck. In the obscurity beyond crouched her cats, rosettes of green tied around their necks.

"A tableau, by God," said Al, and the picture did look unreal and posed, like a bad composition by an indifferent artist. One could easily imagine that Mrs. Moran had heard our step and sprung nimbly from the wings before the audience.

"What are we doing here?" Al whispered, as though astonished at himself. And then he rang the bell.

The harpist frowned, half rose, sank back again. She heard us certainly. The dark eyes remained preoccupied, intent. The white hand in the frill of crimson rippled languidly across the strings. Al was a simple male. He scowled and rang again impatiently.

This time the harpist woke from her absorption, started. The long crimson draperies swirled, swept forward. Breathless, eager, welcoming, Mrs. Moran herself, complete with cats, was at the door. A wave of perfume greeted us. The foyer reeked with it. She favored musk and tuberose.

"At last," she cried, and stretched out ringed, dramatic hands. They were scented, too. "I'm so very, very happy you could come. Please forgive the informality. I thought that Hannah—"

The loud blast of a radio from the vicinity of the kitchen placed the remiss maid to my satisfaction. No doorbell could have penetrated such an uproar. We could hardly speak above it. Mrs. Moran frowned and closed a door.

"I'm a bad mistress," she explained, flurried and apologetic. "Servants always find me out. But Hannah loves the radio serials, and with her affliction she has very little pleasure. She forgets her duties and I—well—I suppose I humor her."

She was too concerned by a triviality, embarrassingly apologetic, like a nervous hostess who suspects her cook is tippling. Obviously the little scene was spoiled by Hannah's absence. I knew I should feel sorry for the hostess.

"Let me help you with your coat, Mrs. Blake. Oh, what a lovely sweater!" As it happened, my skirt and sweater were in a serviceable shade of red. The dark eyes opened wide. "How extraordinary! I believe you must *feel* color, too. Is Friday also red for you?"

I was wholly lost.

"Friday's crimson for me," she said confidentially, "just as Thursday is yellow. A deep sulphur yellow. Saturday is always green. Sunday's white, of course, and Monday's blue. Electric blue. I hate navy. Navy's pure poison to me always. Not on other people, naturally," she added hurriedly, with a doubtful glance at Al's unencouraging face. "Men are different, of course. They don't understand our feminine foibles, do they, Mrs. Blake?"

I began to grasp the secret of the wardrobe that had held Harriet spellbound at her window. Order ruled the wardrobe, the crashing procession of changing color. Mrs. Moran dressed not to suit the time or place or season, but to suit her own peculiar concept of the proper color for each day. She ran the spectrum every week, and then began again.

"I never vary," she said earnestly. "You should see my closet. My system is so practical, once you grasp it. As I often say, I'm not a slave to style or fashion. I dress to please the day. Even with Gog and Magog—"

At that point Al stepped on Gog, which turned out to be the black cat's name. When the snarling and spitting of the outraged animal had subsided, when Mrs. Moran had caught him to her breast and comforted him, she finished out her point.

"Gog and Magog *feel* color, too. My darlings are affected deeply if Hannah forgets to change their ribbons."

Eyeing Gog, I almost felt that might be true. It was evident that he'd already decided Al was a mortal enemy. Al, who didn't care much for Gog and who had always dressed to please himself without recourse to a calendar, clung to his hat as we were piloted into the shadowy living room. The bank had provided the solid furniture, the orthodox sofa, the upright piano, the sprinkling of Windsor chairs. Mrs. Moran had supplied the overlay. Hers were the India scarf that draped the piano, the rococo mirrors and meaningless hits of statuary, the crowded what-not, the fringed and decorated Chinese lamps, the Buddha incense burner, the scores of photographs.

It was impossible to ignore the photographs or the scrawling purple-inked inscriptions. The collection was definitely of the theater, definitely of another day—handsome men in opera cloaks, women of a classic, opulently old-fashioned type of beauty draped in clouds of tulle or peeping coquettishly across feather boas or enormous feather fans.

In a glance I solved the name that had baffled Merristone. To those lost, outmoded people, to the matinee idols and the pouting soubrettes, to the frowning tenor dressed like Caruso in short striped tights, Mrs. V. Moran had been Veronica. The purple ink gushed the name: *To darling Veronica, may your successes multiply. Dearest Veronica, play on. Veronica, Veronica, in heaven let us hear you still.*

A recollection knocked at my mind, a fugitive memory. Veronica Moran? Wasn't there a musical figure—a harpist—who had enthralled the unsophisticated youth of an earlier generation?

Veronica Moran leaned her dyed black head against the golden curve of the harp. "My dearest treasure," she said, "or so I thought it once. We were reunited today, after a separation of many months. I play seldom now, and badly. Long ago they used to call me the heavenly harpist."

"My parents thought you were wonderful," said Al, in an effort to redeem himself. "They heard you in Carnegie Hall. On September 7, 1915."

She looked flattered and surprised. I was confounded.

"Father recalled the occasion all his life," Al continued, and even forced a smile. "He and Mother often mentioned it. The fact is I was born that night."

My husband's long suit wasn't tact. It was one thing for our hostess to date herself, and quite another for him to assist her in the process. Veronica Moran, who had played her harp the night that Al was born, sat down at the tea table as though suddenly she were worn and tired, exhausted by our very youth.

Her hands trembled at the samovar. She could paint her face and dye her hair, but enameled nails could not conceal the knotted knuckles, the clawlike, aging hands. I had felt uncomfortable before, and alienated. Suddenly I found I really pitied her.

The machinery of the party was creaking badly, and she had tried so hard. Thought and effort were implicit in the greenhouse flowers rushed from the village, in the fussy sandwiches, the samovar, the pitted old bottle of brandy.

"Calvados, 1928," said Mrs. Moran, with a bright determined smile. "I suppose I shouldn't boast, but I brought it back with me from Paris the last time I was over. I've saved it ever since for an occasion. Will you do the honors, Mr. Blake?"

She handed Al the dust-encrusted bottle. My glance stilled his protest. With marked reluctance he twisted out the cork.

Mrs. Moran kept on trying. "I can't recommend the cake," she confessed, and laughed nervously as she offered the Merristone Bakery's finest. "Hannah doesn't bake and declines to learn. But we've been together so many years, I'd be lost without her. In the country particularly—I'm wholly at her mercy. I'm such a fool I never learned to operate a motor car. I was brought up to believe my hands were priceless."

Servant talk wasn't what she wanted. She wanted praise and admiration. I gazed desperately around the room. The *Merristone Journal*, folded to the social items, lay on the piano bench. That was revealing, and pathetic, too. We'd discussed the frock, and with Al sitting there, I didn't dare resume the topic of the crimson Fridays and sulphur-yellow Thursdays. But she wore an unusual, old-fashioned locket—shaped like a lily with an opal in the heart. I'd noticed it several times before on those occasions when we'd passed her on the road. I could admire the locket, and lucklessly I did.

"Capri," she said at once. "I was in Capri a summer long ago. An Italian summer when all the world was filled with song and romance. A young Italian was courting me, and one day we stopped on the Bridge of Sighs and in a tiny shop saw this very locket...."

We heard the embarrassing anecdote in full. Its only point was that she had once been young and beautiful, courted by an Italian count who'd called her his Roman Lily. No woman past 18 should have ventured the recital. Few women would.

I couldn't look at her. I wished that I was anywhere but there. It had been a mistake to return. Pity couldn't help this affected, babbling woman. Why had she asked us there? Al and I couldn't give her back her lost importance. I sent him a covert, wretched glance.

Veronica Moran was foolish, but she wasn't dull. To my horror, she intercepted the glance and correctly read its meaning. She had been holding out the lily locket. It dropped from her fingers. Sudden tears spilled from her eyes. She bent over the tea tray to hide them.

I wet my lips, and no words came. The only sound was the far-off mutter of the radio. Situations often escape Al, but he'd seen the tears. Our eyes met above the bent head. Gog padded across the room, eyed Al malevolently, and jumped softly into his mistress's lap. Magog rubbed against her knees.

The dyed black head came up at last. The dark eyes were now quite dry, and very bright. "I've lived in cities, all my life," said Veronica Moran. "Paris, Rome, New York. People call cities cold and unfriendly. Those people don't know Merristone."

In an instant I saw, or thought I saw, the truth behind the artifice, the posing and posturing. Bitter loneliness was the explanation of our invitation, the explanation of the too elaborate entertainment. She had acted a role she thought we'd find appealing, a role successful in the vanished, radiant past, and she had failed. Thus, she had failed with the village itself—she'd made herself conspicuous to attract attention and companionship, and she'd attracted attention only. Merristone had been devoured with curiosity, but Merristone had not called.

"I thought of buying here," she said. "This house. My old friends are dead and scattered. Years and years ago, I lost my husband and my babies. A typhoid epidemic brought me tragedy, before you two were born. But I was young enough to build up a new life then. When that life went too, I thought foolishly I had sufficient courage to try once again here in Merristone with new surroundings and new associations. You have shown me my mistake."

At that moment Al's sweating hands undid him. The glass of lukewarm tea, laced with brandy, escaped his grip, upset upon the floor.

He started mopping with his napkin.

"Never mind," said Mrs. Moran. Suddenly she stood up. "I'll ring for Hannah. Let it go, Mr. Blake. I insist. I'm afraid I've already delayed your dinner."

It was a clear dismissal. Al reddened and dropped the napkin. I rose at once. Simultaneously the distant radio went off. The low, monotonous chatter had run like an uneasy thread beneath our labored, uneasy conversation. Abruptly all was silence.

"The serial's run its course," I said inanely, and then paused, confused.

Mrs. Moran wasn't there. One instant our hostess had been standing at the bell, a set conventional smile upon her face. The next instant she was disappearing through the foyer. There was no word of apology or explanation. She simply went. We had the living room to ourselves.

"What lovely continental manners!" Al said. "Where's your bonnet, Jane? Let's get out of here."

"She's coming back. She just recalled our groceries or—or something."

"Come on, Jane. I'm serious. Aunt Mildred's bones were right for once. Something's wrong about that woman. Wrong about the pair of them. Mrs. Moran hasn't spoken a word of truth all afternoon. Not even about her brandy."

I glanced toward the tea table.

"That bottle didn't come from Paris," Al said. "I had a chance myself to buy it in the village. Dust and all. It was the last of Humbolt's stock, and the most expensive. Furthermore, the Bridge of Sighs isn't in Capri. It's in Venice."

"She was posing for effect."

"She's created it," Al said grimly. "I believe she even invented the typhoid epidemic. Don't be a sentimentalist, Jane. I don't trust that woman."

But I wouldn't go like that. Before he could stop me, I went quickly toward the kitchen. I expected to find Mrs. Moran and Hannah there, and to hear some simple explanation of the sudden disappearance. Through a half-open bedroom door, I glimpsed our hostess. She stood beside a silent radio. I saw her eyes, and the expression in them. She was angry—angry with a sort of cold, implacable rage foreign to my experience. The dark eyes were cold with fury. Cold and hard as stone.

Except for her, the room—a frivolous, over-decorated kind of place— was empty, and there was nothing unusual in it except that a half-shelled pan of peas rested on a chair pulled up beside the radio.

Al's instincts had been sounder than my own. I knew that quite suddenly. The eyes had told me. I started a noiseless retreat. She heard me, turned. In a twinkling the look was gone. Her eyes warmed again, within the fraction of a second. The foolish, conventional smile curved her painted lips.

"Mrs. Blake! Do forgive me. I just ran back to get your parcels— your—your fruit and coffee."

Another lie, and a clumsy one. Obviously our groceries wouldn't be kept in the bedroom. In the kitchen beyond a footfall sounded. "There's Hannah now," said Mrs. Moran, and moved swiftly in that direction. I was in complete confusion about the household now—a household where the mistress waited on herself, and the maid apparently prepared her vegetables and played the radio in the master bedroom. As we entered the kitchen, the back door closed.

It was like a fantastic game of hound and hares, with Hannah fleeing on before us. But I'd had enough. My groceries were lying on the sink, and I grabbed them.

Outside a car motor started. Mrs. Moran ran to the window. The battered top of the roadster moved swiftly past along the drive below. Evidently Hannah was going somewhere else, and I, for one, didn't blame her. At first I thought that Mrs. Moran meant to fling up the window and scream out an angry summons. But my presence must have stayed her. Her fingers gripped the sill until the knuckles whitened, but she didn't move or call. Somehow I didn't want to see her eyes again.

In an afternoon of complete insincerity, I had identified one emotion that was real, and I had no wish to investigate it.

"Goodbye," I said, and left her standing there, staring out the darkening window.

Chapter Six:
FOUND IN THE CELLAR

A moment later Al and I were on the road and headed home. Al wasn't impressed by my account of what had happened in the kitchen. He was too tired and hungry to be interested in discussing the emotions of Veronica Moran or the behavior of the maid.

"Hannah probably forgot something in the village. You imagined the rest of it. Unless Mrs. Moran was irritated because Hannah settled in her bedroom. I know I wouldn't want her shelling peas in mine."

"Really, Al. This was pure fury. Her eyes were awful. Hannah was running off, that's what I think."

We had walked about half a mile. At the point where Copston Road made a sharp, right-angled turn, I paused and glanced back. Across the open country fields, the Moran house was still visible. A light was shining from the master bedroom, shining down into the driveway. The driveway was on our side. Astonished, I stared at it.

Hannah hadn't gone to the village. The battered roadster was pulling up again beneath the bedroom window. Even as we gazed in that direction, the headlights snapped off. Simultaneously the bedroom light was doused, and the car was lost in gloom. The first flakes of snow fluttered from a rapidly darkening sky.

"Hannah wasn't running off," I said blankly. "She's already back. I think—"

"Listen, dear, we can't solve their problems. We've got dinner guests. Sarah and Frank are probably there already. Let's try to beat the storm."

We left the solid footing of the road and took the shortcut through the woods, but it was already snowing hard when we staggered into Aunt Mildred's yard. Frank's car was in the garage beside our own, and we found him in restive possession of the living room, entertaining himself by studying the real oil portraits of various departed Blakes. He greeted us with considerable relief. I asked at once for Sarah. It seemed to me that Frank hesitated.

"She's in the village. I dropped her at Selby's office and came on out."

"At the office," I said, surprised. "Why?"

"She had something she wanted to discuss with Selby. Or so I judged."

"But Selby is coming to dinner. They all are."

Again Frank hesitated noticeably. "You know our Sally when she gets a notion in her head. Prompt action is her motto. Grass doesn't grow when Sarah operates. Anyhow, I promised I'd pick her up at half-past six."

He was talking much too fast. It suggested that he was concealing something. Al looked at him narrowly.

"Why didn't you stay with her, and save yourself the second trip?"

"I wasn't asked," Frank said dryly. "In point of fact, Selby wasn't in his office. Sarah insisted I come on out, and she'd wait a while by herself." He glanced at his watch. "I'd better be getting started. It's nearly quarter past now."

His air of elaborate concern did not deceive me, or conceal the fact that Sarah evidently meant to take up with Selby some matter she meant to keep from the rest of us. She never went to his office. Was Selby in some kind of difficulty? If that was so, Al was the one to be told. He looked hurt.

I put in a hasty inquiry for Aunt Mildred. It developed that when Frank had arrived a good half hour earlier he walked into an empty house. Aunt Mildred was out. It seemed odd to me; when Aunt Mildred had neuralgia she could rarely be induced to poke her nose outdoors; she said fresh air increased the misery. A moment later I discovered something odder still. There was nothing in the icebox, not even the perfection salad Aunt Mildred invariably concocted for a company dinner. No preparations whatever had been made to feed a lot of hungry people. I flew to peel potatoes, and Frank, who obviously feared he might be further cross-examined about Sarah and Selby, started out the kitchen door. He met Aunt Mildred coming in.

House guests were her special delight, but she greeted Frank almost curtly. When he went on she didn't even ask where he was going. She offered no explanation of her own absence. In silence she shook the snow from her coat, unwound her muffler and removed her rubbers. And then she bewildered me completely.

"My neuralgia's worse," she said. "I'm afraid you'll have to excuse me to the others. Don't bother with a tray. I prefer to rest."

She had felt well enough to go out into a snowstorm, but she firmly gathered up her wraps and climbed upstairs. It was incredible. I was too occupied, however, to attempt to fathom Aunt Mildred or Sarah either. Al set the table, and I whipped up a salad for seven people and rushed the steak to the grill. At that, no one was on hand at seven. The dinner was doomed from its inception. Frank and Sarah got back about 7:15, but the others still weren't there. Irritated by the pangs of hunger and troubled about his brother, Al tackled Sarah at once.

"What's this about you and Selby? Is something wrong? What were you two conferring about in his office?"

"Nothing," Sarah said. "I haven't seen Selby, Al. I waited over an hour, but he didn't show up. Miss Hawkins said he went out at noon and didn't come back."

Of course that wasn't what Al desired to know, but Sarah eluded him by going upstairs to inquire into her mother's state of health. Almost immediately afterward Belton and Ruth walked in. Selby stayed outside long enough to park the car, but a moment later he entered the dining room.

Sarah's behavior had planted the seed of worry in my mind. I viewed Selby with sharpened eyes. As he passed beneath the old-fashioned chandelier, I saw that he looked rumpled and untidy—an unusual thing with him. Suddenly I wondered if he hadn't grown a little thinner the last few weeks, without our noticing. His voice, however, was quite natural.

"Sorry to be late," Selby said apologetically. "It's all my fault. Ruth's quite put out with me, aren't you, dear?"

It wasn't like Ruth to be annoyed by any small deficiency of Selby's. Yet suddenly I thought I sensed a strain between them. Ruth had slipped into a chair beside her father, and she didn't indicate that Selby was to take the place on her other side.

"You're still delaying dinner, dear," she said patiently. "Do sit down. Janey's steak will be ruined."

"I'm so sorry," Selby said again. "I've had a tough day. I haven't left my desk since morning. I was held up at the office till after seven o'clock."

Sarah had come quietly into the dining room. She drew quick breath, but that was all. At least four people—she and Frank, Al and I—knew that Selby hadn't been held up at his office. Whatever had delayed his arrival at the dinner party, it was not that.

Four people knew he had left his office at noon, and had not returned.

I had never known my brother-in-law to tell an untruth. The small white lies of ordinary social intercourse were foreign to his nature. If Selby saw fit to lie, something was seriously amiss.

As a family we weren't adept at covering up and deceiving one another. Dinner was an odd, uneasy meal. Usually when we were together, we all talked at once, interrupting, laughing and exclaiming. But that night we missed Aunt Mildred. Belton did his best to take her place, for which I was thankful, since his booming voice filled many a silence. Throughout the meal he steadily discussed our cottage and the part he had played in it. Everybody listened. Everybody listened after dinner, too, as he went on and on. He was always pleased to be the center of attention, but once or twice I wondered if his loquaciousness wasn't more than that. There was an almost feverish quality in it.

"Run and get your blueprints, Janey," he said to me. "I want Sarah to see my stairway."

"*Their* stairway, Father," Ruth said automatically.

Grateful for the diversion, I sped into the hall. My purse and gloves were lying on the table. The bulky roll of blueprints wasn't there.

"You had them this afternoon," Al said, as anxious as Belton to keep the conversation rolling. "I remember. I wish you'd keep track of things, my chuckle-headed darling. Look in the kitchen."

I came back empty-handed. The very absence of the blueprints made them seem desirable. Al was now determined that Sarah and Frank, too, should inspect the stairway drawing.

"Maybe you left the blueprints in the cottage, Janey," he said suddenly. "You and Belton were studying them this afternoon. Didn't you have the blueprints in the dining room?"

My mind flashed back. I saw Belton and myself bent at the plaster table, heard the honk of Hannah's car. I'd left the blueprints when I ran outside, and forgotten them. I recalled the very way the thick, curling sheets had lain on the square, rough table.

Belton recalled it, too.

Al decided then and there that we would go at once and get the blueprints. It would be a good opportunity, he insisted, to show everybody how much had been accomplished with paint and plaster. I knew the reason for his inspiration. He wanted action. Anything to break up the gathering.

Snow was falling hard outside, a stiff wind blew. Frank and Sarah went with Al in our roadster, but the rest of us crowded into Belton's coupe. Copston Road was like glass, its twisting hazards further increased by the wind and snow. What I mostly remember of the trip is how Belton drove. Selby had not been quick enough to deprive him of the wheel, and Belton habitually treated an automobile like a balky horse. We skidded from side to side, past fields and woods and unlighted houses, changed now and unfamiliar. Telegraph poles challenged us, and once I was positive a mailbox would come straight through the windshield.

An enormous elm, a giant in the rocketing gloom, marked the division point between the Moran property and ours. I remember that I twisted to get some view of the small, square house, and failed entirely. I had an impression that Selby, who sat beside me, also turned, but that may have been my imagination.

A moment later, we reached the building site intact. Our driveway, blocked with Mr. Thirkle's gear, was of course impassable. We left both cars parked on the road. I don't recall the order in which we staggered across the lawn, but I do remember that I hung back for Frank and I Sarah and that Belton led. The snow was hard and stinging—like blown shot.

Lit only by Belton's flashlight, assaulted by the flying snow, the cottage seemed unfamiliar too. Wholly unrelated to Al and me. A nightmare cottage, ugly and inimical, seen in a nightmare landscape. The dormer windows frowned like hooded eyes, the massive central chimney leaned at a sinister, unnatural angle. Icy scaffolding crawled up the walls like skeleton fingers. All light disappeared as those in advance made the turn. The cottage itself was blotted out.

"Janey," said Sarah.

"Not now, Sarah," Frank said sharply. "Ruth might hear you."

Ruth might hear what? For the moment I didn't care. Ruth was in the cottage, and so was Belton as was attested by his booming voice. We three were the last. With great relief I shut the door upon the turbulent darkness, and surveyed the familiar clutter of the foyer. Flashlight in hand, unperturbed and eager, convinced that what we most desired was a lengthy inspection tour, Belton stood at the stairwell.

"Suppose we start with my stairway," he said. "It goes in here. By the exercise of a little imagination, you should—"

He swept his flashlight toward the ladder that climbed upward, and described a sweeping arc that ended in the cellar below. The swift flight of light, in the encroaching darkness, compelled all our eyes. Seven people looked into the cellar.

"What's that?" cried Ruth. "What's that lying at the foot of the ladder?"

At first glimpse, the body huddled in the cellar, crisscrossed by the shadow of the ladder, might have been a heap of rags. It lay so still. At first glimpse one didn't see the blood, dark and brown, that discolored the upturned face and stained the straggling locks of gray hair. Nor did one see the battered earphone that lay nearby.

"It's Hannah," Al said, and his voice was far away and queer. "Hannah Wilson—Mrs. Moran's maid. She's fallen down the ladder."

"Fallen?" Belton said, and his voice, too, was strange and harsh. "That woman didn't fall. Her whole skull's crushed. She's been murdered—beaten to death."

Chapter Seven:
THE VANISHING KEYS

The flashlight slipped from Belton's hand, and plunged through the rungs of the ladder toward the cement below. The falling light raced across Hannah's body in a fantastic, spinning arc, blazed into the dead, unseeing face, touched the blood-spattered hair, caught other light from the thick spectacles that screened the wide-open eyes. Her whole skull had been crushed by some heavy weapon wielded many times; violence was implicit in her death.

There was, however, no sign of struggle. Her clothing—the cheap, heavy coat, the uniform beneath—was not disordered or awry. Beside her was the shabby purse she carried to the market, topped by her decent, neatly mended gloves. With the rough concrete as her bier, Hannah lay almost as though prepared for burial, unresisting, defenseless and resigned—her old, work-worn hands with the chipped, broken nails folded peacefully upon her breast, her lean, cotton-stockinged ankles carefully crossed. Circled by its own broken cord, the shattered earphone lay within reach of the quiet fingers as though she herself had dropped it, arranged her purse and gloves, adjusted her cheap felt hat, smoothed her bloodstained hair and lain down to die.

The picture was mercilessly clear, and then was gone. Glass tinkled as the flashlight struck. The light went out.

One of the women drew a soft, gasping breath, and after that the silence was like death. For an awful moment it was as though all of us were trapped in blackness in the unfinished foyer, with the dreadful cellar opening like a well beneath us. Seven people stood absolutely motionless. Then someone stumbled, and someone else—Belton I think it was—said querulously:

"In God's name, where's the switch? Thirkle's got some sort of lights attached. Near the dining room, Al."

The darkness bustled. A plank fell over, and a pail handle rattled. My fingers closed on a swinging electric cord. I found a plug, and connected it. Light blazed on, but the bulb was in the cellar. We were still lost in semi-gloom above, a crowd of ghosts collected around a fiercely brilliant opening in the floor. I gasped and backed away. Ruth put one hand across her eyes, and with the other reached automatically toward Selby. Sarah was the first to step forward.

"Please let me by, Janey. I'm going down. I suppose there's nothing to be done, but—"

"You stay here," Frank said, and caught her by the arm. He peered over, went very white. "The woman's plainly dead. Been dead a long while too, I—I'd guess. One would almost think—"

A look flashed between him and Sarah, as though they shared a similar perplexity, and then Al pushed past and went scrambling down the ladder. For what seemed like a long time, he bent over the silent body. Illumined by the brilliant overhead glare, he knelt below us, motionless, intent, and, on the whitewashed wall beyond, his monstrous shadow knelt. His eyes studied Hannah's folded hands, paused long upon the peaceful face, shifted to the earphone. With maddening slowness Al straightened up and removed his coat to spread it like a shroud. Before he dropped the muffling folds, he hesitated, and again stooped over to gaze at the clasped hands as though they held the secret of Hannah's death. I saw him pick up the purse. I could bear no more. Several doors opened off the foyer. As I turned blindly toward the living room, I felt Belton's shaking hand on my arm.

"Steady, girl," he said, apparently under the impression that he was quite calm himself. "We—we'll have to pull ourselves together for the police."

"The police?" I repeated stupidly. Until then, I had been wholly preoccupied with the horror of the moment, with the tableau in the cellar—Al's tedious examination of the body, his curious air of hesitancy. I hadn't really comprehended that we—Al and myself and, for that matter, all of us—had been personally projected into a fearful crime. Dreadful as it is to say, my first coherent thought was self-centered and realistic. I wasn't fond of Hannah and couldn't pretend to be. I wished most urgently that the disagreeable old servant hadn't met a shocking and mysterious death in our cottage.

"What was Hannah doing in our cellar?" I asked aloud and then added foolishly, "We saw her at half-past four this afternoon."

It was then that Sarah called down to Al, "Can you tell—have you any idea how long she's been dead?"

"A long time," Al said. "Hours, I'd think, though I'm not really qualified to judge."

"Would you say she'd been dead since seven o'clock?"

It was Selby who asked that question, and I was dimly aware that

Sarah had turned to look at him. Al himself must have wondered that his brother had fixed upon a specific hour.

"That's an expert's province, Selby. We'll have to let Dr. Traphaven decide. All I know is, she's been dead a good long while."

I have some numbed recollection of looking at my watch. The small gilt hands met at midnight. Then the ladder creaked, and through the opening Al's head appeared. He swung over to the foyer. An endless moment passed before he spoke. Standing against that dismal background, with the piled-up planks, the scattered pails and tools, he seemed hopelessly confused, unable to get his thoughts in order. But at last he found words.

"Hannah wasn't beaten to death down there in the cellar," he said. "It simply isn't possible."

Belton's hand dropped from my shoulder. Ruth's head came up. Selby was looking down at her, and I couldn't see his face. Neither Sarah nor Frank showed surprise. Those two, whose brains were quick and clever, in many ways so much alike, had read the truth at a glance. The oddly peaceful position of the body, the careful disposition of the earphone, the gloves and purse, the small amount of blood in the whitewashed confines of the cellar—those details had told them the story. Hannah hadn't smoothed her own hair, folded her hands, lain down and quietly expired. Someone else had arranged the scene.

"The poor old soul was dead when she was carried down the ladder," Sarah said. "There's no possible weapon down there, Janey. Besides," she finished awkwardly, "there's so very little blood. The police can tell at once...."

"But I don't understand—"

"Neither do I," she said. "Unless someone brought the body here, intending to get you and Al in trouble."

"That—that's fantastic."

"What other answer is there, Janey?"

I felt the first sharp stab of a different, an incredible kind of fear. Any deliberate attempt to involve Al and me in another's crime, postulated an enemy—and a dangerous enemy. We had no such enemies. Or had we? Belton's thoughts must have run like mine, because he so valiantly attempted to produce another possibility. His voice was loud and overconfident, like a little boy who whistles in the dark.

"Sounds like the behavior of a maniac to me. No one can account for the doings of a homicidal maniac. Was the woman robbed?"

"No," Al said, and added curtly, "Someone will have to drive for Sheriff

Blandish. Selby, will you—?"

"We'll take my car," said Belton.

It flashed through my mind that Selby would do better by himself. And then when I glimpsed his face I wasn't sure. It was white as chalk, dazed and stricken. Nevertheless, he started toward the door. In the semi-gloom and in his haste not to be left behind, Belton lurched against a length of scaffolding. Sarah reached out and turned on the foyer light. The sudden brilliance was dazzling. I blinked my eyes. It was then that Ruth screamed.

Leading from the ladder, splashing the shavings and the sawdust, an irregular crimson line wandered across the littered floor. The crimson line broke off abruptly at the threshold of the dining room.

I don't remember who jerked open the door. But I remember what we saw. Hannah had died in the cottage after all. She had met her violent death no more than 20 feet from where her body rested.

The dining room was freshly plastered. Blood spattered the chalk-white walls and dyed the baseboards. Except for a built-in corner cupboard and a backless chair, the only piece of furniture was the square, crude table where Belton and I had conferred that afternoon, bending companionably over a roll of blueprints. Blood stained the table in a dark-brown tide, seeped into the wide cracks between the plaster-smeared boards, discolored the floor beneath. Soaked and crumpled, my blueprints lay toward the center of the table in a crimson pool.

I had perched upon the table. But Hannah had pulled up the chair. One could almost picture her seated at the table—lean ankles crossed, skirts decently adjusted, an old, deaf woman in an empty, unoccupied house, oblivious that death approached her from behind. One could picture her reaching idly for the blueprints, and the blueprints slipping, roiling, as she toppled under a sudden crushing blow. Her assailant had caught her unawares. She had had no chance whatever to fight or struggle. With the first assault she had fallen forward, collapsing where she sat. In the soft wood of the table, deep dents were visible—mute evidence of the savagery of the attack upon an already dying or unconscious woman. In at least a dozen places the plaster crust was cracked, and inch-deep depressions marred the wood beneath.

"I—I wonder where the weapon is," Sarah said, as white as the plaster walls. Like one hypnotized, she stared at the table. "It wasn't an ax, or anything like that. Those aren't cuts. They're dents."

The next few seconds are blurred in my recollection. Someone must have closed off the hideous dining room. A banging door informed me that Selby, with Belton at his heels, had rushed outside toward the cars. I believe it was Al, with Frank's assistance, who herded the rest of us back across the foyer toward the living room beyond. That room had been freshly plastered too; the wrinkled canvas spread to protect the floor was damp. Drops of moisture gathered on the window panes, the air was thick and humid. I have some dim recollection of dusting off a sawhorse, and sitting down with Ruth. But when I tried to light a cigarette, she had to hold the match.

Curiously enough, a part of my brain was rational. I didn't wonder at the time what had brought Hannah to the dining room, but nevertheless I think I must have known—as Sheriff Blandish was to know at once—that in order to solve a peculiarly difficult and complex crime, we would need to learn the reason for the old woman's presence in our cottage, just as we would need to learn why her body had been so mysteriously transferred to the cellar. I am sure that Sarah's thoughts ran in a similar channel.

She stationed herself beside Frank at one of the watering windows, but she spoke to Al. Her tone was oddly hesitant. "Listen, Al. Don't you think we should have some sort of—of explanation for the Sheriff?"

"What kind of explanation do you mean? We don't need to solve the murder, Sarah. My guess is Blandish will find that hard enough himself."

"That isn't what I mean. After all, it's your house, Al. You saw Hannah just this afternoon. Did you get any idea she was coming here tonight?"

"Of course I didn't. Really, Sarah, I don't see much point in this."

Sarah hesitated. She looked up at Frank. I seemed to sense between them some secret anxiety, unshared by the rest of us. He, too, hesitated.

Then, "Al's right," he said uneasily. "Let the authorities do the thinking, Sarah. Let them get the ideas."

"It might be better to be—prepared."

"Prepared for what?"

"For the question they're bound to ask," Sarah said slowly. "That poor old woman didn't come here and sit down in that dismal dining room just to amuse herself. She came here of her own accord, Al. That's obvious."

"Well?"

"I don't believe she wandered in by chance. The police won't either, Al. Not on a night like this."

Sleet dashed against the windows. It was over-warm inside with the furnace blazing in the cellar to dry out the plaster—but bitter chill crept through the cracks, and wind sighed in the chimney. Subconsciously I listened for the throb of Belton's motor. The only sound was the whispering and the rustling of the wind.

"If we could only think of something," Sarah said, almost feverish in her urgency. She was usually so calm and collected. "Some reasonable explanation—"

"You've thought of one already. What is it?"

She drew a long breath. "Hannah came here to meet someone, Al."

There it was. I knew that Sarah was right. The police would know too, would immediately reach the same conclusion. It was inevitable. Ruth's hand clutched mine. Her fingers were like ice. Al's face went a little white, but he chose to argue against his own convictions.

"Look, Sarah. Why should Hannah come here to meet someone? It's ridiculous. She had a home."

"Not exactly. No servant ever really has a home in that sense. That's what we'll have to show Blandish. Hannah could have been meeting someone without your knowledge. Suppose she wanted privacy, or even secrecy—"

"We ought to notify Mrs. Moran," Al said suddenly.

As he spoke, his expression changed. A silence fell. The five of us looked interrogatively at one another. In the silence of the overheated, disordered room, Veronica Moran rose like a phantasm. She rose before us all—crowned with her dyed, black hair, bedecked in her floating draperies and veils, trailing the heavy scent of musk and tuberose. Al and I had seen Hannah that afternoon, but we had seen her mistress too. The strangeness of the association that had rocked the village had been vividly impressed upon us. Hannah hadn't appeared to serve our tea, and our hostess had been restless, artificial and uncertain, and, afterward, I had seen her in her bedroom, standing beside a silent radio—a look of cold and terrifying rage in her eyes. What had happened between Mrs. Moran and Hannah, after Al and I went away? What had happened after the battered roadster circled the field and came back?

I didn't know. But one thing was certain. In all the world one person had been close to Hannah. One person had known her well.

"Mrs. Moran!" cried Al, and relief rang in his tone. "You may have hit on something, Sarah. Maybe we should investigate. But it's Mrs. Moran we want to talk to. The minute Selby gets back from town—"

He paused to stare at Frank. Posted beside the window, Frank stood in an obvious attitude of listening. Ears cocked, eyes intent. Sarah was listening, too,

"Are you sure they ever started?" Frank asked slowly. "I haven't heard a car."

"Of course," Al began, and broke off.

Through the vaporous, sweating glass nothing of the outer world was visible. Nothing could be heard. Suddenly Frank turned around and rubbed vigorously with his palm. A smeared aperture appeared. Gleaming indistinctly through the frosted pane, the headlights of both cars—Belton's coupe and our roadster—shone into the living room. Selby and Belton had left the house some minutes earlier. Parked and motionless, the cars stood on the road exactly where we had left them.

Al ran outside immediately, and I fell over my own feet in my haste to follow. Sarah paused long enough to snatch up Mr. Thirkle's electric lantern, and Frank waited for her. Ruth maintained a terrier grip on my elbow. Stumbling and sliding, we raced past unidentifiable obstructions, and down the slippery drive. I don't know what I expected to see, but I know I was surprised to see Selby, armed with a flashlight, disappearing up the road on foot. I was even more surprised to see how Belton was occupied. The door of his coupe stood open, and he had stepped into the headlight glare. In the midst of a snowstorm he had removed the carpet of his car, and was energetically shaking it. Al reached him first.

"What seems to be the trouble?"

"I can't find my keys," Belton said. He shook the carpet again. "That's the trouble. I left them in the car. They're not there now."

"They're probably in your pocket," said Al, in a frenzy of nervous impatience. "Stop shaking that carpet, and try to talk sense. Where's Selby headed? I don't suppose he means to run all the way to town. If he does, he's started in the wrong direction."

"He's gone to use Harriet Strings' phone. He—I—we didn't want to alarm the girls."

"Why didn't you use our car instead of Selby's going off half-cocked? I *know* I left my keys."

With that Al leaped into our car, reached automatically toward the dashboard. He dropped his hand in bewilderment. Careless by nature and further demoralized by life with me, Al never removed his keys from the car. Indeed he frequently exasperated Selby by remarking blandly that he let his brother's insurance company do the worrying. Fifteen minutes earlier the keys had been in the ignition lock. I was positive of that. Together we gaped at the lock. The keys were gone.

"I knew you'd left your keys," said Belton, half hysterical and yet triumphant too. "You always do. I told Selby so. Someone took them. Someone stole the keys of both cars while we were inside." Again he added, "We didn't want to alarm the girls."

Speaking for myself, Belton had alarmed me thoroughly. So far as I could judge, there was one answer only to the disappearance of the car keys. While we were in the cottage, perhaps at the very moment we stumbled upon Hannah's body or opened the door of the dreadful dining room, a killer had been in the neighborhood. Within a few hundred yards of us. I didn't reflect upon the purpose behind the disappearance of the car keys. I was too shaken by the fact itself.

Frank stooped over to examine the drifted snow around the two cars—a quite futile piece of business. It was impossible to identify any specific footprints in the maze of footprints that were visible on the trodden ground and that were rapidly vanishing beneath the continued assault of the falling snow. Sarah flashed her valiant light into the brush that encroached upon the road, and she and Frank carried their unsuccessful investigation some distance from the cars. It was Sarah's idea. She seemed determined to find footprints, some clue to what had happened.

None of the rest of us showed any disposition to assist them, by venturing into the bustling, blowing darkness. The air was bitterly cold, but a more bitter chill ran through my veins. My teeth were still chattering when finally the two returned, and we started back into the cottage.

"I'm scared too," Ruth said faintly. "Scared stiff. Where's Al going?"

"Going?" I whirled around. A second earlier, as we began stumbling up the drive, Al had been beside me. He had managed inconspicuously to melt away, and was moving not toward the cottage but away from it. Moving so speedily that I barely glimpsed his departing back. I broke all records in catching him. My little sister-in-law made it, too. I must confess Al wasn't pleased to have two women overtake him.

"You girls go back at once," he said sternly. "The police will soon be here. Until then you stick with the others. It isn't safe for you...."

"Safe! What about yourself? What are your plans, I'd like to know."

"That doesn't matter."

"It does to me. You can come back with us yourself! You're alone, unarmed. I know you, Alan Blake, when you set your head...."

Al sighed. "Talk some sense into this nitwit, Ruth. Tell her that her husband's not a hero. I'm not going to start beating the bushes on a futile manhunt. Not me. I mean to do something far more definite, and to the point."

"What?"

"I'm going to have a talk with Veronica Moran," Al said grimly, and started up Copston Road.

Chapter Eight:
GOG AND MAGOG

It's difficult in emergency to behave as the police authorities would choose. Difficult if not impossible. Sheriff Blandish and Dr. Traphaven, the merry-eyed, spade-bearded little coroner who followed him like a faithful shadow, were contemporaries of Aunt Mildred's, and as such had been family friends practically forever. Indeed Aunt Mildred seemed to feel that in her far-off youth she could easily have married either of the pair. She often regretted that she had settled for Uncle Ned.

Family friendship, as we were soon to discover, has nothing to do with the official attitude in a murder investigation. In the first place Sheriff Blandish bitterly resented our delay in summoning him, despite the valid reason. As puzzled as was Al himself by the car key incident and its extraordinary termination, he nevertheless appeared to hold us at fault for making the incident possible. "You shouldn't have left your keys," was the way he put it. As for our call upon the Moran menage, Sheriff Blandish more than resented that; he was as furious as the physician who arrives to discover that the patient owns a copy of *What to Do Before the Doctor Comes*. In that one respect his resentment was justified. We would have been better advised had we stayed away from the small, square house that adjoined our cottage.

Ruth and I accompanied Al, of course. As I've indicated, he started off alone, crashing along the ice-encrusted shrubbery that lined Copston Road. The road was like a sheet of glass, its familiar outlines totally invisible. Snow poured from the sky, and sky and snow alike were swallowed up in blackness. I believe that Ruth would have given up and returned to the cottage. I'm a more determined type, however, and when I started in pursuit of the crashing noises she chose to follow. A second time, beneath the giant elm, we overtook Al. A second argument ensued.

"Go back, you dames. I mean it. This may be unpleasant."

"Exactly. You're the only husband I've got."

"You're my only brother-in-law," Ruth's voice quavered. "Let's all go back to the others. Selby will wonder where I am. He'll be back soon himself. Dad's probably already noticed, and begun to worry."

Al sloughed ahead. Unwelcome and unwanted, Ruth and I floundered in his wake, making tedious work of a trip that by daylight could have been accomplished within three minutes. It would have been more sensible to cut across the field, I suppose. Possibly none of the three of us, and that included Al, really desired to hurry. None of us, I am sure, had any clear idea of how we meant to conduct an interview with Veronica Moran, of precisely what we meant to do. Personally I had arrived at that state where action—imprudent or otherwise—was necessary. I was convinced in advance that Veronica Moran, who had been so close to Hannah, was deeply implicated in the murder.

I must confess that I was trembling when we came abreast the Moran grounds, pressed through the icy branches of leafless sumac and elderberry, and started up the footpath. Had a night ever been as dark? We couldn't see the path; the shrubbery guided us.

The Moran house was lost in whirling snow, was only a darker part of the inky landscape. One had to guess its outlines. Across what was the open field the pinpoint lights of our cottage wavered dim and far away, as unreal as witch lights. They seemed to float in space. I wished we'd brought one of the other men along, and then, with a sinking heart, I remembered we hadn't even announced where we were going. It struck me that our expedition might have been better planned. Somewhere in the distance I thought I heard Belton shouting.

"They're hunting for us, Al."

"Let them hunt. This isn't a convention." And then Al paused to say, "You two keep quiet. I'll do the talking. Watch Mrs. Moran's reaction, when I tell her Hannah's dead."

It flashed through my mind, must have flashed through all our minds, that Veronica Moran might require no notification of the tragedy. The three of us joined hands to mount the steps of the little balustraded porch, half buried in drifted snow. We felt our way toward the door. No chink of light penetrated the blind eyes of the curtained windows. Silence, thick as felt, blanketed the dwelling. Al fumbled for the bell. Suddenly the quiet quivered, trembled, broke. From within the deepest recesses of the house came a distant sound—a sound like far-off wailing. I gasped.

"What's that?"

"I—I don't know," Al said, and rang the bell.

It echoed and re-echoed, but no one came. Again we heard the wailing—unearthly and inhuman. Ruth drew a little whimpering breath.

"Let's get away from here. That—that sound!"

"Nonsense. It's just those cats of hers. Gog and Magog. I'd forgotten. They must be trapped somewhere."

"Trapped?" My own scalp prickled. "Listen, Al. Let's go. I'm scared."

"It's too late now." He tried the doorknob. The unlocked door gave so quickly that we almost fell inside. At first glimpse the hall was as dark as the night, and as bitterly cold. Cold with a chill that struck at the marrow of the bones. A gust of snow blew in behind us.

"Mrs. Moran! Mrs. Moran!" Al shouted.

No one answered. Unless the thin, far-off wailing of the cats could be called an answer. The blackness equaled that outside. We might have stepped into a vault. And then, as my eyes became adjusted, I saw against the floor a thin razor line of flickering light. With a gasp of relief I located the living room door, and jerked it open.

I stared inside. For an instant it was as though time had queerly reversed itself and blotted out the recent past and carried me back to tea at five o'clock. The hostess alone was missing.

The golden harp sat exactly where it had sat that afternoon, the outmoded photographs smirked and simpered from the walls, the littered cups and saucers, the samovar, rested undisturbed upon the table. Nearby, now dried into the rug, was the glass of tea that Al had over turned hours before. No one had cleaned the stain or bothered to pick up the glass. The fire had long since burned out, but the candles that had been brave and tall, still shed uneven, dying light. They guttered in the candelabrum, leaped and flamed from collected pools of melted wax, cast their final radiance everywhere. Even as we stared, one of the candles hissed and expired.

"She's gone," I said uncertainly. "She isn't here. It looks as though—"

"As though she went in a tremendous hurry," said Ruth, peering across my shoulder. "A long time ago. Those candles have been burning for hours."

"Since tea time," I said.

Al had already dashed back into the hall and was racing through the house, banging into empty rooms and then on, shouting loudly for the woman who wasn't there. Ruth sped after him. Moved by an impulse of a different kind, an impulse I hardly understood myself, I stepped into the living room that spoke so loudly of tea at five o'clock. Tea for three. My nerves, my deepest instincts informed me that all of us, particularly Al and I—were going to be called upon to explain Veronica Moran. She had got away. We were left behind.

I bitterly regretted that we had ever come to tea. How would that look? Tea with a woman who, in a period of many months, had entertained no one else; tea followed, perhaps almost immediately, by the brutal murder of her maid. The body of the maid discovered in our cottage. Taken in combination, these circumstances could not fail to make the authorities wonder.

Without volition, I found myself walking toward the glass that Al had upset on the carpet. My intention must have been to pick up the glass, to make some feeble effort to obliterate the plain evidence of the gathering held that afternoon. As I stooped over, however, my brain awoke. I shrank from the glass as though it would burn me, scrambled to my feet, and backed away from the tea table.

My palms were sweating, as though I'd escaped a sudden danger. It would be impossible to hide the fact that Al and I had been the guests of Veronica Moran. Better that Sheriff Blandish should learn from us than from some other source. Shocked at my own heretofore unknown capacity to go against the law, to consider the law an enemy, I told myself that Sheriff Blandish was a friend of ours. A close friend. But I couldn't make myself believe it.

At that moment I must have become aware that Al and Ruth had stopped their running and banging doors. Where were they? All was silence. I went back into the hall, just as Ruth emerged from the master bedroom. She was shaking with excitement. Her blue eyes were blazing, as she cried out to me that Mrs. Moran wasn't in the house, but that her room was all torn up.

"She's made an utter mess of it, Janey. Come and see. It's absolutely incredible!"

Two steps carried me there. The elaborate, over-decorated bedroom had been in order that afternoon. It was now in complete and total confusion. Someone had pulled the embroidered coverlet from the bed, and the little pillows and sheets were wadded all together, so that the mattress was exposed. The peas that had been on the boudoir chair were scattered everywhere—sown like seeds in every corner. The painted Italian desk where Mrs. Moran kept her press book and her treasured clippings, was a wreck. All the cubbyholes had been turned out, and clippings and personal correspondence—old and yellowed for the most part—flung helter-skelter. A bottle of ink had been upset, and ink stained the back of the press book that lay upside down upon the carpet. No degree of haste could explain that scene. It almost looked deliberate.

But the strangest thing was yet to be revealed. Gog and Magog were imprisoned in the clothes closet, and scratching frantically. Al was just going to let them out.

Bedlam broke loose as he opened the door, but the animals did not rush forth. Something held them. I approached and saw what it was. Gog and Magog were tied.

Whoever had shut them in and wrecked the adjoining bedroom had inexplicably decided to protect the contents of the closet. The crimson rosettes that decorated the two crimson collars had been unwound and looped securely through a window fastening. The outraged cats had managed to claw the wall and window curtain, but they had been held back from committing further damage.

Displayed on hangers at the opposite end of the long, narrow space, blazing with raw, harsh color, Veronica Moran's remarkable wardrobe was safely out of danger. It was a surprising exhibit in more ways than one. There were exactly seven hangers.

Each hanger was labeled like a calendar—collared with a little printed ticket which named a single weekday, Monday through Sunday. From each hanger was suspended one of the amazing, solid color gowns with matching shoes tucked underneath, a matching veil and scarf hung overhead. A single hanger was empty, and that hanger was labeled Friday.

"Mrs. Moran went off in the crimson," I heard my own voice say mechanically. "All her other things seem to be here. She didn't even take a coat."

"That should make it easy for the Sheriff," cried Ruth, still sustained by sheer excitement. "She'll be caught at once. Dressed like that, she hasn't got a chance."

I didn't share my little sister-in-law's optimism. Even then, I believed that Veronica Moran would not be captured soon or easily. Al thought that, too.

Without a word he dropped to his knees and began struggling to free Gog and Magog from their tangled, twisted ribbons. Between the frenzied leaps of the indignant animals and his own clumsiness, he was severely scratched before he was able to snap the ribbons. Released, the cats fled screeching toward the kitchen.

"They've not been fed," I said, clinging to one tiny commonplace in the midst of general bewilderment. "The poor beasts are starving."

The blazing light died from Ruth's eyes, as she glanced from Al's set, stern face to me. Suddenly she looked forlorn and small—a little frightened.

"I'll find some milk," she said, and left the room.

Al dropped the torn, crimson ribbons. One of his thumbs was bitten, and he staunched the wound with his handkerchief. The small injury seemed to require his full attention.

"I'd hate to undertake to tie those devils up," he said. "It was hard enough to get them loose. Gog darn near took my hand."

For some reason, that irritated me. Probably because I was so keenly aware that his mind wasn't on the thumb, or on Gog's disposition either. I turned around to survey again the wreckage of the bedroom. Even the dressing table had not escaped. The scarf that protected the glass top had been jerked violently to the floor, and the jars and bottles, the hairbrush and the mirror, the enormous atomizer, had tumbled off into a wastebasket. Unless Mrs. Moran had gone berserk, I couldn't understand it.

"I can," Al said grimly. "Without half trying. In the general confusion we were meant to overlook the desk. Not to notice it particularly, I mean."

I frowned.

"Wake up, Janey. We're going to need to be wide awake. The desk is all that matters. Someone went through that desk, made a desperate search of it. The rest is only a stupid attempt to cover up."

"Someone searched the desk? Do you actually mean that Mrs. Moran herself—?"

He leaned toward me. "Mrs. Moran left this house hours ago, Jane. Keep that in your mind. It's important."

"Why?" I stammered, alarmed by the alarm I could feel in him.

"Why? That's easy, too. The desk has been searched in the last half hour. Maybe in less than that. Look at the press book, Janey. Go on over and look at it."

The press book, pasted with notices and criticisms of concerts given long ago and long forgotten, was an ornate volume, brassbound and with a vellum cover. The ugly blot of ink on the cover had dripped over to stain the floor and carpet. I touched the vellum cover. It was wet A little ink came off on my finger. It was a deep purple color.

"Ink evaporates," Al said, "in no time at all. That explains the disappearance of our car keys, doesn't it? Very satisfactorily. Just that stain of wet ink." His voice was savage. "Someone had to make an opportunity to reach this bedroom and go through the desk before the police were on the scene. That's why the car keys went. It certainly wasn't Veronica Moran who took them."

I wet my dry lips. "Someone? Who?"

Al's own voice broke. "Janey, I'm afraid to think."

With a numb lack of any feeling, I gazed at the Italian desk. At the tumbled papers, the scattered clippings, the old programs and the older letters, souvenirs of the bygone days of the owner's glory. A feather pen, sunk in a cup of shot, remained miraculously in place. Like the ink, it was a deep purple color. I touched Al's hand.

"But why? Why? What was in the desk that could be that important?"

His voice was now dead and lifeless. "We're in the middle of a murder case, Janey. Every one of us. Can't you realize that? In a murder case, people consider their necks important. I don't know what was in the desk, but I have a pretty good idea it might have hanged someone." He wasn't speaking of Veronica Moran. He was speaking of one of us. I had seen Veronica Moran that afternoon with cold and murderous rage in her eyes; from all appearances she had fled almost simultaneously with Hannah's murder; but she hadn't stolen our car keys, or gone through her own desk in frenzied, desperate haste. Veronica Moran had been close to Hannah, but I no longer felt assured that she alone was in that position. She could have hated Hannah to the point of murder, or feared her, but that didn't mean that the enigmatic harpist was alone in such fear and hatred.

These thoughts passed through my mind, as I looked at Al. I have never seen such wretchedness in his face.

"Please leave me, dear," he said.

On legs that felt stiff and wooden, I moved toward the door. At the threshold, I looked back. Al had stooped and was sopping up the ink stains with his handkerchief. I didn't ask him why. I knew. Sheriff Blandish would soon arrive, was undoubtedly rushing toward us at that very moment, and before he surveyed the bedroom Al meant that the telltale ink stains spilled across the book, and shining on the floor and carpet, should be quite dry. If Al could help it, Sheriff Blandish should not know something of which we were both convinced—that one of us had deliberately removed the car keys in order to gain time to search Mrs. Moran's desk. Sheriff Blandish could inspect the bedroom, and no doubt like us would conclude that the desk was all that mattered. Once the stains of ink were dry, however, he would be unable to decide when the devastation had occurred. Al intended to see to that. I left him at the task.

As bewildered and wretched as I've ever been, I went out toward the kitchen. Several minutes passed before I had the heart to enter.

After the bedroom, the kitchen looked almost peaceful. It wasn't neat, but then it had not been neat that afternoon. Everything was exactly the same. Half of the bakery cake and a crumb-smeared knife lay on an enamel table. Several dried-out watercress sandwiches, left over from the supply in the living room, rested on the drainboard beside an open canister of tea. Gog and Magog were dancing frantically around the table, attempting to reach the cake. Ruth stood at the icebox. I had meant to conceal my own feelings, but my sister-in-law was too perplexed herself to notice anything amiss with me.

"This is the strangest house, Janey," she said. "I'm beginning to think that Mrs. Moran wasn't just peculiar. She was mad."

I walked over to the icebox. It was entirely empty. No milk, no butter, no eggs. Nothing. The meshed wire shelves were as bare as a ballroom floor. Mrs. Moran's refrigerator was like one of those glistening porcelain affairs exhibited in a showroom window, or used as a prop on a stage. There wasn't even ice.

"Where in the world did she keep her milk?" Ruth demanded. "Except for the peas in the bedroom, and that cake and stuff, there's nothing here to eat. I haven't looked in the cabinets yet, but I shouldn't think—"

As though they understood, Gog and Magog wailed louder. The black cat attempted to climb the table. Ruth glanced uncertainly at the cake.

"Try the porch," I suggested.

As she opened the door that led to the dusky, screened-in place, I glimpsed in the dim light a jumble of domestic overflow—a garbage can, the hard shine of a tilted broom handle, an old-fashioned washboard, all partly hidden by a portable wooden clothes rack hung with frozen garments rustling in a ghostly way. There seemed to be no outdoor storage place for provisions, but with that instinct people have to satisfy themselves, I started over there.

"Nothing here," Ruth said quickly, and closed the door.

My vague surprise at her manner was lost in my discovery of something that both of us had overlooked before. Reposing in the sink was a can of patented cat food. The can was open. I remembered seeing it that afternoon. Gog and Magog went wild with joy and recognition as I transferred the contents to a plate. I could hardly get the plate upon the floor. Biting and clawing, each fighting to outdo the other, the cats fell upon the food as though they hadn't eaten in months. Gog, the violent brother, was determined to have it all. Ruth stooped to push him off. It wasn't necessary. Abruptly at the second mouthful Gog gave up the struggle, lifted his sooty head, howled in an unearthly fashion and leaped across the kitchen toward the porch. But the door was closed, and he reversed himself, and, still howling, fled into the foyer.

"Whatever in the world," I began, and suddenly recalled tales of animals who sensed what people couldn't.

From far away, like an echo to the unearthly howl of the cat, came the clang of an ambulance bell. Distinct and unmistakable, hurtling across the open field, came the clang of the hoarse-tongued bell. The Merristone ambulance had pulled up on Copston Road before our cottage.

Chapter Nine:
A LADY SUDDENLY MISSED

I probably broke Gog's record in the speed with which I quit the kitchen. I expected Ruth to follow, but she bent over to pick up the plate that Magog, left in sole possession, had already emptied. Waiting in the living room, Al was hurried but practical enough, and quite calm. In emergency he can always pull himself together. To Al the arrival of the ambulance simply meant that the police were in possession at the cottage.

"Blandish always gets there first. Call Ruth. We've been here much too long already."

"The ink?" I said.

Al wanted to forget that part, to push it from his mind. He spoke with no feeling whatever, as though discussing something that had happened long ago to someone else. "Blotted dry. And I've cleaned my hands. Do hurry, dear. I'd much rather they didn't find us here."

We had underestimated Sheriff Blandish. Outside, I heard a sudden rush of footsteps on the porch, the urgent ring of a doorbell. Almost simultaneously the door banged open, and the foyer light snapped on. With mutual surprise Sheriff Blandish regarded us, and we regarded him. A startled deputy peered over his head. The Sheriff spoke first: "So this is where you are. May I ask why?"

Al spoke a shade too quickly. "We came to tell Mrs. Moran about Hannah. We thought—"

Sheriff Blandish frowned. It developed at once that he preferred to do the thinking himself. "Where is she?"

"Gone," I said, too hurried myself. "We think—"

Again he frowned, and I was silenced, Sheriff Blandish was as large as Belton, but entirely bald. His eyes we blue—swift, quick-moving eyes, trained to take in the essentials. The speed of the blue eyes was disconcerting. In a single sweeping glance they encompassed the whole of the living room, took in the guttering candles, the overturned glass on the floor, the stain of tea.

"That—the glass is not important," I felt impelled to say. "Al did it this afternoon. We had tea here."

"I see," he said, as though he didn't see at all. "I wasn't aware that you were acquainted with Mrs. Moran, or with her maid."

No response to that occurred to either Al or me. What I had anticipated was happening. The tea table suggested intimacy. It was impossible to explain how meager was extent of our acquaintanceship with Mrs. Moran and Hannah, without sounding too defensive.

Our presence in the house at that moment was definitely a mistake. It, too, suggested that we had felt privileged to make ourselves at home. With shock, I realized that we'd left the cottage a good half hour earlier. We could have discovered very quickly that Mrs. Moran was gone and returned to the others. Something as small as a blot of ink—moist and wet, spilling across a vellum-covered book—had prevented the return. Sheriff Blandish looked hard at us both, then turned to his deputy.

"Go and round up the others. Tell them the lost are found. Get help from the cottage if necessary. Doc won't need Evans and Smith much longer. At any rate, I want everybody located and here inside ten minutes."

Located? My heart sank as I glanced at Al. He said with more assurance than he felt, "I gather the others, my brother, my cousin, aren't at the cottage. Have they been hunting us?"

"Quite some while," said Sheriff Blandish. "Your brother was seriously alarmed. I must say I wasn't. Though I'd like to add I consider your behavior—theirs, too—extraordinary. We had to lead ourselves, Dr. Traphaven and I, to the body of a murdered woman. First time in my experience."

"I—we thought—"

"Hereafter, if you'd just not think, Mr. Blake, I believe we'll get along a little better. You might pass that suggestion on to your relatives and friends." And then, with chill politeness, he added, "Sit here and wait, please. I'll want to talk to you."

With that he turned on his heel and went quickly through the house, apparently to find out for himself whether Mrs. Moran was really gone. He stayed several minutes in the master bedroom. The door squeaked as he went in, and squeaked again as he emerged and crossed the foyer to return to us. He seemed to be in no hurry to begin the questioning. He switched on the electric lights, blew out the few remaining candles, pushed the harp aside, and planted himself upon the sofa. Only then did he address himself to us. The blue eyes held a most peculiar expression.

"House in this condition when you came in? I have reference to the bedroom. Is that how you found it?"

"Exactly," said Al, and looked him unwaveringly in the eye, which was more than I could have done.

"Curious," said the Sheriff thoughtfully, "whoever tore through there like a tornado seems to have been of several minds. Pulled the bed apart, threw those peas like birdshot, wrecked the desk—that's significant—upset a bottle of ink, and then turned around and wiped it up. Not too consistent, is it?"

I looked at the floor. But it seemed to me that his eyes were burning through my head, and I felt sure a much duller man could have heard the thumping of my heart. Somewhere in the snow and darkness outside, the deputy was bellowing like a bull, shouting for Frank and Sarah Belton and Selby. He sounded like a schoolmaster summoning a reluctant class to order. But the crowded living room, seen now in a harsh blaze of electricity, was entirely silent.

"Mrs. Moran—" I began, in a choked voice.

"An odd woman, unquestionably," said Sheriff Blandish. "But that bedroom—the condition it's in—goes several steps beyond sheer oddity. I can't see it would be to Mrs. Moran's advantage to leave it in that shape. Any more than it would be to her advantage to kill her maid and then turn tail and run. In my line of business, flight is usually a confession of guilt."

I didn't pluck up hope at that. I daresay I wasn't meant to. With the greatest effort, I managed to leave off my study of the carpet.

"Mrs. Moran wasn't stupid, was she?" asked the Sheriff gently.

"We hardly knew her."

"She wasn't stupid," Al said. "No, Sheriff Blandish. Mrs. Moran wasn't stupid in the least."

The Sheriff sighed, and I remembered times when he had dropped by to argue with Aunt Mildred that certain taxes were necessary to run even a small community. Suddenly the blue eyes regarding us weren't cold and hard. They were troubled and distressed, and infinitely more terrifying. Abruptly the Sheriff got to his feet.

"Nevertheless, Mrs. Moran is—missing. There's no doubt of that."

"If you'd like a description of her clothing," I said.

He accepted the description. Indeed he requested minute details, particularly of the shoes and jewelry—the height of the stilt heels, the type of leather, the shape of the lily locket, the metal, the kind of jewels that encrusted the petals, the size of the opal that burned in the golden heart. One would have thought that Mrs. Moran was to be recognized and arrested in her flight by a mere identification of her ornaments and shoes. It did not occur to me that these were the least perishable items of her costume. Perhaps I didn't desire to follow the Sheriff's trend of thought, or to wonder whether Veronica Moran, like the murdered Hannah, might not be gone forever.

Still moving slowly, Sheriff Blandish went to the telephone, plucked off the china-headed, fluffy-skirted doll that hid it, gazed at the frivolous object in mild surprise, and then made the calls that were to send Veronica Moran's description humming up and down wires strung the length of the Atlantic seaboard. By morning Merristone was to be famous. A missing harpist, dressed from head to toe in crimson, her murdered servant found in the cellar of an unfinished house belonging to "a prominent young advertising executive"—the story had everything.

Sheriff Blandish replaced the telephone. "They'll want photographs, I suppose." He glanced around the collection on the walls and frowned. "I see she's not represented here. Well, the picture can wait till we get at her press book."

"I can describe her car," said Al. "A roadster, black, two dented fenders, a 1937 model...."

"Never mind, Mr. Blake. I understand she didn't drive. At any rate, I know she didn't drive her own car off."

With that he picked his way across the crowded room and flung up a window. Snow was still falling but softly now and lightly. Like a flight of moths, tentative and uncertain, flakes of dazzling white fluttered across the flashlight which he shone onto the drive below. Blanketed in white, until it was like a drift itself, sat the battered roadster. The snowfall had started at 5:45. I didn't need Sheriff Blandish to inform me that the car had not been used since. Al and I saw it pull up beside the house and abruptly stop. The glistening driveway, smooth and unbroken as a stretch of placid water, was proof enough.

Outside, through the open window, I heard Belton's querulous, complaining voice. The first to enter, he came in, shaking snow like a sea lion, chilled to the bone, and annoyed with everybody. In a minute it seemed to me the living room was filled with people: Selby and Frank as chilled as Belton but less vocal about it; Sarah, who had fallen into a drift and was soaking wet; the puzzled deputies who had either stuck to firmer terrain or had been less interested in running down three people old enough to take care of themselves. Comparatively speaking, the deputies looked quite comfortable.

No one remarked that we might have been less reticent about our plans, or realized that our absence might cause certain natural concern, but viewing the bedraggled group I felt like a dog. Sarah observed that Frank's feet were wet, quite unaware that her own were sopping, and asked no one's permission to go over and build up a fire. Al's conscience hurt him, too. He got the kindling away from her, before Frank could do it. In the confusion and babble of the arrival, even Sheriff Blandish's compelling personality was almost lost. Indeed, Dr. Traphaven managed to slip in without my noticing, until across Sarah's head I glimpsed his spry, familiar figure, his little quivering beard. He was whispering to the Sheriff.

I knew then that one phase of the dreadful and fantastic evening was at an end. The coroner's presence meant that Hannah's body had been removed from the cottage. Silently, and without the clanging bell, the ambulance would carry her body to the village. Sheriff Blandish nodded to Dr. Traphaven, walked into the center of the room and took a position that hushed the babble as though by magic.

"Now that I've finally got you all together—" and he hesitated, frowned vaguely, glanced around.

It was then that Selby spoke. "Except Ruth," he said. Still shaking from exposure, blue to the lips, but apparently too exhausted to move toward the blazing kindling, Selby sat huddled in the chair nearest the door. "Where's Ruth, Janey?"

Far below the surface of my conscious mind, wholly occupied with what was going on, I must have felt some minutes before that Ruth was spending an unconscionable length of time in the kitchen. Subconsciously I must have wondered why the noise and confusion of the various arrivals had not brought her running to the living room, just as subconsciously I had wondered why she hadn't followed me, and had paused instead to pick up a plate. I had not missed her. Ruth, whose blond head barely reached Al's shoulder, was so little she could be overlooked in any crowd. But somehow I must have realized several minutes earlier that she was not with us.

"Where's Ruth?" Selby asked again, in a slightly louder tone.

I jumped to my feet. "In the kitchen. I'll call her."

I had thought my voice was calm. But Belton jumped up too, and Selby's thin, drawn face turned white. The scrape of his chair was like the shriek of chalk across a blackboard.

The Sheriff said, "In the kitchen? I didn't see her there."

Chapter Ten:
BEHIND THE LATTICE-WORK

Ruth wasn't in the kitchen. Magog was sleeping peacefully underneath the stove, curled up beside a plate that was licked bare and clean. Ruth had picked up the plate and then laid it down again. On the porcelain table beside the bakery cake was the tin can I'd emptied, but the plate was on the floor. On a chair nearby lay a pair of bright blue mittens. Ruth had stripped her hands, as she stepped to the icebox. The mittens belonged to her. But Ruth wasn't there. Where had she gone?

Ruth never did impulsive, heedless things that would worry other people. She hadn't wanted to come to the house in the first place. She'd only come because of Al and me. It was incredible that she would leave without telling us. Forty steps, perhaps even less, separated living room and kitchen. Al and I were in the living room all the time. From the kitchen Ruth could have heard the Sheriff arrive, the sounds of the others flocking in soon afterward. But she hadn't stayed in the kitchen. Why? *Where had she gone?*

With the others at my heels, I ran out on the back porch. The screen door stood open upon a short steep flight of steps that descended to the kitchen yard. A little snow was drifting in. The yard below was invisible. The blackness of the night rose like walls, shutting in the house like a little lighted island. Ruth wasn't on the porch.

It was then that panic struck us all—all of us who loved and knew her. Behind me I heard Selby's voice, loud and desperate: "Something's happened to her. She's afraid of the dark. Terribly afraid. She wouldn't leave the house of her own accord."

He went plunging down the steps to the kitchen yard, and most of the others went after him. The next few seconds weren't real to me. People were running through the house, calling Ruth's name, other people—Belton and Selby like two mad men—were stumbling through the darkness of the bitter night, fanning out from the house, playing flashlights on every heap of brush, calling, calling. Their futile progress could be followed by the rising hysteria in their voices.

Where had she gone? She couldn't just disappear. I walked stiffly past the chair where Ruth had dropped her mittens. I looked at the plate that she had picked up from the kitchen floor, and then inexplicably laid down again. Something must have caused her to lay down the plate, something had prevented her from coming to the living room and led her from the house. What?

I could think of nothing. Like Selby, I repeated senselessly, "But Ruth wouldn't leave of her own accord. I know she wouldn't. She'd have stayed here in the kitchen."

Sheriff Blandish, who alone refused to yield to general panic, had stuck at my side. He, too, looked around the kitchen, commonplace and ordinary in the brilliant light.

"Sometimes, Mrs. Blake, the people we know best do unexpected things. I'm convinced your sister-in-law left the kitchen voluntarily. Why?" He hesitated. "Partly because of the way she set down the plate, carefully, in the spot where it had been before. Partly because nothing could have happened to her here. It isn't possible. You and your husband were in earshot every single minute."

I had thought of that, even in my terror and bewilderment. If Ruth had seen anything to alarm her, if she had screamed, Al and I would certainly have heard her. She had vanished without a sound. Apparently without a trace.

"Was the back door closed when you yourself left the kitchen?" Sheriff Blandish asked me. "I mean the door opening on the porch."

"She closed it herself," I said mechanically, and suddenly remembered something.

I saw Ruth standing on the kitchen threshold, peering out upon the dusky porch. I saw her close the door as I approached. Very quickly, almost as though she meant to cut off my vision of the shadowy, screened-in place, piled up with the garbage can, the washboard and the tubs, the rack of frozen garments. The Sheriff called a rapid question, but I had run out on the porch again.

He paused long enough to switch on the light. But there was nothing out of order. The washboard and the tubs were in place, and the garbage can. The clothes rack was arranged across a corner, and the stiff, unnatural folds of the suspended garments curtained a three-sided space behind. In his own frenzied investigation, Selby had gone there first, I had gone there myself, but the shadowy three-sided space had been empty.

Nevertheless, Sheriff Blandish went straight toward the clothes rack. It was difficult to peer over the contraption, and he lifted it, clothes and all. The garments creaked and rustled in his arms. With a smart bang he set down the rack, and turned to continue his examination of the corner.

At that point, something caught in the icy ruffle of a petticoat rattled to the floor. Simultaneously we turned around. Lying beside the clothes rack was the buckle of Ruth's belt.

The buckle hadn't fallen from her belt. It had been ripped from the heavy cloth material. A few broken threads clung to the metal shaft.

I saw the Sheriff pick up the buckle, saw the metal flash in his hand. It was a small, square buckle of some shiny composition. The clinging threads were sapphire blue. Ruth's woolen frock had matched her eyes, and over it she had worn an unbelted reefer coat. The buckle had been torn from the belt of her dress. With a numb lack of any feeling I saw the buckle flashing in the Sheriff's hand. I heard him speak.

"We should have made a thorough investigation of the porch," he said, and then he added, "The buckle wasn't *really* hard to find. I don't believe your sister-in-law is away."

I made nothing of that, or of the curious expression on his face. It was as though my brain had stopped functioning. When Sheriff Blandish walked from the screened-in porch and started down the steps to the kitchen yard, I followed like an automaton. In the distant darkness the others were calling and shouting. They had rushed through the kitchen yard and on.

Sheriff Blandish paused on the bottom step of the short, steep flight of stairs. From that vantage point he moved his flashlight, inch by inch, across the gleaming snow surrounding us. The kitchen yard was defined by a picket fence. So far as I could see, the enclosed space, carpeted in glistening white, was barren and empty. There wasn't even a tree of any size. Closer and closer the light crept toward where we stood. I leaned against the guard rail of the steps, my aching eyes fixed upon the creeping spot of light. There was nothing.

Disappointed, evidently frustrated in some personal theory, Sheriff Blandish seemed about to give up. Suddenly he thought of something, whirled around and swept his light up and down the steps.

I screamed.

The steps had sides of flimsy, crisscrossed latticework. Through the latticework directly below us one end of Ruth's belt emerged. Like a bright bit of sapphire ribbon it curled across the snowy ground. One end only; the other end was out of sight. Sheriff Blandish had been right. Ruth wasn't far away. She was underneath the steps.

My scream brought Sarah and Dr. Traphaven on a dead run. Selby was there an instant later. Ruth had been thrust head first, like a lifeless dummy, into the aperture underneath the stairs. The latticed side had been removed, and carefully put back into position. We had to jerk it out again before we could reach her.

Within that incredible hiding place, Ruth lay white and still like a sleeping child. The sharply angling stairs formed the ceiling of her prison, the bare and frozen ground the floor. As though some fantastic effort had been made to protect her from the bitter chill, her coat had been securely wrapped around her and the doormat from the porch placed beneath her fair head. But her head was smeared with blood. Her hands were folded upon her breast precisely as Hannah's hands had been folded. The sapphire belt that had led us to her, bound them together. Her own handkerchief had been stuffed into her mouth.

I was sure that she was dead, as Selby pushed the others back and started to lift her in his shaking arms, and then I saw the flutter of her eyelids. It was only then that I began to cry. Sarah was crying, too.

"You'd better let me carry her," Dr. Traphaven said. "She may be badly hurt."

As the physician gently touched her head—she had been struck from behind—I thought Ruth winced. When he stripped the handkerchief from her mouth and unloosed her hands, her eyelids fluttered again. But the blue eyes didn't open until Dr. Traphaven had carried her through the kitchen and into the nearest bedroom. It was Hannah's bedroom.

He laid Ruth on the narrow cot, so at variance with the luxurious bed in the room adjoining, thrust a pillow underneath her feet, and ordered Selby to open the windows. He had spied the brandy in the living room; I could bring him that. Everybody else, including Sheriff Blandish, he firmly invited to wait in there.

"Particularly you, Sheriff. The child's going to be all right. But she's not fit to be questioned now." He stooped over to make a thorough examination of the injury. Gently he parted the fair, blood-smeared hair. I saw a flicker of perplexity cross his face, saw his sure, professional fingers reach quickly for Ruth's wrist. He and Sheriff Blandish were closer than most brothers. As they exchanged a glance, the perplexity passed from one man to the other.

Dr. Traphaven said slowly, "The blow's a surface injury. It's not serious. But of course you can never tell with shock...."

Selby had already fallen to his knees beside the cot. "Darling, darling, can you hear? You're safe now."

The blue eyes opened then. I found out what the doctor meant by shock. The eyes weren't Ruth's eyes at all. In a dead white face, with the pupils enormously dilated, they were black as coal. She drew a long shuddering breath.

"Don't try to talk, dear," Selby said. "Try not to remember. It's all over now. Now we've got you back, nothing matters, darling. Nothing."

His eyes were on her face. Ruth looked at his bowed, dark head, and then around the group. Selby might have been a stranger, and Sarah and myself. Still in a dazed, uncertain way she looked at Dr. Traphaven and then at Sheriff Blandish. A crease between his brows, the little doctor was staring down at her.

I don't suppose it was deliberate, but Sheriff Blandish had paused beside the washstand where Hannah's personal possessions were ranged. Spread on a neatly folded towel was a toothbrush in a glass, a ten-cent comb caught with a few gray hairs, a can of talcum powder. Piled on a shelf underneath was a heap of tattered magazines, containing the western stories and tales of romance with which Hannah had whiled away the dreary, empty hours of her leisure. Ruth looked at the pitiful array, and perhaps like myself she thought of the murdered Hannah. It seemed to me her eyes grew blacker still. She tried to struggle up in bed.

Selby cried out, "Lie back, dear. Your head."

"It hurts very little, Selby." Ruth pushed aside his restraining hand and managed to sit up. "I'm all right, really. No, Dr. Traphaven," she said feverishly, "I won't drink that. I won't be treated like an invalid. I want to know—"

What did she want to know? Sarah and I halted on the threshold. Ruth's voice had been desperate in its urgency, but she didn't finish out her question. It was as though she was unable to find the proper words. Unable or unwilling. Sheriff Blandish turned away from the washstand. Again, as on the porch, I glimpsed on his face a most peculiar expression. He gazed at Dr. Traphaven and then steadily at Ruth, and waited. She didn't ask her question.

"I'm sorry I gave everybody such a scare," she said in the confused and feverish way. "I was scared myself. I still am, I guess."

"Don't talk, dear."

"Where's that brandy?" demanded Dr. Traphaven.

Sarah and I left the room, but the coroner didn't request a second time that Sheriff Blandish wait elsewhere. In some subtle way his whole attitude had changed. It had changed the moment he picked up Ruth's wrist and took her pulse. As I closed the door, Sheriff Blandish was pulling up a chair beside the cot. His attitude had also changed. One was reminded that he was in charge of a murder investigation. My final glimpse was of Ruth shrinking back from him. Sarah saw it, too.

"Something's wrong," she whispered. "Something's got into Ruth. She's not like herself. I'd almost think—"

We were standing in the hall. The other men had come in from outside, and in the living room Belton was arguing with Al and Frank, insisting that he should be taken instantly to his daughter. I was fond of Belton, but I felt the situation was far too complicated for him to go crashing into the bedroom.

"We'll have to keep him out," I said. "Or you will. I've got to get the brandy, Sarah."

Sarah held on to me. Indeed she stood so close that I was pressed against the door.

"Don't you know what's wrong? Didn't you see? The doctor's not interested in the brandy." Sarah leaned toward me, and whispered in my ear. "Ruth's not badly hurt. Dr. Traphaven knows it. She was conscious when we found her. Didn't you notice how loosely she was bound? If she'd made any kind of struggle she could have freed herself."

"Shock," I said, over my own terror and bewilderment. "Shock could account for that."

"Sheriff Blandish could figure out another answer. He probably has. That's what terrifies me. If it weren't Ruth, I know what I'd think—"

I wet my lips. "What?"

"That Ruth was playing for time. Waiting to find out how much we know, before she told what happened on the porch."

"I don't believe that. It makes no sense at all."

"Listen, Janey." Sarah's whisper was almost desperate now. "Let me tell you why I wanted to talk with Selby before dinner. I've got to tell someone. Frank and I saw him last Monday in New York. Monday at lunchtime. We were crossing Fifth Avenue at Forty-second Street, and were caught by a traffic light. Selby didn't see us. He was getting in a cab on the other side."

I was utterly at sea. Selby seldom went to town, and usually complained about such a trip long afterward. He hadn't spoken of any visit to the city. But surely he had a right to travel 40 miles and hail a cab on the Avenue, without taking the whole family into his confidence.

"Selby wasn't alone," Sarah said. "There was a woman in the cab. I saw her, too."

"A woman?"

"It was Hannah. Hannah Wilson, earphone, man's coat, and all. Hannah was no stranger to Selby. They were going somewhere together. At lunchtime in New York last Monday."

"But, Sarah—"

"Selby knew Hannah quite well. Blandish is bound to find it out. Frank and I are not the only ones who know. I spoke to Selby's secretary this afternoon."

"Miss Hawkins?"

"Miss Hawkins told me"—again Sarah clutched my hand—"that Selby has seen Hannah repeatedly in his office. He's been seeing her since last November."

Chapter Eleven:
CONFUSION, DELIBERATE AND COMPLEX

When I returned to Hannah's room, I walked on legs of lead. Sarah's information had changed everything. Why had Selby met Hannah in New York at lunchtime on Monday? The answer to that question seemed less important than the fact itself.

In all our agitated family discussions of the mysterious outlanders in the neighborhood—Veronica Moran and Hannah—Selby had never indicated in any way that he was acquainted with the maid. On the contrary, he had taken pains to convince us all that both maid and mistress were total strangers to him. We had discussed the pair for months, and Selby hadn't shown the slightest interest except—I remembered with a sinking heart—that he had always tried to lead the conversation elsewhere.

To hear that Selby had met Hannah in New York five short days before her murder was more than bewildering. It was appalling.

When I slipped back into the room and set down the brandy bottle no one noticed me, which was fortunate. My face would probably have given me away. But no one there was in the least concerned with me. Even before I Looked around, I felt the strain and tension in the bleak and poorly furnished room that was so evocative of the murdered Hannah.

Dr. Traphaven, usually voluble and expansive, was silently folding up a length of bandage and replacing it in his bag. Sheriff Blandish, seated in the chair beside the cot, looked very tired. Tired and oddly depressed. Selby was on his feet, but he leaned against the iron footrest of the ugly cot as though he had run a long hard race and lost it.

For one awful moment I was afraid that Sheriff Blandish, in some inexplicable fashion, had discovered that Selby was well acquainted with Hannah—well acquainted enough to meet her 40 miles from Merristone and take her "somewhere" in a cab. But the Sheriff's eyes were fixed on Ruth.

Ruth was propped high with pillows. A little color had come back into her cheeks, and beneath the bandage that Dr. Traphaven had fixed on her head the blank, black look had faded from her eyes. At first glance she looked almost like her old self again. And then I saw that her recovery only touched the surface. A new and unfamiliar expression had come into Ruth's eyes. They were wary, guarded, watchful. Lying there among the pillows, constrained, remote, unlike herself, she made me think of a little, cornered animal—defiant but frightened, too.

I knew at once that she had told her story. I knew, too, that Sheriff Blandish was far from satisfied.

"One point I don't understand," he was saying gently, "is why you left the kitchen and stepped out on the porch."

It was a natural question, and one that had troubled me. Troubled me from the instant I recalled Ruth peering out into the jumbled place, and then closing the door before I could join her. Under some circumstances the question might have been calculated to be reassuring, to start Ruth off from the beginning. Ruth wasn't reassured. I saw for the first time the little nervous quivering of her mouth that was to increase in the coming days. She raised her hand to her trembling lips.

"I don't remember," she said. "I tell you I don't remember. It must have been an impulse. Unless I was looking for milk to feed the cats."

"But you'd discovered several minutes earlier that no food was stored on the porch. Indeed, as I understand it, you and your sister-in-law had already fed the cats."

"That's right, too. I—I'm mixed up, I guess. So much has happened that I'm all confused."

Sheriff Blandish was very patient. "Maybe I can help," he said slowly. "Try and think back. You were standing over by the stove, with the empty plate in your hand. Your sister-in-law had just gone. Gog had run from the kitchen and—"

"That's it," cried Ruth in sudden triumph. "I do recall! I thought Gog had run out on the porch, and I went after him." She caught my eye, faltered, said, "Don't you remember, Janey, how he ran?"

I remembered exactly. Gog had fled in the direction of the living room—not toward the back porch but away from it. When Ruth walked across the kitchen and stepped outside, pausing long enough to close the door behind her, she certainly had not gone in pursuit of Gog. I opened my mouth—and closed it.

Sheriff Blandish was watching me, just as Ruth was watching. She and I had always been like sisters, sharing all our thoughts and little secrets. With shock I realized that Ruth's mind was closed to me, that she was like a stranger.

"Were you about to speak, Mrs. Blake?" asked Sheriff Blandish.

"No," I said.

He smiled persuasively. "We were discussing the black cat. Did you also see him run out on the back porch?"

"Magog went under the stove," I said steadily, "but I didn't notice Gog. Except that the ambulance bell terrified him, and he left his food."

"Gog hadn't gone to the porch," Ruth broke in with stumbling eagerness. "But I thought he had. So I went after him, and then—"

Sheriff Blandish said absently, "Odd. The black cat shot through the front door and off into the dark as we entered. Still, I suppose one might become confused."

To my surprise he dropped the topic there. Possibly he might have pursued it except that the door opened just then. Belton came in, followed by the others. With Sarah's assistance, Al and Frank had kept the architect from the room a good 15 minutes. Belton was in a state of outrage and suspicion. Brushing Dr. Traphaven aside, he bore down upon the Sheriff like a white-thatched, angry bear.

"What are you doing to my daughter? Why have I been kept from her? Why isn't she allowed to go home? She's in no condition to withstand a cross-examination! Selby, I'm surprised you put up with this! I'm this child's father, and I demand—"

"Please, Mr. Weaver." Sheriff Blandish managed to stem the sizzling phrases. "Your daughter is talking to us of her own free will. Indeed, at her own request."

"That's quite true, Father," said Ruth in the odd, stiff, unfamiliar voice. "No one's mistreating me. The trouble is Sheriff Blandish and I don't agree about what happened on the porch."

"Don't agree! Rubbish! What's there to agree about? You've been hurt and—"

A little smile flickered across the Sheriff's mouth. Something seemed to please him. He leaned forward in his chair. "Your father hasn't heard your—story, nor have the others. Tell them what happened on the porch."

Sarah flashed a glance at me, and I recalled our conversation in the hall. Ruth's reluctance to talk to her own father was unmistakable. Her blue eyes remained fixed upon the tumbled bedding, and her voice was very low.

"I've told it several times, Father. She was on the porch, when I stepped out there. Hidden behind the clothes rack. It was she who struck me from behind. I heard her draperies rustling, I smelled her perfume—"

A puzzled crease between his snow-white eyebrows, Belton stared down at the cot. To this day I can see him standing there, the look of growing bewilderment on his face. I can see Sheriff Blandish bending forward, hands clasped around his knees, the overhead light shining on his great bald head, his eyes gleaming and intent. The pause lengthened out, to be broken finally by Belton.

"Her, Ruth? Her?"

"Veronica Moran," said Ruth.

Perhaps I should have been prepared, but I wasn't. For an instant I thought I hadn't heard correctly, or that Ruth's mind was wandering. I know that Sarah started violently. She and Frank stood near the flimsy bedside table. As Sarah caught the table edge the brandy bottle tinkled. and one of the tattered magazines slid off on the floor. Al stooped automatically to pick it up, and I saw his eyes. They reflected my own incredulity.

Even in the first moment I felt positive that Veronica Moran was miles away, still fleeing toward escape or perhaps already ensconced in some "safe" hiding place. In the light of what we knew, it was virtually impossible to picture the flamboyant Mrs. Moran crouched behind the clothes rack on the porch, less than an hour earlier. A dozen objections flashed into my mind. Al and I had been in the living room throughout; the authorities had arrived almost simultaneously with Ruth's disappearance. Dressed in the flowing draperies, hampered by four-inch heels, Mrs. Moran would have had little if any opportunity to effect an escape. Within five minutes the house had been ringed with searching men.

"Veronica Moran was on the porch," Ruth said a second time, and in a rising voice. Her face was pale but set and stubborn. "Hidden behind the clothes rack. I stumbled over something—a broom, I guess it was. Anyhow, I fell. Mrs. Moran came out and hit me on the head. I was on my knees, I had no chance to fight back or even to turn around. I heard her draperies, I smelled her perfume and—and that's all I remember."

Belton stood quite still. He didn't release Ruth's hand, he didn't question anything she said. No one questioned her or asked for fresh details. I daresay we were all too wretched and bewildered. Every word my little sister-in-law had spoken sounded unreal and rehearsed. Her very tone was wrong. She was like an actress letter-perfect in her part, but with no inner conviction to lend the role reality.

Ruth pulled her hand away from Belton. Color stained her face. "I can see you don't believe me. None of you. Any more than Sheriff Blandish does. Well, I should know what happened!"

She might know, but I for one believed that she did not choose to tell. Her indignation was as unreal as her story. As though she had rehearsed her emotions too. I tried to reach the stranger who was my sister-in-law.

"Ruth, my dear—"

"You needn't ask me questions, Janey," she said hostilely. "That's all I know. I don't remember being carried from the porch. I was unconscious then. But I remember that Mrs. Moran came out from behind the clothes rack and hit me on the head. I've no idea why, it's no use your asking, Sheriff. Unless she meant to kill me just as she killed Hannah."

The hand that struck down Hannah had been sure and murderously certain; Ruth had not been badly hurt. I recalled the buckle lying on the porch, the belt emerging through the lattice-work of the stairs. Whoever had concealed Ruth underneath the steps, wrapped her coat around her and placed the floor mat beneath her head had either been extremely careless or had meant that we should find her quickly. Would Veronica Moran behave in such a fashion? I could not believe it. What else was there to believe?

The air was heavy with the weight of unasked questions. And then in a puzzled, stumbling fashion, Belton spoke: "Ruth, my dear, I—we all understood that Mrs. Moran had run off early in the evening. Shortly after the murder. It seems unlikely that she'd come back here."

"Mrs. Moran did not come back," said Sheriff Blandish in flat and positive tones. "Nor was she on the porch. Your daughter is—mistaken."

Ruth sat up in bed. Bright and defiant, almost hard was the gaze she turned from her father to Sheriff Blandish. Her lips quivered and she steadied them until her mouth was as set and stubborn as Aunt Mildred's.

"Mistaken, Sheriff? Suppose we stop equivocating. What you really mean is that I'm deceiving you deliberately. Isn't that correct? You think I am inventing what I heard and what I smelled. Perfume has a definite odor. Let me tell you that I smelled real perfume, I heard real draperies rustle...."

"You didn't see Mrs. Moran," he said, still gently. "Suggestion is a powerful force. It wouldn't be surprising if in an excited state you heard and smelled what you subconsciously expected. But I know that Veronica Moran was not responsible for what happened to you on the porch."

"How can you know that?"

"By the facts themselves. By what occurred. Considerable physical strength was necessary to knock you unconscious, carry you from the porch, and shove you underneath those steps."

"Well?"

"Mrs. Moran is fifty at the very best. Not too well preserved a fifty at that, I'm convinced in my own mind she wasn't capable of such a feat."

He put his finger on the inconsistency that caused the whole narrative to collapse. Even before he spoke I must have perceived the absurdity of the idea that Veronica Moran, alone, unaided and in desperate haste, had sufficient strength to haul Ruth down the steps and thrust her out of sight. Whether my sister-in-law was honestly mistaken or whether she had concocted an explanation with the deliberate intent of implicating the missing stranger was something I didn't care to speculate about. Perhaps that is why I undertook to argue against my own convictions.

"Mrs. Moran carried Hannah down the ladder," I said aloud.

"A physical impossibility," said Sheriff Blandish. "She couldn't have done it. Dr. Traphaven bears me out. If Mrs. Moran killed her maid, she had an accomplice."

I heard him with a queer lack of surprise. In some far-off corner of my brain I must have known that to apprehend Veronica Moran was, in itself, not enough to solve our mystery. The solution of the crime was not to be clean-cut and simple. Hannah's death was to change and alter everything and plunge us all into tragedy.

The room was absolutely silent. So silent that when Dr. Traphaven closed his bag, the rasping of the catch was clearly audible. Sheriff Blandish sat back in his chair and crossed his knees. He even took out his handkerchief and mopped his bald and glistening brow.

Ruth had sunk back among the pillows, and lay there quiet and unstirring with her father gazing down at her. Frank's eyes and consideration were for Sarah. He gripped her hand, as though he wanted to protect her from the bleak and troubled future. Sarah seemed unaware of the silent pressure of his hand.

She had looked instinctively toward Selby. I looked at Selby, too, and so did Al. I had the queer fancy that my brother-in-law had braced himself just as if an expected blow had fallen.

I had to check an impulse to cry out, to beg that he explain why he had met Hannah in the city. It might have been that my nerves were overwrought, but suddenly it seemed to me that the room was filled with secrets. Selby knew more than he was willing to tell anyone, even Ruth. She wasn't in his confidence, I felt positive. Anyone who loved them could sense the change in their relationship, as though in a single evening their mutual trust had slipped away. Ruth herself, Ruth who had always been as open as the day itself, had lied to all of us.

Belton slowly straightened up. Beneath his turbulent ruff of hair, his face looked old and tired. His usually blustering voice was quiet.

"I'd like to get this straight, Sheriff Blandish. For all our sakes. We've taken it for granted that Veronica Moran killed her maid. Now you say if she's guilty, she had help. There is, of course, another possibility. Is it within the realm of possibility that Mrs. Moran herself is innocent?"

Sheriff Blandish hesitated. I saw him glance toward Dr. Traphaven.

"It's a puzzling case," he said at length, evasively. "In order to solve the crime, it's obvious that Veronica Moran must be—found."

"Mrs. Moran had a motive for murder—" began Dr. Traphaven, and then, abruptly, was silent. He flushed a painful red; it was obvious that the garrulous little doctor had spoken out of turn. For the first time, and with mixed sensations, I became aware that the authorities themselves were holding back information, that they knew more about the case than they were admitting. That single inadvertent statement was the only blunder of officialdom; no further information was forthcoming. Dr. Traphaven picked up his bag, and, like a guilty schoolboy, scuttled from the room.

"What was Mrs. Moran's motive for murder?" I asked, but in vain.

Sheriff Blandish ignored me. "I want you all to appreciate the situation as it now stands," he said. "Let me repeat: If Mrs. Moran killed her maid she had help."

"Help?"

"An accomplice. Someone who helped her commit the murder, and who very possibly helped her get away sometime early in the evening. Dr. Traphaven tells me that Hannah Wilson died sometime between six o'clock and seven. From all appearances Mrs. Moran made her escape around that time, probably directly afterward. But how? Certainly she didn't use her own car, nor did she call the local taxi or take a bus. I've checked." Sheriff Blandish got up from his chair. "Nevertheless, Mrs. Moran is gone. But someone remained behind. Hannah Wilson's murder was violent, hurried, evidently committed in the heat of passion, without plan and very possibly without premeditation—but after the murder occurred someone began to think. Someone decided quite deliberately to confuse and complicate the case. It may well have been this—this accomplice who was hidden on the porch. I'm inclined to believe it was. Just as I believe that the person who remained behind had something to do with the wrecking of the master bedroom."

"But why?"

Again he ignored the question and went calmly, courteously ahead. "Those cats weren't tied by accident in the clothes closet. Nor was the ink spilled accidentally and then wiped up. I don't know the purpose behind those seemingly demented acts, but I mean to find out. This I know now. A consistent and deliberate campaign has been carried out this evening to make things appear what they are not."

"Why do you tell us this?"

"Because I have every reason to believe," Sheriff Blandish said politely, "that the person I describe—the person who knows the answer to Hannah Wilson's murder—is present in this room."

With that he turned on his heel and walked out. He didn't even look back. We heard Dr. Traphaven call him from the master bedroom.

Chapter Twelve:
BLACK AND SHINY

Six minutes later, I was in Mrs. Moran's kitchen looking for my coat. A deputy had come to Hannah's room and told us we were no longer needed, that we might all go home.

Bright and commonplace in the glare of lights, the kitchen was deserted. The others were helping Ruth out to a car, but I had been convinced that the best way I could help my sister-in-law was to stay away.

I wasn't interested in Mrs. Moran's kitchen, in the bareness of her shelves and cabinets, in the emptiness of her refrigerator. I wasn't interested in the mystery. All that I desired to do was to shut thoughts of Ruth and Selby from my mind. But when I buttoned on my coat and turned to go, I turned back again.

Almost without volition, I moved slowly across the kitchen until I stood on the threshold of the porch. The overhead light still blazed on the clutter there—the garbage can, the old uniform of Hannah's suspended from a nail, the empty vegetable bin, the clothes rack hung with frozen garments.

I did not know what had happened on the porch, but in a kind of frenzy I realized that had Ruth remained in the kitchen she would have been quite safe. Why had she waited until I left the kitchen, and then immediately gone out on the porch? The answer came at once. Ruth had seen something. When we were searching for food to give the cats and she had looked outside for milk, she had seen something that aroused her curiosity. When she hurriedly closed the door before I could get a clear view myself, she had already decided to venture forth and investigate. Of that I was positive.

My memory of the scene was accurate and distinct. Each detail came back to me. I saw Ruth open the door and look out—I heard her call, "No milk, Jane!"—I saw myself approach. Through the swiftly closing door I had received a single flashing glimpse of the porch beyond.

Shivering in my heavy coat, I looked at the porch again. The litter and confusion suggested nothing to my mind. Like a person acting out the details of a dream, clear and unforgettable, I stepped back until I stood exactly where Ruth had stood. From that angle she could not have seen behind the clothes rack. In any event I doubted that she would have gone outside, had she suspected some person was hiding on the porch. Ruth had seen some—some object. What was it?

Suddenly I recalled that the porch light had not been burning. I reached out, and snapped it off. The porch became as it had been when I had received my single glimpse—dusky, shadowy, confused and crowded. The porch was precisely the same. But was it? Vaguely, in the dimmest kind of way, I missed something. My head hurt with the effort of concentration. The clothes rack swam before my eyes, steadied. I jumped a little, as I solved the problem.

A broom was missing. I had glimpsed the shiny handle emerging from behind the clothes rack. The handle, dark and highly polished, had caught the kitchen light. I remembered the hard, high shine.

"What became of the broom?" I said, aloud.

"The broom?" echoed a soft voice behind me.

I turned around. Sheriff Blandish was standing at my elbow. "Suppose you and I locate this disappearing broom, just to satisfy our curiosity," he said quietly—and with the utmost affability. "Surely, Mrs. Blake, you're willing to help me find a broom."

When he took firm hold of my elbow, I considered various objections and discarded them. I did not like his change of manner, or his calm pretense that I would be pleased to assist him. Underneath we both understood quite clearly that he menaced me and mine. But I could not fathom how an ordinary house broom could play a part in our mystery, and, to tell the truth, I was curious too.

With mixed emotions, I followed Sheriff Blandish out upon the porch. There was no broom there. Between us we carried out an exhaustive and quite futile search. We explored every inch of the porch; we turned the clothes rack upside down, peered behind the garbage can, lifted Hannah's uniform from the hook. We even left the house and went outside. We looked underneath the steps and all around the kitchen yard. The broom had vanished.

Sheriff Blandish was obviously puzzled. "Are you sure it was a broom you saw?"

"A broom or mop," I said. "I only glimpsed the shiny handle. The handle rested on the floor; the sweeping end was out of sight."

"You mean," asked the Sheriff doubtfully, "that the broom was upside down?"

"I don't know," I replied, and I told the truth. "What I saw was the handle. About a foot of the handle, coming from behind the clothes rack. Tilted at an angle, as though the broom head rested against the wall. The handle was very shiny. Black and shiny."

"Well, both broom and handle have disappeared," the Sheriff said with finality, and sighed. We turned back into the house.

The Sheriff and I had been occupied in our futile and puzzling search for some 15 minutes. Selby's party had already gone, and Sarah and our two men were awaiting me in the kitchen. Al was in a state of nerves and irritation, and neither his temper or Frank's had improved by the delay. Characteristically, Sarah had taken advantage of it to explore Mrs. Moran's barren refrigerator, and her equally barren shelves.

"I wish you two would look," she was saying. "Our absent hostess must have been on a starvation diet. This place looks like a summer cottage two hours before the owners have packed up to close the house and go back to town."

"Doesn't it?" said Sheriff Blandish.

The men looked up at that, and Sarah quickly turned around. Her straight, black brows were drawn together, as though something in her own words had startled her. She dropped the lid upon the yawning bread box and then on impulse picked up the box and shook it. The box had been cleaned and scrubbed. Not even a solitary crumb fell out.

"You've asked a lot of questions, Sheriff Blandish," Sarah said abruptly. "I'd like to ask one myself. Why did Mrs. Moran clear every scrap of food out of the kitchen? Except the food she served this afternoon."

"I think what you think, Miss Blake."

"Speak up, Sarah," I said, still fretted by the puzzle of the broom. "Don't be so mysterious. We've had enough of that."

"You can't make a complete cleanup of a kitchen in a minute, Janey," Sarah said. "It takes time and preparation. You know how long Mama takes to get her kitchen ready when she plans to visit me in town. She needs at least a week."

I had no idea what Sarah was getting at. Despite my familiarity with Aunt Mildred's careful, tedious ritual on those rare occasions when she planned to close her own house and go elsewhere—she always stopped the milk a day too early and parceled out the last few grains of coffee and wouldn't buy an extra loaf of bread—the condition of Mrs. Moran's kitchen carried no implication to my tired brain. "Well?"

Sarah said slowly, "It strikes me that Mrs. Moran must have had in mind to close and leave this house. Before tonight, I mean. Some time before tonight. Several days ago, at least."

Al scowled, and Frank bit his lip. A burst of housecleaning, the careful clearing out of a kitchen, didn't look much like the prelude to a brutal murder.

Sarah went on. "After all, this previous plan to go away—supposing it existed—might have precipitated the murder. If we could figure out what was in Mrs. Moran's mind—"

My tone was sharper than I intended. "Mrs. Moran certainly wasn't planning to leave Merristone this afternoon, Sarah. Al and I saw no signs of it at five o'clock. She invited us to tea; she served elaborate refreshments. Those peas that were in the saucepan must have been intended for her supper. There was food to feed the cats—"

I glanced toward the can that had held the cat food. I had forgotten all about Magog, and now I looked around for the white cat, wondering who would take charge of him. The plate that he had cleaned with eager greed lay beside the stove, but Magog had crept away and crawled underneath the set tubs. There he lay, apparently still sound asleep.

The set tubs were located in a distant, poorly lighted corner near the pantry. In the thick shadow cast by the metal overhang, the cat was a vague blur of white. Blandish idly flicked his flashlight in that direction. Light spilled in a yellow circle. I stared hard. The white cat was stretched out in an odd, uncharacteristic posture. He was turned over on his back, his four furry legs were extended stiffly in the air, his small pink mouth was wide open.

"What's wrong with that cat?" the Sheriff asked in a peculiar way.

"He's asleep," I said, and wondered why my heart suddenly began to beat so hard. I called, "Magog, Magog."

Magog didn't move or stir. Sarah and Sheriff Blandish crossed the kitchen simultaneously. The Sheriff bent over and touched the small, furry body.

"This cat's not asleep, Mrs. Blake. He's dead."

"Dead?"

"He's been poisoned, Janey," Sarah said. A lock of hair fell across her forehead, as she dropped to her knees. She gazed intently at Magog's wide-open mouth, at the dreadful arch of the small spine. "Arsenic would be my guess from the effect it's had. The laboratory tests will show. Whatever did you and Ruth feed him?"

"From the can, of course," I stammered. "That is, I fed him. Ruth had nothing to do with it. The can was open in the sink, lying ready...."

Sheriff Blandish had already returned to the sink and picked up the can. I had emptied it with a lavish hand, but a few sticky crumbs clung to the rim. He shook them on the table. The crumbs were dark in color, but the dark color was faded by streaks of fine white powder. Powder, finer than salt and difficult to see unless one looked for it beneath strong, bright light, had been thoroughly mixed in the food. Someone had prepared the tin of patented cat food to serve as Gog's and Magog's last meal on earth. But I had fed it to them. Shocked and shaken, I opened my mouth to enter into a fumbling, and unnecessary defense.

"I am quite sure, Mrs. Blake," said Sheriff Blandish, with grim humor, "you do not carry around a supply of arsenic. That's what this stuff is. I am quite sure you had no reason for poisoning Gog and Magog. But I'd like to know the source of the supply. I'd like to know who wanted to poison those cats—and why."

At that moment Dr. Traphaven called urgently from the master bedroom. Sheriff Blandish left the kitchen at once. The four of us glanced bewilderedly at each other, and then went trailing in his wake. Sarah led. She and the men crowded the doorway. I had to rise on tiptoe to peer around them.

Sheriff Blandish and Dr. Traphaven stood at Mrs. Moran's beruffled dressing table. Lying on the glass top, among the fallen perfume bottles, was a miniature trunk—a doll's trunk covered with faded, flowered wallpaper. For an instant I imagined that the trunk was the discovery that Dr. Traphaven was heralding so excitedly.

And then I saw that the little physician held in his hand a theatrical make-up box with a broken lock. In his other hand was a large paper bag, cracked and yellowed with age, tied with frayed and rotting twine.

"We had to break the lock," Dr. Traphaven was explaining to the Sheriff. "The box was well hidden, shoved far back in the dressing-table drawer behind the little trunk. But there's no question of what we've found."

The Sheriff did not interrupt him.

"But what is it?" I called, unable to restrain myself.

"Arsenic," said Dr. Traphaven. He poured from the paper bag into his palm a little heap of the fine crystalline powder. "Pure white arsenious oxide. Veronica Moran kept enough hidden here to poison half the population of Merristone."

We had discovered the source of the poison that had been mixed with the cat food. But I thought we had discovered something else. Mrs. Moran had not only planned to leave her house and go elsewhere. Before she left, and for a reason incomprehensible to me, she had planned to poison her two helpless pets.

Chapter Thirteen:
EAVESDROPPER OR DECOY?

An hour later Al and I were back at Aunt Mildred's and in bed—almost too spent to realize where we were. After the discovery of Mrs. Moran's secret supply of arsenic, Sheriff Blandish had sent us home. An officious deputy drove us in his car, just as a second deputy had previously served as chauffeur to Selby's party. I don't know how their deputy behaved, but I know our personal watchdog was keenly alive to the responsibilities of his position.

Mr. Bleakly followed Frank and Sarah to their respective bedrooms and bustled about inspecting their sleeping arrangements for a full 15 minutes. In the process he made noise enough to wake the dead—much less Aunt Mildred. To our general surprise and relief, however, and with no thanks to Mr. Bleakly, she did not put in an appearance. Having disposed of Frank and Sarah, the deputy then tracked Al and me to our room, and kept us waiting while he examined each of the three windows separately and satisfied himself of the steepness of the drop to the ground below. That accomplished, he went noisily downstairs, pulled the sofa from the dining room to block the stairway, and stretched out in comfort to await developments.

None of us had troubled to inform him that a rear stairway leading to the kitchen was also accessible to the second floor. Had any of us chosen to escape, the way was wide open.

In some ways I suppose we should have been grateful to the deputy. He provided us with a safe topic of conversation.

"If Mr. Bleakly expects me to climb out a window and head elsewhere before morning," I said to Al, as I collapsed in bed, "he's in for a sad disappointment. An earthquake wouldn't stir me."

Al reached out and snapped off the light. My manner did not deceive him. The springs in the old bed creaked a little, as he turned over and smoothed back my hair and kissed me. "You're a good girl, Janey. Smart but generous and good, and when the going's tough that's more important. Or have I told you all this lately? Sometimes I wonder why you ever took me."

"Because you've got curly hair, my sweet. Or have I told you lately?"

"No, seriously, Janey dear, when you married me you took on my—

my family. I thought of that tonight. I'm thinking of it now."

"Then don't," I said, pretending not to understand. "Don't think of anything. Let's go to sleep."

It was quite useless. In the familiar darkness of our own bedroom, with only the marble top of the bureau gleaming palely beneath the faint shine of the mirror, Al and I were not alone. Fear was in our bedroom with Al and me, fear of what the morrow would bring forth.

The Sheriff might be investigating Veronica Moran, but it wasn't Veronica Moran of whom we thought. Mrs. Moran might have mysteriously decided to poison the pets whom she had decorated with garish ribbons and walked daily along Copston Road; she might have owned and hidden away a large supply of arsenic, but Hannah Wilson had not died of poison. Hannah had died in violence under a brutal rain of blows.

Al turned again, and put his arms around me. "That bloodhound talks about Veronica Moran and lets us in on her secrets, but he's got his reasons. I know he's on the track of my own—"

"Don't say it, Al."

"Why not say it? Don't let the Sheriff's manner fool you, Janey. Blandish will say soon enough that he wants Selby's explanation. It was Selby he had in mind tonight, with all that talk about an 'accomplice.'"

"No, Al, no."

"Selby could have stolen the car keys, Janey. Who would Ruth protect except Selby? When he ran up the road to telephone, he had ample time to stop and go through Mrs. Moran's desk. Suppose we caught him there, suppose he heard us come in and got as far as the back porch—"

"You know that Selby would not hurt Ruth."

"I don't know any more what he *would* do," said Al in that dead hour of the night. He could feel the beating of my heart. "Sarah told me, dear. We've got to face the fact that my own brother is seriously involved in—"

"We needn't face anything, Al. Not yet. The Sheriff may be bluffing. He can't know that Selby was acquainted with Hannah."

"We know, Janey."

Before that simple statement, I had to force myself to simulate a confidence I did not feel. "There's probably some quite—quite natural explanation. You talk to Selby tomorrow, and I'll see Ruth. Things will be different in the morning. You'll see."

Al was silent. But I knew that his tired brain was twisting, turning—flashing back to him pictures from the past when his big brother had acted in his dead father's place. The two boys had lived out their youth with Aunt Mildred and her daughter in a manless household—in a house where men and masculine pursuits were held in low esteem because of Uncle Ned's defection. It was Selby who had seen that Al got his bicycle and his catcher's mitt, he who had successfully fought through the issue of the junior driver's license. I put my hand on my husband's cheek, and it was wet.

"Trust Selby, Al. Trust him till it's no longer possible. Everything's complex and complicated—that's been proved. If you must think, think about Veronica Moran."

"I've thought myself into a mental vacuum. I've used up all my questions and got no answers."

All that I could produce myself were questions. "Where is she now, Al? How did she get away? What was her motive—the one Dr. Traphaven knows—for wanting to get rid of Hannah? Was she really making preparations to close the house and leave? Why did she put poison in the cat food? Or did someone else find the arsenic and—?" I broke off abruptly. "What is it, Al?"

Beside me, I had felt him go rigid. In the darkness was the faint shine of the mirror above the paler marble of the bureau top, nothing else. Slowly, cautiously, Al moved in bed. He placed his lips against my ear.

"Go on talking, Janey. Talk hard. Someone's listening outside our door. I heard the rattle of the latch."

I heard it, too, the faint, surreptitious rattle, followed by the sudden silence. As though someone stooping had struck the latch. Someone crouched and immobile now, listening at the keyhole. For an instant I had no voice.

And then I said loudly, "I'm sure you agree, Al, that we should concentrate our efforts on Veronica Moran. She's the important one, she—"

Beside me, the blankets slid back slowly, cautiously, and I felt the mattress give as Al slipped noiselessly to the floor. Rag rugs dotted the floor, and the rugs were thick. Long familiarity guided him past the massive wardrobe, the useless, ugly washstand that Aunt Mildred was unwilling to discard. Without a sound, stepping from rug to rug, he crept toward the door. He would have made it, except for his own shoes—as usual dropped where he had shed them. He stumbled, the small rug skidded beneath his feet, he clutched for the bureau, and caught the mirror frame instead. The heavy glass fell with a resounding crash.

By the time Al reached the door, it was too late. The hall was empty. We had left the hall light burning, but the light was off, and the narrow corridor was dark and deserted. Al swore. I fumbled for the bedside lamp. It cast a brave glow through the open door, illumined the gloomy vacancy beyond.

"Our friend the deputy," I said uncertainly, "is the keyhole type." And then we heard Mr. Bleakly, who had taken prudent refuge behind his couch, shouting loudly from his barricade below, "What's going on up there?"

By that time other doors were opening. Sarah was calling from her doorway and Frank had appeared in his. "What fell? I heard something fall."

"I stumbled over my shoes," Al began.

"Your shoes!" snapped Sarah. "Well, they shook the foundations of the house." She pulled on her dressing gown and peered forth suspiciously. "Who turned off the light? I thought we decided to leave it burning."

"I guess Janey forgot," said Al.

"Well, I wish someone would turn it on." The men were in bare feet and pajamas and Sarah had her heavy, sensible dressing gown, but she shivered suddenly. "The switch is at the rear stairway, Frank. Did anyone think to lock the kitchen?"

It was an odd question, but no one commented. Frank walked down the hall toward the switch. He walked straight into the end of a door that should not have been open—the door that closed off the rear stairway. It certainly had not been open when we retired to our bed rooms. Everybody in the family had been trained to be extremely careful about that door, a habit which had been firmly established since the time Sarah fell down the unprotected stairwell and missed her high school graduation because of a broken ankle. I knew that none of us had carelessly left it open.

Frank took one look at the door, jabbed the switch and then, without a thought of possible danger, shot down the stairs and disappeared. Al paused long enough to grab a pair of heavy candlesticks—evidently on the theory that an inadequate weapon was an improvement on none— and went plunging after Frank. Marooned in the front hallway and apparently determined to stick there, Mr. Bleakly continued to bellow his insistent and quite futile demands for enlightenment. I let Sarah handle him. As I followed Frank and Al down the back stairs to the kitchen, I heard her calling soothingly, "Go back to sleep Mr. Bleakly. My cousin Jane just saw a mouse."

The men had turned on all the kitchen lights, and in the cheerful, commonplace glow, everything seemed to be in order. There was no one in the kitchen. Not that I expected to see anyone crouched in the jelly closet or hidden behind the stove. Whoever had knelt in darkness at our keyhole, and rattled the latch, now had a good head start.

Al had divested himself of the candlesticks, and he and Frank were talking quietly together. They weren't pleased at my arrival. I soon saw why. The back door, a door that led from the kitchen to a small porch and from there to the dense blackness of the winter night, stood open. Wide open, as though someone had left in too great a hurry to close it. The door was swinging to and fro, creaking across the worn linoleum.

"It could have blown open, Jane," Al said to me.

"A good stiff breeze," I said, "that went on up the stairs, and blew that door, too. You know it's got a patent fastening."

Al did not argue. Together he and Frank stepped outside to the porch—a porch that was much like Mrs. Moran's—a general catch-all, jumbled and confused. There was no clothes rack hung with frozen garments, but there were mops and brooms and cleaning things, a barrel of winter apples packed in sawdust, a kerosene jug, a clumsy ash can that stayed sometimes in the cellar and sometimes on the porch, and was seldom where you wanted it. The men found no signs of an intruder. Had they known where to look, however, they would have found something that would have saved us a deal of future trouble.

Barefooted as they were, they left the porch and stepped into the snowy yard beyond. There the investigation ended. We ourselves had disturbed and trampled the snow, when we returned home an hour earlier. It was futile to attempt to track an intruder farther, or even to decide in which direction he had gone. But one thing was certain. Whoever had crept through the kitchen into the upstairs hall had been well acquainted with the ways of the household—well enough acquainted to know that we never locked the kitchen door.

I said bitterly, "It's a complete mystery to me. What could you and I say, Al, that would be worth taking such a risk to hear?"

"Nothing," Al replied, and glanced at his partner. There was a queer expression on Frank's face. He hesitated. "I'm wondering if that was the—the intruder's real purpose. Eavesdropping at your door. Someone who got through the kitchen and up the stairs without being heard—well, that person was pretty careful. It seems odd your latch was rattled."

"An accident."

"Maybe." Frank glanced toward the thick, chill blackness of the night. "But it's also odd that both doors were left wide open. It wouldn't have taken a second to close them. In point of fact, it would have delayed pursuit."

"I don't get your point," said Al, and frowned.

"An open door is like an invitation to certain temperaments. A temperament like yours, Al. Suppose—oh, well—I guess I'm nuts...."

"Go on."

"Suppose," Frank said slowly, "you were *meant* to follow, Al. Suppose you were meant to go outside—alone."

I went cold from head to foot. Except for the accident of the broken mirror, and the accompanying crash, that is precisely what would have happened. Moving swiftly into the empty hall, Al would have discovered the open stairway door, and would have rushed down to the kitchen and on outside—alone. One murder had already occurred that night, and we were deeply involved in it. Possibly we knew and suspected too much. Except for the crashing mirror, Al would have left the house alone, in bare feet and pajamas, without a weapon, and placed himself at the mercy of the unknown.

My husband has more than an ordinary amount of valor, too much valor on some occasions and too little sense, but his laugh was uncertain. Fortunately at that moment Mr. Bleakly appeared and put an end to the discussion. Neither Al nor Frank nor I had cared to speculate about the possible identity of an intruder who was so familiar with the house. With actual relief I saw Mr. Bleakly. Trembling like a leaf, pointing before him a large gun that he held as though it was extremely hot, the deputy entered the kitchen to investigate our voices. I daresay he was surprised to find us gathered there. At any rate, he tried to hide his gun, and with high indignation demanded an immediate explanation. By now Al had pulled himself together.

"We came down to lock the back door, Mr. Bleakly. It's a pity you didn't think of that yourself."

The deputy watched suspiciously as Al snapped the lock. I watched too, and it seemed to me that I watched the closing of an era. A careless, happy era when we hadn't bothered with house keys, and danger was remote, and fear was far away from us.

Al and I did not discuss the incident, or attempt to figure it out. Perhaps we didn't dare. But as I was drifting into troubled sleep I heard Al get out of bed and lock our door, too. It was then, when I heard the ugly grating sound of the key, that I wondered why Aunt Mildred hadn't been aroused by the uproar and why she hadn't joined our colloquy in the hall.

Chapter Fourteen:
BLAKE HOUSE

When I woke up in the morning, the first thing I saw was the broken mirror that Al had clutched at on his journey to the door. But even in that cold gray winter dawn, the intruder of the night before became an impossibility. Something not to think about by the light of day. Somewhere I heard Aunt Mildred's stricken voice riding high above the sounds of moving furniture. I sat up in bed and listened.

Aunt Mildred was in the lower hall, browbeating Mr. Bleakly. The accompanying noises were the sounds of the sofa being returned to its proper place in the dining room. Aunt Mildred did the talking, and Merristone's first deputy did the work.

When I dressed and went downstairs I found the sofa where it belonged to the inch, between the sideboard and the china closet, directly centered by the hideous real oil portrait of Uncle Ned. In the light of her own frequently expressed opinion of her deserting spouse, I sometimes wondered why Aunt Mildred kept the portrait on view. Personally, I would have retired the mustachioed, red-cheeked gentleman, leering from a four-inch gilded frame, to the upstairs attic. Perhaps she liked the frame, or it may be that she felt the prominent position of the flamboyant canvas was necessary evidence of her marital status. Aunt Mildred had a grownup daughter, but it was perilously easy to think of her as a spinster.

She and Mr. Bleakly were in the kitchen. It was evident that the exhausted Mr. Bleakly, after a thorough cross-examination, had yielded up all that he knew about Hannah Wilson's murder. Her curiosity satisfied, Aunt Mildred in no uncertain terms was engaged in telling him what she thought about his presence in her home.

"We'll soon see," she informed the wretched deputy, "whether a decent, law-abiding woman has to put up with supporting a common spy—a spy who's never earned an honest penny in his life—on her premises. Drink your coffee, and find your hat. I'm telephoning the Sheriff what I think of his saddling us with a know-nothing like Aaron Bleakly. If he wants my family watched, let him come and watch himself."

Mr. Bleakly greeted me with outright pleasure. Aunt Mildred delayed long enough to pour me a cup of coffee and get out the cream—she had offered top milk to her uninvited guest—and then marched to the telephone. The operator immediately informed her that the Sheriff's office was receiving none except official long-distance calls.

That was my first intimation that the search for Veronica Moran was spreading miles away from Merristone. It did not surprise me. I had not expected to awake to the news that the harpist, dressed in her veils and draperies of flowing crimson, crowned with her dyed black hair, had been quickly and easily apprehended.

Aunt Mildred, who considered her own business should take precedence over anybody else's, returned indignantly to the kitchen. She was about to refuse Mr. Bleakly a second cup of coffee, when I seized the opportunity to mention the broken mirror.

Aunt Mildred's eyes opened wide. She frowned, and then said a shade too quickly, "I never liked that mirror anyhow." She asked for no explanations whatever. Mr. Bleakly turned out to possess the rudiments of intelligence. His eyes narrowed. "Don't you sleep upstairs? That mirror made a hell of a lot of noise when it fell. I'd have thought—"

"What?" Aunt Mildred asked sharply.

"Nothing," he muttered.

He had been shown his place, and he subsided into it. But I kept on wondering. There was something distinctly odd about the soundness of Aunt Mildred's sleep the night before. She saw me gazing at her.

"Is your neuralgia worse?" I asked.

"Much improved," she said. "After all, a good night's rest—"

She didn't look as though she had slept well or soundly. Her color was bad and her eyes were dulled and ringed by deep, tired lines.

With Mr. Bleakly sitting there, it was impossible to go into the story of those two open doors. But I stood up abruptly and stepped out on the porch to look around. I caught my skirt on the ash can, and I started to push it farther back against the wall. Just then I heard a snorting car and saw Harriet Strings drive into the yard. I reentered the kitchen in a hurry.

My intention was to escape upstairs. But the deputy had also seen the car, and he straightened up expectantly. Aunt Mildred gave him a look of clear dismissal.

"You can take your coffee to my parlor, Aaron. Mind you're not to smoke your smelly pipe in there, or start snooping through my things. And don't set those dirty pants of yours on my best needlepoint chair."

Suddenly Mr. Bleakly balked. "My duty's here, madam," he said coldly. "It's my bounden duty to check on the doings of this household, and that includes their company. My dirty pants—Mrs. Bleakly cleaned these pants just last week—stay here in the kitchen."

In consequence Harriet caught us all. She was full of talk about the murder, but I had the impression that she would have preferred to see Aunt Mildred privately, that for once she would gladly have dispensed with the extra audience. I must say that if Harriet's plans were upset, she made a swift readjustment.

She was a new person that morning, reborn and revitalized. Harriet was fairly trembling with excitement, like an ancient fire horse, long at pasture, who hears a distant bell. After 40 years of dealing in meager scraps of gossip, striving and struggling to lend importance to trivialities, Merristone's town crier had come into her own. The village had a genuine mystery, and Harriet Strings was to play her own small part in it.

"No coffee, thanks, Mildred. I have several calls to make." She rubbed her long cold nose against my Aunt's, and I wasn't quick enough to avoid a similar caress. "I'm sticking by you, dear, in your trouble," Harriet informed me with a fervency indicating that nothing would pry her loose. "I came here purposely to show Merristone where I stand. I stand with my lifetime friends. Let people talk and gossip all they like. Words can't hurt you, Jane."

Since I felt that Harriet would do her share of the talking, I was perhaps less touched and grateful than I should have been.

"Besides," said Harriet with an abrupt change of manner, "I want to talk to Al."

"He's still asleep."

Nevertheless, and despite her air of hurry, Harriet sat down and loosened the Afghan that covered her scrawny neck and shoulders. She took out a handkerchief and blew the long cold nose. When she was assured of general attention, she fixed me with a somewhat dubious eye. "Well, I suppose, Jane, that you'll have to do. I tried to stop Al yesterday. It's about Mrs. Moran's harp case."

"Harp case?" I echoed, mystified. So many things had occurred that it was difficult to cast back my mind to the moment when Al and I had seen the three-sided wooden crate rattling along Copstom Road in Hannah's wake. "What about it, Harriet?"

"Are you sure Mrs. Moran received a harp case from New York yesterday?"

"Certainly. We saw it."

"Well, what was in it?"

"Her harp, I suppose." I said ironically.

The irony was a boomerang.

"That's where you're wrong," Harriet cried triumphantly. "The harp has been in Mrs. Moran's house for months. It came over a year ago with all her other furniture. I watched the van unload at the time. Now what do you suppose was in that crate?"

I was too startled to reply. Mrs. Moran had taken pains to assure Al and me that the harp had been unloaded and placed in her living room immediately before our arrival at tea, that she and Hannah had just removed it from the crate. It seemed such a meaningless piece of deception even on the part of an almost pathologically deceitful woman. Why inform us that the harp had just been received from storage when it had been in her home more than a year? What had been contained in the clumsy three-sided crate?

"Why don't you go and ask the Sheriff, Harriet?" I suggested dryly. "He's probably opened the crate, and looked inside."

"Oh, I have talked to the Sheriff," replied Harriet, innocent of the self-revelation in the remark. "That's just the point. Since yesterday afternoon the crate has disappeared."

"Disappeared!"

"Sheriff Blandish is looking everywhere for that crate. I came by the Moran place just now," said Harriet importantly. "The crate is nowhere on her premises. Men were hunting through the woods, and all. They even wanted to go trampling through mine, and believe me I had a time keeping them off my property. The Sheriff certainly wants to locate that harp case."

Harriet had appeared before eight o'clock. It must have been past eleven when Sarah and I put on our heaviest wraps and drove to the village to do the marketing. Mr. Bleakly offered no objections. I fancy that he did not wish to take up arms with Aunt Mildred. "Whatever happens," she had remarked as she produced a lengthy grocery list, "men go on eating. Mind you watch the butcher, Sarah, when he weighs the roast. Otherwise you'll buy his hand."

Except that we were obliged to use Frank's car—our roadster was still marooned at the building site—on the surface it might have been any ordinary Saturday. Frank and Al always stayed in bed until noon; Sarah and I always did the marketing; Aunt Mildred always warned us to beware of Merristone's honest tradesmen.

In the beginning, Sarah and I pretended valiantly that we had nothing on our minds except Sunday dinner, and the burning question of whether we would serve grilled kidneys or honey waffles for Sunday morning breakfast. Both of us pretended we had not met in the upper hall the night before. I made no comment when Sarah chose an inconvenient, roundabout route to the village. The direct route led along Copston Road. Sarah felt obliged to offer explanation. "I thought," she said with elaborate carelessness, "that we'd leave Copston Road till we came back. Of course you'll want to arrange about moving your car sometime today."

"No hurry," I said quickly. I had no more desire than Sarah had to pass the curtained Moran dwelling, where Sheriff Blandish was looking for a large wooden crate. I did not want to stop before the building site that had meant so much to Al and me. "Suppose we go to the bank first, Sarah. I need to cash a check."

"The bank it is." Sarah negotiated a treacherous turn. A thoughtful expression crossed her face. "That's not a bad idea, Janey. I'd like a chance to talk to Arthur Cleat."

I was surprised. Arthur Cleat was the village banker, and conversation decidedly was not his forte. It was difficult to induce him to express a clear-cut opinion of the weather. He always hedged to be on the safe side.

"Why talk to Arthur?"

"Mrs. Moran banked there," said Sarah slowly. "The bank owns the house she rented. Arthur could tell us something about the woman. Her finances, anyhow."

"Arthur never tells you anything except that you're overdrawn," I said. "And he shuts you in a closet and whispers that. Or writes it on a little piece of paper and slips it in your hand when no one else is looking."

Sarah didn't smile. The illusion that this was a usual marketing expedition was slipping fast. On ordinary Saturdays a visit to the bank did not suggest possibilities for detective work. We drove a while in silence, and then my cousin said, "By the way, did Selby telephone this morning?"

She put it in the form of a question, but she knew as well as I that Selby had not telephoned. We had not heard from him since he and Belton had been permitted to take Ruth home the night before. With Ruth hurt, it would have been natural for Selby to call and tell us how she was. Belton got us on the wire nearly every day, but there had been no word from him about his daughter.

The Merristone Enigma, the woman with the fantastic wardrobe and the dyed black hair, the woman who had hidden pure white arsenic in her dressing table and very possibly mixed it in the food to be given to her pets, had worked well. Missing, her whereabouts unknown, she had nevertheless sown the seeds of mistrust and separation in what had been a singularly united family.

"No, Sarah," I said. "Selby didn't telephone."

Beyond the closed and frosted windows of the car, a cold wind blew. Snow, dry and powdery, was spinning, whirling through the air, but no snow fell from the leaden sky. Barren, drifted fields shot past, and woods unrolled, and scattered farmhouses, with shutters tightly drawn, punctuated the desolation. No one was abroad in the frozen countryside.

Sarah's eyes became as bleak and bitter as the day. "I don't care who murdered Hannah Wilson. A poor old woman better dead. I hardly even pity her. She's out of it. We aren't. I care for Selby and for Ruth. I care for you and Al, and Frank and Mama. Belton too. What's to become of us, Jane, when the truth comes out?"

"The truth is that Veronica Moran is guilty. She killed her maid and ran away. That's got to be the truth, Sarah."

"Has it? Whom did Ruth see on the Moran porch last night? She certainly didn't see Mrs. Moran. Why did Selby meet Hannah in New York on Monday? Why has he been seeing her since last November?"

I did not answer.

Suddenly a car horn shrilled beside us. An indignant face peered from a passing window and grew startled and alert, as Mrs. Sanders of the Garden Club recognized two participants in the murder she had just discussed exhaustively with eleven people. Without noticing, Sarah and I had come into the village. The shopping section lay ahead; we were abreast the frozen Green. Set like jewels among ancient elms and pines, Merristone's fine old houses marched around the Green and turned their backs upon the huddled stores and filling stations two short blocks ahead.

Selby's home, built in 1675 and restored by Belton as a wedding present to his daughter, was the finest and oldest of the lot. Sarah looked across the Green at Blake House, at the serene facade that architects came from everywhere to study, at the lovely double doors that had opened to receive Lafayette, at the particular window of which Selby was so proud, where Aaron Burr had once scratched his signature with his daughter's diamond ring. As Ruth often said, when she lamented the single inconvenient bath, "Anyway, Blake House reeks of history." Sarah drove around the Green and stopped. Before I could protest, she stepped to the curb. Her face was set and resolute.

"I'm going to talk to Selby, Jane. Believe me, this is not curiosity. I only want to help. But I must know what the situation is, and what story he means to tell. I've got to know what kind of help Selby may need very soon."

"Don't."

She had already pushed through the swinging wooden gates that led to Blake House, passed beneath the towering sentinel box, and started up the crazy path. The first Selby Blake, homesick in a foreign land, had laid such a crazy path from his memories of far-off Surrey, and the years had obliterated every trace of it, until Belton, stone by stone, had laid the path again. The boxwood trees had triumphed over time. But in the two centuries since a homesick Englishman had remembered Surrey and spent a fortune to build another gracious country home in a wilderness, Blake House itself had changed inevitably with the new demands of each new generation. Two centuries of changes had been erased in the five years of Selby's marriage. Blake House, inside and out, was as it had been in 1675.

Tirelessly, tediously, with fanatical attention to detail, Belton had restored the dwelling to its original form until it had become a local landmark and a source of unadmitted pride to all the family, except Aunt Mildred. She saw no sense in Blake House, and I suppose, practically speaking, it was absurd that a struggling insurance salesman should dwell in a mansion that cost so much to heat. It was absurd that Belton's funds and enthusiasm had collapsed just as he reached the problem of the plumbing.

But Blake House suited Selby. I thought of that, even as I swiftly followed Sarah. The paneled library suited him, and the spacious ballroom that was so seldom used, and the secret stairway—no secret to anyone in Merristone—where Revolutionary soldiers long ago had hidden and warmed themselves by the adjacent chimney and heard the heavy footfalls of loyal English bailiffs walk up and down the room beyond. Yes, Blake House suited Selby. It was built by a proud and romantic man, in an age when arrogance was the natural right of gentlemen. Selby was like his long-dead ancestor. His pride was of a more subtle, deceptive kind perhaps, and was well concealed by his usual gentleness of manner. But no one could move Selby or talk to him unless he chose.

Sarah stood on the doorstep, lifted her hand to the great brass knocker. I caught her arm.

"You're making a mistake. You're in no mood to handle Selby." And then I glanced toward the old carriage house, used nowadays as a garage, and saw the open doors and realized that the deep tracks in the snow had been made by Selby's car. With relief, I said, "Anyhow, he isn't here. He's probably at his office."

Sheer desperation had carried Sarah from the street. The desperation faded from her eyes. She looked relieved herself. "I'm glad, Jane. I'd have made a scene just to relieve my nerves, and accomplished precisely nothing." She shook herself, as though to clear the dreadful fancies from her brain. "It's all right now. I'll stop imagining things."

She raised her hand again, hesitated and glanced at me. We both thought of Ruth.

Even standing at the familiar door, I was tempted to turn away. I felt that Ruth was as much in need of help as Selby, but I lacked Sarah's single-minded determination. I would not press my help on anyone. Let Ruth call on me when she desired.

A consideration of a different kind decided me. I had never passed Blake House in my life without stopping; every trip to town meant to me a cup of tea with my sister-in-law, a few pleasant minutes wasted in family chat and gossip. I could not break that custom lightly.

"Now we're here," I said slowly, "suppose we stop a minute. But I want your promise, Sarah. You're not to worry Ruth with questions."

"Certainly not!" said Sarah irritably. "We won't discuss last night." And then she added gently, "I wouldn't trouble Ruth for anything. You should know that, Janey."

I reached over and gave the knocker three soft raps in quick succession. Because strangers often stopped in from the road and asked to be taken through Blake House and even demanded the privilege on occasion, Ruth and I had invented the special knock. *Let me in*, it meant.

Several minutes went by. The iron-jawed widow woman who came to Blake House by the day to "help out" had an air of deceptive competence, but, as I was well aware, Mrs. Simpkin managed to spend most of her time curled up with the portable radio that she thoughtfully carried to every job. I rapped three times again, more sharply. And then a third time. Eventually, breathless as though she had run a hard race from a heavy washing, Mrs. Simpkin did appear. She opened the door a narrow crack, and peered out.

"I'm sorry, ladies. Good morning to you both. Mrs. Selby Blake isn't in."

"Of course she's in," snapped Sarah. "She isn't well. Tell her it's her cousin, Sarah Havens, and her sister-in-law."

"Oh, she knows," began Mrs. Simpkin, and went the bright red of a beet.

But Sarah, impatient and sure of a welcome, had already pushed the door wide open and started to step across the threshold. Beyond the rich dark oak of the foyer; and through a second door, a corner of the paneled library was visible. The corner with the fireplace and the facing chimney settles where Ruth and I had sat so often and shared our after-dinner coffee, while Al and Selby sprawled on the mammoth sofa that was out of sight.

Ruth was huddled in the chimney corner before a dying fire. The bandage that bound down her curls gave her the pathos of an injured child. A handkerchief was crumpled in her hand, and her eyes were wet with tears.

The eyes met mine and paused and turned away. Then was no warmth or welcome in them. There was no flurry of embarrassment. There was stark misery, and nothing else. Ruth needed help and comfort and reassurance. But not from me.

Chapter Fifteen:
TESTING DIFFERENT DENTS

Sarah and I tried to keep it from each other that we had been turned away from Blake House. But when we walked back slowly to the curb, Sarah did not get in the car.

"You can wait here, Janey. I have an errand."

Because of her mood, I guessed the errand that had so suddenly occurred to her. Dr. Traphaven's bachelor residence was also on the square, indeed was next door to Blake House. Sarah looked in that direction.

"The authorities know a lot more about the case than the simple fact that Veronica Moran is missing. Sheriff Blandish is a hopeless proposition, but I'm ready to gamble on the doctor. After all, he took Al and Selby through chicken-pox and measles, and me through appendicitis."

"He won't talk either, Sarah. Why should he?"

"Maybe not. But Dr. Traphaven's got a heart, Janey. I intend to ask him flatly just what motive Mrs. Moran had for killing Hannah."

I thought she might ask in vain, but again I followed her along the sidewalk. Dr. Traphaven's house was, by long odds, the newest and ugliest on the square. Despite the anguished cries of half of Merristone, Dr. Traphaven had built to please himself. His home was made of stucco; the asbestos shingles were bright blue in color, and, because the little doctor liked lots of light, the many windows were of the plate-glass variety. The iron deer, sprinkled about the snowy lawn, had been bought up at country auctions.

Most of Dr. Traphaven's private income, a large income for Merristone, was spent upon his abiding passion—which was criminological investigation. The little doctor's enormous library was devoted to the subject of crime and the corollary art of detection. For years Dr. Traphaven had read and studied in our law-abiding community, and all the while had lain in patient waiting for a first-class murder mystery.

"He's got it now," Sarah said, and rang the bell.

The doormat was thick with fallen snow. The manservant who presently appeared, had evidently just got out of bed. At any rate, he was pulling on his coat.

He informed us that Dr. Traphaven was in his study. We followed the white coat across islands of Navajo rugs, and through thickets of lamps, toward the strangest room in Merristone. The servant didn't bother to knock, he simply opened the study door. The 20-foot room contained perhaps 2,000 books, relating in detail the bloody tales of old and half-forgotten murders. Six steel files held newspaper clippings of sensational cases that, through years of crime-tasting, had struck the little doctor's fancy.

There was other equipment in the study. A clumsy fingerprinting outfit squatted beside a ghastly-looking plaster model of a shoe that had once figured in a famous San Francisco murder case. Crowded between two of the overflowing bookcases, enclosed in a glass cabinet, was the doctor's prized collection of weapons—guns and knives, a hatchet and a hammer, a short stout piece of rope. Each of these grisly objects had once served as Exhibit A in a murder trial, and each was neatly labeled. The photographs—and there were many on the walls— were also labeled. Each of the men and women represented there was a convicted killer.

The fierce overhead lights that blazed into every corner had been copied at considerable expense from the lights used in the "line-up" at Police Headquarters in New York. The lights were burning, but Dr. Traphaven was alone, and far too absorbed to be aware of the opening door.

He stood before a thick cork mat which he had placed in a cleared space on the floor. Beside him lay a heavy gnarled stick of wood, an ugly, three-cornered piece of rock, and a length of lead pipe. Just as we stepped in he raised the pipe high in the air, and brought it smashing down upon the thick cork mat. He was about to compare the resulting dent with the dents that had been produced by his other make-shift weapons, when he heard me gasp.

He dropped the length of pipe at once, and looked embarrassed. No explanation was offered, and none was necessary. Dr. Traphaven was attempting to decide the weight and type of weapon that had produced Hannah Wilson's mortal injuries. My knees went weak and wobbly, and Sarah's high bright color faded. She cleared her throat.

"I'm sorry, Dr. Traphaven. Maybe we shouldn't be here, but I had to come. I—I wish that you'd be honest with us." And then her question burst out. "Do you really think that Veronica Moran killed her maid?"

"It hardly seems a woman's kind of crime," the little doctor said slowly, and in a troubled way. He glanced toward the stick of wood, the poker, the marred cork mat. His eyes that had been warm and almost sympathetic hardened slightly.

"Great passion might explain it," Sarah said.

"I suppose so—yes," he said with no conviction.

There was a chair pulled up at a crowded table a few feet away. I walked to the chair and sat down. On the table was the doll's trunk that I had last seen on Mrs. Moran's dressing table. Beside it was the paper bag of arsenic. But the oddest exhibit was a black card on which lay a single long gray hair. The hair had been delicately cut in three pieces, and the separate sections clipped to the card. The black card rested beneath Dr. Traphaven's powerful microscope.

I was only vaguely aware of that surprising array of seemingly disassociated and unrelated objects. My attention was upon Sarah. She intended to go through with the interview.

"I should tell you, Doctor," she said steadily, "why we're really here. We're anxious, naturally. Do you think it's fair to keep us in the dark about Mrs. Moran's motive?"

The doctor looked exceedingly uncomfortable.

"My dear young lady," he began, and made a speech the gist of which was that police officials must naturally work in privacy.

Sarah was not yet defeated. "I can think of only one motive," she said bitterly, "that could conceivably move that woman."

Dr. Traphaven waited politely. His eyes were bright but somewhat absent, his small neatly trimmed beard cocked sidewise. "Yes, Miss Havens?"

"Money," Sarah said.

I could not imagine how Mrs. Moran could hope to benefit financially from Hannah's death. But I was looking at the doctor. His eyes flew open, his mouth made an astonished O. His reaction seemed to indicate that Sarah had literally read his mind. But he refused to give us any further satisfaction, or to explain how Veronica Moran could obtain money from the demise of a penniless dependent. As he urged us toward the door, he said:

"I realize you're anxious, both of you. But please take a piece of advice from an old man. Don't try to do our—our sometimes unpleasant work for us. You may find out something you don't want to know."

His wise advice fell on deaf ears. Sarah was still set on talking to Arthur Cleat, the banker. Ten minutes later we entered the Merristone First National Bank. The bank was thronged and boiling with talk, but when Sarah and I appeared a complete silence fell. The Saturday morning line collected at the cashier's cage froze like a row of statues. Twenty pairs of eyes turned from Sarah to me. No one spoke.

Sarah lifted her head in the air and stalked through the staring company toward a little anteroom in the rear. She planted herself before a frosted glass door marked, "Arthur Cleat, Acting Vice-President. Private," and rapped vigorously.

No answer was forthcoming. The electricity was burning behind the frosted pane, and I thought I heard murmured voices from within.

"Arthur's busy, Sarah. Really. And I'd rather go cash my check, and leave."

"After that silent treatment"—Sarah's face was red—"should think you'd want to solve the mystery." Again she rapped imperatively. The muffled voices within broke off, and a chair scraped back. Unshaven, in shirt sleeves and suspenders, the acting vice-president appeared at his door. Across his office a second door, a private door that opened into an alley behind the bank, was just closing.

I had never seen the slightest sign of emotion on Arthur Cleat's impassive face before, but that morning he looked genuinely upset. His office, usually exceptionally neat, just as he himself was usually as neat and ordered as the vault adjoining, was buried in a blizzard of newspapers. Newspapers spilled from the rolltop desk, emerged from all the wastebaskets, carpeted the floor as though Arthur had glanced at each sensational story, groaned and cast the sheet away.

"You shouldn't have come here, Sarah. You either, Janey," was his hospitable greeting. "If you had to see me, why didn't you walk through the alley?"

And then he stepped aside and let us enter. Unfortunately for the banker, his acquaintanceship with the family dated back for many years. Sarah had been his classmate in high school, and it was always rumored that, except for Sarah Havens, Arthur Cleat would never have passed in second year chemistry.

"I hope you don't mean to stay. God knows there's been enough talk already." He cast a bitter glance at the scattered newspapers. "The publicity is ruinous. It's going to hurt the town, and hurt us too. The bank has been mentioned in every single story about the search for that wretched woman."

He glared at me, as though I personally had invited Veronica Moran to come to Merristone and rent a house belonging to the bank, and open an account with them.

"What am I expected to do? Investigate every client on the theory that she's going to kill her maid, run off and get our name splashed in print? How was I to realize what was going to happen?"

"I'm sure I don't know, Arthur," I said, and then with a shade of malice, added, "It's a great pity the bank owns her house."

Arthur started as though a bee had stung him. "We don't own the house," he said violently. "You'll read that in the papers tomorrow, I suppose. We sold the house to Veronica Moran a good six months ago."

"Sold!" I said.

Sarah sat up in her chair. "But, Arthur, everybody understood she only rented. The deed was not recorded."

"That was her affair, not ours," he said firmly. "Our responsibility was at an end when we accepted her offer—quite a fair offer, too—and delivered the deed. It wasn't my concern if the buyer didn't choose to let everyone in Merristone know her business. In point of fact, I myself didn't even meet the woman."

Sarah opened her eyes. "It must have been a distinctly awkward transaction, if you didn't meet the buyer."

"A bit unusual, perhaps. But we desired to sell a piece of property and this Mrs. Moran desired to buy. It wasn't necessary for her to appear in person. I wasn't curious at the time."

The office was not overheated, but Arthur had begun to perspire. I gathered quite easily that his lack of curiosity concerning the transfer of the house had something to do with the "fairness" of Mrs. Moran's offer. The Copston Road property, taken in lieu of payments on a mortgage, long had been a liability to the bank.

"Unusual, yes," Arthur repeated, as though, having found a satisfactory word, he meant to cling to it. "At any rate, Sheriff Blandish seems to think so. Unusual the transaction may have been—because of the buyer's wish for privacy—but I assure you the sale was not in the least irregular." He choked a little. "The maid, this Hannah Wilson, brought in the cash, and I delivered the deed to her last July. She had the written authorization of her mistress, and was in every respect a legal and proper agent."

I glanced at Sarah, and became aware that she had abruptly stopped listening. Her fascinated gaze was fixed on Arthur's desk. Lying in an open drawer, I could see several long yellow sheets of paper covered with neat blue figures. Sarah had discovered that the yellow paper contained the official and highly confidential record of Veronica Moran's account and business dealings with the Merristone First National Bank. The banker had sent for the record for his personal perusal. He sprang across his office and slammed the drawer.

Sarah raised her eyebrows, as though mystified by his rudeness. Her face was innocent of guile. "If you say you weren't curious, Arthur, I suppose you weren't. But I must say the whole affair does seem extraordinary. Not a bit like you. You're usually such a careful soul."

"What's care got to do with it? Naturally, I'm careful." Arthur looked suspiciously at Sarah, still unsure how closely she had observed his precious records. "A banker must be, if he expects to stay in the banking business."

"Still, with just a little care," said Sarah musingly, "you might have spared the community from ever harboring the woman. I mean at the time Mrs. Moran first began to rent. I understand you waived all references, because she paid six months' rent in advance."

"That's untrue," he retorted, struck at his most tender point. "You're simply repeating village gossip. When Veronica Moran came to Merristone more than a year ago, she came highly recommended."

"Highly recommended!" said Sarah incredulously. "Who recommended her?"

Arthur bit his tongue. He looked exceedingly unhappy, and then, suddenly, he squared his shoulders. He drew a long, deep breath. "An old and trusted friend of mine recommended Mrs. Moran to me as a desirable tenant."

"What old friend?"

"Your cousin, Selby Blake."

I gripped the arm of my chair to brace myself, and then I spoke.

"You're mistaken, Arthur. Al and I have met Mrs. Moran, but Selby did not know her a year ago. She is a stranger to him."

"It's you who are mistaken," said the banker. "You're bound to find out soon. You may as well learn from me as from the public prints. Selby not only recommended Veronica Moran, he actually selected the house for her. Something over a year ago, sometime in August of '39, he came to me and asked me for our list. I gathered that Mrs. Moran was an acquaintance of his, elderly and unsociable by nature, looking for a quiet country place."

I didn't hear the door behind us open, but I saw the look of horror on the banker's face. I pulled myself around.

Selby had entered quietly from the alley. The sudden glare of electricity after the gloom outside must have momentarily blinded him. He blinked, shrugged a few flakes of snow from his shoulders, and then he saw Sarah and me.

Something flickered in his dark eyes—fear or anger or a combination of both—but he kept his mouth quite steady. Within a second, he even smiled.

"Morning, Sarah. Morning, Jane. I didn't expect to find you here. Sorry, Arthur, I didn't realize you were occupied."

"Come right in," cried Arthur, with a pretense at ease that wouldn't have deceived a child of ten. "We were just discussing—that is—well, the girls and I were talking about the situation in general."

"Then I'll be running on," Selby said politely. "You've changed, Arthur. I always thought you considered loose talk dangerous. I still do. I just came back because—" He hesitated. Arthur waited.

With effort Selby produced his excuse. He looked around the office as though hunting something, looked at the umbrella stand, at the chairs, at the desk.

"I thought I might have left my stick," he said lightly. "I seem to have mislaid it somewhere. It isn't here."

Arthur frowned. "You mean that blackthorn cane? No, Selby, you didn't have the cane in here—"

Selby cut him short. "Oh, well, I daresay the stick will turn up. At that, I don't believe I carried it this morning. I remember having it last night at dinner. You might look for it, Jane, if you can spare the time from your other activities."

His tone was cold. But when he turned around and left, we followed him. Sarah made one attempt to break through the barrier he had raised between us.

"Selby, dear," she said, "why did you hide it from us that you knew Veronica Moran so well?"

"You've been misinformed," said Selby, in a voice like ice. "I don't know Mrs. Moran. She isn't even an acquaintance. I never saw the woman in my life."

He removed Sarah's fingers from his arm, walked down the alley, got in his car and drove away.

Chapter Sixteen:
THE ENIGMA OF COPSTON ROAD

I was so sick at heart that I wanted to go straight home, to feel Al's arms around me, to have him assure me, as I had assured him, that there was some innocent explanation of Selby's behavior. But Sarah stopped at the grocery store, and with grim efficiency tore Aunt Mildred's list in two and divided it with me. The grocery store was as crowded as the bank and as silent. By the time we got through the marketing ordeal—even Miss Frisbee, the boarding-house keeper, stopped pinching lettuces to watch us make our purchases—we had both forgotten any intention to visit the building site.

As it turned out, Frank had gone to the cottage and driven our roadster back to Aunt Mildred's. When Sarah and I finally got there, he was just pulling into the garage. I was surprised to see our car. I had supposed it would be necessary to call the wrecker and have it hauled to a garage until new keys could be made. Without explanations, Frank alighted and crossed the snowy yard to help us unload our packages.

"You girls have been gone a hell of a while," he said, and grinned. "That's no way to treat an admirer, Sarah. To run off and leave him breakfast with her mother. Besides, I wish you wouldn't."

Frank suspected quite correctly that Sarah had been investigating the murder. His voice was gruff, but it was gentle, too. It was queer to see Frank attempt to be protective with Sarah, and rather sad that she never realized or appreciated the impulse, and usually began an argument. I kept on looking at our car.

"How did you get it started without a key, Frank?" Like most women I am wholly ignorant about combustion engines. "Did you short-circuit the wires, or something?"

"No," he said quickly. "No. Luckily Thirkle found your keys. Here they are, with my compliments. Or I should say Mr. Thirkle's compliments. He's quite a fellow, your builder."

Frank tossed over the keys, picked up a bag of vegetables, and would have closed his accounting there. I looked at the keys in my hand. They were mute and unrevealing. "Where, Frank?"

Frank started. "Where'd Thirkle find the keys? Oh, lying in the yard just in the road. Both sets fairly close together. He phoned us about noon, but hadn't reached Belton yet. The keys weren't any trick to fund by daylight. They were in plain sight."

But that wasn't the point, and Frank knew it. The point was that our keys had not been stolen; they had merely been tossed away by someone who desired to delay us at the building site and gain a few minutes of vital time before a murder was reported. Instinctively, without thinking, I began to rub the keys against my jacket. As though after a night in the open, telltale fingerprints might still remain. Very slightly Frank shook his head.

"It isn't necessary, Janey. I took care of that myself."

In silence we walked into Aunt Mildred's kitchen.

Al had long since finished with his twelve o'clock breakfast, and pushed his tray aside. But he was still at the table, and before him lay a heap of morning newspapers. He was plowing stubbornly through the lot, as though somewhere in the long, printed columns he might find an answer to his own unrest.

"The gentlemen of the press," Al announced, and grimaced at the headlines, "have undertaken the job of locating Veronica Moran. They might do slightly better if they depended less on lurid phraseology, and published a few photographs of her."

"She probably hasn't faced a camera since her days of glory," I said. "And has changed so much it wouldn't matter."

But I looked in surprise at the New York papers. Working in their own inscrutable ways, the great dailies had obtained a dreadful flashlight of Sarah taken at a chemists' dinner, a photograph of Al in the mortarboard he wore when he was graduated at Yale, and a really distinguished view of Blake House with Belton standing proudly in the doorway. But there was no picture of Veronica Moran and her harp.

"She'll show up in the evening papers," Frank declared confidently. "Mrs. Moran's career might have ended in 1915, but she'll be filed away in lace and lavender in the records of some theatrical agency. My guess is that at least twelve New York reporters are inches deep in dust this minute."

I frowned. "But that takes time, Frank. Mrs. Moran must have had pictures around her home. She had that press book, and all those clippings. I should think that Sheriff Blandish—"

"I didn't notice any pictures," Al said slowly. "Veronica Moran had fifty grinning tenors and pompadoured sopranos on display, but she wasn't there herself with her harp. Maybe she wasn't photogenic."

That concluded our discussion. It was then nearly three o'clock. At half-past four Sheriff Blandish telephoned, and asked us to report at his office. Frank and Sarah rose to go along, but Al shook his head.

"Blandish wants just Jane and me."

"Why?" I inquired, when we went outside to the car.

"Apparently he wants to ask a few more questions about Veronica Moran," said Al, and added bitterly. "The Sheriff seems to consider that you and I, having met the woman, ought to be a mine of information."

My heart sank. If Arthur Cleat had talked to Sarah and me, he had undoubtedly talked to the authorities. Selby would be the natural one to question. I wondered if we were being called downtown to discuss and to explain Selby. How were we to do that?

To my great relief Sheriff Blandish was alone in his small, sketchily furnished office. There was nothing frightening or forbidding in his manner. In the chill winter twilight the Sheriff sat before a rolltop desk and looked depressed and baffled, like a man who has wrestled overlong with a problem that grows increasingly more complicated and complex. Al asked at once whether any trace had been discovered of Veronica Moran.

"None at all. In those striking clothes and despite that striking appearance, she's managed to vanish like a puff of smoke. It seemed odd at first. It seems less odd now."

Al raised interrogative eyebrows.

"The woman had made careful plans, plans that go back many months, that infinitely simplified her disappearance."

A wall clock ticked loudly in the silence. My heart began to beat. My husband merely looked perplexed.

"I don't follow you. I suppose of course you've tried to trace Mrs. Moran through her musical connections."

"Did you ever hear her perform on that beautiful concert harp?" Sheriff Blandish asked abruptly.

"No, Mrs. Moran didn't play for us yesterday," Al said, frowning. "She was sitting at the harp when we went in, but she explained she was badly out of practice." He paused, vaguely startled and confused. "But then, she told us the instrument had just arrived from storage."

"The harp had been in her house since the day of her arrival," I said.

"None of the neighbors ever heard it," said Sheriff Blandish. "Harriet Strings went by the house every evening and sometimes stood outside and listened. The harp was kept in the parlor, but it was never touched."

"Well?"

"Hasn't it occurred to you," said Sheriff Blandish, "that the woman was unable to play at all?"

"Unable! Veronica Moran!" Al stared. "She was a famous harpist in her day. My parents heard her play."

"They heard *this* Veronica Moran," said Sheriff Blandish.

A folded evening newspaper lay on his desk. He unfolded it, and handed us the front page. Frank's prediction had turned out to be correct. A tedious search through the files of the Globe Theatrical Agency had uncovered a photograph of the harpist who had thrilled an earlier generation. A two-column photograph in the middle of the page was captioned: *Veronica Moran, the harpist, as she appeared in Carnegie Hall, June 2, 1910.*

Al and I gazed at the picture of a slender young woman seated at a concert harp. She was tiny with tiny hands and feet, made even smaller by the massive background of her harp, the airy, ascending pattern of the strings that reached high above her. Her curling hair was gold and piled in an elaborate pompadour that seemed almost too heavy for the delicately modeled head to carry, just as the pale, luminous eyes seemed too large for the wistful, lovely face.

The picture had been taken 30 years before, but in 30 years that fragile girl could not have turned into the Veronica Moran of Copston Road. Some changes do not occur in 30 years. Height does not change appreciably, coloring does not change, nor do eyes that are tender and light in hue change into eyes that are cold and hard and black. We were looking at an entirely different person.

I spoke first. "There—there must be some mistake. This is not Veronica Moran."

"There is no mistake, Mrs. Blake. You are looking at Veronica Moran, the harpist, at the age of twenty."

"But what does it mean?"

"It means," said Sheriff Blandish, "that the Veronica Moran of Copston Road was an impostor. When she arrived in Merristone, she had stolen another woman's identity and reputation. It means we don't even know the name of the black-haired, black-eyed woman that we're hunting for."

Chapter Seventeen:
PERHAPS A CRIMINAL RECORD

I don't know how long Al and I sat beside the rolltop desk staring at the photograph of the tiny gilt-haired girl posed at the concert harp. Finally Al cleared his throat.

"But the real Veromica Moran? This girl. What became of her?"

"The girl of the photograph is dead, Mr. Blake," said Sheriff Blandish gently. He glanced at the lovely, wistful face of the harpist, at the quaint, old-fashioned clothes "The impersonation did not harm or hurt her; she never learned of it. This talented musician whose career was so brilliant and so brief, grew older. She died, forgotten by her public and her friends, almost two years ago."

The Sheriff took a notebook from his pocket, studied it a moment and put the book away. The information listed there had resulted from a dozen phone calls, but it hardly filled a single page.

"Veronica Moran, the harpist, died of tuberculosis on April 3, 1939," Sheriff Blandish told us. "She died in the charity ward of a New York hospital, destitute and quite alone. Her personal effects, a few sticks of furniture, ornaments, books, pictures, her music and her instrument, were put up at auction to satisfy a board bill and pay her funeral expenses."

The public sale of Veronica Moran's pitiful personal effects, the mementoes of her vanished fame, had been held at Silver's Auction Rooms on August 27, 1939. A black-haired, black-eyed woman had attended the sale, and bid on everything that the little harpist owned. She had paid $500 for the lot.

"The woman we must still call Veronica Moran, for want of another name," said Sheriff Blandish, "in effect paid $500 for the dead harpist's identity. With $500 she erased her own past and became another person."

"But who was she?"

Again the Sheriff sighed. "We can only guess, Mrs. Blake. We can guess that she was someone whose own name was such a burden that she was eager to cast it off. Someone with a past that she intended to blot out and forget."

"But if you have located the auction room—"

"I needn't tell you that a period going on two years is a long time in New York, or that a metropolitan auction room is a very busy place. I've talked by telephone with the Mr. Silver who handled the transaction, and he has no memory of it whatever. Veronica Moran outlived her reputation by many years; her possessions were of small intrinsic value, and of little interest either to the general public or Mr. Silver. The bare record of the auctioneer's books is all we know of the story. The buyer paid cash and, of course, was not called upon to identify herself."

"In other words," I said bitterly, "she attended the sale without a name, and left as Veronica Moran."

"Exactly. Two weeks after the sale, equipped with a truckload of convincing personal effects and a brand-new identity, accompanied by a maid who very possibly shared her secret, the impostor arrived in Merristone."

To locate Veronica Moran, the harpist, had proved to be a laborious assignment. To locate a woman who was not a harpist, whose name was not Veronica Moran, looked virtually impossible. Unless—

All too vividly I remembered the visit to the bank, what Sarah and I had learned from Arthur Cleat, and had not learned from Selby. Had my brother-in-law been aware from the beginning that Veronica Moran was an impostor, or had he too been deceived when he went to the banker and asked about a suitable house for "an elderly acquaintance, unsociable by nature, seeking a quiet country place"? Why didn't Sheriff Blandish speak of Selby? I sat back, and tried to simulate a calmness that I did not feel.

Sheriff Blandish's manner was calculated to be reassuring. "Obviously," he said, with an air of taking us into his confidence, "it's imperative that we identify the black-haired, black-eyed woman. Find out who she is. The woman herself has made it extremely difficult. She prepared in advance for investigation."

"Surely she had personal possessions of her own," Al said. "Something that might identify her. Clothing—"

"No labels," said the Sheriff briefly.

"Correspondence?"

"Most of the correspondence consisted of letters sent years ago to the true Veronica Moran. The impostor destroyed all photographs of the harpist, but she kept her press book, her clippings, the pathetic personal letters that no one had the heart or wit to destroy."

"But she got mail herself," I said slowly, remembering agitated conferences between Harriet and Aunt Mildred, bi-weekly bulletins rushed from the local postmistress. "She got mail here in Merristone. Or so I've heard. Several letters every day, sometimes five or six."

"I'd like to show you a sample of that mail."

Sheriff Blandish opened a drawer, pulled out a handful of envelopes, and dropped them on his desk. He invited us to examine them. Al drew forth a glossy little booklet that explained in glowing terms how to become a well-paid cartoonist in ten easy lessons. He frowned, selected another envelope and glanced in perplexity at an illustrated pamphlet describing the manufacture of a well-known brand of stockings.

My envelope yielded up a printed letter which began *Dear Madam*, and listed several recipes calling for a well-known brand of gelatin. I picked up a second envelope and then a third. I discovered that for ten cents in stamps the requested sample of Swampmilk facial cream had been promptly forwarded. I discovered instructions for knitting a sweater from yarn of virgin wool. Another printed letter offered to teach hotel management to anybody willing to study at home, an envelope in azure blue produced an enthusiastic recommendation of a course in public speaking, a sheet of stationery in bright pink suggested the immediate purchase of a small whistle that would reproduce any "wanted" bird call. Each of the two dozen envelopes contained advertising matter in praise of two dozen widely different products, and each was as impersonal and unrevealing as a quart bottle of morning milk delivered on the doorstep.

Since Al was in the advertising business, we arrived at the answer very easily. The false Veronica Moran had clipped from newspapers and magazines countless coupons and sent them everywhere, and had received in return sufficient correspondence to satisfy the local post mistress and Harriet and Aunt Mildred and everybody else in Merristone who might be interested. Without friends to write her letters, she had, in an ingenious way, provided for herself a respectable amount of correspondence.

"Is that *all?*"

"That's a fair sampling of the mail that the Veronica Moran of Copston Road received in Merristone. The mail tells us nothing, except that the woman was patient, careful and determined not to be found out."

"Careful or not, I should think—" Al paused and frowned and glanced at me. "You're a woman, Janey. You should know your sex. Or am I crazy? If you were running away from your past, could you bear to leave absolute everything behind? Wouldn't you hang on to something— some small thing—of your own?"

I looked instinctively at my wedding ring.

Sheriff Blandish followed the direction of my eyes. He hesitated. "That's rather shrewd, Mr. Blake. We did come across one thing in the Copston Road house that might conceivably lead somewhere. An item not listed at the auction room as among the harpist's effects. Evidently it had some personal meaning for Mrs. Moran herself. At any rate she carried into her new identity a miniature, doll-sized trunk."

"The trunk that was in her dressing table!" I exclaimed, and recalled my glimpse that morning of the pretty, paper-covered trifle, so out of place in Dr. Traphaven's macabre study.

"Apparently," said Sheriff Blandish, "the woman bought the trunk herself long ago, and kept it out of sentiment. Or so we believe. Did she ever mention a child to you?"

We stared at him.

"The trunk is packed with little clothes, in an infant's size. Little dresses and caps and shoes, worn and yellowed with age. Put away as though they were no longer needed, but kept nevertheless."

During our single interview with the impostor, she had spoken vaguely of a husband and children, carried off long ago in a typhoid epidemic. Even at the time, Al had put no stock in the tale of the epidemic and the little family. Mrs. Moran's tears had fallen too quickly and too easily. In the light of what we had learned since the tea party, I found it impossible to credit that the missing woman was a bereft and grieving mother. The Sheriff seemed equally dubious; although he scribbled a few brief notes covering the conversation.

"The story doesn't ring too true," was the way he put it. "I'm afraid it won't help identify Veronica Moran."

"Her 'sentiment' doesn't ring true either," Al remarked. "Or it's a queer variety. She kept the little trunk hidden way, cheek by jowl with a bag of arsenic." For a moment he was silent, and then he leaned forward in his chair. "I'm not telling you your business, Sheriff Blandish, but I suppose you've thought of fingerprints."

"We thought of fingerprints, Mr. Blake." The Sheriff smiled grimly. "After a reasonably thorough investigation of the house on Copston Road, we haven't turned up a single fingerprint of the missing woman. None whatever."

I was dumbfounded. Indeed I started to argue that Dr. Traphaven, whose reasonably thorough investigations were famous locally, must have slipped for once.

"But Sheriff Blandish, she poured out tea for Al and me. I saw her handle the samovar, the cake plate, the brandy bottle with my own eyes. Surely...."

"The samovar, the cake plate, the brandy bottle have been examined. The fingerprints—including yours and Mr. Blake's—have been carefully wiped away. Mrs. Moran handled her toilet articles every day, but they've also been wiped clean. She turned out her bedside lamp every night—an excellent surface, but completely free of fingerprints. She entered the bathroom and touched the tiled walls. No luck there either."

At that a corner of my bewilderment lifted, and I glimpsed dim, uncertain light. A mere thread of light, but something. I knew at last what Sheriff Blandish and Al had sensed at once—that Veronica Moran's hidden past was criminal. No honest woman would wipe her fingerprints from her brush, her comb, her bedside lamp, no honest woman would scrub the bathroom walls and electric fixtures or touch them cautiously with gloved hands, but a woman who was a criminal might do just that. A fanatically careful woman whose fingerprints were in police records somewhere. Such exceeding caution strongly suggested that the woman, who anticipated investigation and insured against it, had been again prepared to commit a criminal act.

Al said restlessly, "All this planning, all this preparation—doesn't it seem to indicate—well, that Mrs. Moran intended to kill Hannah when she first came to Merristone? It almost looks as though, from the very day of her arrival, Mrs. Moran had murder in her mind."

And then my husband halted.

"I do not doubt Mrs. Moran's intention," the Sheriff said quietly. "I believe myself that she intended to kill her maid. And from the day she settled in the village. But surely you perceive that her plan, whatever that plan may have been, was not carried out last night."

Some minutes before, I had perceived the direction in which we were headed. The very perfection of the false Veronica Moran's impersonation, the untiring care that had gone into it, went to show that she would not lose her head. She would not lose her head, beat another woman to death in a moment of frenzy, and then admit guilt by panic-stricken, ill-considered flight. If Veronica Moran plotted murder, the first requisite of her plot would be the establishing of her own innocence. Something had happened to the patient, tedious and unknown scheme of the woman who had lived out her secret months in the house on Copston Road. Something had destroyed the plan.

I was thinking desperately, and it seemed to me that we had proved Veronica Moran's criminal intent only to prove simultaneously that she had not committed the violent murder which had occurred the night before. Where then was the woman with the bold, black eyes, and the untidy hair bound in veils of crimson? What had become of the impostor?

"That's what I want you two to find out for me," said Sheriff Blandish gently. "That was my purpose in calling you here."

Al started, as though he hadn't heard the words correctly. I looked up. Sheriff Blandish had opened the drawer of his desk a second time. I watched in silent horror as he drew forth the long yellow sheets that had lain that morning in Arthur Cleat's desk at the village bank. Sheriff Blandish had visited the bank, as I should have realized from the beginning, instead of being deluded by his expansive air of sharing a policeman's problems with us out of sheer good will. The Sheriff knew as well as I did that Selby had rented the house for the impostor, and throughout the interview he had known that Selby was the one to talk to and to question.

"I have talked to your brother," Sheriff Blandish said to Al. "At length and quite in vain. Selby Blake asks me to believe that he never met the impostor, but that he rented a house for her, that he had important business dealings with her, that—"

Al's face was ghastly. Every drop of blood had gone from it. When I reached for his hand, he pushed my hand away and picked up one of long yellow sheets that recorded Veronica Moran's monthly deposits. Below her printed name marched a long row of cold, blue figures crediting the account with $500 on the 15th of every month. I had not been interested in Mrs. Moran's finances that morning, nor had I thought that they concerned Selby in any way. Now, with cold fascination, I stared at the figures.

"I am convinced," said Sheriff Blandish, "that Selby Blake can explain the source of Mrs. Moran's mysterious income, though he insists that he cannot. He could tell us all we need to know about her, if he wished." And then the Sheriff turned to me. "Selby Blake knows Veronica Moran much better than even you realize, Mrs. Blake. I want you and your husband to go to him and make an appeal that he come clean on his story. Maybe you two can persuade him it would be wiser for him to tell us what he knows, than to let us find out for ourselves."

"My brother—" Al began in a voice unlike his own.

"I have proof," said Sheriff Blandish, "of Selby Blake's close association with this woman, whom he stubbornly and foolishly professes that he has never met. Proof that goes far beyond a simple matter of his renting a house for her. I have proof sufficient to arrest him any time I choose."

With one deft gesture, he swept the long yellow sheets of paper to one side. Lying underneath was a cancelled check. The authorities had been unable to discover how the false Veronica Moran had got her income, but they had discovered from the Merristone First National Bank how she had spent it.

On the 27th of December, three weeks exactly before Hannah's murder, Mrs. Moran had made out a check which had virtually wiped out her sizable account. She had made out a check for $4,720 to Selby Blake, and Selby Blake had cashed it. His familiar signature, with the dashing loops and curlicues, was scrawled across the back.

Chapter Eighteen:
TEN WEATHERBEATEN BUSHELS

We went at once to our futile, hopeless interview with Selby. It was nearly six o'clock. Blake House was lighted, but instinct led Al down the block to the insurance office. Everything in Merristone was crowded on a single business street—the police station, the bank, the grocery stores, the undertaking establishment where Hannah Wilson's body lay awaiting burial. We were obliged to pass the small square building with the droplight over the door and the painted sign, but I kept my eyes upon the sidewalk.

We found Selby alone in his office. Miss Hawkins had closed her desk and left at noon, as she always did on Saturday. The heat had gone off at two o'clock. Selby had preferred his chill and solitary office to his home. During the long, lonely hours of the afternoon he must have gone over and over the unconvincing details of the unconvincing story he had decided to stick to until the bitter end. Selby was prepared for Al.

I don't like to remember that short, bitter talk between the brothers who had always been so close—the lies and evasions on Selby's part, the wretchedness and baffled anger of my husband.

"Surely you can tell us why you located a house for this woman?"

"Of course I can. Something over a year ago an acquaintance of mine wrote asking that I find a house for the woman and her maid. It was very little trouble. I located a suitable place and had Cleat communicate with Mrs. Moran."

"An acquaintance? Who?"

"The—the name has slipped my mind. Unfortunately I've lost the fellow's note. Doubtless it was someone I met in the line of business. I've been looking through my files." Selby pointed to a steel filing cabinet as though that would prove his story.

"I see," Al said quietly. "I suppose this acquaintance of yours, the one whose name you can't remember, might explain Mrs. Moran's income."

"Her income?"

"I am wondering if this acquaintance, who asked your assistance in settling Mrs. Moran in Merristone, provided her with $500 on the fifteenth of every month."

Selby said nothing for a full minute. Al's remark must have been a terrible shock to him. A thin white line appeared around his mouth, and he visibly braced himself. Somewhere deep inside I am sure he felt his brother's despair and longed to respond to it, but he did not.

"I know nothing about Mrs. Moran's income. I am ignorant of her past and private life. The sole point of contact between us was this acquaintance whose name has slipped my mind. Until Sheriff Blandish informed me, I had no idea the woman was an impostor. If I had suspected in time—"

"What?"

Selby was silent.

But Al was relentless. "If you had suspected the impersonation in time, do you mean you would not have accepted that check? Or have you forgotten that Mrs. Moran handed you a check for $4,720 and that you cashed it?"

"Please don't use that tone with me." Selby's own fear took the form of anger. He must have walked the length of his office a thousand times that day; he paced it off once again. "Naturally I have not forgotten the check. Nor was it handed to me. The check came to me by mail, shortly after Christmas. How many times must I tell you that I have never met Mrs. Moran?"

Selby went on to say sullenly that he had placed the money in his safe deposit box at the bank; it was in a plain brown envelope; Sheriff Blandish was at liberty to impound the envelope and contents whenever he desired. The sooner the better. And then he did let something slip. "Maybe Mrs. Moran had that money in her possession, but she had no more right to it than—"

Just as my brother-in-law failed for a fractional second to guard his tongue, he also failed to guard his eyes. They were alive with hatred, and when I saw the white blaze in them I knew that he despised the Veronica Moran of Copston Road.

Al seized upon the words. "Ah, that's interesting. Very interesting. So you didn't feel that this money belonged to Mrs. Moran. Why? Why would you have any feeling, if you were as ignorant about her affairs as you say you are? How did you persuade this woman—a virtual stranger to you—to write you a check that almost wiped out her account?"

It was then that we heard the incredible part of the story. Selby drew himself up to his full height, squared his shoulders and regarded us as though he was already in his mind's eye facing a judge and jury. "There was a—a private business matter between us. Mrs. Moran and I made certain arrangements by telephone. There was nothing wrong about this transaction, but until she is apprehended I am not at liberty to explain it."

"Why not?"

"I gave my personal word to Mrs. Moran that I would keep the—the whole matter strictly confidential. I do not break my promises."

My heart sank. Selby sounded like the woodenheaded hero of an old-fashioned melodrama. Even supposing he had given a promise, Mrs. Moran's subsequent behavior made it imperative that he break the promise and speak out.

Selby had no intention of speaking out. He picked up his overcoat and pulled on his gloves to signify that the interview was at an end. I rose at once. Al rose more slowly, his shoulders sagging, his face a mask of bewildered misery. But he wasn't yet ready to admit total defeat.

"Was Hannah Wilson your go-between?" he asked suddenly. "Yours and Mrs. Moran's? Surely you didn't carry on all of your mysterious arrangements by telephone. Were you discussing this 'private' business matter with the maid on the day Sarah saw you with her in New York?"

Al had shaken his brother at last, penetrated the armor in which he had encased himself. Selby's fingers fastened on the edge of his desk. I saw them close and tighten. The sewn fabric of his glove grew taut, and his voice was like a thin fine wire stretched to the breaking point but still too strong to snap.

"What sharp eyes our cousin Sarah has! I wonder, Al, if you and Sarah realize what you're doing. Believe me, you aren't making my position any easier. I'm trying to do my best for the family."

"The family!" Al said, startled. "What's the family got to do with it?"

Selby didn't seem to hear the question. "I want you to listen to me, Al," he said. "I do not know who killed Hannah Wilson. If I knew I'd be talking to the Sheriff now. I did not kill her, if that's what's behind your sudden interest in my personal affairs. My personal opinion is that Veronica Moran is guilty, and when she's found I'm willing to match my story with hers. Until then, I have nothing more to say."

When we left him in his chill, deserted office, wearing his gloves and overcoat but unwilling to follow us even to the sidewalk, I wondered whether we would ever see Veronica Moran again. I had no conviction that Selby would ever have the opportunity to match his story with the story of the impostor. And if Selby stuck to the account he had given Al and me, I thought it very probable that within a few days or even within hours he would be arrested as an accessory in Hannah Wilson's murder—provided, of course, he escaped being charged with the murder itself.

In his desperation Al decided to go and see Ruth, but when he approached Blake House his heart failed him as I had known it would. He next thought of Belton.

"Selby must talk, Jane. Maybe Belton can make him listen to reason; one of us has got to do it. Selby is protecting someone. I'm sure of it. My brother never killed a helpless, deaf old woman, and I'm going to prove it in spite of him."

Belton had built fine houses for other people, but characteristically enough he preferred to occupy two tumbled untidy rooms at the Merristone Hotel. Belton was not at the hotel. When we drove toward Aunt Mildred's, however, along the winding twists of Copston Road, we found him.

His car, still pulled up before our building site, was blanketed in drifted snow, but the engine was going and the lights were burning. Al stopped at once, got out and approached it. "Funny, Belton's not in the car, Jane. But he can't have gone very far."

Instinctively I had averted my eyes from our cottage, and looked only at the road. Now I turned. It wasn't much past six o'clock, but the early darkness of winter had fallen. A few stars pricked the high black heavens, and a slender moon had risen.

The workmen had all gone home, but I thought I heard distant voices. Suddenly beyond the cottage that bulked palely in the gloom, on the side away from the road, I caught the flicker of a flashlight. A transitory flicker that danced into view and immediately disappeared.

"Let's go on, Al," I said nervously. "We can't talk to Belton now. Someone's with him."

But Al was curious. "It's only Mr. Thirkle, Janey. I think I hear his voice. What do you suppose the two of them are doing?"

I was more interested in reaching Aunt Mildred's than in finding out, but when Al started across the littered yard I would not remain behind. We had no flashlight. The high moon shed no light at all. I suppose we had stumbled forward perhaps 20 feet, when the voices guiding us abruptly died away. There was no sound whatever. And then the silence was broken by the unmistakable and anguished wail of a cat. The wail, rising to an agonized and piercing crescendo, was suddenly choked off.

My hair rose on end. Al shot around the house and left me to follow as best I could. It was a strange sight that greeted me 30 seconds later. Mr. Thirkle was squatted on the snowy ground, apparently engaged in peering underneath the flooring of the dining room. Al knelt beside him. By the bright illumination of Mr. Thirkle's flashlight I saw that it was Belton Weaver whom they were regarding with such fascination. Flat on his stomach, Belton lay half underneath the cottage and half outside, caught in that position by his own ample middle. As I ran up to them, he managed to jerk one arm free. Clutched by the scruff of the neck, he held a black cat draped in shreds of faded green ribbon.

"Meet Gog again!" gasped Belton. "And, for God's sake, someone take the animal off my hands."

Gog looked more dead than alive when Al handed him to me. All the fight had abruptly left him, although Belton, scrambling to his feet, bore evident marks of battle. There was a long scratch across his cheek, and he had a badly bitten thumb which he examined ruefully.

"The little devil crawled under there to die, I suppose. It might not have been such a bad notion to let him do it."

"That's what I said," remarked Mr. Thirkle with an air of quiet satisfaction. "You've torn your good coat, Mr. Weaver."

Belton had the guilty expression of a man caught out acting on his better nature. He began to brush the snow and mud from his expensive tweeds, and grinned at me.

"I've done my part, Jane. The future problem of Gog is now yours. The cat will undoubtedly live, though he seems undecided at the moment. He's evidently been under the house since he ran off last night."

Gog had absorbed less arsenic than Magog, and mercifully the worst effects of the poison had worn off. Quiet, miserable and resigned, he lay limply in my arms. Mr. Thirkle eyed him with considerable disfavor.

"I don't like that cat," he snapped. "I didn't like Mrs. Moran either. Snooping around this place, where she had no mortal right to be. Maybe you folks don't know it, but the last few weeks that woman spent a lot of time on your property."

I almost dropped Gog in my astonishment.

"It's gospel truth I'm telling," said Mr. Thirkle. "Ask Mr. Weaver if it isn't so. He saw Mrs. Moran in your yard late one evening just last week. Isn't that right, Mr. Weaver?"

"Yes," said Belton a shade uncomfortably.

"Twice, myself," continued Mr. Thirkle, angry and yet triumphant, too, "when I came back for something I caught her—veils, high heels, cats on leashes, and all. Standing out there by my rubbish pile, Mrs. Moran was. It was no use complaining to you folks, Mr. Blake. I knew exactly what you'd say."

Mr. Thirkle then launched upon an old, time-worn grievance. Casual, uninvited visitors had long been in the habit of stopping at the building site, particularly after hours—village people who desired to see for themselves how Al and I were wasting our substance. From the first Mr. Thirkle had wanted to eject these trespassers, but we would not permit it and finally we had refused to listen to the builder's grumbling and complaints.

It was impossible for me to believe that Veronica Moran had been a casual trespasser, any more than Hannah Wilson, who died in our dining room, had been a casual trespasser. On the other hand, it was equally difficult to believe that she also had used our cottage for a rendezvous. A maid might be obliged to leave home to keep a private appointment, but surely a mistress, desiring secrecy, would send away her servant and remain in her own comfortable living room.

"She didn't go in the house," Mr. Thirkle said emphatically. "And I can tell you why. She found what she wanted outside the house. And took it too. That fine lady, with all her veils and airs and graces, was a common, ordinary thief."

"A thief!"

"She stole from my rubbish pile," said Mr. Thirkle, and turned his flashlight in that direction.

His rubbish pile rose from the field nearby. It was made up of worthless odds and ends of lumber, bits of lath, curling shingles from the old roof, all the leftover debris incidental to any building project. Al and I had done our best to persuade Mr. Thirkle to haul away the stuff, but he had remained stubbornly convinced that we might find future use for some bit of junk. I looked at the rubbish pile and thought of Veronica Moran, and had a hysterical impulse to laugh.

"Laugh if you like," said Mr. Thirkle venomously. "Maybe it sounds funny, but it's true. That woman came here with a flour sack, and she filled it from that pile. It stuck out underneath them veils she wore. A great big sack. She almost dropped it when she went hightailing off for home."

I simply stared at him.

Al closed his mouth, and opened it again. "What in heaven's name did she take? Have you any idea, Mr. Thirkle?"

The builder looked embarrassed.

Belton gave a ghostly little chuckle. "Thirkle knows that pile like the palm of his own hand. After he discovered what was missing he decided he'd better hold his tongue and forget the matter. Indeed I advised it. We thought you'd laugh, if he suggested filing criminal charges."

Mr. Thirkle's face was red, but still indignant. "Stealing's stealing, Mr. Weaver. But Mrs. Moran did take a kind of funny thing. She carried away old shingles."

"Shingles!"

"That's all she took," admitted the builder reluctantly. "Just those shingles from the old roof. But she took a lot of them. At least ten bushels. Ten bushels is a sizable load. She had to make a lot of trips with that flour sack."

"What do you make of it?" asked Belton, obviously perplexed but unable to repress his amusement.

I made nothing of it whatever. Mrs. Moran's theft of our shingles, shingles so old and dry and weatherbeaten that they almost crumpled in the hand, sounded like sheer insanity. There had been no shingles in her house. What had she done with the shingles, or planned to do with them? How could ten bushels of old shingles fit into her scheme—assuming she had a scheme—to commit a murder?

I was thinking of these things as we bade goodbye to Mr. Thirkle, and followed Belton to the road. In the flurry of rescuing Gog, in my perplexity at Veronica Moran's surprising theft, I had almost succeeded in thrusting Selby from my mind. But when Belton got into his car, Al paused beside the running board.

"I'd like to talk to you a moment. Jane and I just saw Selby."

In the dash light glow the amusement faded from Belton's face. He looked suddenly quite old. "Talking's useless, son. Take an old man's word for it. You can't jaw your brother into changing his nature one jot or tittle. I should know. I tried to talk to him myself."

"Then you—you've heard about that check?"

Belton nodded.

"I suppose he told you," Al said bitterly, "as he told us, that he received a $4,720 check from Veronica Moran in the ordinary course of business."

"He told me that," said Belton, "and, God help us all, I believe it. Hasn't it occurred to you that Selby's business is insurance? Think that over. How could Veronica Moran get money out of Hannah's death, except by insuring her?"

His big foot stamped on the starter. Without another word he drove away. Al and I stood there in the road, long after the red eye of the tail light had disappeared

Chapter Nineteen:
MINIATURE CLOTHES

When we reached Aunt Mildred's, Sarah took immediate charge of Gog, for which I was thankful. Indeed, directly after supper she dosed him with a sedative and transferred him to her own room. Al stayed downstairs with the others, but I retired very early and took a sedative myself.

It was nearly noon on Sunday and the others had long since breakfasted when I awoke heavy-eyed and unrefreshed and went downstairs. Everybody was collected in the kitchen, including Gog, whom Sarah had wrapped in her favorite sweater and tucked beside the stove. Aunt Mildred was complaining about the cat, and meanwhile chopping liver for his lunch. Al and Frank had brought in the radio, and with Sarah were listening to reports of the futile search for Veronica Moran. At noon on Sunday, nearly 48 hours after Hannah Wilson's murder, the pretended harpist had not been found, nor had her true identity been determined.

As it happened I entered the kitchen just as Dr. Traphaven's old and battered car drove up in the yard outside. Al snapped off the radio. No one spoke as the little doctor, dainty as a cat himself, picked his way to the porch, stamped and scraped his feet and came inside. Dr. Traphaven didn't hide his feelings like Sheriff Blandish. He looked grave and depressed. His boots were caked in mud, despite his efforts with the mat. He apologized for tracking up the kitchen, but did not explain where he had been to get into mud and slush so deep that it went well up his trousers legs. Instead he said, "I've only got a minute. But I'd like a cup of coffee. Just one lump of sugar, please, but don't spare the cream."

He drank the coffee before he opened his bulging briefcase and took out the paper-covered doll's trunk. It was my first close view of the little trunk that had been hidden in Mrs. Moran's dressing table beside a bag of pure white arsenic. I had almost forgotten its existence.

The Sheriff himself had once believed that the tiny yellowed garments the trunk contained might be an important clue to the past of the black-haired, black-eyed impostor. But that was before he discovered a check made out in the amount of $4,720 to Selby Blake. Sheriff Blandish had lost interest in the quaint, old-fashioned little trunk, and on that bitter winter day was working feverishly in other directions—a fact of which the doctor was well aware. He had just left him with a band of volunteers, who had divided up in groups to search the thick woods that encroached on Merristone. Sheer goodwill and nothing else was responsible for Dr. Traphaven's call on us. As he was to tell me later on, "In the last analysis I suppose I'm rather shy on manhunting instincts. I'm not like the Sheriff. He has to get convictions. Justice—the truth— was all I ever wanted."

So now he looked around at us a bit uncertainly and said, "I'm asking a favor of you ladies. That's why I brought the little trunk. I'd like your opinion of these—these baby clothes."

With an unconscious air of drama he opened the trunk lid, and spilled the jumbled, untidy contents upon the kitchen table. I hadn't seen the wardrobe before, and I leaned forward in my chair. Little caps and shoes and capes and dresses were mixed together in a tumbled heap. My first impression was of dirt. All of the tiny garments were frayed and worn and badly soiled—so soiled that it took me a second to perceive the oddity of the materials and the colors. Very few of the long swaddling dresses were white. The rest were in vivid garish hues, and they were made of expensive velvets and satins, sewn with beads and gewgaws and elaborately embroidered. I picked up a handkerchief- sized frock that flashed a sign in circus spangles.

"No child ever wore that!" cried Aunt Mildred with outright horror. I myself could not imagine any self-respecting infant tricked out in such a rig. The size was all right, the cut was passable, but surely no mother would dress her baby in brocade and spangles.

"Mrs. Moran might," said Frank, out of his profound wisdom as a bachelor. "The dress is on the gay side, but so was she."

Dr. Traphaven was also a bachelor, and Al was not a father. The two of them nodded in slightly puzzled agreement. We women protested in chorus.

Sarah spoke for us all. "Nonsense, Frank. It's more like a—a doll's dress. Something for show. Though it seems expensive for a doll. Let me see, Jane."

"Monkey clothes is more like it." With acute distaste Aunt Mildred turned over a little cape, stiff with dirt at the hem, and embellished in threads of tarnished silver. She lifted and hurriedly dropped a minute and filthy pair of velvet shoes. "Sentiment! Well, maybe Mrs. Moran was sentimental, but she let her cats sleep in the trunk."

Indignantly she brushed several long black hairs off on the floor. Sarah examined the neckline of the little spangled frock and found no label, and I was not surprised. Obviously a wardrobe so bizarre had been made to order, and Dr. Traphaven would have discovered the labels had they existed. As Sarah laid down the dress, I spied the tiny boxing gloves. A pair of boxing gloves made of soft brown leather, thickly padded, laced at the wrists—an absurd miniature of the larger model. The gloves were shaped to fit coin-sized fists.

I had not believed that any of the clothing had been fashioned for a child of cradle age, despite the size. I knew it then. No infant in my experience had ever needed a pair of boxing gloves. But why Mrs. Moran had acquired that extraordinary wardrobe and why she had kept it was beyond us all.

"Well, then—" Disappointed in some obscure way, Dr. Traphaven got up to go. He walked as far as the door and even opened it. Suddenly he changed his mind, turned around, looked at Al with a grave and troubled expression, and asked to speak privately to him. To Aunt Mildred's annoyance, Al went outside with Dr. Traphaven and conferred with him beside his car.

I stepped to the window, and watched the two across the yard. Heavy clouds banked the west, and the distant figures of the men had borrowed from the cheerlessness of the day—the little doctor talking earnestly and Al bending down to listen. Once I saw the white flash of paper as Dr. Traphaven pulled a typed sheet from his pocket and handed it to Al. Al read the paper and gave it back, and presently the doctor drove away.

When my husband started slowly back across the yard, I went out and joined him. I didn't need to ask, I knew the news was bad. I slipped my arm through his, and together we walked away from the house and up the country road. I gave Al time, and kept my questions to myself. I tried to hide my relief when he told me Dr. Traphaven had shown him a copy of his report on the autopsy. My fear was that the paper had been an official document of another sort—a copy of a warrant for Selby Blake's arrest.

"Dr. Traphaven made a careful examination of Hannah's body," Al said listlessly. "He was kind enough to think I might be interested in the results. He did find something rather—queer. Although in the circumstances it seems somewhat academic."

I lost a step. "Didn't Hannah die of a fractured skull? Is—is that changed?"

Al shook his head. "The poor old woman died of multiple fractures of the skull, all right—seven separate fractures produced by some heavy and unknown weapon. She died sometime between six o'clock and seven on Friday evening. That's what happened, Jane. But the doctor is interested in what didn't happen."

I waited.

"Except for that fractured skull, Hannah Wilson might in time have died much more painfully and tediously. Died of mineral poisoning."

"The arsenic!" My thoughts returned to Gog, huddled beside the kitchen stove. "Dr. Traphaven found arsenic in Hannah's body."

"Not a fatal amount of arsenic," Al said with bitter emphasis. "Just enough arsenic to make the average person start to fail, have vague pains in the joints, mysterious stomach upsets. Enough to suggest a campaign of slow poison."

Afterward I was to read the autopsy myself, and was to learn something of the ineradicable evidence that repeated doses of arsenic leave in the human body. Evidence that the most cunning and skillful poisoner cannot hope to conceal, once the laboratory technician steps in. Dr. Traphaven had found traces of arsenic in Hannah's broken, work-worn nails. Her gray hair, short and scraggly and badly tended like her nails, was impregnated with the drug both at the ends and at the roots. Dr. Traphaven knew that the growth of human hair averages half an inch a month, and thus a single gray hair, cut delicately in three sections, carefully tested and then measured, told him that Hannah Wilson had been absorbing minute quantities of a deadly poison over a period of many months.

On that winter day, I was glad I hadn't read the terse, technical phrases of the coroner's report. Even without it, I felt sickened. Poison, that subtle, silent weapon that destroys life secretly, without violence; poison that is so often accepted by a trusting hand, is not a pleasant thing to think about. I did not like to picture Hannah warming her old bones with a cup of tea, or sharing a glass of milk with her mistress, or allowing herself to be urged to accept the last sandwich on the tray.

"It looks as though slow poison was intended to serve as Mrs. Moran's method," Al said dully. "A pretty stupid method of murder, if you ask me. Laboratory technicians are too advanced today to be fooled by arsenic. Mrs. Moran must have counted on getting away without a postmortem. Her motive is certainly plain enough. She planned to collect a thumping insurance policy on Hannah's life. Of course Dr. Traphaven knew about that part from the very first."

"How?"

"Hannah went to Dr. Traphaven weeks ago to take a physical examination so she could get insurance. Selby was the agent. He himself sent her to the doctor. Not that any of this matters now. The Moran plot did not go through."

Again, with ice-cold water running through my veins, I waited. In silence, hands caught together, we walked six steps up the road, seven and eight. And then Al stopped.

"Surely you've guessed why Dr. Traphaven came today. He's known Selby all his life, he still has some faint hope of his innocence, some faint hope that the answer to the murder may be hidden in Mrs. Moran's past. He begged me to tell him anything—suspicions, surmises—anything that might bear on the point, and help identify her. But Sheriff Blandish won't wait. Tomorrow he's going to arrest Selby. He's already asked for the warrant."

I had expected the blow so long that I received it numbly. I put my arms around Al's neck, and laid my cheek against his hair. "Selby didn't do it, dear. We'll get a lawyer, the best lawyer in the world. Things can surely be delayed till Mrs. Moran is found."

"Don't you understand?" Al's own voice broke. "No one thinks that Mrs. Moran is still alive. They think she's dead and buried. That's why Sheriff Blandish and a hundred volunteers are hunting high and low this afternoon for the missing harp case. They expect to find her body in it."

Chapter Twenty:
IN THE ASH CAN

I don't know how Frank and Sarah occupied themselves that endless afternoon. Aunt Mildred wrapped up and went off to make her usual Sunday call on Harriet Strings, and left them to themselves. There was no word from Selby, but toward five o'clock Belton dropped by and said that Selby had gone to his office and that Ruth was locked away in Blake House—and that both were out to everybody, including him. Sarah talked to Belton; Al and I did not go down.

We remained upstairs in our own room, locked away like Ruth and Selby. I lay on the bed, and Al walked the floor and tried desperately to think of some way to fathom the secret of the Merristone Enigma.

"They can arrest Selby, and convict him maybe. But Dr. Traphaven's right. They'll never learn the truth until they pin a name on that woman."

Personally I saw no hope of accomplishing the feat. Sheriff Blandish had not accomplished it. Although I did feel, as Al felt, that the Sheriff had forgotten the importance of identifying the missing woman, and was bending all his efforts upon the search for the harp case. Even without the harp case, he had Selby. The warrant charging Selby with Hannah Wilson's murder had already been requested. Once the warrant was served and Selby was behind bars, the Sheriff could wait comfortably until his prisoner chose to talk, secure in the conviction that the right man had been arrested, that Selby could furnish all the necessary facts about the impostor.

"I don't believe that, Janey. Somehow the woman tricked Selby, too. It's up to us to dig up the story of her past."

Well, I didn't argue. Al did all the talking. As a starting point, he began with the premise that Veronica Moran's hidden past was criminal. Otherwise she would not have taken such elaborate precautions to conceal it. "Murder is my guess," he said grimly. "I'm willing to bet that she once figured in a famous murder case. That's what she was hiding, Jane." He continued walking up and down the room.

"If we only knew her real name," he said later, out of his burning restlessness, "we could go to Dr. Traphaven's library and search his files, and maybe find her listed there."

But we didn't know the impostor's real name. A thorough search of Dr. Traphaven's library would require days or even weeks, with no real promise of success.

It was past seven o'clock, and high cold winter stars were shining through our bedroom windows, when Al eventually gave up. I stepped to the bureau and combed my hair for dinner and daubed powder on my nose. I looked into the cracked, spoiled mirror, but I didn't really see it. Nor did I think about how Al had broken the mirror in his futile rush toward the hall two nights before. The mysterious visitor to the house, who had crept into the hall and rattled our latch and swiftly fled leaving two open doors to invite pursuit, was distant from my thoughts. I had no idea how soon we were to learn that the unknown had attempted to place in our hands the key to the very problem that absorbed us.

Aunt Mildred was still away when Al and I descended to the kitchen. No preparations had been made toward the evening meal. Sarah announced that she and Frank had also been attempting to decide upon a method of identifying Veronica Moran.

Dr. Traphaven had either forgotten to take the little trunk, or had left it purposely. The two of them had carefully examined each of the baffling little garments, and come to no conclusions except that the wardrobe was expensive. Tossed aside, the garish little dresses, the hats, the capes and velvet shoes, the tiny boxing gloves, lay in a tumbled heap on the kitchen table. Frank laid down a little cap, decorated with wheels of bright red ribbon, tilted back his chair, crossed his legs and sighed.

Al looked at his partner rather hopelessly. "Any ideas, Frank?"

Frank hesitated and admitted to an idea. Simultaneously he conceded that research and time would be necessary to carry it out. Knowing how much his mind worked like Al's, I imagined he had arrived at the same conclusion. That the only way to identify Veronica Moran was to assume a criminal past, and go on from there. As it turned out, however, Frank's approach was somewhat different.

"I'd use for my essential clue—my beginning point—the fact that the woman chose to pose as a harpist."

"How is that a clue to her real identity?" I asked irritably. "She had a chance to buy a harpist's effects."

"It's a rather specialized profession, Janey. No matter how badly the average woman needed to change her identity, she'd hardly dare pass herself off as a harpist. Would you try it?"

"No," I admitted. "But what's your point?"

"My point is that only someone in the arts would be likely to attempt the role. A woman too vain to choose a commonplace personality, a woman with a little acting ability—can't you see that woman deciding to become a harpist overnight? Another musician, maybe. Or an—an actress."

"We might settle down," I said ironically, "and start making out a list of all American actresses since 1900. Once that's done we can pass on to Europe...."

"It's simpler than that," said Frank, without resentment. "If I were in New York, I know exactly how I'd go about it. I'd start with the sure knowledge that if Mrs. Moran was an actress she wasn't extra good at it."

"So—"

"So I would decide she must have reached her blooming sometime in the '20s, in the good old expansive days when a little talent and a lot of brass went a long way. Cheap shows and tawdry acts were a dime a dozen then."

Suddenly Frank began to enjoy himself. He had the quick enthusiasm of the advertising man, the enthusiasm that was the bread and butter of the firm he had founded with no help from anyone in the dismal '30s when old established houses were failing by the score. His shining eyes made me recall the day we met him first; the day he had sought out Al, newly down from Yale, discouraged, jobless and disheartened in a strange, unfriendly city. On that day Frank had led us both to a mountain top, indeed had made our marriage possible with the offer of a job much better than a novice deserved. On occasion Frank's compelling enthusiasm almost caused me to forget that some of his ideas were sound and some were not, and that he always ignored the difficulties.

"Provided with a date to shoot at," he said, brisk and incisive, and as though the date were an established fact. "I'd go to the offices of one of the theatrical publications—*Billboard* or *Variety,* say—and I'd look at *their* files. Those sheets are jammed with photographs. If you saw a picture of Veronica Moran, even if it were taken years ago and captioned with another name, you'd recognize her."

"You aren't in New York, Frank," I mildly reminded him. "You've got no chance of getting there."

Frank looked startled. Like a man rudely awakened from a dream, he glanced toward Sarah. She usually rushed to his defense in any argument he had with me, reserving to herself the right to differ. But Sarah was looking across the kitchen, an odd and absent expression on her face. I followed the direction of her eyes, and saw that they were fixed on Gog. Wrapped in the yellow sweater, the black cat lay sleeping underneath the stove just as Magog had lain and slept underneath another stove.

"Gog could tell us everything we want to know," Sarah said. "Isn't that strange to think about? Gog should be the real clue."

Gog heard his name. The cat's glazed, sick eyes opened, and gave us all a look that was almost human. A queer, cool little silence held the room. Gog indeed could tell us what we needed to know about the mistress who had poisoned him.

For a queer, cool instant the four of us sat very still. And then Frank brought down his chair. His hand brushed the doll's trunk, the heap of overdecorated little clothes.

On sudden impulse, and with a half-smile for Sarah, he picked up the tiny boxing gloves and held them out toward Gog.

"Tell us, Gog," he said. "Tell us if your mistress really bought these things, and what they're for. Tell us what a pair of little boxing gloves meant to her."

It was then that the extraordinary thing occurred. As though Frank had given a signal, the sick cat shook off the folds of the sweater, rose to uncertain legs, moved staggeringly across the floor. When Gog reached Frank he stopped. He stopped, stood up on his hind legs, balanced there and held out two black paws. Nothing could have been more clear than that the tiny gloves had been fashioned to fit the two extended paws, and that Gog expected Frank to lace them on.

Sarah gasped, and I stared in dumb incredulity. But Al's eye lit with sudden illumination, and Frank's blazed with triumph and amazement.

"Trained cats!" he cried. "There's your answer, people, part of Mrs. Moran's past. We know her profession, anyhow. She had an animal act."

With that he swept up a handful of the dirty tinseled dresses, the spangled capes and velvet shoes.

"Tell them, Gog. Tell these people how you and Magog used to wear this silly stuff, and box before the public and maybe do a little dance. Tell them how this woman, who tried to poison you, once earned her living in the theater by the talents of her pets."

The black cat still stood upright, balanced perfectly, with his paws extended. In unprotesting patience, Gog waited until the gloves were fitted on and laced. He rose to the very tips of his back legs, threshed his gloved paws in the air, and began a feeble dance, just as Aunt Mildred walked through the door.

"Listen, Mother," Sarah called excitedly, and then she paused.

Both of us caught the look on Aunt Mildred's face as he gazed at Gog in the convolutions of his absurd and ridiculous dance. It wasn't amazement that was on her face or amusement either. It was a look that seemed almost close to fear. Most people would have stopped to exclaim at the spectacle of a dancing cat. Aunt Mildred didn't stop at all. She walked straight through the kitchen and on upstairs.

Sarah glanced at us uncertainly, and went after her. Frank followed. Everything had happened very quickly. Gog was still moving through the figures of his stage routine.

"Well!" I said, and stooped and picked up the cat. I unlaced the little boxing gloves, and silently carried Gog back to the stove. And then I had to say, "Aunt Mildred didn't seem to enjoy our show."

Al didn't comment, and I regretted my remark. I started upstairs myself.

But Sarah appeared at the upper landing and called down to me. "Mamma isn't feeling well, Janey. She should have worn her other coat, I guess. She's had a—a chill. Will you ask Al to fire the furnace?" Without further explanation, she returned to her mother.

Aunt Mildred's chill had struck with remarkable suddenness. She had felt well enough that afternoon to go out and call on Harriet. Her health hadn't troubled her until the moment she had seen Gog, wearing boxing gloves, rise on tiptoe and begin to dance.

Al went immediately to the cellar, without his usual complaints. I was alone in the kitchen. Moved by some obscure impulse, I replaced the boxing gloves in the doll's trunk, repacked all the gaudy little clothing and dropped the trunk lid so the things were out of sight. Presently Al, from the cellar, shouted up for me.

Aunt Mildred's cellar was a place of neatness and order. She could easily have entertained her company there. The concrete floor was swept every day and scrubbed once a week. Al stood beside the furnace, with a helpless expression on his face. The lower door of the furnace was open, and he had just removed a shovelful of ashes. He held the loaded shovel in his hands.

"I can't find the ash can," he said plaintively. "Where is it?"

In Aunt Mildred's house, unless he or I moved them, things were seldom out of place. I looked toward the spot where the ash can should have been. The poker hung in its usual position upon the wall, and beside it hung the scrubbing pail. Two neat stacks of wood rose from the floor, with a vacant space between. The metal ash can wasn't there. A teasing memory flickered through my mind. I had seen the ash can somewhere lately.

"Did you carry it upstairs to empty?"

"I emptied it last Monday," said Al, "and I'm dead certain I brought it back. God knows Aunt Mildred's worked hard enough to train me. Where is it?"

Suddenly I said, "I believe it's on the porch. I think I saw it yesterday morning."

A strange expression crossed Al's face. The shovel shifted in his hands. His mind flashed back, as mine had done.

"By God, Janey, you're right. The ash can is on the back porch. You saw it Saturday morning. I saw it Friday night."

"Friday night!"

Unbidden, the marauder of Friday night came into my mind. I remembered how Frank and Al had dashed through the kitchen and out upon the porch only to discover that the intruder had vanished. Al was remembering too. But his thoughts were focused upon the mystifying transfer of the ash can from the cellar to the upstairs porch.

"I fell over the damn thing, Janey. I had to push it from my way. It was in the middle of the floor."

With that Al dropped his shovel in Aunt Mildred's spotless cellar, and shot back upstairs. Wholly bewildered, I followed. There was no electric light on the porch. Al was striking matches, and fumbling through the dusk that smelled of cleaning rags and kerosene and the spicy scent of winter apples. A stiff breeze was blowing. The breeze blew his matches out.

The ash can wasn't hard to locate. It was exactly where Al himself had pushed it on Friday night, against the wall next to the barrel of apples. For two days we had come and gone across the porch, and no one had wondered what the ash can was doing there. I still couldn't fathom it.

"Surely, Al, the can wasn't moved up here so you would stumble over it. That isn't sensible."

"No, it isn't," said Al.

His last match was gone. The kitchen light, shining through the open door, provided only faint illumination. Al's dusky figure bent, and I heard him try to heave the can. The receptacle was securely wedged against the wall, and was very heavy. A sharp clatter sounded as he snatched off the metal lid. I heard the soft, sliding sound of ashes, and then the unexpected crackle of paper.

"There's something in the can, Janey. Papers. Have you got another match?"

With trembling fingers, I struck a match. In the brief yellow flare, I saw the inside of the can. It was three-quarters full of ashes, but a compact bundle of papers lay atop the ashes. At first glimpse the bundle resembled a newspaper, folded by some newsboy, flung into a vacationer's yard and long left outside in the rain. The bundle of flimsy, crumpled sheets was not a newspaper. It was a collection of advertising dodgers, old and yellowed by time, held together by a rubber band. Cheap throwaways of a type seen seldom nowadays.

"Whatever in the world—!"

Al had already grabbed the paper bundle and run into the strong light of the kitchen. When he tried to slip the restraining band, the rubber was so rotten that it snapped. Like a pack of playing cards, a score of paper dodgers fell upon the kitchen floor.

They were all alike—bits of cheap and yellowed paper struck off long ago by the same indifferent printer. The photograph that filled one side of the page was bad and blurred, but it showed a woman with bold, black eyes and a mop of wild black hair, dressed in flowing draperies and posed between two cats—one black and the other white. The printing that filled the other side of the dodger read:

COMING!
See the Notorious Valerie Maple.
See the Cat Woman Who Trained her Pets in Prison
See the Cat Woman Who Paid Society her Debt
Help Valerie Maple to her Redemption.
Majestic Theatre
Saturday Thru Monday, August 3-5.

The woman of the blurred, bad photograph, the Valerie Maple who had trained her cats in prison and paid off her debt to society, was in her early 30s. The white cat and the black cat tricked out in velvet capes and little bonnets, were distant ancestors of Gog and Magog, but I instantly recognized the Veronica Moran of Copston Road.

"You recognize her! So do I!" said Al, and his voice was as bewildered a voice as I have ever heard. "We were meant to recognize and identify

Valerie Maple. Don't ask me why. All that's penetrated my thick skull is the purpose of that housebreaking episode Friday night. This stuff was planted, Jane, and placed deliberately on the back porch so we would find it."

Chapter Twenty-one:
THE CASE OF THE PICNIC MILK

We didn't announce our discovery to the others. Al swept the advertising dodgers from the floor, stuffed them in his pockets and ran outside to the car. I delayed long enough to grab our coats, but I caught him in the drive.

"Where are we going?"

"Straight to Dr. Traphaven."

I didn't ask him why. Valerie Maple's own name was the key we needed to unlock her past. Without the name we were helpless. Someone else had realized that, and, at considerable personal risk, had placed the telltale circulars on our premises. Why?

"I've no idea," Al said. "At the moment I don't even care. If Valerie Maple's story—the story she tried to hide—isn't in Doctor Traphaven's library, he can tell us where and how to find it."

I have no recollection whatever of our wild ride to the village. I do remember our breathless arrival at Dr. Traphaven's dwelling, and his immediate appearance at the door, the agitation of his manner. His hair was tousled, his small neat beard was all awry.

"Oh," said the doctor blankly, "it's you. I've been trying to locate Blandish."

"I hope you reach him," said Al with fervor.

The doctor stepped aside. "Come in. I want to show you two something."

He fairly pushed us along the hall into his study. The overhead lights were off. The packed shelves of books, the filing cabinets crowded with the accounts of old murder cases, were lost in shadows. The guns and glittering knives were softened by the dusk. Enclosed in a green shade, a single lamp burned at the rolltop desk where Dr. Traphaven sat to ponder crime and the ways of criminals. Illumined in a pool of greenish light lay an open book. I glanced at it. The book was entitled *Famous Poison Cases*. The page to which the book was turned was headed: *The Strange Tale of Valerie Maple and the Picnic Milk. Was She Guilty?*

Even with the knowledge of Veronica Moran's real name, I had expected to spend fruitless hours of research among the 2,000 volumes of that highly specialized library. But I was beyond surprise. When the doctor pulled out a chair, I sank into it limply. He seated himself at the desk, and picked up the book.

"I didn't stumble across this volume by accident," he began, his beard quivering angrily. "It wasn't by accident that I came across the facts of Valerie Maple's ghastly past. I was directed to the book."

"Directed?"

"Someone had the audacity to leave this in my mailbox. I don't know how long it's been there. I haven't gone to the post office for several days."

He flung on the desk a crumpled circular that was a duplicate of ours. There was one important difference. Printed slantwise across the pictured face of the false Veronica Moran—defacing the cheeks and forehead like a brand—was a date. The printing was crudely done in pencil. The date was July 2, 1916.

"We were directed too," Al said, and emptied his pockets and spread out our circulars for inspection. "Someone *wanted* us to know the truth about Veronica Moran. Can you think of any possible explanation?"

Dr. Traphaven didn't answer immediately. In the greenish light, the bearded face became grave and sad. For years the little doctor had reveled in his voluminous reading on crime, but when murder struck in Merristone and encompassed his friends and neighbors, it was plain he didn't like it. He pulled himself together.

"Someone here in Merristone knew all about the woman. That's obvious. Someone knew and hated her. God knows, Valerie Maple had earned hatred in her time. But I'm guessing there was a further reason behind this—this planting of information."

He gestured toward the circular and the crudely printed date that crossed the face like an ugly, malicious brand.

"I'm guessing that this person, who knew the facts and who was unwilling or afraid to come forward publicly, banked on Valerie Maple's past. Hoped, in other words, that her past was black enough to convict her out of hand of murdering Hannah Wilson. Valerie Maple was a killer, all right. A convicted murderess. She wouldn't have hesitated to kill her maid. But she never in this world would have used a bludgeon. Her method was poison."

"Arsenic, I suppose?"

"Arsenic," repeated Dr. Traphaven. And then he sighed, and leaned back from the desk. "A great deal of nonsense is talked about the criminal type. But Valerie Maple was a pathological case unquestionably. A born criminal—one of those women who bring death and endless misery to all who come their way. Suppose I tell you her story.

"On July 2, 1916," he went on somberly, "Valerie Maple was twenty-seven years of age, beautiful in a flamboyant way, vain, restless and dissatisfied within herself. She had everything any normal woman could desire. A pleasant home in the suburbs of Chicago, a devoted, hard-working husband, three lovely little children."

"She did have a family then?"

"She had a family, yes. One of the children was her husband's by a previous marriage, but two were her own flesh and blood. She treated them all alike. The typhoid epidemic of course was pure fiction. Valerie Maple's family met a different fate. On July 2, 1916, this apparently happy wife and mother committed the crime that should have ended her career on the gallows. She took her husband and her helpless babies on a picnic in a Chicago public park. With her own hands, she unpacked the picnic basket and fed poison to them all."

Dr. Traphaven laid down his book. I looked at the open page. He saw me glancing at the title—*Was She Guilty?* In a sudden spurt of wrath, he banged his fist against the volume.

"Sometimes writers annoy me. 'Was She Guilty?'" He mimicked the words. "This woman was guilty as hell. Her husband and two of the children died in agony within the week, and the third survived only by a miracle. Pure white arsenic was what she mixed in the picnic jug of milk, and she alone did not drink it. There was some fraudulent defense that she used arsenic as a complexion aid—and that it got in the jug by accident. It was proved in open court that Valerie Maple deliberately put arsenic in the milk, that she meant to wipe out her family. There was no doubt about her motive."

Al looked his question.

"She had a sweetheart," said the doctor quietly. "A sweetheart more fascinating and more desirable to her than her husband, her little son and daughters. To him she did show a certain twisted loyalty, for she refused to disclose his name. Valerie Maple poisoned her whole family so she could be free to marry, join this man in the East and go on the stage."

It was a terrible and chilling story, but it had happened long ago. I had hoped that Valerie Maple's past would lead us to the truth of Hannah Wilson's murder. What I had really hoped, I suppose, was that it would prove her guilt.

I listened dully as the little doctor explained that Valerie Maple had been convicted of murder, that she had gone to prison, and had been pardoned nine years later. I listened while he declaimed indignantly on the stage career that had been terminated eventually by the petitioning of outraged women's clubs. It was only dully that I heard Al say:

"But I don't quite understand why Valerie Maple took such terrible means to get her freedom. Why didn't she divorce her husband, or simply run away?"

"Money," said Dr. Traphaven.

I woke up at that.

"She had insured them all," he said. "She meant to profit by the deaths of her husband and her children, and use the money to finance herself in her new existence."

It was then that Al took my arm and led me from the study. Dr. Traphaven followed us outside. Next door, across an untrodden sheet of snow, the lights of Blake House were shining. None of us looked in that direction. We got into our car, and the doctor went off in his to hunt for Sheriff Blandish.

The Sheriff had not returned either to his office or his home since early morning. He and his band of exhausted volunteers were still beating through the woods in search of the harp case. They had moved far away from Copston Road. The doctor drove to the west, and we went north.

As we drove along in silence, I tried to bring order out of my own confusion. Our visit to Dr. Traphaven had only served to deepen the mystery. It seemed to me that Valerie Maple, even protected by the name of Veronica Moran, must have been insane to plot a crime so similar to the crime which had sent her off to prison 25 years before. Arsenic and insurance. She had insured her family, poisoned them with arsenic, and had been caught.

Her second essay at murder, her plot to kill Hannah Wilson, had gone wrong. Its details were still obscure. But evidently Valerie Maple had again planned to insure her victim, and commit the murder with arsenic. How had she hoped to succeed?

"Do *you* think Valerie Maple is still alive?" I asked Al.

"No," he said, and turned off the main road.

Once again we were on Copston Road. The moon rode high and shed lustrous unreal light upon an unreal world. The huddled trees were silver, and the twisting familiar turns in the winding road were like a length of tangled silver ribbon. As we approached the building site, Al instinctively slowed down. I moved closer to his side. Our cottage was unreal too, as illusory and unsubstantial as a dream. The trampled snow around it sparkled like a shining hill. A queer fancy came to me. Almost I could see Veronica Moran stealing across the moonlit lawn, carrying from the rubbish pile her incongruous loot—our shingles.

"Al," I said.

He was looking straight ahead. The Moran house was partially hidden by the giant elm, but light flickered through the barren branches. The Moran house was lighted.

"Someone's there, Janey."

Suddenly the flickering light behind the tree blazed up a clear bright yellow. Al pressed his foot on the accelerator. A second later we were abreast the dwelling that adjoined our cottage. The curtains that cloaked the Moran living room were closely drawn. Flickering yellow light, more dazzling by far than electricity, danced at all the windows. The curtains were in flames.

"The house is on fire!" With that, Al leaped from the car and ran up the path to the balustraded porch. He was hammering at the door when I joined him. The door was locked, and the fire inside seemed to be gaining rapidly. The curtains in the living room were dropping in flaming fragments from the rods.

"Stand back, Jane."

Al rushed the door once, and then again. The lock gave under his third assault. Choking and coughing, we stumbled into the foyer. It was filled with smoke. The living room beyond was blazing with incredible brilliance. The door into the foyer was open and acted as a draft. Al ran forward to slam it shut.

There was a bonfire in the center of the room. It rose as high as the concert harp. Shingles, old and dried with age, had been heaped in a great pile upon the carpet and deliberately touched with a match. The blazing pile popped and crackled like pine knots, and flung fiery embers everywhere.

Al slammed the door. His face was white.

"Where's the phone, Jane? The whole house is going, unless the fire department gets here quick."

"There's an extension in the master bedroom."

I tried to stop him, but he ran immediately toward the rear of the house. By the time I caught up, he had already opened the door of the master bedroom. The smoke that rolled out from there forced us backward.

The fire in the bedroom wasn't burning brightly. Indeed we couldn't find it for the smoke. Al clapped a handkerchief across his nose and mouth, reached around and switched on the electric light. A column of thick white smoke rose from Valerie Maple's frivolous bed, but the foolish little pillows and the embroidered coverlet were still unscorched. The underside of the mattress seemed to be burning.

Al shook off my hand, and dashed across the room toward the bed. The little pillows sailed in all directions, as he grabbed the mattress and the coverlet and jerked them aside.

The fire was at once revealed. Through the lacy pattern of the metal springs, it burned a fierce, three-sided design upon the floor. The harp case had come to light at last. It had been pushed underneath Mrs. Moran's bed and set afire. Shingles, soaked in kerosene, surrounded the clumsy wooden box and fed the flames.

In the sudden gush of air the lid of the harp case crackled, crumpled and collapsed. The dazzling radiance of its own consuming flames hid the contents. But sparks flew upward, and with them went a gauzy shred of material. It was crimson. The material flashed like tinder, and then sank in powdery ash.

The ash was all that was left of the costume Valerie Maple had worn on the afternoon she entertained Al and me at tea.

Chapter Twenty-two:
CAUGHT IN THE COUNTERPANE

I had no doubt whatever that the blazing harp case was Valerie Maple's funeral pyre. We were too late. Within the space of seconds, the ominous crackle of wood announced that the floor supporting the incredible bonfire was giving way. The legs of the bedstead spraddling the harp case abruptly disintegrated. White hot with heat, the metal springs tilted and crashed upon the blaze. At once the harp case lost its form and shape. A pillar of fire climbed redly toward the ceiling. Zigzag cracks appeared in the plaster overhead.

Sparks and fiery embers rained down like the falling sparks of Roman candles. Miraculously the rug had not yet caught. Only the distant corner of the master bedroom burned, as the corner of the newspaper touched by a match flashes into flame before the whole is consumed. The Italian desk was still intact; the bedside table, although scorched and blackened, stood firm beside the burning sea. The smoke parted, and I saw a picture slide as gently from the wall as though someone had cut the string. Uncomprehendingly, I watched an organdy curtain billow from a window, catch and instantly disappear. Like the shred of crimson, it was there one second, gone the next. Rooted to the threshold, at once stupefied and fascinated, wholly unafraid, I stared inside.

Al was the full length of the room away from me. He had gasped a summons for the fire department into the telephone, and flung the instrument on the floor. Between him and the rising heat of the blaze, he held the barrier of the mattress. Through the thickening smoke, he whirled around and shouted, "Get outside, Jane!"

"You?"

"I'll follow."

There was still a slim chance to check the fire, or rather to confine it to the master bedroom and the living room. I daresay Al had the human desire to do it. At any rate he dropped the mattress, and ran into the adjoining bathroom, slamming the door behind him. Afterward I was to learn that he arrived in Hannah's room, just as it also caught fire. The arsonist had been thorough. Al didn't dream I would disobey his instructions, or leave the safety of the hall. I had no intention of going off without him.

With a handkerchief clasped across my mouth and nose, too concerned with Al's imprudence to realize my own, I started after him. I fumbled my way into the room and around the dressing table which was placed against the wall most distant from the mounting flames. Almost immediately I discovered my mistake. In order to reach the bath connecting with Hannah's room I had to pass within a few feet of the corner bonfire. That was now impossible. In less than a second, so rapid was the progress of the fire, the situation had entirely changed.

The harp case and the bed had vanished. A hole was opening in the floor. Tongues of flame now leaped from its edges, and raced across the room. I turned to dash back into the hall. Simultaneously the flimsy skirts of the dressing table ignited. The way was cut off. I was trapped between two fires.

I tried to scream for Al, and filled my lungs with burning, acrid smoke. A spasm of coughing shook me. My senses swam, and steadied. I didn't mean to die without a fight. Nearby lay the mattress Al had hauled from the bed, and beside it in a wadded heap, sheets and blankets, the heavy, crumpled counterpane.

I couldn't lift the mattress, but I managed to scoop up the counterpane. With the thick material as a shield for my head and shoulders, and with a little prayer for luck, I rushed straight at the flaming dressing table and once again around it. Fire hissed and roared in my ears, there was the stench and fumes of burning cloth, but when I passed the dressing table I knew that I had won. Six steps more carried me back to safety. Not until I reached the hall, not until I banged the door that shut off the inferno of the master bedroom, did I really comprehend the narrowness of my escape.

My unprotected hands were blistered, my breath was rattling in my throat. Smoke was gathering in the hall. Again I tried to scream for Al, and had no voice. Choking, gasping, coughing, chilled and hot by turns, I fought with deathly sickness. The scorched, charred mass of the counterpane still filled my arms. Like a shapeless laundry bundle it slid to the floor.

Something was caught in the middle of the counterpane, hooked securely in a fold of the material. The fold fell apart. The object clattered free, rolled over once and stopped. Selby's cane lay at my feet. Through waves of nausea, I stared at it.

Between us, Al and I had rescued the final bit of evidence that was needed to convict his brother. Evidence that except for us would have gone up in flame and smoke, disappeared in ashes like the harp case.

Al had stripped the bed, and hadn't seen the hidden cane or guessed the extent of the evidence that someone had intended to destroy. If Valerie Maple's body was wholly consumed, a second murder would be impossible to prove. Al and I, however, it seemed to me, had virtually fixed on Selby the responsibility for the first. Between us, we had saved the cane that otherwise would certainly have burned. I had carried State's Exhibit A into the hall, along with the counterpane.

Selby's cane was the weapon that had killed Hannah Wilson. There was no doubt of it. The shaft was splintered, the metal head was scarred and dented. Fire hadn't touched or marred it. The polished wood wasn't even scorched. The dark brown stains discoloring the raw edges of the splintered wood were Hannah's blood.

Outside, I heard or thought I heard the clanging bell of the village fire engine, shouting voices, pounding footsteps. Somewhere Al was calling. Or did I imagine that? I leaned over automatically to pick up the cane. What I meant to do with it I don't know. Even as my fingers gripped the dented head of Selby's cane, the door of the living room crashed and fell. A column of smoke rolled through the opening and down the hall. A storm of coughing racked me. I attempted to straighten up, and could not.

Instead I slumped over to the floor, and my consciousness slipped away.

Hardly a minute later Al, still calling frantically, groped through the smoke and found me huddled there. As he knelt to lift me in his arms, half a dozen firemen poured in from outside and into the hall. Sheriff Blandish was with them.

The firemen had little opportunity to swing their energetic axes or spray their chemicals. Aunt Mildred always insisted that the Merristone force, composed of enthusiastic volunteers, was more destructive than any fire. They were spared from demonstrating their talents at demolition. The kerosene, the dried old shingles that had set off the conflagration had too good a start. Fires were raging in a dozen different places. The living room was gone, the master bedroom was about to go. Within five minutes the hardiest of the volunteers were driven out.

Al had barely time enough to grab me from the floor and rush outside. Sheriff Blandish, however, had sufficient time to discover the stained, discolored blackthorn cane. It lay immediately beside me. My fingers were closed around the splintered shaft. Sheriff Blandish unclasped them gently, and took the cane, and told Al to take me home. He didn't need to question me. His case was quite complete.

After that he did not delay. Most of Merristone was gathered on the trampled lawn when the Moran roof collapsed, but Sheriff Blandish wasn't there. Many of the villagers, swaddled in coats and blankets, stamped their feet through the bitter hours of the night and waited patiently until the dwelling burned to its foundations. Most of them had heard that Valerie Maple's body was in the house. Shivering in the chill, they soon observed that police deputies were assisting the firemen in the futile battle. The most powerful hose was directed upon the wing that had once contained the master bedroom. The hose cart had been driven from the road, and stationed there. Gallons of water poured into the cellar. There must be hope, the villagers whispered, of saving some portion of the harp case. When and if that occurred the freezing watchers wanted to be present.

A few of the earlier arrivals—Harriet Strings among them—had seen Sheriff Blandish rush to his car and roar off downtown. But no one knew the Sheriff had discovered the weapon he had sought so long, or how fortuitously he had discovered it. No one knew that Sheriff Blandish had gone to Blake House and put Selby under arrest.

The charge was murder in the first degree, and Hannah's name alone appeared on the warrant. But the Sheriff did not conceal his own belief that Selby had killed Valerie Maple too, and fired her dwelling to conceal the fact. The part that Valerie Maple had played in the arson plot, the fact that she herself had collected the incendiary materials, didn't interest him.

"No doubt Valerie Maple did plan to burn up her house and Hannah Wilson in it, and then turn around and collect a thumping insurance policy for an 'accidental' death. But that's not what happened. There's been too much emphasis on Valerie Maple's intentions. Too much talk about her past."

And then he handed Selby the warrant. My brother-in-law read it through and offered nothing in his own defense.

Ruth had her desperate, despairing say.

"How can there be too much talk about that woman's past? Valerie Maple was a convicted murderess, she poisoned her whole family, she came to Merristone hoping to commit another insurance murder. Many people must have hated her. Selby didn't, he never even met her, he—"

"Your husband isn't charged with killing Valerie Maple," said the Sheriff grimly. "What the State intends to establish is that he killed Hannah Wilson in a quarrel over an insurance policy that was applied for, paid for to the extent of $4,720 and never issued by the company. I have every belief that the State will prove its case. Prove why Hannah Wilson died, and at whose hands, and exactly how she met her terrible death."

With that Sheriff Blandish, who had been shocked and sickened, did a cruel and uncharacteristic thing. He exhibited Selby's splintered, bloodstained cane. Afterward I suppose his conscience bothered him, because he waited at Blake House until Belton arrived to stay with Ruth before he removed my brother-in-law to the village jail.

Chapter Twenty-three:
THE STRANGE TELEGRAM

I didn't hear what had occurred at Blake House until morning. When I regained consciousness I was still nauseated, but I was back at Aunt Mildred's and tucked into my own bed. Al had swaddled me with blankets, and Sarah had bandaged up my hands and done a skillful job at it. But I was not allowed to talk.

In the morning the news of Selby's arrest could no longer be kept from me. It was known to all the world, splashed in print across the pages of the New York newspapers. When Dr. Traphaven called to dress my hands, he had the whole story. He sat down beside my bed and outlined the case that our prosecuting attorney was even then engaged in putting into shape for presentation before the Grand Jury.

The case against Selby was much blacker than even Al and I imagined. Working with the patience of a fanatical beaver, Sheriff Blandish had uncovered and turned over to the prosecutor facts of which we ourselves were ignorant. Thus, for the first time we learned the story that Annabelle Hawkins, Selby's secretary, had to tell of Selby's relations with Hannah Wilson and her mistress.

The circumstantial evidence against my brother-in-law had been appalling enough, but I had comforted myself with his apparent lack of motive. On that bitter January morning we learned that the State was confident it could establish a motive—a motive that was cold-blooded, mercenary, without one mitigating feature.

The prosecutor was equipped with ample evidence to establish the precise nature of the "private business matter" that Selby had handled for Valerie Maple. It concerned a $50,000 insurance policy that Valerie Maple, "otherwise known as Veronica Moran," had desired to take out on the life of Hannah Wilson.

In the middle of November, weeks before our tragedy, Hannah had appeared in Selby's office and explained that she wished to insure her life, with her mistress named as beneficiary. Fortunately for the State, Selby's secretary had been present at this interview.

Miss Hawkins was a spinster of indisputable veracity who had worked for Selby since he first opened his office. She was devoted to my brother-in-law and had hated to talk. But she talked, and was reluctantly prepared to testify about the initial interview between Selby and Hannah Wilson and other interviews that followed.

In the beginning, according to Miss Hawkins, Selby had seemed loath to accept Hannah's business. Indeed he had pointed out that the servant's age—Hannah was well over fifty—would greatly increase the premiums demanded by his company. To discourage the insurance seeker, he had produced his actuary tables and explained that the initial premium required on a policy of $50,000 would be $4,720. In her apparent eagerness to please her mistress—it was evident throughout that Valerie Maple desired the policy—Hannah had not protested or demurred at the cost. At her insistence, and after several other office calls, Selby had sent the servant to Dr. Traphaven for a physical examination.

Hannah had passed the examination with flying colors, and had again returned to Selby. When questioned about her resources, Hannah had admitted that she lacked the money to meet the premium payment, but she had added that her mistress would be willing to advance it. At this point, Miss Hawkins who had been listening with avid interest, had been called away to the telephone. It was the secretary's impression that Selby had intended to refuse to handle the business. If this were true, there was direct evidence to show that Selby had changed his mind.

Only five days later, on December 27th, Valerie Maple had mailed to Selby a check for $4,720. A covering letter asked him to obtain the $50,000 policy at once, and deliver it to her maid. The letter was not in Selby's files, and had presumably been destroyed. But again Miss Hawkins had seen and read it. Indeed it was Selby's secretary who had carried the fatal check to the bank, cashed it and brought the money back to Selby.

Long before affairs had reached this stage, it was Selby's duty as an agent to communicate with the New York offices of his insurance company and advise them of Hannah Wilson's application for a $50,000 policy. Selby had not communicated with his company then or ever. The company was left in total ignorance of the entire transaction. Bewildered officials, subpoenaed in the New York offices, were expected to testify to that effect. In short, Hannah Wilson, through Mrs. Maple, had paid for insurance but had not received it.

"The prosecution," said Dr. Traphaven, "will claim that Selby never had the slightest intention of requesting the policy. That his sole object was to defraud Hannah, or Mrs. Maple. Take your choice. There's the motive. Theft, pure and simple."

"I don't believe it," Al said. "Selby might commit a murder under some other kind of circumstances. But Selby a thief! It's preposterous! Money means nothing to him."

Dr. Traphaven sighed. "Blake House—its size and elegance—will work against him. The prosecutor will play on prejudice, ask how a man living on a tiny income can afford to maintain a mansion. The answer's easy. He had to steal to do it. Steal, and then kill to cover up his theft. There seems to be little doubt that Hannah, backed up by Mrs. Maple, was threatening to appeal to the company, demand the policy and bring the whole matter out into the open."

"The ubiquitous Miss Hawkins again?" Al asked wryly.

The doctor nodded, and went on with his recital. After the delivery of the premium payment, Hannah had called repeatedly at Selby's office. Because Selby had expressly asked his secretary to step into the reception room, Miss Hawkins had not been actually present at any of these interviews. But the door was thin and above the not too determined clicking of her typewriter, Miss Hawkins had heard her employer and his visitor quarreling, had heard high words exchanged about the non-appearance of the insurance policy. She had put through to Selby several telephone calls from Valerie Maple. Virtue had triumphed over curiosity here. Miss Hawkins had not listened in on the extension, but the subject matter of the conversations between Selby and Valerie Maple seemed clear enough.

"It looks like an airtight case," said Dr. Traphaven. "Selby had the motive, and the opportunity. He had the weapon."

It looked like an airtight case indeed. I didn't need to be told that an indictment was a foregone conclusion. Dr. Traphaven had no comfort to offer us, although I had an impression that he himself was vaguely dissatisfied.

"Gregg's a shrewd and clever prosecutor," he said heavily. "He'll use Selby's association with Valerie Maple to blacken Selby, and at the same time do his damnedest to keep the defense from entering her past into the evidence. Regardless of what turns up in the ruins of the Moran house, Selby will never in this world be charged with murdering Valerie Maple."

"Why not?"

"Because Valerie Maple wouldn't make an attractive victim," said Dr. Traphaven with sudden anger. "A murderess, who poisoned her husband and three small children to run off with a lover, wouldn't appeal to a

New England jury. An impostor with murder in her own mind—our prosecutor will tread very carefully when he mentions Valerie Maple, and speak softly. Even Mortimer Gregg should see," the little doctor concluded indignantly, "that the two crimes are linked, and should be so presented to a jury."

But then Dr. Traphaven was obliged to disclose that Selby also lacked an alibi for the night before. After an early dinner with Ruth, he had gone out for a solitary walk. It was a long walk, from which Selby had returned shivering with cold and fatigue only a few minutes before the arrival of Sheriff Blandish and the warrant. According to his own statement my brother-in-law had been nowhere near Copston Road, nowhere near the Moran cottage, but the statement was not susceptible of proof.

"It's a pity," Dr. Traphaven said a little later, "that you two drove along Copston Road last night. If the alarm had been delayed even half an hour, the Moran house would have been a roaring furnace. No one would ever have entered it. A lot of people would have believed that Valerie Maple did kill her maid, that she came home, set fire to her own place, and lay down on her own bed to die by violence as she had lived. Without that cane, Selby could hardly have been brought to trial."

Dr. Traphaven wouldn't have made that remark had he himself been convinced of Selby's guilt. A flicker of hope shone in Al's eye.

The little doctor's expression didn't lighten. He got up from his chair.

"The more I study crime, the less I know about it—the more I depend on hunches, intuitions. Personally, I don't believe we've solved this case or even scratched the surface of it. I've seen Selby, and I think he's innocent. God knows why; maybe because I brought him into the world. But I'm convinced he's holding back, concealing something." Dr. Traphaven paused and looked at Al. "Suppose we go back to the time he located the house for Veronica Moran. Why won't he name the person who wrote asking about a suitable residence for her?"

Neither Al nor I replied. The obvious answer was that the mysterious acquaintance, whose name had slipped Selby's mind, did not exist.

"Well, maybe," said Dr. Traphaven restlessly. "But if this—this acquaintance was an invention, how did Selby himself meet up with Veronica Moran? That is, before he settled in Merristone. He seldom leaves the village; it's highly unlikely their paths would ever cross. Actually"—the doctor smiled faintly—"it's much more likely that you and Jane might have met the woman somewhere in New York."

Al looked somewhat taken aback, but Dr. Traphaven was quite right. We had only recently achieved the status of ex-New Yorkers. At the time Valerie Maple had attended a New York auction sale and became Veronica Moran we had been living in the city. So had Sarah and Frank. However, I felt certain that none of us had written Selby sponsoring Veronica Moran. Certainly I hadn't. Dr. Traphaven sighed.

"I suppose that leads nowhere, but it's an interesting point. Now let's think about that insurance policy a minute. If Selby's aim had been to embezzle the premium payment, why did he attempt to discourage Hannah? The prosecution will try to make out that was a form of subtle salesmanship, but it wasn't. Selby definitely didn't want the business."

"Then why did he accept it?" Al asked bitterly.

"One might almost imagine," said Dr. Traphaven slowly, "that a form of pressure was applied. My mind keeps going back to the 'mysterious acquaintance.' Suppose this individual did exist, suppose it was to favor him or her that Selby capitulated.... By the way, you should suggest to your brother's lawyers that they attempt to track down the source of Valerie Maple's income. The prosecution won't do it. They've dropped that angle like a hot potato—Gregg isn't interested in any information that might upset his case."

Dr. Traphaven walked over to the window and gazed out. Massive clouds filled the sky in ranked battalions. No sun shone. Presently he turned around, and again he sighed.

"Mind you, I can't fathom Selby's behavior. I'm satisfied that he never had the slightest intention of requesting the policy. He must have known his company wouldn't touch it with a ten-foot pole."

We stared at him.

"No reputable company would approve such a policy. The whole proposition reeks of fraud—is virtually an invitation to murder. A servant insuring herself in favor of her mistress in the sum of $50,000, the mistress meeting the premium payments—it's fantastic on the face of it. Unless Selby conspired with Valerie Maple to conceal the circumstances and deceive his company, she hadn't a Chinaman's chance of insuring Hannah's life. I'm in a position to know Selby was not conspiring with Valerie Maple."

We waited.

"When Selby sent Hannah to me for the physical examination," Dr. Traphaven said quietly, "he expressed a strong hope that she wouldn't pass. Personally, although I had not mentioned it, I was surprised that

Hannah had been able to pass a physical examination. She was more than fifty years of age, and evidently had lived a hard, exhausting life. And if Valerie Maple had been secretly dosing her with arsenic . . . I know, I know." Dr. Traphaven pulled his little beard impatiently, as though we had questioned him in a diagnosis. "The fact is that arsenic can sometimes improve the general health, provided it's taken in small enough amounts. When I examined her, Hannah was certainly suffering no noticeable ill effects from the drug."

Suddenly Al sat forward in his chair. "I don't understand the arsenic angle now. Since last night, I mean. If Mrs. Moran was planning to make Hannah the victim of an 'accidental' fire, why did she give her arsenic?"

"I've wondered about that myself," confessed Dr. Traphaven, restive and uncertain. "I've asked myself whether it was possible that Hannah was dosing herself. Sometimes foolish women, the vain ones, take arsenic to benefit their complexions. They develop a remarkable immunity to the drug, and in the end definitely crave it. Arsenic can be habit forming, too. Not that Hannah Wilson seemed the sort to worry about her appearance. Still, it's hard to say. She was an odd woman."

"Odd! She struck me as quite ordinary, unless you mean she was unusually disagreeable. What struck you as odd about her?"

"For one thing, she was remarkably healthy for a woman of her age."

"Forgive me, if that seems a little hard to credit. She was deaf, she was half blind, she—"

"That's just it," said Dr. Traphaven, perplexedly. "You must remember I examined Hannah. Her hearing and her sight wouldn't necessarily affect her general health, and anyhow I felt that her ailments were imaginary."

"Imaginary!"

"In my opinion Hannah Wilson could see and hear quite well. I so noted on my report, and listed her as a hypochondriac—one of those unfortunates suffering from illnesses that are the products of their own unhappy minds. That might explain the arsenic, of course. Possibly she was taking it for some fancied ailment."

Al and I looked at each other. Dr. Traphaven had drawn a strange picture of the brusque, efficient Hannah, thrown a strange light on her. But, after all, what did we know of Hannah? Very little beyond the fact that she worked for Valerie Maple, and had somehow been persuaded to apply for insurance on her life.

"In the uproar about Valerie Maple," said Dr. Traphaven, very slowly,

"Hannah Wilson has been overlooked. Valerie Maple's past has come out, but we know nothing of Hannah's past. We don't know how or where the two women met, nor do we know how Hannah was prevailed upon to become a pawn in an insurance plot. That's strange, too, when you think about it. Why wasn't Hannah suspicious of her mistress? Didn't it ever cross her mind that she was putting herself into a dangerous position, once she got that policy? Didn't she ever wonder about Mrs. Maple's motives when she kindly 'advanced' that premium payment?" In a baffled way he pulled his beard. "I'd expect a child of ten to be brighter. Hannah must have been extremely dense. Yet it doesn't seem like her to be so stupid. Any more than such an apparently unimaginative woman seems the type who turns to hypochondria. But what was Hannah Wilson really like?"

With a queer little start, I realized that neither Al nor I could make a cogent reply. Except for two brief conversations on the day we had been invited to tea, we had never talked to Hannah. On those occasions we had spoken only about arrangements for the tea party. We had never addressed a single personal word to Hannah, or thought of her save in her connection with Valerie Maple. She had become familiar to us from her daily appearances in the village, from our many glimpses of her working around the Moran place, but always she had been overshadowed by the high-colored personality of Valerie Maple. Now, abruptly, it occurred to me that in her own way Hannah Wilson was as enigmatic and mysterious as her mistress.

"Apparently," said Dr. Traphaven, "Hannah Wilson was alone in the world. So far as we can discover, Valerie Maple was her only contact. She received no mail, had no visitors. No friends or relatives have come forward since her death. No inquiries have been made either to the authorities or at the undertaking parlors. That's significant—isn't it?—like her life somehow. An old woman dead by violence, done with living, and no one at all to claim her body."

It struck me as pathetic and rather sad, and I started to say so. At that moment Frank opened the door. Sarah was bringing up my tray, and he was assisting her. They caught the doctor's final words. Frank turned and looked at Sarah.

"No one would claim me either," he said involuntarily. "Unless you would, Sally."

He used the familiar name, but his tone wasn't light, and the remark wasn't like him. Possibly the way the family had rallied about Selby had brought on one of those occasional bitter and lonely moods of his.

Or perhaps the picture of Hannah, lying at the local undertaking parlor with no one to mourn her passing, had moved him as it had moved me. He smiled a little wryly.

"We're not discussing the problems of a self-appointed bachelor, after all. Sorry, folks. I've been wondering myself about Hannah Wilson's life before she came to Merristone. Maybe a check with employment agencies—"

"That's been done," said Dr. Traphaven, and added, "without result."

And then the doctor picked up his bag, advised me to take it easy, and walked out the door. He had something more to say, but apparently he preferred to keep it until Al and I were alone. He spent five minutes with Aunt Mildred in the kitchen, and then, after Sarah and Frank went down, he popped back upstairs again.

"By the way, I almost forgot to tell you. I do have one line out on Hannah Wilson. It may amount to nothing, but this morning"—the doctor hesitated—"I had a sudden brainstorm. I telegraphed the warden at the prison."

"The prison?"

"The Illinois State Prison, where Valerie Maple served nine years for murder. I thought the warden might have some information about where Hannah Wilson and Mrs. Maple met."

I looked at him blankly.

"Do you think Mrs. Maple met Hannah in prison? But that would mean—"

"It would mean Hannah was a criminal too," Al said excitedly. "That would explain her lack of friends and relatives—her apparent lack of background; it might even explain Valerie Maple's hold on her."

Dr. Traphaven was silent.

Encouraged, Al went enthusiastically ahead. "It will be easy to find out whether Hannah had a prison record. We've got *her* fingerprints. Gosh, you had a real brainstorm, Doctor," he finished admiringly. "I wish I'd been that bright myself."

"Are you sure you weren't?" asked Dr. Traphaven in a peculiar voice.

Al's jaw dropped. "What do you mean?"

The doctor frowned. "I want you to tell me frankly, Alan. Didn't you wire the Illinois prison regarding Hannah Wilson?"

"Me! Of course not. Do you mean someone else had the same idea?"

"Precisely," said Dr. Traphaven dryly. "Someone became interested in Hannah Wilson's record and telegraphed the warden, considerably before I got around to it. Someone here in Merristone."

"Someone in Merristone! Then surely the local telegraph office—"

"The message was shoved underneath the door after the office was closed. It was printed on a regular telegraph blank, and left with a dollar bill to cover the cost of transmitting."

"When?"

"Late Saturday night, or sometime Sunday. The office was closed all day Sunday. The telegram was dispatched when they opened Monday morning. To tell the truth," said Dr. Traphaven, with a little cough, "there's the explanation of my own sudden interest in Hannah Wilson's past. The prison warden sent on an inquiry to me today. Naturally, I'd like to know who was responsible for that first message."

"Wasn't there any signature at all?"

"Yes, there was a signature. Printed carefully like the message."

"Whose?"

The doctor's face again assumed the peculiar expression—an expression that was a mixture of irritation and perplexity.

"My name was signed."

"Yours!"

"My name was printed at the bottom of the message," repeated the doctor wrathfully. "Naturally the local telegraph office supposed I'd left it underneath their door. I'd never done such a thing before, but telegraphers aren't paid to use their brains."

"How did you learn about it?"

"I learned," said Dr. Traphaven grimly, "when the warden of the Illinois State prison replied to a telegram I hadn't sent. He wired me this morning asking that I send on Hannah's fingerprints so he could check his records."

"But, Doctor—"

"Don't ask me who this mysterious forger was," snapped Dr. Traphaven. "All I know is this: It was someone who knew me well enough to print my signature in full, and spell my middle name correctly. In other words, someone who badly wanted to direct my thoughts to Hannah Wilson!"

Chapter Twenty-four:
THE ANCESTRAL PORTRAIT

It wasn't until late the following day—Tuesday—that Al had his interview with his brother, and that I saw Ruth at Blake House. Dr. Traphaven had ordered me to spend the day in bed, but late in the afternoon I rebelled, slipped on a dressing gown and went downstairs. In order to avoid unnecessary argument, I waited until Al went to the bathroom to shave for dinner before I made my noiseless descent. My intention was to stretch out on the dining room couch, and thus to obey the doctor's injunction in the spirit if not in the letter.

Despite the fact that the dining room was done in browns and greens, and crowded with Aunt Mildred's heavy furniture, it was a cheerful, homely kind of place. The sofa had been installed sometime around 1910 for the comfort of great-grandfather Blake, who had liked to take "forty winks" after thumping, midday meals. Aunt Mildred's ideas on household decoration were impervious to change and fashion.

Nevertheless, something seemed oddly different about the dining room. As I approached the sofa, I had a vague sense of vacancy, of loss. I sat down and looked around. From the kitchen I could hear Sarah and Frank engaged in low-voiced conversation, and Sarah beginning dinner preparations. The dining room itself was very quiet. The wan sun of the late winter afternoon shone across the worn old carpet, touched the sideboard, gleamed on the china cabinet. Frowning, I regarded the sideboard, the neatly disposed row of chairs, the table, decorated as always, with a bowl of unconvincing wax bananas. Everything seemed to be as usual. My vague sense of loss persisted. I raised my eyes a little. My mouth fell open.

The portrait of Uncle Ned had disappeared.

For as long as I could remember, the dashing figure, wearing the tight black suit and sporting the checkered vest, had commanded the dining room. Overnight and with startling abruptness, Uncle Ned had been supplanted. A flight of energetic seagulls, streaming in the wake of a seemingly quite stationary sailboat, now filled the four-inch, gold leaf frame.

The mystifying transfer had been hurried. Hurried and recent. Glue had been used lavishly. A few drops spattered the elaborate frame. The glue was damp. I pulled down a corner of the canvas, and saw that Uncle Ned was not concealed underneath.

His portrait had been carefully cut from the frame and carried elsewhere.

Suddenly I heard Sarah and Frank start toward the dining room. For no particular reason, I didn't want to share either my discovery or my bewilderment with them. As they approached, I pushed the seascape back into place, shot into the main hall and on upstairs.

As I left the stairs and started toward our bedroom, I thought I heard a muffled sound. I stopped and listened. The sound was coming from Aunt Mildred's room. I approached it. Aunt Mildred was inside. I could hear her. She was crying.

At first I couldn't believe my ears. Weakness—even a momentary weakness—and Aunt Mildred were wholly incompatible. I had heard Sarah say that she herself had never seen her mother cry. The low, heartbroken weeping continued. It was more than I could bear.

The fact that Aunt Mildred might prefer to be alone did not occur to me. I knocked, opened her door and entered. Aunt Mildred was on the opposite side of the bedroom. Her back was to the door, and I could not see her face. One didn't need to see her face to read her utter wretchedness. She wept as those weep who weep alone—without hope of comfort. For once in her life, the indomitable woman who managed everybody seemed to be in need of the help and advice that she always forced on others.

She stood near her dresser, illumined by the last rays of the dying sun. The missing portrait was in her hands. Her tears were falling on the wrinkled canvas.

I suppose it's difficult for the young to realize that their elders may have emotional complications, too. It had not occurred to me that Aunt Mildred might feel any lingering tie to the man she never mentioned except to criticize, or that she might have her own hours of loneliness and despair, her own secret life. All I knew at the moment was that I should not be there. I started to retreat. Unfortunately she had heard me enter.

"Who is it?"

"It's I. Jane," I said, and muttered something about the portrait.

"The portrait?" She clutched the canvas to her heart as though it was a treasure. I had a confused impression that she meant to conceal it from me, and had suddenly become aware it was too late. Still she did not turn around. In an agony of embarrassment, unable to advance or to retreat, I clung to the doorknob.

"Close the door," she said presently, in a much calmer voice.

A full minute must have passed before she turned around. Within that minute she had pulled herself together. The transformation was amazing.

"Well, Jane? What did you want? Something important must have brought you bursting in on me."

It was rather wonderful—that calm way of putting me on the defensive. I found it impossible to mention her tears, almost as impossible as it was to believe that the tears had existed. To offer sympathy was patently absurd.

Again I mumbled. "I was wondering about the portrait. I was so surprised when I missed it."

"Surprised?" she said coldly. "What's surprising about moving my own things around, and placing them as I choose? Am I expected to take the whole house into my confidence if I decide to change my pictures?"

Her second attempt to put me on the defensive was less successful. Some women might choose to rearrange their household furnishings in the midst of tragedy, but for Aunt Mildred to do so was to revolutionize the whole pattern of her habits and her thinking. Besides, she hadn't rearranged her pictures. She had merely removed a single portrait from its conspicuous position in the dining room.

"For more than twenty years," said Aunt Mildred, in her cool, collected way, "Ned Havens has watched me eat my meals. I got tired of it. Sick to death just of looking back and thinking of him. So I took the paring knife and made the change. Now I hope you understand." I understood less than ever.

Silently she rolled up the canvas and placed it in her dresser. She might have folded and put away an ordinary housedress in just that manner. But then she locked the dresser drawer, and dropped the key in her pocket. Evidently she felt some additional explanation was necessary.

"I hope you won't mention this matter to the others," she said stiffly. "It's not important. You and I have talked too much about it already, though I must say I don't know why."

Actually we had not discussed the incident at all. I was defeated by her bland pretense that everything was quite as usual, that a sudden whim had caused her to lock that particular canvas in her dresser drawer after a storm of passionate weeping.

Like many people who possess the eyes of hawks and the ears of watchdogs, Aunt Mildred was of the opinion that others never used their eyes at all, and that they were without curiosity. Apparently she had convinced herself that none of us would notice or comment on the passing of the portrait.

Completely baffled, I left her standing beside her dresser. I met Frank and Sarah coming up the stairs; Al was at their heels. Sarah was in a state of great excitement.

"Where's mother? The most astonishing thing—father's picture—"

"I know," I said, and when we went downstairs I told them what had happened to the picture.

Sarah and Al looked confused. Frank looked astonished too, and something more than that. He looked uneasy.

"Why don't you go on up and talk to your mother, Sarah?"

"Apparently she's done her talking," Sarah said dryly.

"I don't mean that. But I believe I'd suggest she put the picture back."

Sarah opened her eyes. "Why should I do that? I'm not fond of it myself. Anyhow, you know Mama. She does exactly as she pleases."

Frank hesitated. "I don't suppose it really matters. But if your mother's object was to distract attention from your father's portrait, keep people from thinking about him, she's gone about it in the worst way."

"Whatever are you talking about?" Her voice was sharp

"Policemen notice such little things," he said uncomfortably. "And start wondering. It's none of my business, and I hate asking. But when did your father leave Merristone?"

"When did my mother divorce him, you mean," said Sarah half annoyed, and a little tart. "When I was in pinafores. Five, or so."

"And you're twenty-seven now," said Frank with a kind of obscure relief.

"Thanks for the compliment." Sarah relaxed, and even flashed a smile at him. "Maybe Mama told you that. But my birthday in November was my thirtieth."

Frank did not smile back. Indeed his face became so dark and grimly intent that I was startled. Al turned suddenly on his heel, and walked into the dining room.

I could not fathom the significance of Sarah's age. A moment passed before I did a simple sum in subtraction. Aunt Mildred's marriage had collapsed when Sarah was five years old—exactly 25 years before. That meant that in 1916 Uncle Ned had vanished from the family scene— 1916 was a year we all would have reason to remember. In 1916 Valerie

Maple had gone on a picnic in a Chicago public park, and had fed her husband and three small children a bottle of poisoned milk. Two of the children and her husband had died in agony so that she could be free to join a sweetheart whom she had refused to name. Instead of freedom and a comfortable fortune in insurance Valerie Maple had received a prison sentence. That was in 1916 too.

Automatically I moved toward the dining room and Al. Frank and Sarah followed. The seascape—the foolish flight of gulls and the ponderous sailboat—might command the table, but Uncle Ned was with us all in spirit.

Until that afternoon Ned Havens had been only a name to me—a painted figure clad in tight black trousers and a checkered vest. A figure as remote as great-grandfather Blake, and one who had apparently left less imprint on the family. I had never considered Uncle Ned as mysterious or provocative, or worthy of interest or speculation. What Al knew about his uncle by marriage I knew, but that was little. I had gathered that Ned Havens was successful in business, that during his brief and ill-starred marriage he had traveled a great deal, spending more time away from Merristone than in it. Somehow I had always assumed that those frequent absences were the simple and uncomplex answer to the divorce, that one day it had been easier for Uncle Ned to stay away from Aunt Mildred than to come back. On occasion I had clearly understood his point of view.

Now suddenly it struck me that the answer might not be simple at all. Had Uncle Ned's travels ever carried him to Chicago? Dr. Traphaven still believed that the key to our riddle lay in Valerie Maple's past. Could Ned Havens illumine that past, and was Aunt Mildred aware of the fact? She had moved the portrait and locked it in her dresser. Surely that was significant.

Where was Ned Havens now?

"I have no idea," said Sarah dully. "I haven't heard from my own father in years. When I was a little girl he sometimes wrote me postals, always from different addresses. I imagine he still travels from place to place on those promotion schemes of his, although that's only guesswork. I remember he used to send little presents that Mama promptly carted off to the church bazaar. They weren't ever suited to my age. I know he sent a doll on my sixteenth birthday; that's how close we were. I don't suppose I'd recognize my father if he walked into the room this minute."

It was Aunt Mildred who walked into the dining room just then. Two spots of color burned in her cheeks, but her head was high and her eyes were remarkably steady. In her hand she held the portrait of Uncle Ned, unrolled again and like a banner.

"There's no reason you should recognize your father," she said in a level, quite unemotional voice. "Nor is there any reason why Ned Havens should occupy this dining room, but since there's been so much pother about the picture I prefer it go back in place. Alan, will you kindly oblige me?"

She made Al mount a chair, and fit the picture back into the gold-leaf frame. Her effort was valiant, but, so far as I was concerned, unsuccessful. From that moment on I was convinced that Uncle Ned had played some part in Valerie Maple's past, and that he would figure in our own oblique drama.

Chapter Twenty-five:
FOUND IN THE ASHES

Possibly we should have gone straight to Dr. Traphaven and reported the incident of the portrait. But we had nothing to offer except suspicion, a date that might be sheer coincidence, the bare fact that Aunt Mildred had removed a picture of her husband from the dining room and later returned it.

"That's not enough to get Selby out of jail," Al said grimly. "Not with Selby refusing to talk."

"Aunt Mildred knows something, Al. I'm sure of it—something that made her worry about the portrait. Something that concerns her separation from Uncle Ned—something that concerns this case. I'm going to find out what it is."

"Please don't."

"Why not?"

"Selby himself wouldn't want it. Selby," Al said bitterly, "is a romantic. As out of date in this day and age as a horseless carriage. And as stubborn and hard to manage. I swear I believe Selby would rather die than have us wash all the family linen in public."

Well, that might be. Until Selby was willing or able to explain, there was little we could do for him. Also, to be quite frank, I did not know any favorable way of persuading or coercing Aunt Mildred to tell me anything she had decided to keep to herself.

All the next day I temporized, and late in the afternoon something occurred which temporarily distracted my mind from the matter. At half-past five Sheriff Blandish telephoned that Selby wanted to see and talk to Al. I was hardly sufficiently recovered to go outside, and Al exhibited his own kind of pride by flatly refusing to let me see his brother at the jail. In the end, however, he agreed to take me as far as Blake House. I had not seen Ruth since Sarah and I had been turned from the door. Actually that was only three days before, but in the interval all of us had lived a lifetime.

It must have been shortly after six o'clock when I had my talk with Ruth. A queer and broken talk that took place in the master bedroom of Blake House—a room so vast that I often thought it would serve nicely for a minor coronation. When Selby was at home, a great fire was usually roaring on the hearth. It was one of my brother-in-law's vanities that he cut the wood himself, and daily supplied the many fireplaces.

There was no cheerful heartening glow on the hearth that bleak winter evening, and the blazing chandelier poured light as cold and icy as its crystal prisms. I found my sister-in-law looking like a little frozen ghost, removing her clothes from the tremendous wardrobe and throwing them into a bag. Selby had insisted that she leave Blake House. It was his one request of her.

"I don't know why," Ruth said listlessly. "It doesn't matter, anymore, where I am. I'd really rather stay than bother. But Father is taking me to his place at the Inn."

Muffled in an extra sweater, Belton was attempting to be helpful without notable success. When I went over to him, he was examining one of Ruth's little shoes as though he'd never seen a shoe before, and pawing the closet floor in blind search for the mate.

"The Inn's not much," he admitted, "but I must confess I do begin to see certain virtues in the modern furnace. Surely, my dear, you've got two of these."

"Let me do that," I said, and took the shoe from him and located the mate at once. "Of course you can't continue to stay here, Ruth. Even with your father with you, the house is just too—too big."

What I really meant, I suppose, was that it was too crowded with memories. Memories of Selby strolling around outside, clipping the privet hedge in summer, raking leaves in autumn, clearing the paths in winter. Memories of Selby seated in the paneled library below, or rising with a slow pleased smile to greet a guest. Most visitors wanted to be shown through Blake House, and Selby was only too delighted to oblige.

I could see him now moving up the lovely curving stairway to show the ballroom, pausing to describe "the possibly apocryphal visit of Lafayette, though we Blakes have some documentary evidence that the General did stop overnight on his way to Boston." I could see Selby standing at the threshold of the birthing-room where so many Blakes had first seen the light of day, walking down the hall to point out the cherished window in the guest room where Aaron Burr had scratched his name. The secret stairway that was his special pride was entered from the library.

Like a small boy parading his treasures, Selby always waited until the end of the tour before demonstrating the secret that hardly seemed a secret, so simple was the device. But Selby loved to stroll casually toward the fireplace, hesitate at what seemed to be an orthodox Dutch oven, turn a great iron key and open the door to reveal a narrow, hidden staircase that led upward along the chimney to the roof. The staircase had always seemed too cramped to me to shelter anyone, but I could hear the very intonations of Selby's voice as he told of the Revolutionary soldiers who had crouched in hiding there, sometimes packed together like barley bags.

All these pictures and more too passed through my mind. I was so familiar with the house I could have gone from cellar to attic blindfolded. I had always loved it. For the first time that night I understood Aunt Mildred's very different sentiments. For the first time it seemed to me that for all its austere, authentic beauty, for all its proud history, Blake House was a fragment of the past that had outlived its day and usefulness. Cold and lifeless like a tomb. Perhaps, I thought confusedly, the heart of Blake House had gone when the master went away. And something oppressive and forbidding, something inimical had come instead.

Suddenly Ruth shivered. "I—I feel that way too, Janey. Nerves, I suppose. Nerves and worry. Blake House used to feel like home before—before—"

"The Inn has its points," Belton broke in to say briskly, and yet with no particular conviction.

"Ruth isn't going to the Inn," I said, and quite deliberately shook off my own sense of oppression. "She's coming home with me. That is, if she will."

My whole attention was fixed on my sister-in-law, but I had a vague impression that Belton was relieved. Ruth didn't speak. Again I had an impression that her father would have liked to point out the inconveniences of the Inn, and urge the superior comforts of Aunt Mildred's house.

"Please come, dear," I said. "Take the room next to Al's and mine. None of us will bother you with questions."

Still she didn't speak, but she nodded and her eyes filled up with tears. When I put my arm around her, and pressed her wet cheek against my own I suppose we had our reconciliation. Neither of us ever mentioned afterward the brief estrangement.

I knew that Ruth had not talked to Selby since his arrest. But she had her own story to tell—her story of what had happened on Valerie Maple's porch. Nothing would have induced me to press her confidence.

Ruth herself had apparently reached the point where she had to talk. She sat down on the tester bed and looked at me with devastated eyes, and held her hand against a mouth that twitched with nerves.

"Selby's innocent, Jane. But I've learned something these past few days. Only the truth will clear him. Anyway, you probably know what I saw on Mrs. Moran's porch, partly sticking out from behind the clothes rack. You saw it yourself."

"I saw a broom," I said stupidly. "And later on it was gone."

"You saw Selby's cane."

I felt no surprise, except a kind of numb astonishment at my own stupidity. Seen only partly and through a swiftly closing door, the shaft of a cane would be like a broom handle. Why had the cane been transferred from the scene of Hannah Wilson's murder to the Moran cottage? With a sinking heart, I perceived that it would be to Selby's advantage to hurry his own cane from the scene of the crime. But if he had been pressed for time, he might have been obliged to conceal the damning piece of evidence in a temporary hiding place, intending to return for it later. We had made no real search for the missing weapon. During the confusion that followed our discovery of the murder, Selby had ample opportunity to regain possession of the bloodstained, splintered cane. Suppose he had done just that, recovered the cane and run to the Moran house only to be trapped by our unexpected arrival.

"The prosecution," Ruth said dully, "means to convict Selby with that cane. Actually it's the cane that proves to me he's innocent."

I stared at her.

"Selby lied to me about the cane. That's how I know."

"Do speak more plainly, dear," said Belton testily. "If you're going to tell your story, tell it so that Jane can follow."

"Selby lost his cane almost a week before the murder," Ruth said dully. "Or anyhow it disappeared."

"Selby *lost* his cane!"

"Almost a week before the murder, Jane. I missed the cane, of course, and spoke to Selby. He told me he'd left it at the office. But when he didn't bring it home next day, I happened to run into Miss Hawkins at the drugstore and asked her to remind him. She was very much surprised. It seems Selby had told her he left his stick on the train going into New York."

I began to tremble inwardly.

"When was this trip?"

"On the Monday before the murder. He had some kind of business in the city, and Miss Hawkins says he had the cane when he started for the train. She doesn't ever remember seeing it afterward."

Selby's business in New York had been with Hannah Wilson. Surely the fact that he had lied about the cane meant only that he was unwilling to explain to Ruth or his secretary the circumstances of its loss. Surely he would be compelled to explain now. If Selby had really lost his stick and we could prove that someone else had got possession of it, that would be an important step toward clearing him.

How were we to prove it?

"Selby's cane was on Mrs. Moran's porch," said Ruth. "I recognized it at the first glance. That's why I waited till you left the kitchen and then went outside. But someone else had the cane. Someone was hidden behind the clothes rack and holding the other end of the cane. I found that out when I stooped over."

Ruth spoke quite calmly. She had gone beyond any reminiscent dread. As Belton's and my eyes met, I think we felt for her the fear she did not feel. The calmness of her words could not eradicate the terror implicit in the picture. A small blond girl, alone on a shadowy, screened-in porch, approaching a clothes rack hung with a curtain of creaking frozen garments. A small blond girl who stooped to brush the rustling garments aside and reach for a half-hidden cane. She saw only the splintered shaft and tip. She was wholly unaware that the heavy, blood-stained head of the cane was gripped in a killer's hand. A killer crouched into the corner of the porch, shielded from immediate discovery by the wall of frozen petticoats. But the killer had a weapon, and Ruth was alone and quite defenseless. When she stooped, she was lost.

"You have no idea who was behind the clothes rack?" I said quietly.

For a moment Ruth was silent. And then she lifted her eyes to me. "You probably won't believe me, Jane. No one believed me before. But I still think it was Valerie Maple."

"Valerie Maple!"

I could only repeat the name incredulously. I had been certain that Ruth had deliberately concocted the theory that Valerie Maple was her assailant. Since Selby's arrest, however, she had decided that only the truth would clear him, that she was through with evasion and deceit. And I believed her. Her eyes were starkly honest.

"It's true I didn't see Valerie Maple, Jane. After I stooped, I really saw nothing except the cane. Just as I reached out, the cane was pulled away. It was there, and all at once it moved. Moved beneath my fingers. I knew then that someone was on the other side of the clothes rack. I was petrified. Before I could straighten up or really get my wits together, I was knocked unconscious. Whoever was behind the rack rushed out and struck like lightning. There was hardly a second's gap, but in that second I heard and smelled and felt."

"Yes, Ruth."

"I heard the swish of Mrs. Maple's draperies—a soft, silky swish. Some soft material—one of Mrs. Maple's floating chiffon veils, I think now—brushed my cheek. Just as the blow came, I smelled her perfume. A wave of perfume, Jane, an almost sickening wave. I did not imagine those things."

I believed Ruth, and almost wished that I did not. There was no possibility, or I could see none, that Valerie Maple had been crouched behind the clothes rack.

"Valerie Maple was dead, Ruth, at the time of your attack."

"Then," Ruth said stubbornly, "someone else—her murderer, I suppose—had taken her clothes."

"What would be the point of that?"

Neither Belton nor Ruth replied. My own mind gave me back no logical answer. All pretense of packing had been abandoned while Ruth told her story. Belton had dropped to an old trousseau chest, and was apparently absorbed in the carved initials of one Alameta Blake who had died of "the fever" shortly after the war of 1812. Suddenly he looked up.

"No one knows that Valerie Maple is dead," he said harshly. "No one knows that she's been murdered. Everyone has assumed the woman was killed about the time Hannah Wilson was, that her body was put in the harp case and concealed somewhere in the woods. Everyone has assumed that her body was carried to her house and burned last night with the harp case. Why?"

He glared at me. I looked meekly back, and opened my mouth to reply.

Belton had the floor and he kept it.

"Maybe, Jane, you and all the rest of us are thinking what we're supposed to think. Maybe we're the victims of an—an illusion. You saw the burning harp case, you saw a scrap of burning dress material. You saw no body, did you?"

"No," I admitted. "But—"

"There's no proof," he said firmly, "that Valerie Maple has been murdered. No real proof that she's not still alive and in hiding. Actually she herself could have rigged the whole affair of the burning house."

"But why?"

"If that woman did kill her maid," he said, irritated by the interruption, "it would certainly be to her advantage to get herself declared dead. You can't deny that. At any rate, I'm going to find out what—if anything—the authorities have discovered in the ashes of that house."

With that, he stamped downstairs to telephone to Dr. Traphaven. During his absence Ruth and I finished the packing, snapped the locks on her two small bags. During his absence, too, something else occurred. Ruth asked my advice. She asked me whether she should perjure herself on the stand and give Selby an alibi for the time of Hannah's murder.

"It might not hold up," she said. "That's all that stops me. I'm terrified the police will learn where Selby really was on Friday evening. Learn where he was just before we came to you for dinner."

Belton and Ruth and Selby had arrived to dine with us at 7:30. They were late, and I recalled the time exactly. Just as I recalled that Hannah Wilson had died in our cottage sometime between six o'clock and seven.

"Selby was at your cottage on Friday, Jane. He was there a few minutes before we came to dinner."

"How do you know?" I whispered.

"We *saw* him, Jane." She meant her father and herself. Selby had not appeared at home by seven o'clock, and Ruth had fretted over the ruin of our dinner and eventually telephoned Belton. The two had started off without Selby, intending to present his apologies. But when they drove along Copston Road, Belton had seen his son-in-law leave the building site, step quickly from the yard and start walking up the road toward Aunt Mildred's. Selby's appearance had been so sudden and unexpected that Belton had almost run him down. They had stopped of course and picked him up.

"Did Selby explain?" I asked with dry lips.

"No," Ruth said. Her tears were spent, her eyes were dry. Only her voice was tortured. "But I think he must have gone to the cottage to meet Hannah."

I thought that myself. And when Ruth asked again whether she should invent an alibi for Selby, swear that he had returned as usual from the office and been at Blake House with her, I had no advice to offer. Both of us had forgotten Belton until we heard his lagging footsteps on the stairs. Even before he entered I guessed that he had reached Dr. Traphaven, and that his news was also bad. Crushed and disappointed, Belton came on inside.

"My idea," he said, "has gone up in smoke. They'll never be able to decide precisely what did happen to Valerie Maple. But there seems to be no question that she's dead, her body cremated."

And then he gave us the details of the excavation of the cellar of the Moran house, and a description of what had been recovered in the rubble there. For more than 24 hours Sheriff Blandish's band of volunteers had shoveled and dug through mountains of still smoking debris, one man stepping forward as another dropped out to go home and fall into bed. Early that afternoon the search had been repaid.

Paradoxically enough, the fierce heat with which the harp case had burned was responsible for a partial preservation of its contents. The floor of the bedroom had caught and burned through, dumping into the cellar the bed, the springs, the flaming harp case. The cellar of the Moran cottage had an earthen floor, and the earth was damp, soaked with winter snows and rain. Such objects as came into direct contact with the damp ground were not destroyed. The flanges of the harp case were intact, a portion of the sides and bottom, and mixed in with the char and ashes the searchers had recovered particles of human bones.

"Not enough," said Belton awkwardly, "for you and me to call human. But the doc's a scientific man. He's busy working now to—well—establish that the bones are Valerie Maple's."

Ruth turned pale at that, and I rose quickly and suggested that Belton carry down the bags. A few minutes later, the three of us walked from the house. Ruth and Belton did not look back. But as we walked down the crazy path, beneath the towering box and toward the street, I turned for a final glimpse of Blake House. Dark and deserted in the winter night, locked against intruders. And again I thought that, without Selby there, the house was cold and lifeless—like a tomb.

Chapter Twenty-six:
A PLAN THAT DIDN'T WORK

In the meantime, while I was listening to Ruth and later taking her to Aunt Mildred's, Al was having his interview with Selby. Sheriff Blandish wasn't cruel or inhuman. Although he believed Selby to be a double murderer, he allowed the brothers to talk in the reception room of the jail. A guard was posted directly outside the door, however, and when Selby was brought in he was in handcuffs.

The ostensible reason for the interview was to discuss arrangements for obtaining a lawyer. Al could not hide his own conviction that in the circumstances a lawyer was useless. Indeed, he accused his brother directly and at once of having guilty knowledge of the murder, and of shielding someone else. To him it was the only explanation of Selby's attitude.

"I'm armed with my own innocence," Selby said oddly. "But I'm not a fool. If I knew who committed these murders, I would certainly tell. Nothing—no considerations of family or personal loyalty—could persuade me to protect anyone I believed to be a killer."

"Nevertheless you're holding back, protecting someone."

"Maybe, Alan, the strong are obliged to protect the weak. I am well aware that my situation looks very black. At that, I feel that I am more able, better qualified to prove my innocence than—"

"Than whom? Whom are you talking about? You have reference to some specific person."

Selby refused to explain his strange remark. He sat down on the other side of a long pine table, and placed his manacled hands underneath and out of sight, and presently began to talk. While Al listened in silent horror, Selby admitted to the most telling part of the prosecution's case against him. Hannah had come to him in the middle of November and sought to take out a $50,000 insurance policy in Valerie Maple's favor. From the first, according to his own account, Selby had felt that the policy should not be allowed, that fraud was intended.

"Naturally, I suspected fraud. Any agent in the business would have been warned by the very nature of the proposition. With Hannah's first words I was suspicious."

"Why didn't you notify your company to that effect?"

Selby had been speaking quite freely, like a man who at long last has decided to lay down a heavy burden. Indeed, as Al was to tell me later, his brother seemed to have achieved a kind of weary peace.

Now he hesitated.

"Possibly I wanted to investigate Mrs. Moran's intentions for myself. After all, suspicions are not facts. You must remember at the time I was ignorant of Mrs. Moran's past history, or of her real name."

"It wasn't your job, Selby, to investigate Mrs. Moran's criminal intentions. Besides, how could you possibly hope to circumvent her?"

"I did my best."

"How?"

"By trying to show Hannah Wilson," Selby said bitterly, "the deadly danger of her own position. If she took out that policy she placed herself at the mercy of her mistress, and I so informed her. There was a queer relationship between those two. I do know that."

"How do you mean?"

"Hannah wouldn't listen to a word against Mrs. Moran," Selby said, and seemed honestly perplexed. "She trusted her utterly. Most people would feel a little gratitude if you pointed out they were proposing to make themselves prospective murder victims. Not she! The more I talked against the policy, the more determined Hannah became to take it out. I argued with her more than once, and over a period of several weeks, before I sent her off for the physical examination."

"Why didn't you confront Mrs. Moran?"

"Because I found it impossible."

"Impossible?"

"Of course I tried to see Mrs. Moran, or I should say Valerie Maple," Selby said, as though Al should have known without being told. "It was she whom I suspected of plotting an insurance murder. Hannah was only a pawn—and a stupid, stubborn pawn at that."

But had Hannah Wilson been a stupid woman? Even in the midst of his consternation at Selby's behavior, Al once again felt a sharp wonder at Hannah's determination to put her hand into a lion's mouth.

Selby went on. "I managed to reach Valerie Maple by telephone. On two occasions I made appointments with her; she broke them both. When I arrived at the Moran house only Hannah was there to present lame excuses. I thought then and think now she was afraid to face me."

"Then it's true that you never saw Valerie Maple?"

"Quite true."

Almost in spite of himself, Al believed his brother. But he could not forget the weak point in the whole account, the point that would be the very core of the prosecution's case. "If your suspicions were so thoroughly aroused, why did you keep the whole matter to yourself? Why didn't you appeal to your company, or even to the police? Did you ever intend to apply for the policy?"

"No," said Selby.

"Then why; in God's name, did you accept that check as payment for the first premium?"

"I felt it necessary," Selby said slowly. "If I could gain a little time, I might be able to show up Valerie Maple for what she was—a would-be killer, cold and mercenary and without mercy."

Before he spoke Selby's hesitation had been perceptible, and the dark eyes that had been raised in bleak candor dropped to his handcuffed wrists. Al remembered Dr. Traphaven's suggestion that some unknown pressure had been brought to bear, and no doubt he remembered, too, that we had never learned the name of the "acquaintance" who had been responsible for Mrs. Moran's arrival in Merristone. Possibly his mind went to the portrait in Aunt Mildred's dining room. I don't know. I do know that he had no opportunity to speak or to demur.

As though to block questions or interruptions, Selby quickly went ahead. "I was wrong, of course. Too arrogant and cocksure of my own ability to clean up an—an ugly mess. I realize that now. Indeed, I realized it very soon."

And then Selby told of how swiftly the situation had changed after he accepted the premium payment. Hannah quite naturally had expected to receive her policy upon delivery of Mrs. Moran's check. Presumably spurred by her mistress, she had warned Selby that the canceled check would serve as a receipt—a fact of which he was thoroughly aware.

By his own act, his position had become completely untenable. He admitted it. Admitted that after December 27th he was bombarded from two directions—by threats from Mrs. Moran on the telephone and by threats from Hannah in person. Miss Hawkins had heard high words exchanged in the office. Selby confessed that quarrels between him and Hannah Wilson had taken place, that he had put off Hannah with evasions and excuses. He told how he had temporized—temporized until the day the outraged servant informed him she was at the end of her patience, that she was going straight to New York, prepared to lay the whole matter before his company.

"I followed her in," Selby said, averting his eyes from Al's stunned, bewildered face. "I expect that's when Sarah saw us. On that day I was desperate. I couldn't have the company dragged in. That would have been ruinous. My whole plan depended on—"

"Ah! You had a plan to resolve this situation!" As he leaned forward, Al must have felt his first hope. "That's interesting. I'd like to hear it."

"My plan didn't work," said Selby, with the closed look in his eyes again. "To reveal it would do me no good, would only do harm. You'll have to take that on trust for the present, Alan. Please understand that even now I'm not completely hopeless. I'm innocent. There's— well—there's still a chance things will work out."

"Don't you realize where you are?" Al asked brutally, "You're in jail, son, charged with murder. You're not a free agent any longer. How are you to do anything to accomplish this miracle?"

"You'll have to take that on trust too, I'm afraid. Let's get back to Hannah and that Monday in New York. I've had time to think, and figure. Now that it's too late, I see Hannah lied to me about the purpose of her own trip. My good sense should have told me she wouldn't dare appear at the company offices."

"Why wouldn't she dare?" Al had just lit a cigarette, and now he carefully stubbed it out, and carefully kept his own gaze fixed upon the table. "You'd accepted her money, or Mrs. Moran's money; you'd' evidently promised to obtain the insurance—"

"My cooperation," said Selby, with a flash of bitterness, "was necessary, or there'd be no insurance. If I was in a cleft stick, so were those two women. Without me, without my deceiving my own company, trading on the company's trust in me, no policy was ever possible. Hannah had some other object in making that New York trip. I've wondered about that since. If we could find out her real purpose in going to the city, maybe it might help."

To Al, Hannah's purpose in traveling to New York City on the Monday before her death was beside the point. It seemed trivial and unimportant. Selby had drawn too clearly the picture of his own desperation at the prospect of her call upon the New York office of his company. He had been so convinced of the imminence of his own exposure that he had followed the servant to the city. He had got into a cab with Hannah, had talked to her.

What had he said to change her mind?

"I argued first," Selby said. "Again it was useless. She seemed adamant. At one point she even gave the driver the company address. I argued until finally I—I had to do something else."

"Yes?"

"I promised Hannah that I would act. I promised to deliver her policy on—on Friday."

"My God!" said Al. He looked at his brother, as though Selby was a stranger. Selby's own story had made him out a stranger, alien and unfamiliar, with no resemblance to any Selby Al had ever known. The Selby of our experience was stubborn and proud, with rigid ideas of conduct and honor, inflexible in any course that he considered right. Now Selby asked his only brother to accept him as a weak and vacillating man, victimized and browbeaten by two women, one of whom he was convinced was a criminal.

At any time Selby could have gone to the police, advised his company of the situation, or simply refused further dealings with either Hannah or Mrs. Moran. He had done none of these things. Why?

Al was too sick at heart to put the question. Selby must have felt it.

"I needn't tell you," he said, "that I was playing for time. By Friday I hoped—well, never mind what I hoped. Everything went wrong. It was on the New York trip, of course, that I lost my cane."

"Lost your cane!" Al exclaimed, as incredulous as I had been.

"In a way," said Selby, suddenly very pale, "I lost it."

"In a way! What do you mean?" Al's mind worked faster than mine had worked. "Do you mean you know where you left it? If we can show someone else had the cane—"

"That won't help."

"You're crazy! If we knew who had the cane, who carried it to our cottage—"

"I do know."

"Who?"

"Hannah Wilson," Selby said.

"Hannah?" Al echoed blankly. "I don't understand."

"It's quite simple," Selby said. "I left my cane in the cab with Hannah, that day in New York."

Still, Al was uncomprehending. Selby had been upset and overwrought when he had left Hannah in the cab, and had not missed his cane until he was on the train returning home. Hannah had brought the stick back to Merristone. So much Al understood. But why had Hannah taken the cane to our cottage?

"That's simple too, once you know." An overhead light shone on Selby's wan, pale face. New lines were etched around the mouth that always before had been firm and steady. His mouth twitched and then was quiet. He hesitated for a moment before he spoke. "Hannah carried my stick to the cottage because we were meeting there. She meant to give it back to me!"

It was simple, once you knew. Too simple to have occurred to anyone, and yet the explanation dovetailed perfectly with the physical circumstances of Hannah Wilson's murder. Al had forgotten, as I had forgotten, that even Sheriff Blandish believed the murder was unpremeditated, committed the heat of passion; that the skill and planning had come afterward. It had not occurred to us that when Hannah walked to our cottage and her doom, she had carried the instrument of her own destruction. It had not occurred to us that the killer, blind with frenzy, had seized and employed the weapon close at hand. A heavy-headed cane, laid down carelessly by an unsuspecting victim.

A full minute passed before Al spoke again. "But you did meet Hannah at the cottage?"

"Someone else met her first," Selby said. He braced himself, threw back his shoulders, as though to fight for Al's belief. "She was dead when I arrived, although I didn't know it."

Beads of sweat came out on his forehead. Instinctively he reached toward a handkerchief. The manacles clanked and he quickly dropped his hands, shoved them underneath the table. When he resumed, his voice was low, and the fight had left it.

He had not expected, he said, to meet Hannah at our cottage that fatal Friday evening. The appointment had originally been made for the Moran house, and when Hannah phoned to change the arrangements he had objected. And then Selby made another of those curious and provocative remarks of his—remarks hinting at the "plan" he was withholding with such stubborn determination, and at such great personal peril.

"Not that I really minded. I'd have met Hannah anywhere that day. This may be hard to credit, but on Friday afternoon I thought I had the situation solved. It soon turned out I was mistaken. Anyhow, I went to the meeting confidently. A few minutes after seven o'clock I arrived at your cottage. I—I almost trapped the murderer, Al."

For a moment the bare reception room was absolutely silent. Not even the ticking of a clock relieved the silence. In the hall beyond the two men heard the restless shuffling of the guard. Their time was running short.

"Of course I didn't know it," said Selby. "Suppose I tell exactly what happened. When I arrived, your cottage was dark. That surprised me, rather. I was a little late myself, and I expected Hannah to be there. I blundered around outside and finally went on in through your kitchen way. I was stumbling over hardware and stuff piled on the floor, hunting for an electric switch, when I heard movement in the dining room."

"What kind of movement?"

"Someone walking. Not an alarming sound. In fact, I thought it was Hannah. Why would she be waiting in the dark? Maybe, I thought, she was afraid of lights showing on the road. I hadn't found the kitchen switch myself. I called and she didn't answer. But she was deaf."

"Dr. Traphaven says she wasn't."

"She'd convinced me," said Selby grimly, "that she was deaf as a post. I'd been yelling at her for weeks. I yelled now. Yelled her name."

Again he had received no answer. Standing in the dark confusion of the kitchen, Selby had been uncertain and perplexed but not at all alarmed. Eventually he had fumbled forward, located the swinging door, and pushed on into the dining room. There had been no one there. Even as he entered, however, he heard the sound of rapid footsteps in the foyer, followed by the hard slam of a door. He had run across the dining room in that direction.

"I didn't mean to let her get away."

"Her!" Al stared. "Are you saying you thought it was Hannah who went through the foyer?"

"Exactly."

"But you were in the dining room, where she died. The room was stained with blood, the walls, the plaster table—"

"There was no light," said Selby dully. "The incredible truth is that I didn't see the dining room. I just ran through it, ran so fast I actually banged into the plaster table. My whole mind was bent on catching up with Hannah. I thought she was starting back home. Going with my blackthorn stick, at that." Selby paused and drew a deep breath. "I had my reasons—we needn't go into them—for wanting a good, long talk with Hannah. And with Valerie Maple, too. I told you I thought I had the situation—solved. Anyhow, I ran outside. It was dark as pitch, as dark as your cottage, and snowing hard. I barked my shins on a length of scaffolding, slid down the mound of fill. I got completely turned around, and blundered off into the fields. Anyhow, I didn't see a soul. But when I finally reached the road, and got headed toward the Moran house, a car came along."

Ruth and Belton were in the car, of course, and Selby had no recourse except to get in with them. It was then 7:25. What had happened in our cottage had taken longer to describe to Al than it had taken to occur. Until Selby stepped into the car he had no time to ponder various inconsistencies in his own thinking, his own assumptions. Until then he had no idea that he had run across the dining room in pursuit of a woman, already dead and murdered. No idea that he had visited the scene of a crime. In the car, however, he had happened to glance at his own hands, clearly revealed in the dashboard glow. There was a smear of blood, wet and sticky, upon his palm.

Selby did not describe to Al how his mind had flashed back to the plaster table that he had pushed aside in his first, mad dash toward the foyer. Nor did he describe his sensations in the moving car, or tell how quickly he had jammed his hand into his pocket lest his wife or father-in-law should see. He said nothing of his subsequent emotions when the dinner at Aunt Mildred's had dragged on, and finally we had all decided to make an inspection of our cottage.

Again the small reception room of the jail was silent. The guard in the hall beyond was growing restive. He opened the door and looked in. "Five more minutes, boys," he said in a not unkindly way.

Al got up from his chair. He had sat a long time, and felt cramped in body and very low in spirit. It was his task to obtain a lawyer for the defense, and he guessed in advance how his brother's narrative would impress any lawyer. "I want to ask one more question, Selby. When Ruth and Belton came along in the early evening, they stopped your going to the Moran house. Did you go there later? After we discovered Hannah's body, during the time all of us were scattered?"

"No," said Selby violently. "I had no reason for going there. I went straight to the Strings'. It was someone else who took the car keys."

"Someone else?"

"The killer, I suppose. Someone who needed desperately to make an opportunity to visit that house before the police arrived on the scene."

"Why?"

"I can only guess, Al. The murder was committed on the spur of the moment, in such haste that there was no time to work out a campaign. There must have been something in the Moran house that the police could not be permitted to see. I'm convinced the wrecking of the bedroom was only meant to be confusing. Furthermore—" Selby paused for a moment.

"Yes."

"I have a theory—a queer theory—about the guilty person. He or she is—well—distinctly unusual."

"Unusual? How?"

"Like any other killer, this one has acted to protect himself. What makes the situation extraordinary is that he hadn't wanted to gain his own protection at the expense of other people."

"I don't follow you."

Selby rose from the table. His face was grave and sober, intensely earnest. His dark eyes met Al's directly. "Before God," he said, "I don't know who the killer is. But I know one thing about him. He didn't mean to involve you and Jane in the crime, or me either."

"How do you figure that?"

"In the first place," Selby said, "I interrupted the murderer at the building site. It wasn't ever intended that Hannah's body be left in your cottage, or the dining room left in that condition. Except for my arrival, I am positive the body would have been moved off your premises. The cellar was a temporary expedient, necessary because I came blundering in. And, as for me—"

"Yes?"

"All the killer had to do to convict me out of hand," Selby said, "was to leave my cane beside Hannah's body. That wasn't done. The murderer himself, whoever it may be, did his very best to get rid of my stick, destroy it utterly."

"I see," Al said slowly. "I do see now, though I can't quite grasp the object—"

"I can," Selby said. "The killer's plan—the very heart of it, the only plan he had—was to pin the guilt for Hannah's murder on Valerie Maple. There's a kind of ironic justice in that, after all. The only trouble is—"

"The trouble is," Al said, "the plan didn't work." And then he reached out and grasped Selby's hand, and walked swiftly from the room before the guard could enter and lead off the prisoner.

The interview was over.

Chapter Twenty-seven:
WITH COPPER ARTICULATION

Few crimes are ever solved by any single line of inquiry, I suppose, or few criminals entrapped by any single clue. In Selby's story, however, was a clue or rather a suggestion that was to be important in our swiftly unfolding drama. But when Al left the jail and walked to the drugstore to telephone Aunt Mildred's for transportation—Ruth and I had taken our car from Blake House—he was not aware of it. I daresay he was too concentrated with puzzling over the part of the story Selby had withheld.

When Al stepped from the drugstore telephone booth and sat down at the soda counter to await the car, his mind was far from the minor problem of Hannah Wilson's trip to New York City on the Monday before her death. Even then, rattling toward Merristone on a bus, was a bright, birdlike little man who was prepared to illumine her surprising purpose in going there.

His name was Whistler, and though he entered the case late Mr. Whistler was to contribute a small but vital bit of information.

As it happened, I actually saw the little man at the moment he arrived in the village. After Al discovered I had returned home from Blake House, he expected me to stay there and that Frank alone would drive the car back downtown. I was too anxious for an account of the interview with Selby to submit to that. In consequence I was present when Frank was obliged to pull up with a sharp jerk, as a bus on the road ahead of us came to an abrupt stop.

It was the through bus from New York, and only one passenger got off. A mild little man without luggage, but bowed down by the bulk of an overcoat that could have done service for a polar sleeping bag. Mr. Whistler looked confusedly around, and then hailed us. Frank had already pressed the accelerator, and I wasn't inclined to stop again.

"It's probably some reporter."

"He doesn't look like a reporter."

Frank backed up, and with considerable relief the little man trotted toward us to ask directions. Exactly where was Merristone? The scattered lights of the shopping section shone directly ahead.

"You're in it."

"Oh," said Mr. Whistler blankly, and then added sheepishly, "Guess I'm not used to the country. I'm city born and bred myself. I'm looking for a—a Dr. Traphaven. I've been reading the papers, and I'd like to talk to him about the case."

My own opinion was that Dr. Traphaven had more important things to do than to chat with this bright-eyed, birdlike little stranger. Our case, like all cases treated sensationally in the press, had attracted its fair share of cranks. If the little man had any serious purpose, I thought he would have asked for Sheriff Blandish.

But we had stopped beside the village green, and Frank obligingly leaned out the window and indicated the doctor's house.

Mr. Whistler glanced uncertainly in that direction. "You mean the big dark place?"

"No," I said shortly. He had pointed to Blake House. "It's the place next door with all the lights."

He thanked us, pressed his card in my hand and we drove on to the drugstore and Al. As we alighted there, Frank said thoughtfully, "He didn't smell like a reporter either. Did you notice that odor?"

I did recall I'd vaguely caught an odor—faintly antiseptic, reminiscent of a hospital corridor or a doctor's office.

"Iodoform," I said. "Or moth balls maybe from that coat. I daresay, being city born and bred, he trots it out just to make these daring forays into the wilderness."

My thoughts weren't upon Mr. Whistler but upon the story Al had to tell us. For the next half hour the three of us sat in one of the drugstore booths, while Al described in detail his talk with Selby. It was when I got up that the card I had quite forgotten slipped from my lap and to the floor.

"What's that?" Al asked.

"Nothing," I said, numb and dazed by Al's recital. As I picked up the card I automatically glanced at it—a small neat business card printed in small neat letters: *E. A. Whistler—Arco Surgical Supply Company.*

Frank raised his eyebrows. "Well, the little man's profession is solved, Janey. A salesman, no less. I must say he picked a poor time and approach to sell the doc a new set of forceps."

But Al had turned over the card. Mr. Whistler had evidently used the back surface to jot some notes for his own use. There were six penciled words. Small and neat like the printing. They said: *One framework, female, with copper articulation.* And beneath was penciled: *1/13/41.*

The words might have meant something to E. A. Whistler, but to me they were incomprehensible. They were words and English words, but in combination they had no meaning.

Frank and Al looked equally baffled, and then Frank pointed to the penciled figures.

"I can't define 'copper articulation,'" he said, "or tell you what a 'framework' is, but I can solve the figures. It's just a date. January 13th, this year."

"The day Hannah went to New York," I said involuntarily. "Maybe—"

"Maybe we'd better stop off at Dr. Traphaven's," Al said slowly,

And then he swept up our checks, flung a bill on the drug counter and almost ran to the car. The eagerness with which he seized on that slight evidence, as though by finding out the meaning of a few incomprehensible words he could be of help to Selby, was a measure of our desperation. Al was still clutching the card when we arrived at Dr. Traphaven's house.

During the past few days we had grown almost fond of Dr. Traphaven, and used to his ways. Al dispensed with the lengthy wait expected of the average caller, coming into contact with the doctor's couple. He simply rang the bell and entered, with Frank and me behind him. Similarly he went straight to the study door, rapped and announced us all.

"It's us—the Blakes. We've got my partner along."

There was a brief hesitation, and then Dr. Traphaven bade us enter. Mr. Whistler was still with him. The little man, whom I had given such cursory attention, had shed his tremendous overcoat, and, without it, looked less birdlike and eccentric and even somewhat larger. He recognized Frank and me, and beamed at us as though we were old and tried friends of his.

Dr. Traphaven was not smiling. His face was preoccupied and grave.

"Sit down," he said.

The smile faded from Mr. Whistler's face, as though by request. His face became grave and sober, too. When I sat down beside him, I discovered that he scrubbed his hands with some strong surgical soap. I shifted my chair a little closer to the window.

For a moment no one spoke. Then Mr. Whistler cleared his throat.

"You can see," he said to Dr. Traphaven, "how I thought it was doubtless a practical joke. People do at times have such odd ideas of humor."

"They do at times."

Mr. Whistler received that remark like an accolade. He looked setup and relieved. "Well, that about covers it. Of course this Hannah Wilson didn't seem—well—like a prankster, and I couldn't understand her undue concern about the type of product she desired. That's why I wondered."

Mr. Whistler's alert bright eyes shifted to the doctor's desk. A folded towel was lying there. Almost casually Dr. Traphaven turned back the fold. I saw Frank start, and then turn pale. Al started too, and reached for my hand. I stared at the littered objects on the towel, and felt absolutely nothing.

Even though I knew that shards of human bone had been recovered in the ashes of the Moran house, I failed at first to identify the blackened fragments that were carefully arranged upon the snow-white cloth. To a layman like myself, the display was so completely unrecognizable that it was robbed of any shock or horror.

"These," said Dr. Traphaven, "are segments of human bone. I won't harrow you by describing the structural difference between human hone, and the bone of other mammals. Just take my word for it. These fragments, recovered from the Moran cellar mixed with wreckage of the harp case, are undeniably of human origin."

I did not doubt it. I wondered why he felt it necessary to hammer at the point.

The doctor hesitated, and then spoke again. "Nevertheless, Valerie Maple's body was not burned with her house."

Al was seated on the other side of the desk. He got up from his chair. "But, Doctor, how can you possibly say that?"

"Valerie Maple's body was not burned," repeated Dr. Traphaven. "Nor was her body concealed in the harp case. Mr. Whistler has just told me so. Although actually I knew when this was brought in."

He took a pair of tweezers from his desk and delicately lifted from the towel one of the burned and blackened bone splinters. Clinging to the splinter, securely fastened, was a small loop of twisted copper wire.

"What's that?"

"It's known in the trade," Mr. Whistler said with dignity, "as copper articulation. So that the framework will give proper service we articulate the important joints—you might say reinforce them—with copper wire."

In surgical supply circles "to articulate" meant to join. *Framework*, Mr. Whistler explained, apparently surprised that we didn't know, was also a trade word. It meant *skeleton.*

On the Monday before her death, at 2:30 in the afternoon, Hannah Wilson had called at Mr. Whistler's place of business. Before she left the surgical supply house, she had ordered and paid for a human skeleton. Ordinarily Mr. Whistler's customers were doctors or laboratory workers, but he had not been surprised at Hannah's purchase. He had, however, been surprised by the several conditions she set.

"Miss Wilson," he said, unhappily, "was most emphatic about what she wanted, and what she didn't want. She desired a female framework, and on that score I was in a position to satisfy her. We do classify our products more or less by age and sex. But in our business it is the usual custom to connect the important sections with copper wire. I explained to Miss Wilson that this copper reinforcement added years of service to the product. She insisted she didn't want it. We always try to please our customers, and I did attempt, without success, to locate a female framework of the unusual type that this—this lady specified. All of our own stock, being of the highest quality, was of course equipped with the copper articulation. I did my level best to meet the exact conditions of the order, but when Thursday came—"

Hannah had been equally emphatic in her request that the skeleton arrive in Merristone on Friday morning by the latest. More than that, she desired that it be shipped in a box which she herself provided. "A clumsy-looking, three-sided box," in Mr. Whistler's phrase. It was our missing harp case.

"When Thursday came," said Dr. Traphaven, "Mr. Whistler decided to ship from his regular stock, hoping his customer wouldn't object too much. A lucky thing he reached that decision. If Hannah's order had been met exactly—" He hesitated. "I probably would have believed until my dying day that Valerie Maple's body was consumed in the flames of her own dwelling. It would have been impossible to establish whether she had been murdered, or whether she had secretly returned home and committed a dramatic kind of suicide. No one would have doubted, however, that Valerie Maple was dead. You can see how very little of the skeleton we recovered in the ashes. But the loop of copper wire remains to identify Mr. Whistler's shipment. It tells us the truth. No body at all was cremated in the house."

Al was still standing. "I do see," he said stupidly, "but what—what does it mean?"

"Ask yourself, son." The doctor glanced around the quiet study. His eye stopped on Frank. "Or ask your partner. He's guessed some of it."

"Only a little." Frank raised a distracted hand to his forehead. "But one thing's clear enough. All our thinking up to now has been based on an entirely false premise. We misunderstood Mrs. Maple's intentions, missed the whole point of her original scheme. But let me get it straight.

As I understand, the harp case wasn't exactly shipped to Hannah."

"The harp case and contents," said Dr. Traphaven, "was addressed to Veronica Moran."

"Exactly." Frank kept his eyes fixed on the doctor as though for encouragement. "Surely that indicates that both women, maid and mistress alike, were plotting the insurance fraud. Outright murder was never intended. Hannah wasn't a fool; she didn't mean to die. She wasn't a stupid pawn, she was in the confidence of her mistress. If Hannah simply disappeared from Merristone, wasn't seen again, and the house burned down and human bones were recovered—"

"Payment on the insurance policy could have been demanded," Dr. Traphaven said at once, and then added dryly, "Provided, of course, that the policy on Hannah's life had ever been issued. The fraud was set up on the mistaken assumption that the insurance would be in force by Friday night. All necessary steps had been taken. The incendiary materials had been collected and concealed somewhere, the skeleton had arrived, Mrs. Maple or Hannah had thriftily cleaned the kitchen in preparation for the fire. Poison had been mixed with the cat food."

"I don't understand the poison," said Frank.

My flashes of intuition are few and far between. But I had seen Valerie Maple many times with her cats, a veiled and solitary figure walking along a country road preceded by her leashed, beribboned pets. "Mrs. Maple was fond of Gog and Magog," I said. "But they had to die. It would be amazing enough if she herself escaped the holocaust she had in mind. She could substitute a body for Hannah, but that wouldn't work with the two cats. I suppose poison seemed more merciful to her, more quick and sure, than suffocation."

"My idea exactly," said Dr. Traphaven approvingly. "Everything possible was done to provide against any slipup. No doubt Hannah's hiding place was arranged in advance, every detail carefully worked out. The mistress was to remain behind and do the talking. And she'd have talked against a background calculated to win her sympathy. I can picture Mrs. Moran-Maple now, demanding double indemnity on the insurance policy, and meanwhile weeping copiously and loudly at the 'bier' of her devoted maid."

Al gripped the back of his chair. "Can you picture her?" he said, almost savagely. "Well, I cannot. Don't you realize, any of you, that we've lost Valerie Maple again? Last night we knew, or thought we knew, what had happened to her. What are we to think now? Where is that woman?

What's become of her? Did she kill Hannah, after all? Is she hiding now in the place where Hannah was supposed to go?"

Frank was watching the doctor. I looked at him, too. Suddenly a strange look came on the bearded face, an intent and questioning look, mixed oddly with another expression that was like dawning comprehension.

"By God," he said, "age doesn't improve the wits. But at last I see where the end is." And then he swept the folded towel into the drawer, sprang to his feet and cried, "Get out, you kids, get out! Take Whistler with you. I've got work to do."

My final glimpse was of Dr. Traphaven snatching up his telephone. I saw this through the closing door. But I didn't see Frank slip behind one of the tall glassed-in cabinets.

Chapter Twenty-eight:
THE SECRET STAIRWAY

With Mr. Whistler between us, Al and I found ourselves upon the sidewalk. The little man was wholly bewildered at the precipitateness of our dismissal from the scene. I was less bewildered than he, and considerably more annoyed. The doctor's electrified manner as he shooed us from the study and seized his telephone, the dawning comprehension on his face, had told me with the utmost clarity that the end was in sight, the end of all the mystery. And I resented the fact that we'd been sent away to wonder and to worry.

It wasn't until we guided Mr. Whistler to his bus, accepted his effusive thanks and returned to our car that I missed Frank.

"I don't believe he ever left the study, Jane. I hope to heavens he manages to get some news for us. Eavesdropping has its points at times."

Just then we heard Frank's footsteps approaching. A moment later, breathing hard, he appeared at the curb. "Those cabinets are plenty high enough to hide behind," he said. "Unfortunately the Doc's got sharp eyes, and a suspicious mind. He put through the phone call all right, but he discovered me just as he began to talk. And out I went."

"Who'd he call?"

"The Illinois prison."

"The prison!" I was surprised and disappointed. "Isn't he trying to find out what became of Valerie Maple? Surely he doesn't think she's hiding *there!*"

"I don't know, Jane. I can't explain the doctor's great idea, or the workings of his mind, but listen—"

There was something excited and unnatural in Frank's manner. Something which made me wheel from the curb and gaze instinctively toward Blake House. It was in Blake House that all my own anxieties were rooted. Several hundred yards from where we stood, faintly visible against the midnight sky, rose its grim, forbidding bulk. In the summertime the house would be shut away behind barricades of greenery. Long since the foliage had fallen from the giant trees; the shrubbery, the towering hedges were bare and leafless.

Two hours earlier Ruth and Belton and I had locked and bolted Blake

House, made it secure against intruders. Ruth had one set of keys, Selby had carried the second set along with him to jail. There were no others. Nevertheless, someone was in Blake House now. A light was shining from the library. Even as I raised my eyes, the light went out.

"I saw it from the doctor's study," Frank said in the tense, unnatural whisper. "Who do you suppose is in there?"

"Valerie Maple!" I said at once.

My conviction, born of nerves and strain, was instantaneous, positive, allowing of no doubt or argument. My first, indeed my sole concern was to keep from the authorities the knowledge that the vanished woman, for some reason of her own, had mysteriously returned to pay a visit to Selby's home.

The end might be in sight, but I didn't want it to come with the capture of Valerie Maple in my brother-in-law's library.

I clutched Frank's arm. "Did the doctor see the light?"

"I don't think so. No. He was busy at the phone, but I just happened to glance out the window. Anyhow, I'm prepared and ready to investigate."

Frank was prepared indeed. Suddenly, as if by magic, a gun had appeared in his hand. The gun had very obviously been selected from the doctor's cherished collection. Pasted across the sturdy barrel was a meticulously typed label that named the female bandit who once had used it.

"I hope to God the thing is loaded!" cried Frank. "And that the doc doesn't mind a temporary loan. In a good cause, of course. You folks stay here."

With that he leaped the fence that enclosed the grounds of Blake House and started floundering forward through the snow and darkness. We followed naturally, though we did run around to the gate. The box hedge that lined the crazy path was like a tunnel. Once we entered it, the heartening glow of lights from Dr. Traphaven's vanished, and all signs of Blake House itself were swallowed up in darkness. The icy branches of the hedge creaked and protested, whipped across our faces. Snow sifted from the laden branches overhead, sliding, whispering, unseen. At last we reached the open, mounted the shallow steps that led into the chill dampness of the winter vestibule. It was darker, almost, than the night.

Frank was already there. I gasped when I felt the touch of his hand.

"You shouldn't be in on this, Jane. You either, Al. There may be trouble, but I could have handled it myself."

I didn't doubt the trouble. Nor did I need Frank's whispered adjuration to keep quiet. Blake House was as quiet as the grave. The vestibule was as hushed and clammy as a vault, and as uninviting.

"Let me go first," whispered Frank. "I've got the gun. Stand back. I need room to rush the door."

I heard Al fumble in his pocket, strike a match. As the match blazed up, the vestibule became homely and familiar. I felt a little foolish. The foot scraper was commonplace and reassuring, as was the worn old mat, the pair of abandoned rubbers lying beside the great oak door.

"No one's here," Al said loudly. "It's idiotic. That woman wouldn't come here. I'm damned if I'll break in my brother's house because you two think you saw a light. We'll wait and get Ruth's key."

"That won't be necessary." Frank moved swiftly, noiselessly toward the door. It was unlocked, and standing slightly ajar. Ruth had closed and locked the door two hours earlier, and taken away the key. Immediately, without an instant's hesitation, Frank stepped through the unlocked door into the foyer beyond.

We followed.

The foyer was silent, cold, and extremely dark. However, I was no longer frightened. The door that stood ajar had convinced me that we were too late, that the visitor to Blake House had already gone. I bore the thought with equanimity.

Almost cheerfully I fumbled past the umbrella stand, and felt for the switch. My fingers found the paneled wall, froze there.

The silence was shattered by a sudden sound. A sound as startling and unexpected as a pistol shot. A door slammed in the library. Slammed as though it had escaped the hand of someone in a tremendous hurry, slammed violently, and with a peculiar, hollow reverberation that echoed throughout the house.

One door in Blake House and one alone produced a sound like that.

"The secret stairway!" I screamed, but Al and Frank had already rushed past and on into the library.

My feet seemed rooted to the floor, my fingers glued to the paneled wall. The library was immediately adjoining, the library with the secret that Selby had always loved to show. I had serious doubts that I would ever rally sufficient strength to reach it. Confused sounds came from there. Footsteps pounded against floorboards, thudded against a stone hearth. In total darkness the men raced for the false Dutch oven set in beside the massive chimney. The poker fell over, the fire tongs crashed. As a light flashed on, I tottered to the threshold. Across the book-lined library, framed by the cavernous fireplace and the matching chimney settles, Al and Frank were struggling with the Dutch oven door. Al was assaulting the wooden panels with the poker, Frank was using the butt of the doctor's gun to attack the lock. Above the uproar, both of them wild with excitement, they were yelling at each other.

"She's on the stairway now!"

"Isn't there a key to the oven door?"

"Inside! She's locked herself in from the inside!"

In his efforts with the poker, Al had apparently forgotten that the secret stairway opened at both ends. Whoever was crouched on the other side of the door, safely out of reach, didn't need to wait obligingly until they broke down the barrier. There was an exit in the cellar, another to the roof. Just as I appeared, Al recalled that important fact.

Dropping the poker, he rushed from the room, shouting that Frank was to prevent an escape from the roof while he took charge in the cellar. Presumably I was to remain where I was.

Al almost knocked me down in his own departure, and Frank completed the process when he dashed outside to guard the roof. Fortunately I landed in a chair. It happened to be Selby's worn old leather chair. I sank into it, limp as a dishrag, wondering why men so often acted first and reserved their thinking for afterward.

Frank had bent and flattened the fine old metal hardware on the Dutch oven door, Al had scarred and splintered the lovely panels.

In the soft light of the single lamp the library seemed quiet and peaceful, far removed from violence. The tremendous leather couch where Selby stretched out to read the evening paper flanked the Governor Winthrop desk. At the desk Ruth sat to do her telephoning and catch up her correspondence, pausing from time to time to smile at her husband. She and Selby had spent their happiest, completest hours in that room.

Presently I got up and went over to examine the damaged door that concealed the secret staircase. I placed my ear against the panel, listened, and heard nothing. Because of the near proximity of the chimney to the hidden stairway, the slightest sound inside was enormously magnified. Standing as I stood, one could hear the softest footfall on the stone stairs, the most surreptitious movement. In a generation long ago, hunted men who took refuge there had been betrayed by a cough, an inadvertent whisper.

There was nothing. Once again as I listened, rigid, tense, my ear against the paneled door, it came to me that we were too late. There was no one on the other side of the door. No one at all. The secret stairway was quite deserted. Al would watch in vain the cellar below. Frank, freezing on the lawn outside, would peer vainly toward the roof. Somehow, in a way I could not fathom because the time had been so brief, an escape had already been effected. I felt sure of it.

Half disappointed, half relieved. I straightened up. The lamp was placed behind me, shining across the hearthstone, shedding a gentle glow into the fireplace. Feathery ashes, gray and dead, stirred lightly from the draft above. Blake House had been hastily closed. Ruth hadn't shut the dampers or bothered to clean and sweep the fireplace. Among the feathery ashes, buried deep, I saw the glint of a live coal. Instinctively I leaned forward to extinguish it.

The glint was not a coal. The light behind was shining softly on the shaft of a wrought-iron key. The key to the secret stairway had been tossed into the ashes of the fireplace, and had almost sunk from sight. Even when I picked up the key and looked at it, I didn't comprehend the full significance of my discovery.

I only knew that the Dutch oven door had not been locked from the inside. The key had been turned from the outside, turned from the outside by someone who stood on the hearthstone where I stood now. The key had been used from the outside, and then thrown into the ashes. But I had the key again.

I could open the door on the stairs if I chose. I must have reached a decision swiftly, though it seemed to me an aeon passed before I slid the key into the lock. The lock was battered and bent and out of line. The key turned hard, but I turned it. The door that Selby had always opened easily resisted me. It, too, had been forced slightly out of line. It stuck and scraped and squeaked on the hearthstone.

I dragged the Dutch oven door wide open. Once upon a time a false panel hung with copper pots and pans had been placed inside, to assist the illusion that the four-foot door opened into an orthodox Dutch oven. The stairway occupied a cramped space farther back, a space stolen from the angle of the chimney, its existence unsuspected by anyone who didn't go from floor to floor of Blake House with a measuring tape and ruler.

Selby had removed the false panel, the fraudulent pots and pans, so that one could look directly at his cherished secret stairs. The lamplight coldly illumined them, a chill and narrow flight, made of solid stone. Block on block of stone, caught between walls of stone, rising like a steep and jagged cliff.

I stooped, peered up and down the stairs. Upward, step by step to the trap door opening on the roof, downward, step by step to the cellar.

There was no one on the stairway. Someone had been there, though. Someone had spent considerable time in the hidden place, and quite recently. A huddle of blankets at the stairway head, a crumpled pillow, announced that someone had slept in that dark and airless prison, or tried to sleep. Slept a while and wakened, cramped and stiff, and padded restlessly up and down the stairs, up and down, like a captured rat who prowls the narrow confines of his cage.

I could trace the progress of the vanished prisoner by a littered trail that wound up and down the bare stone flight. A sodden, balled-up tissue paper handkerchief lay on almost every step. Whoever had hidden on the secret stairway had been suffering from a heavy cold. Two dozen used and discarded squares of tissue proved it.

I had a sudden hysterical impulse to laugh. Instantly the impulse died. In a second or less, the significance of the key tossed into the ashes of the fireplace swept across me.

I understood the slamming door.

No escape had been made by means of the secret staircase. No one had entered the stairway while we hesitated in the foyer, but someone had left it. The slamming door, combined with the vanished key had deceived us, as it had been meant to do.

How had the unknown eluded us? The only other way to leave was through the library itself. But we were in the foyer, Al and Frank and I, our presence blocking off that escape. No one had slipped past us after the Dutch oven door had slammed. It was quite impossible. How had the intruder got out of Blake House?

Suddenly I whirled around. The single lamp shone softly in the quiet, book-lined library. The Winthrop desk glowed with the magic, tender and multiple fires of wood long preserved and carefully protected. Ruth's telephone was an anachronism.

I stared at it. Suddenly the Winthrop desk and the telephone seemed a long way off. As the rooms in Blake House went, the library wasn't large. Yet the leather couch with the high square back seemed a long way off.

Had Ruth moved the couch, without my noticing? Was there something oddly askew about its placement on the rug? Askew and unfamiliar? Surely the window frame had used to touch the back, and the cobbler's bench in front had not used to be so near. Surely there had not used to be a space between the couch and the wall.

Slowly, on reluctant feet, I started toward the couch. My footsteps tapped on the wide, old floorboards. Louder was the beating of my heart. It was absurd to be afraid of a leather couch, absurd to be sweating with fear in a softly lighted room.

I stopped at the table that held the lamp. I touched the base and steadied myself.

The lamp cord dropped from the table to the floor, and curled along for yards, as did most of the electric cords in Blake House, to disappear at a distant, inconvenient floor plug. The plug was behind the couch. Everything led to the couch. All my attention was focused there, as though a homely, familiar piece of furniture, made of worn old leather and with a high square back, had become the very heart of terror. Surely the couch was pulled askew.

I started to take another step, and did not. My muscles refused to function. My heart hammered against my ribs, and I clung to the lamp that represented security in a world filled with inexplicable menace. Menace emanating from the leather couch. All was silence in the library. But was it? Did I hear the impalpable stir of breathing, a faint muffled sigh? Eyes fixed upon the couch, as though they could pierce the high, stout back and search out the space behind, I listened until my ears rang. I took another step.

At that moment someone sneezed.

Someone sneezed, and I screamed for Al and Frank at the top of my lungs. Screamed and knew that I was not alone in the library, that I had never been alone there, that the unknown was crouched and waiting behind the sofa. I screamed again. Simultaneously, even as I gripped it in my hands, the lamp went out. The connection had been broken at the baseboard. The plug rattled across the floor, the freed wire swished through the air, and darkness smote the room.

In the darkness was the surge of many sounds. The couch was violently pushed aside. Someone scrambled upright. Heavy footsteps were coming straight at me. In a paralysis of terror, I dropped the useless lamp and started running.

It was not my intention to interfere with the escape of the unknown. My sole intention was to make good my own escape.

With that in mind, I fled into the foyer. I could have made a wiser choice. It did not occur to me that the unknown might be as anxious to get out of Blake House as I was myself. At the front door, and in total darkness, we had our meeting. We crashed together with an impact that almost shook the house. I had no breath left for screaming.

Something with four sharp corners like a box struck me squarely in the stomach. I doubled up across the thing, and groaning, tried to let go.

The other person let go first, let go the boxlike object with such abruptness that I lost my scant remaining balance. I fell over backward to the floor. The box accompanied me. This time, it hit me smartly in the nose. With the box atop me, I lay in a huddled heap, expecting instant death.

Instead I heard the front door open, bang back against the foyer wall. The intruder to Blake House was headed elsewhere. The footsteps raced through the vestibule and on outside. The storm door was left open, too, swinging free in the bitter night.

Above the flapping doors, from the distance came other sounds. I thought I heard Frank shout for Al, and wondered dimly if they were setting out in pursuit. I was beyond caring. Several minutes must have passed before I had the strength to totter back into the library. I crawled behind the couch and fixed the floor plug. The lamp went on again.

I returned to the foyer to close the door. The four-cornered leather box was still lying on the floor. Only it was not a box. It was a shabby Gladstone bag.

I carried the Gladstone bag into the library. Valerie Maple had not slammed the door of the secret stairway and crouched behind the leather sofa watching her chance to escape.

She had not remained in hiding in Blake House. Her whereabouts, were still unknown. The mysterious occupant of the secret stairway had been someone else. The identity of that person was quite clear. A name was stamped on the label of the Gladstone bag. The name was Ned Havens.

Chapter Twenty-nine:
IN THE GLADSTONE BAG

After 25 years Ned Havens had come back to Merristone. Uncle Ned had rushed out of the mists of the past and straight into the present. The legendary figure, whom Aunt Mildred had divorced so long ago, and who had never seemed real to me, became a man of flesh and blood to me within a second's time, a man to reckon with in the solution of our tragedies. From the moment he catapulted himself upon the scene, from the moment I saw the Gladstone bag, I knew beyond any doubt that Ned Havens must be linked with Valerie Maple. I had suspected before, and now I knew. Even before I opened the Gladstone bag, I guessed that the presence of Ned Havens in Blake House must be the explanation of Selby's behavior. If Uncle Ned had been able to install himself on the secret stairway, if he had slept there, remained long enough to catch a heavy cold, that could have been accomplished only with the connivance of someone in Blake House.

Selby was the answer. Selby who was locked up in the village jail, refusing to tell a comprehensive story. Selby with his fanatical pride of family, his quixotic notions of family honor.

Selby had acted under pressure throughout, had acted to protect someone else. We had always believed it. It was at Selby's express request that Blake House had been vacated, that Ruth had accompanied me to Aunt Mildred's. Obviously that was done to allow Uncle Ned an opportunity to escape.

With all my heart I hoped that Al and Frank would overtake Ned Havens, and bring him back.

I lifted the Gladstone bag to the table and opened it. The contents were tumbled and tossed together. A collection of dirty shirts, a pair of silk pajamas, were wadded with a wrinkled coat of Harris tweed. A half-used box of tissues, and a dozen soiled handkerchiefs rested atop a pair of English walking shoes, fitted with wooden trees, but stained and stiff from the effects of mud and water. A clumsy and unsuccessful attempt had been made to clean the shoes. Lumps of dried mud, broken twigs and bits of moss, still encrusted the inside heels.

I picked up the coat. A jumble of objects spilled from the pockets. A key ring, a small pearl-handled knife, a tin of aspirin, a litter of correspondence, a Pullman ticket stub. Uncle Ned had not prepared his pockets to face investigation. The ticket stub showed that he had arrived in Merristone exactly five days before. He had arrived at 7:00 a. m. on Friday morning. Late that afternoon Hannah Wilson had died, and thereafter Valerie Maple had been seen no more.

The knowledge that Uncle Ned had stepped off the milk train on Friday morning did not surprise me. What surprised me was that he hadn't seen fit to destroy the tell-tale Pullman stub. The condition of the bag, its contents, told me a good bit about the man who had left the family a quarter of a century earlier.

Ned Havens was still a traveling man. His correspondence had been often forwarded before it reached him. He was untidy and careless. He was extravagant, or he had been extravagant. His clothing was expensive, but it was also shabby and worn. The silk pajamas were falling to pieces, the coat was old, the shoes had been resoled. The shoes suggested that during his five-day stay in Merristone, Ned Havens at least once had ventured from the safe concealment of the secret stairway. I had a strong suspicion that the mud had been acquired on Copston Road.

Turning from the shoes, I stared hard at the scattered correspondence. For some reason I would have preferred to attack Ned Havens's personal letters with others present. I crossed to the quiet library window, looked out, saw no sign of Al or Frank. I went into the foyer and opened the door again and called, and received no answer.

Slowly I returned to the Gladstone bag. With considerable reluctance, I began assorting and examining the contents of the envelopes. Apparently Uncle Ned had no friends who wrote him letters. Most of the envelopes contained bills. Unpaid bills had followed him through hall a dozen western states, forwarded from one hotel address to another, until, worn with travel, they had finally reached him,

The bills were mutely descriptive too, descriptive of the sterile, lonely life of an aging man without roots or family, without too much money, moving always from town to town, with no background save the four impersonal walls of a cheap hotel room. A man who couldn't pay his honest debts, but meant to pay them sometime. Uncle Ned had kept the bills. For the first time I felt a reluctant stir of pity.

I started to thrust the envelopes away, and then suddenly my pity died. A slim gray envelope lay underneath the others. It did not contain a bill. When I saw the familiar handwriting of the address, when I read the postmarked date, my hands shook until I could hardly remove the folded sheet within.

In September of 1939 Selby had written to Ned Havens—16 months before our tragedies occurred, Selby wrote that he had been able to locate a suitable Merristone residence for his uncle's "dear old friend, Veronica Moran."

Why Uncle Ned had kept Selby's note, why he had carried it around for months, I didn't know. I did know who was responsible for the fact that Valerie Maple had chosen Merristone as the scene of her impersonation. It wasn't Selby. He had done a casual, unthinking service for his uncle. Uncle Ned was the acquaintance whose name had slipped his mind.

In frantic haste, all scruples thrown aside, I went to the bottom of the Gladstone bag, tossing its contents helter-skelter. I was convinced that Ned Havens had come secretly to Merristone to see Valerie Maple, and I desired to prove it. The shirts landed on the floor, the coat, the muddy shoes. A toothbrush, a tube of shaving cream, a nasal spray, fell out loosely with the tumbled clothes.

Wasn't there a toilet case? There was. I snatched up the leather box. It rattled. I jerked at the metal catch, opened the case. Something fell out. Something flashed and sparkled, and then hung suspended, turning gently in the air, caught in the metal fastening by a fine gold chain.

I gasped. Caught in the clasp of the toilet case, swinging by the fine gold chain, was an old-fashioned locket shaped like a lily and with opals glowing at the heart. It was Valerie Maple's locket. She had worn it when I saw her last. The clothing she had worn that fatal Friday afternoon, the draperies and veils, had disappeared in flame and smoke, but the locket had not been burned. Again it swung and gently turned, pivoted by the metal catch.

I tried to free the chain, and it resisted me as though determined to remain fastened securely to the toilet case, until it became a noose fastened around Ned Havens's neck. No one had seen Valerie Maple after 5:30 on Friday afternoon, when Al and I had left her with the locket at her wrinkled throat.

Sometime after 5:30 on Friday afternoon, sometime after Al and I had started home, Ned Havens had visited the house on Copston Road. I had proof of it. He had gone there, and when he went away he took along the ornament that Valerie Maple had prized and treasured. I could not believe she would have surrendered it willingly. Nevertheless Ned Havens had got possession of the locket, and had hidden it in his toilet case. Why? What was its importance to him?

The chain parted from the catch, and the golden lily lay in my hand. I turned it over. Engraved on the back was the name of a city, and a date, and beneath two pairs of initials:

Chicago—April 2, 1916—
V. M. from N. H.

My fingers had stopped shaking. They now felt numb and stiff. Valerie Maple was indeed a dear old friend of Uncle Ned's, a dear old friend of a very special kind.

They had met in the city of Chicago in the spring of 1916. In the fall of 1916 Valerie Maple had gone to trial for the murder of her husband and her little daughters, and her motive had been to free herself for a second marriage. She had admitted to the motive, but stubbornly refused to name the other man, the shadowy figure who had inspired her shocking crime. Defiant and alone she had faced the judge and jury, and attempted to convince them that she used arsenic as an aid to her complexion, that it had accidentally contaminated the milk that had swept away three members of her family. She had failed in her fraudulent defense, and had been convicted. Even when the prison gates closed upon her, she had not spoken.

Long ago Ned Havens must have felt that he owed to Valerie Maple a heavy debt. He was the man she had refused to name.

When I pressed the petals of the lily, the locket flew open. Smiling out at me, as he must often have smiled out at Valerie Maple, was a photograph. The picture was old and yellowed by time, but Uncle Ned looked exactly as he looked in the portrait at Aunt Mildred's, even to the reckless eyes, the smiling mouth, the black luxuriant mustache. A few lines of writing ran below the photograph. The purple ink was badly faded. I leaned closer to the light and read:

Courage, Valerie
In the heat of summer
You must strike for the freedom
That belongs only to the brave.

Ned Havens had composed that in April of 1916, and he had signed it. In the heat of summer, in the blazing heat of the following July, Valerie Maple had struck for freedom in a terrible, unnatural way. She had poisoned her husband, her daughters, her husband's little son.

What these mawkish lines meant to Uncle Ned when he wrote them down, I had no way of knowing. But I could judge the precise effect of that foolish scrap of composition had it been produced at Valerie Maple's trial. She would not have stood in the dock alone. It was highly probable that Ned Havens would have accompanied her.

Quite suddenly, as I gazed at the photograph and the faded writing, I realized that Uncle Ned, who had not gone to trial, must have spent years in prison, too. Quite suddenly I understood that he had paid for his folly with his wife and child, his position in society. The public might not have learned his connection with the notorious Maple case, but Aunt Mildred had certainly known when she divorced him.

In some dim fashion, I guessed that Ned Havens must have paid in other ways as well. Valerie Maple had put him in her debt, and it wasn't likely she would forget the fact. Valerie Maple was no normal woman. Dr. Traphaven had described her as a pathological criminal. A murder case can always be reopened, an old scandal be revived.

I saw that Uncle Ned must have been acting under pressure too, when he wrote Selby about his "dear old friend." I wondered whether he had known of Hannah and of the insurance plot, and whether he had knowingly agreed to help Valerie Maple perpetrate the fraud. Had Ned Havens helped until he could bear no more, and then come secretly to Merristone to solve an intolerable situation with murder? I thought he had.

So far my thinking went and no further. I could not fit Hannah Wilson's death into the picture. Ned Havens had good reason to hate and fear the mistress, but he had nothing against the maid. No sensible motive to explain Hannah's murder occurred to me. Hannah menaced no one.

Yet we had found her body.

It was Valerie Maple who had seemingly vanished from the earth. At 5:30 on Friday afternoon she has been in the kitchen, and thereafter she had disappeared. Disappeared utterly and completely, and left no trace of her passing. For 16 months she had lived among us, and now was gone. Her house was gone, her harp was gone, her fantastic wardrobe. The lily locket alone remained as tangible evidence that the Merristone Enigma had existed five short days ago.

Numb and dazed, I stood beside the table and the lamp, staring at the locket in my hand. Scattered on the floor were the shirts and shoes, the emptied Gladstone bag. On the mantel behind me a clock struck two sweet notes.

I stirred and sighed.

At that instant a soft footfall sounded in the foyer. I'd purposely left the door ajar. But someone had entered Blake House without my noticing. It was neither Al nor Frank.

The tiptoed steps came closer. Slowly the door began to open. Simultaneously it struck me that Ned Havens might have shaken off pursuit, reversed himself, and returned to regain his property. My hair rose on end. I made an involuntary attempt to conceal the locket, just as the door opened wide. Belton Weaver stepped noiselessly into the library.

Chapter Thirty:
THE FAMILY SECRET

Across the book-lined room, Belton and I gazed at each other. It had not occurred to me that Belton might have reasons of his own for investigating Blake House, or for suspecting Selby's motive in sending Ruth away. The surprise was mutual. Certainly Belton hadn't expected to find me in possession. Under other circumstances, his confounded expression might have been amusing. But there was something distinctly grim about it.

Eventually I found my voice. "Well," I said, at once relieved and irritated at my own relief, "what are you doing here? You scared me half to death."

Belton's expression changed. He glimpsed the scattered clothing, the initialed Gladstone bag. And then he saw the locket dangling in my fingers. In less than a second he had crossed the room, and seized my shoulder. His face was white with anger.

"Where is he?"

"Who?"

"Ned Havens! I know he's been hiding here, that Selby hid him. I guessed when Ruth was packed off tonight."

I had the evidence conveniently arranged. Belton pounced upon the Pullman stub and Selby's note; he grabbed the dangling locket. His conclusions were as swift as mine, although somewhat different. He seemed to blame me for the fact that Ned Havens wasn't present. "What have you done with him?"

"Nothing," I said coldly. "Please let go my shoulder. You're hurting me."

"First you'll tell me where Ned Havens is. You've got his bag and clothes. You had the locket. He's been here. Where is he now?"

"I wish I knew. He got away. Banged the door and ran outside. Al was in the cellar, Frank was on the lawn. I hope that they—"

"You hope they find a safer place to hide him this time. I don't doubt that, my dear."

Openmouthed, I stared at him.

"I've come to take a hand in this!" cried Belton, and used his hand to grip my shoulder harder. "I know you stiff-necked, stubborn Blakes. To save the family from scandal, to keep the truth from coming out and save Mildred's face, you'd let Selby rot in jail and my daughter break her heart. Well, I'm not so inclined. I'm not proud in that particular way. Where has Al taken his uncle now? Out to Mildred's, I suppose. Or is he trying to smuggle him out of town?"

I got mad myself. "Have you lost your good sense, Belton? Al's trying to catch Ned Havens, naturally. So is Frank. They mean to bring him back."

"Oh, do they?" Belton could hardly speak for rage. "You'll have to produce a more convincing story, my dear. Every one of you Blakes knew that Ned Havens was hiding here. Everyone knew except Ruth and me, and I had to guess. Selby put him here. He hid his uncle in this house, and went to jail rather than admit it. My son-in-law is a romantic fool who'd wreck himself and my daughter's happiness to conceal his family's ugly past."

That I did not deny. No doubt Belton took my silence as an admission of my own complicity. His eyes blazed into mine.

"But the rest of you are in it, too. You'd rather spare the feelings of your aunt and sustain the non-existent family honor, than solve a hideous mystery. The answer to these murders lies in Valerie Maple's past. Ned Havens belongs in that past. He's the keystone of it. He can tell us everything we need to know about what happened here in Merristone on Friday. Why? Because he's the likeliest suspect and has been from the first. You know that, don't you? And you knew he'd been in town since Friday morning!"

"No, no," I said. "You're mistaken, Belton. I didn't know. I only learned tonight."

"Mildred certainly knew."

"I don't believe that."

"I did know," said a quiet voice from the doorway.

We whirled around. I was beyond surprise. Numb and comprehending, I watched Aunt Mildred walk into the library with Sarah at her elbow. Her face was very pale but otherwise composed. She had reached a terrible decision that evening, had shed her tears in privacy and in privacy prepared herself for a revelation that must have been pure agony to a woman of her type and generation. Part of her composure was acting, but I daresay another part was character. It was Sarah who seemed in need of support, as she followed her mother to the nearest chair. Aunt Mildred sank into the chair, and only then did she close her eyes.

"You're quite right, Belton," she said in the quiet voice that was without vitality or life. "I did know Ned was in town. Selby knew, of course, that he was coming. He'd sent for him. I—I wasn't notified in advance. But I've known since Friday afternoon."

"Since Friday!"

"Harriet told me," said Aunt Mildred.

"Harriet!"

"Harriet Strings was at the railroad station on Friday morning," Sarah said, in a voice that shook with bitterness. "Investigating Mrs. Moran's harp case. She didn't even get a chance to see the harp case, but she saw something better. She saw my father get off the train, home again after an absence of twenty-five years. She notified my mother promptly, but no one troubled to tell me. I suppose I should have guessed that Harriet had a secret. It's been obvious enough."

At that, I suppose we might have guessed. In her self-appointed role as newsgatherer, Harriet Strings had long considered it her duty to meet practically all the local trains. Since Friday the town gossip had been bursting with importance, but none of us had bothered with poor old Harriet. Yet Harriet had seen Ned Havens at the instant of his arrival in Merristone; she had recognized and talked to him.

"Harriet," said Aunt Mildred, with some of her old vigor, "was all agog, of course. Being Harriet, she felt morally obliged to mix in other people's business. Anyhow, she took it upon herself to welcome Ned back to Merristone and to insist that I'd love to see him. She made an appointment for me that morning with the man who used to be my husband. I saw Ned at her house late that night."

"Late Friday night!" My mind was spinning, but Friday night came back in all its dreadful clarity. I understood why Aunt Mildred had not been aroused when we returned from the scene of the murder, why she had been undisturbed by the crashing mirror. She had been away from home, closeted at the Strings' menage with the man who used to be her husband.

But if those two had met late on Friday night, they met long after Hannah died.

"Hannah Wilson was dead when we met," Aunt Mildred said. "Dead for hours. Ned and I both knew, of course. You remember that Selby came to the Strings' to phone for the police."

Fascinated and bewildered, I stared at the woman seated in the worn old leather chair. Aunt Mildred sat straight as a poker, and only the trembling of her folded hands betrayed her. She was quite wonderful with her firm assumption that Ned Havens had needed to hear from Selby's lips the news that Hannah Wilson lay dead at the building site.

Momentarily it defeated Belton. I saw him clutch the locket as though he feared his evidence might take wings and fly away.

Aunt Mildred looked around. For the first time she became aware of the rifled Gladstone bag, the tumbled clothing. She started, frowned.

"What are you doing with Ned's things? Why isn't he here? I want to talk to him."

"You want to talk to him!" roared Belton, rousing from the spell that had held him silent. "So do we all. So do the police. He's run off."

"Oh, no," said Aunt Mildred definitely. "Oh, no. This time you are mistaken, Belton. If Ned had cared to run away, he'd have gone Friday night. We urged him to leave then. All of us."

"All of you!"

"Harriet and I. And Selby, of course. Selby particularly. Selby thought—"

"What?"

"Selby thought then, and so did Ned and I—maybe because we wanted to think it—that Valerie Maple had killed her maid. That she alone was guilty." Aunt Mildred's voice fell imperceptibly, grew strong again. "On Friday night there still seemed to be a chance of keeping the family out of it. Maybe I'm a proud and selfish woman. Certainly I'm a mistaken one. I wanted that chance, and Selby was—was fine and generous enough to want it for me. We hoped we could keep the—the old story dark. There was no chance at all, if Ned went to the police."

"If Ned Havens had gone to the police on Friday, our case would have been concluded then and there. He'd have been arrested."

"Unquestionably. But, believe me, Belton, that would not have solved the mystery. Ned himself has no idea what has become of Valerie Maple."

Belton glanced at the locket. Possibly he meant to suggest that Ned Havens in some miraculous way had contrived to kill Valerie Maple without a trace, spirit away her body and leave no sign behind. Possibly the explanation failed to satisfy him. He chose another tack.

"We all know what became of Hannah Wilson. She was murdered! We have got *her* body, and I am convinced—"

"Control yourself, Belton," said Aunt Mildred. "Those rages are bad for a man of your age and weight, and they don't help your thinking. Ned had nothing to do with Hannah Wilson. He wasn't even aware of the maid's existence, until he learned from Selby that she'd been clubbed to death. But he has some—some theory of the mystery and—"

She broke off and turned at the sound of footsteps in the foyer.

Al and Frank came into the library. Both men looked utterly exhausted.

"Ned Havens got away from us," Al said.

"I knew it!" cried Belton. "I knew it all along. We've got to head him off. We—"

"No," said Al, "no, the chase is over, Belton. Ned Havens has gone to the police station. Five minutes ago he went there and surrendered."

Chapter Thirty-one:
THE DAWNING TRUTH

Aunt Mildred was absolutely silent. She may have gone a little paler, but that was the only indication of what she must have felt at the realization that all the efforts at concealment had been futile, that Selby's sacrifice had accomplished nothing, that the old and ugly story of the past must come out.

Sarah uttered a short protesting cry, and stood on her feet. Tears filled her eyes, and, unashamed, she let them fall. I don't suppose that Sarah had ever missed the father she had never known, or felt the lack of a father until the moment she believed that she had lost her father forever. She said dully, "So it's finished and done with then. I suppose my father has confessed."

"I don't know, Sarah." Al dropped into a chair, and rubbed his hand across his forehead. "We saw him dash into the station, and that's all. Sheriff Blandish turned us from the door."

"I knew," said Sarah, "knew in my heart that he was guilty. I don't blame him either. If my father killed that woman and hid her body, I'm glad. If he killed Hannah too, he was driven to it. Valerie Maple is responsible for everything that happened. Morally responsible, I mean." She laughed hysterically, and the tears kept on falling from her eyes.

"Hush, dear." As Frank crossed the room, I saw his face. In that instant of her helplessness and despair, Sarah meant much more to him than I had ever dreamed. It was in his eyes, in the way he put his arms around her and drew her close. "Believe your mother, dear. I do. I believe that Ned Havens has been trying desperately to solve a mystery that he himself can't fathom. And I'm sure—don't ask me why I'm sure, but I am—that soon you'll know the truth. You've got a part of it now. I'm sure of that, too. Valerie Maple was morally responsible for everything that happened."

Frank's words comforted Sarah. They had small effect on Belton. Perhaps he was remembering Ruth, and what Selby's silence had cost his daughter, as he swept up the material evidence of Ned Havens's connection with Valerie Maple. He took the letter Selby had written his uncle, the Pullman ticket stub that showed when Ned Havens had arrived in Merristone. He added them to the locket that long ago a foolish man had hung around the neck of an abnormal and unbalanced woman. He even took the mud-stained shoes.

"The authorities will be wanting these," said Belton.

"Why don't you carry them to the station now?" suggested Aunt Mildred. "You seem to have taken charge of the case."

The irony did not affect him either. Belton remarked that Sheriff Blandish would be engaged, and gathered up his oddly assorted bundle and started immediately for Dr. Traphaven's. Sarah continued her silent weeping against Frank's shoulder. She didn't even raise her head when Belton left the library.

The rest of us, however, trailed him outside, along the trampled snow and toward the house next door. Belton made straight toward his objective, and Aunt Mildred stuck stubbornly at his heels as though she mistrusted his intentions as much as he mistrusted ours. But as we reached the sidewalk, Al paused and turned and glanced toward the dark huddle of the village business section. Most of Merristone had long since gone to bed. Selby's office was dark, the grocery stores, the bank, were hardly more than shadows. The all-night dog wagon had closed for lack of customers at eleven o'clock, as it always did. In the gloom the police station was a brilliant landmark, like a burning torch in an empty field. Lights blazed at every window, cut a path across the white deserted street. On the other side of the street, a dim bulb glowed outside the undertaking parlors where Hannah Wilson's murdered body lay.

Suddenly, Al's hand stiffened on my arm. Ahead the dim bulb had seemed to brighten. A light went on inside the undertaking establishment.

"They've taken him to see Hannah's body, Jane."

"Do you think he killed her?"

"God knows what I think. My thinking stopped making sense some days ago."

I had half expected that Dr. Traphaven would be at the station, too. He was at home, however. Indeed, the little doctor was seated in his study, among his lethal weapons, among his souvenirs of old and half-forgotten crimes, as though he were awaiting the arrival of our delegation. Actually, as I know now, he was awaiting the results of an experiment that Sheriff Blandish was conducting two short blocks away.

Already the doctor knew what the results of that particular experiment would be, because he had learned the answer to that part of our mystery which made its solution so incredibly difficult. Once that part was known, he was able to guess the rest. The truth was almost in the doctor's grasp when we walked into his study, but before he could be absolutely certain of his facts Dr. Traphaven had to receive a report from an institution in a western city, allow sufficient time for a search of yellowing files. Until then he intended to keep his own council. Quite without the knowledge of the Sheriff, Dr. Traphaven had decided to conduct an experiment of his own. Sure of his own essential rightness, sure too that Blandish would be furious, he sat awaiting the inevitable.

No hint of these conflicting thoughts showed in his manner. Dr. Traphaven greeted us courteously and without surprise, and listened politely while Belton summed up his own personal case against a man who had already surrendered.

At the conclusion, the doctor said mildly, "You might put that stuff of yours on the table, Mr. Weaver. We won't need any of it to prove Ned Havens's movements, or to show the part he's played in this case. Ned Havens has talked quite freely."

Belton was, for the moment, deflated. The doctor's eyes wandered to his telephone, and it seemed to me that he was listening. Then his gaze passed on to Aunt Mildred. "Of course," he said, still mildly, "a bad mistake was made when Ned Havens did not come to us on Friday."

Aunt Mildred was sitting very quietly, her hands folded in the familiar gesture upon her lap. Slowly she raised her eyes to meet the doctor's. "The mistake," she said, "was mine. If you're placing responsibility, Doctor, don't blame Ned, don't blame Selby. They were both protecting me in my own folly, sheltering me in an attitude of mind that has spoiled my life. What will people say? What will people think of me? Those are the considerations that have ruled me always."

Never had I heard Aunt Mildred admit to any fault. She was always right, and the world was wrong. A bitter smile curved her lips.

"How shall I explain myself? Because I'm a gossip, I've dreaded gossip. In order to preserve what I've called my pride, so I could hold up my head among my neighbors, I've been willing to resort to any subterfuge to hide an unpleasant, humiliating truth. All my life I've lived like that." She leaned over to the table and picked up the locket. With great effort she held it steady and stilled the trembling of her fingers. "Ned wanted to go to the police on Friday night, and I prevented him. I was afraid. Twenty-five years ago, when Valerie Maple poisoned her family, he wanted to go to the police. Again I stopped him. Again I was afraid."

Belton drew a long hissing breath. She turned cold, contemptuous eyes on him, and then looked around the silent room.

"I was afraid not for my husband, but for myself. Please understand that. Ned was not an accomplice in Valerie Maple's dreadful crime, and he could have proved his innocence had he been allowed to fight it through at the time. That woman had nothing to show against him. Nothing except that he was a male, and a fool. Ned could have told the police how he had been deceived and taken in, how he first met Valerie Maple in a Chicago park, playing with her children, how easily she convinced him she had a cruel husband, was an abused and loving mother—the maternal type!" Aunt Mildred's laugh rose high and, shattering, broke in the middle. "Ned could have told the Chicago authorities how he loved the small daughters Valerie Maple poisoned for insurance, how he spun tops with the little boy who survived. Oh, Ned could have proved his innocence before the world, but only if he publicly revealed the details of his acquaintance with a woman he misread completely, only if he dragged me in."

Again she looked at the locket. She pressed the catch and the locket opened. She read off the fatal foolish lines of writing.

"The locket was a birthday present," she said. "The inscription refers to the divorce that Ned offered to help Valerie Maple get from her 'cruel' husband. And only to that. Oh, I don't deny that this evil woman took hold of Ned's imagination, but even in the first flush of his—his infatuation she had no real hold on his heart." The proud head went higher. "My husband had no idea of breaking up his own family and divorcing me, for Valerie Maple's sake. There was no talk ever between those two of marriage. That was an invention of hers, too. Because it suited her purposes, she twisted a stupid, foolish flirtation into a real love affair."

"But you did divorce your husband," said Dr. Traphaven gently.

Aunt Mildred nodded, and in a low, almost whispered voice, went ahead. On the day the newspapers had first blazoned the name of Valerie Maple, her husband had come to her, needing the support and understanding that some wives gladly give. In her outraged virtue, Aunt Mildred had failed in both. She had insisted upon a divorce. She had demanded that Ned Havens keep his name and hers from being mentioned in the hideous poison scandal.

And he had met those hard conditions.

"Ned was foolish," said Aunt Mildred, "but I was wicked. By my own act, I gave him over into the power of an utterly unscrupulous woman.

Maybe I didn't see that then. But I should have seen, as Ned saw clearly, that it wasn't love of him which caused the Chicago tragedy. It was love of money. Valerie Maple was through with her family, and she wanted to benefit financially by the deaths of her husband and her children. That was her idea of freedom always—money."

"Money," said Dr. Traphaven in a soft, peculiar voice, "and power. Don't forget the power complex. Or the acting ability either. All three are important if you're to understand the riddle of the Merristone Enigma." Startled, I looked at him.

Belton paid no attention.

"This is all very interesting, Mildred," he said harshly. "Interesting and to the point. You've demonstrated very clearly how Valerie Maple held a Sword of Damocles over the head of all you Blakes. At any time she chose she could accuse Ned of complicity and reopen the old case, whatever the merits of her evidence. Selby danced to her tune, and so did Ned. But I'd particularly like to know how Ned got back that locket."

"He took it from the house on Copston Road."

"When?"

"Friday afternoon at six o'clock."

"You mean he took it from Valerie Maple. Are you saying she *gave* the locket to Ned?"

"No, Belton. By six o'clock the house was empty. Ned told me so, and I believe him. He expected to see Valerie Maple, but she was gone."

"Mrs. Maple was singularly elusive that afternoon," said Dr. Traphaven in the same peculiar tone.

"Al and I saw her at tea," I said.

"In a candle-lighted room. By the way," he said oddly, "was she wearing her famous veils?"

"No," I said, surprised.

"But the draperies were closely drawn, weren't they? The light was very poor."

"I suppose so. Yes," I said confusedly.

"Did Hannah serve you tea?"

"No."

"I thought not. I felt very sure that Hannah Wilson did not appear."

I became more confused than ever. "What's your point, Dr. Traphaven? Hannah was in the bedroom, listening to the radio."

"Was she?"

"So Mrs. Maple told us," I said stammeringly.

"Mrs. Maple was not a notoriously truthful woman. But she was surprisingly exclusive, wasn't she?" he said musingly. "She was dependent wholly on the company of her maid, yet the two were never seen in public together. Hannah did the shopping, and Mrs. Maple took her daily walks and otherwise stuck close at home. And even when she entertained at home, she didn't consider it necessary to have Hannah serve."

Belton got up from his chair. "I fail to understand, Doctor," he said impatiently, "how such trivialities concern the situation. We want to know who murdered Hannah Wilson. We also want to know what became of Valerie Maple."

"First," said Dr. Traphaven, with a curious smile, "it's necessary to realize how blind and stupid even sensible people sometimes are. How subject is the human mind to the reception of an illusion. It's been said that Valerie Maple was responsible for everything that happened. It's been shown that she was a subtle, cunning woman, contemptuous not only of the rights but of the intelligence of lesser folk, a woman with an inborn belief in her ability to playact and deceive. Do you follow me, Mr. Weaver?"

"Not exactly," stammered Belton. "Unless you mean her passing herself off as Veronica Moran."

"I mean much more than that. Valerie Maple deceived us in a more important way. She made us misread the evidence of our own eyes, misinterpret the evidence of our own ears. How? By an illusion, built up as deliberately and carefully as a conjurer's trick. When first she came to Merristone this cunning, subtle woman created this—this illusion for purposes of her own. Thus, she accomplished what she herself did not intend. With an illusion, Valerie Maple set the conditions of her own murder."

"Her murder!"

"Valerie Maple is dead," Dr. Traphaven said. "Our whole investigation has been based upon a great illusion. Ned Havens suspected it, wanted to set our thinking straight, but was too personally involved to come forward publicly. So he stayed in hiding, awaiting the results of a telegram—"

"What telegram?"

"The telegram," said Dr. Traphaven, "that Ned Havens sent in my name to the warden of the Chicago prison. The telegram concerning Hannah Wilson's fingerprints. I sent a copy of her fingerprints out west on Monday, but I didn't hear the results until tonight when I phoned the prison. Hannah Wilson was listed in their records. She—"

At that moment the telephone rang shrilly. The doctor leaped to answer it. I received a vague impression that the call wasn't the call he was expecting, that he was startled and surprised. I know that after he said "hello" he listened in silence. But just then the doorbell rang, and two people walked into the study.

One of them was Sheriff Blandish. The other was Ned Havens.

Aunt Mildred stood on her feet. The doctor kept on listening at the telephone, but the rest of us turned around in our chairs.

The study became very quiet.

I stared at Sheriff Blandish and the stranger at his elbow. I had taken no account of the changes that would be wrought by the passage of 25 years. The man who stood beside the Sheriff bore small resemblance to the familiar portrait, the photograph in the lily locket. The thick black hair was almost white, the dashing mustache was gone, the bold dark eyes were sick and glazed with fever. Ned Havens looked incredibly ill, incredibly old. He glanced dazedly toward Aunt Mildred, started to speak, was seized by a paroxysm of coughing.

"Forgive me," he said. "I—I'm feeling unwell. Shock, I suppose. I've just seen the body."

"You're ill," said Aunt Mildred fiercely. "They've no right to torture you. You didn't kill Hannah Wilson."

"I didn't see Hannah's body," said Ned Havens, and added with the querulousness of a sick man, "Hasn't the doctor told you yet? There isn't any Hannah Wilson. There never was. The woman lying at the undertaking parlor, dressed up like a maid and with her skull crushed in, is Valerie Maple."

Chapter Thirty-two:
A VERY ESSENTIAL MURDER

Very quietly Dr. Traphaven replaced the telephone. He turned to us, and sighed. "Thus," he said, "the great illusion crashes. Valerie Maple built it up, and in a very real sense the illusion killed her. Valerie Maple appeared before the world in two separate guises; this actress who found no glory on the stage triumphed as an actress, and that very triumph led to her undoing. In the end," he finished grimly, "the double woman died a single death. Died as she deserved to die."

Sheriff Blandish scowled, and Belton opened his mouth to speak, and thought better of it and was silent. Aunt Mildred went over and sat down beside Ned Havens, and hesitated and then slipped her hand into his. As for Al and me, we stared blankly into space.

Merristone had been deceived and taken in. But he and I had been the most deceived. More than anybody else we had misread the evidence of our own eyes, misinterpreted the evidence of our own ears. Valerie Maple had never appeared in public with her maid. Hannah had never appeared in public with her mistress. No one in the village had ever met them both, or been able to observe the subtle likeness that must have existed all the time between the mistress and her maid. No one except Al and myself.

We had seen and talked to Valerie Maple, had drunk tea with her in a shadowy, candle-lighted room. We had seen and talked to Hannah, had stood with her on Copston Road on a gray and sunless winter day.

So skillfully contrived had been the illusion, so cunningly conceived that I could almost see them still. It was as though they were walking toward me from opposite corners of the crowded study—the mistress and the maid. It was as though Valerie Maple was gliding forward now on her high stilt heels, borne along by a wave of exotic perfume, her bracelets and bangles tinkling, her dyed black hair bound in a flowing veil, another veil flung across a rouged and thickly powdered face. Hannah was clumping forward too, just as she had used to, do, weighted down by shoes as big and clumsy as a man's; straggly locks of iron gray hair escaping from a masculine hat and framing a scrubbed, unpowdered face, eyes blank and distant behind heavy spectacles, one hand cupped behind an ugly earphone.

"They were wholly dissimilar," I said.

"Of course," said the doctor. "In the dissimilarity of this maid and mistress, in their outrageous difference from one another, lay the success of the illusion. Valerie Maple was cold and callous, but she wasn't stupid. In point of fact," he said with a sudden, subtle change of manner, "I've got an interesting notion on that point. You might like to hear it. Valerie Maple went straight to nature for her double masquerade."

The group was tense, on edge with nerves, but suddenly Dr. Traphaven seemed unaware of it. With all of us burning to ask questions, with Ned Havens prepared to tell us all he knew, with Sheriff Blandish obviously restive and impatient, the doctor began to make a speech. The speech was nothing more nor less than an academic dissertation on camouflage in nature. Dr. Traphaven mentioned at some length the brilliant tropical butterflies who pass unnoticed in the jungle because of their very brilliance. Valerie Maple, in the guise of the harpist, had made of herself a butterfly, so conspicuous in her outlandish clothes that no one had wondered at the brightly colored veils that always covered her face, or wondered if the obviously dyed hair might be a wig. The character of Hannah, he went on to say, was at the opposite extreme, copied from the wood owl, brown and inconspicuous, fading into the bark of the trees that are its habitat. But Hannah was obliged to appear daily in the village, and so the thick spectacles and the earphone had been added. The spectacles distorted the dark eyes. The earphone logically explained Hannah's inability to hear questions she didn't wish to answer, and the flat uninflected voice of the deaf in which she always spoke.

Dr. Traphaven then remarked that the cry of the wood owl was deceptive, too. It wasn't like him to be wordy and diffuse, or pointless either. In my restlessness, I began to wonder. It was almost as though Dr. Traphaven deliberately was wasting time. The Sheriff stirred impatiently.

"Of course," said Dr. Traphaven quickly, "I should have guessed that Valerie Maple had invented Hannah for the purpose of the insurance fraud. It was obvious enough."

"Not to me," said Al. "Why, when we were drinking tea with her, and Hannah was playing the radio back in the master bedroom, only, of course," he paused, confused, "it wasn't Hannah. There wasn't any Hannah to listen to the radio."

"Mrs. Maple had turned on the radio before your arrival. A simple enough device to strengthen your belief in the existence of a Hannah."

"But someone turned off the radio while we were there. Someone went out the kitchen door, and drove away in Hannah's car, and then a little later on drove back again. Janey and I saw the roadster when it turned into the drive the second time."

It all came back to me with such vivid clarity that I might actually have been walking along Copston Road again, with Al's hand in mine, walking rapidly away from the Moran house and toward Aunt Mildred's and our dinner party. Once again as our hurrying feet took a familiar turn, we hesitated and glanced back across wide and darkening country fields and saw a battered roadster slide into the drive beside a small, square house, half a mile away.

Once again the lights inside the house went out, just as the roadster stopped outside.

Suddenly I understood why Valerie Maple had quit her home in such frantic haste, and in the guise of Hannah appeared early to keep her appointment at the building site. I knew why she had been so anxious to get rid of Al and me, and with what incredible speed she had changed her clothes and her identity, after our departure, because all at once I knew the precise moment she had left her dwelling. When the lights inside the house went out, she was gone. I could almost hear her flying footsteps, hear the front door slam as the woman who was both maid and mistress left the house on Copston Road forever. Valerie Maple had known who turned off the radio and drove her car away, and she hadn't wished to meet that person, either as Veronica Moran or as the servant of Veronica Moran.

"Who was the person in the roadster?" Al asked quietly, and then answered his own question. "It was someone who knew Valerie Maple very well. Well enough to enter through the kitchen and leave that way, and take liberties with her radio and with her car. It was someone who wanted to see Valerie Maple very badly, but didn't want to see Jane and me."

"But, Al—"

"With the radio turned off, our voices could be heard in the kitchen, Janey. Our voices warned the visitor who was so well acquainted with his hostess that she was not alone, that he must go away. And then when the car came back the second time, the hostess had got away herself. I think I understand her haste. Because I think the meeting Valerie Maple was so anxious to avoid took place later in the evening. About an hour later."

Everybody in the study sat very still, like a group of waxworks arranged in a museum. The surroundings, too, were like those in a museum. The cabinets filled with winking weapons, the plaster cast of the shoes that had once trapped a homicidal maniac, the sashweight that had hanged a woman and her lover. Against that lethal background Belton sat, with an unlighted cigarette raised halfway to his lips. Frozen and immobile, Aunt Mildred sat across the room from him with her hand in the hand of the man who used to be her husband, and he was frozen and immobile, too. Even Sheriff Blandish had stopped his restless twisting, and Dr. Traphaven had ceased his pacing of the floor.

In the strange, tense hush. Al spoke again. "I think," he said, "that the person who drove the car away brought it back, was able to arrange a meeting later. I think Valerie Maple was traced to the building site. She was all dressed up like Hannah, but this person could see through whatever masquerade she assumed, because he knew her so very well. Isn't that what you think, Doctor?"

Dr. Traphaven made no reply. Again I had the feeling that he was deliberately wasting time, was stubbornly unwilling to be pressed or hurried. I knew it when at last he spoke.

"Let's stick to Valerie Maple," he said, with soft insistence, "and the double masquerade. It looked like magic but it wasn't really. I had every chance to suspect the truth." He frowned as though at his own stupidity. "The apparent lack of Valerie Maple's fingerprints around her home was certainly evidence that one woman, and one alone, had occupied the house on Copston Road. I should have been bright enough in the beginning to check that single set of fingerprints with the prison, where they would have been instantly identified. It did not occur to me, until someone else"—he glanced toward Ned Havens—"put the idea in my head. My own misconception, my belief in the maid and mistress, was so firmly fixed that I accepted the only fingerprints in the cottage as those of a real Hannah Wilson, which meant of course I also had to accept that Valerie Maple had lived sixteen months in a six-room house, wiping up her fingerprints as she went along. Fantastic!"

Again the Sheriff stirred impatiently, but the doctor spun on his heel and addressed Ned Havens.

"By the way, you might explain your reasoning when you wired the prison warden asking whether Hannah Wilson had a record. You knew of course that the warden would ask me to send on her fingerprints, and that those fingerprints would expose the double masquerade. But how did you happen to guess the truth?"

"How indeed?" said Belton, in an abrupt unpleasant way. He, too, turned to stare at the wretched figure, huddled beside Aunt Mildred. "In my opinion your conduct still needs considerable explaining. Your helpfulness was rather late in coming, wasn't it?"

Aunt Mildred sent Belton a cold and angry look, but Ned Havens didn't even raise his head. "Very late," he said dully. "I've been a coward and a fool, Belton. But if you're thinking I'm a murderer, you're mistaken. I haven't got the guts. I had every reason to do away with Valerie Maple. I've hated her for twenty-five years, hated her from the moment I found out what she was."

Ned Havens shivered as though he were in the grip of a deathly chill. He was in the cold and crushing grip of memory, and for a moment none of us were there and he was facing by himself the sterile memory of old mistakes, long past and not to be undone.

"Maybe you can't understand"—the tired, sick voice slowed down and almost stopped—"how a bored and restless man, dissatisfied with the restrictions of home, might meet a pretty woman playing with her children in a park, and think that she was warm and soft and tender, and needed him to advise and help her out. But surely you can understand the feelings of such a man when he woke up and discovered he'd wrecked his life to carry on a flirtation with a murderess. A woman who poisoned her husband and three helpless little children to prove something or other. Her own importance, maybe. That meant more to Valerie than the money. Much more. In the last analysis, nothing ever really mattered to her except the power she could wield over the destiny of others."

With that, Ned Havens raised his head, and looked around with dulled and feverish eyes.

"Oh, I hated Valerie enough. She's hounded me for years, kept me constantly reminded that she could always hall me into court on a charge trumped up with a few silly letters, a locket and a foolish piece of composition that could be strained into a different meaning. If I'd had the courage I would have killed Valerie months ago, when she first came to me and demanded that I help her settle here in Merristone as Veronica Moran, a retired and respectable musician. I didn't credit her tale that she was sick of the life she'd lived, that she longed to settle as a peaceful, law-abiding country resident. But unless I helped, she threatened, as she'd so often threatened, to go straight to the newspapers and make it tough for—for—"

"For me," said Aunt Mildred fiercely. "For me and for Sarah. You'd have been glad to face the scandal and publicity, to have the old case reopened so you could prove your innocence. All you ever wanted was to free yourself of that woman."

"That's neither here nor there, Mildred. These people want to hear what I really did. Not what I could or should have done. I wrote Selby, sponsoring Valerie Maple as Veronica Moran. I even financed her stay, by—by request of course. It left me with nothing for myself, but I sent Valerie $500 every month."

"You financed the insurance policy!"

"I didn't know it," he said in the spent and burned-out voice. "Naturally I knew nothing of the fraud she contemplated. Valerie took care I shouldn't know how she meant to involve the family by dragging Selby into an insurance plot, again by threatening to reveal my past, my connection with her long ago. Blackmail was as natural to her as breathing. And she knew her man. Selby would go to any lengths to avoid hurting Mildred. Of course, Selby was foolish too. He tried to handle the matter himself, by appeals to the woman he thought was Hannah Wilson, the prospective victim. At last, and too late, he sent for me. I had a frantic letter, explaining the situation as Selby understood it, advising me that Valerie Maple was attempting to insure and kill her maid. I came immediately to Merristone. I came," said Ned Havens, "with one thought in mind."

"Yes," said the doctor gently.

"I came," Ned Havens said, "with murder in my heart. I let Selby believe I could persuade Valerie to drop the idea of the insurance fraud, but I knew I couldn't. With murder in my heart, I went to the house on Copston Road. I'd have killed Valerie if she'd been there, killed her with my bare hands and done the world a service. I had no opportunity. It was six o'clock, and the house was empty."

And then Ned Havens described his own sensations as he walked through the deserted house. On every hand were signs of the haste with which the dwelling had been abandoned—the flickering candles, the glass of tea upset on the floor, the fire burning on the hearth. There had been something vaguely menacing about the complete desertion of the place. In the master bedroom, however, he had found the locket. That had seemed almost too good to be true.

"Valerie wasn't careless with anything she valued, and she had every reason to value that locket! Later on, I realized how queer the whole thing was. You see, the locket was lying in the master bedroom with a heap of clothes."

"Clothes?"

"Bright crimson draperies and veils, and stuff. There was even a wad of dyed black hair on the dressing table, a switch, I believe women used to call it. But Valerie had reached the age where she might need a switch, or so I thought at the time. It wasn't until afterward that I began to wonder. When I heard about the costume Valerie was supposed to have worn when she ran away, I remembered the false hair on the dressing table and those clothes that were scattered around the bedroom at six o'clock."

"Ah!" A light flashed in Sheriff Blandish's eye. "I begin to see. I do indeed! The clothes were in the bedroom at six o'clock, dropped where Valerie Maple left them when she rushed into the Hannah costume and started for the building site. Later the clothing disappeared. When the body was discovered, the murderer must have realized—"

At that point, with all of us leaning forward in our chairs, Dr. Traphaven took a hand again. Once again he interjected a note of puzzling irrelevance, that seemed calculated somehow. "Let's not go off on tangents," he said, and proceeded to go off on a tangent himself. "I'd like to explain the postmortem I did on the body. I should have known then that Hannah Wilson and Valerie Maple were one and the same. You'll recall that I discovered deposits of arsenic in the hair and nails."

"How would that be of any help?" Al asked uncertainly, puzzled by the doctor's manner. "Was Valerie Maple dosing herself with arsenic?"

"Valerie Maple was an arsenic eater," Dr. Traphaven said gravely. "At her trial years ago, she publicly admitted that she used arsenic for her complexion. But I'm convinced she used arsenic, had used it for years, as other addicts use morphine and cocaine, because they cannot face themselves. With arsenic she could sustain the delusion of her own supreme importance in the scheme of things, her superiority over other people, her brutal lack of feeling where others were concerned."

Sheriff Blandish lost his scant remaining patience. "If you'll just stop talking, Doc," he said irritably, "I'd like to remind you that we're not holding a public forum on the character of Valerie Maple. Our investigation is still in progress. Someone killed that woman; whatever her faults might have been she was murdered. I mean to round up everybody that's involved and—"

"That's quite unnecessary."

Blandish turned red. "Unnecessary is it! My job is to solve this case, that's your job, too. All the other participants are needed here, and at once. Selby and his wife. Sarah Havens and Mr. Phipps. Jane and Al, Ned and Mildred and Belton, we've got already. I want the group complete. All nine of them. Maybe you're still wandering in a fog, but I know this much. The killer is among those nine."

"I don't doubt it," said the doctor.

"Well, then—"

"Nevertheless the group is large enough. Take my word for it, Sheriff. We've gone beyond the need of rush."

Abruptly Dr. Traphaven's unnatural vivacity faded. Slowly he walked the length of his study toward his desk, past the crowded cabinets, past the photographs of murderers who had long since paid the penalty for their crimes, past the pedestal that held the ghostly plaster model of the shoes.

Slowly he sat down at his desk.

"No," he said, "we needn't rush, Blandish. We aren't pressed for time. You see, I know who the killer is. I've known some little while."

Sheriff Blandish sprang to his feet. The rest of us didn't stir. In my fascination with the unfolding drama, I had almost forgotten that a murder investigation was still in progress, that an evil woman had been done to death. Now, sharply and sickeningly, I was reminded.

The guilty person was one of nine, one of the nine I loved most.

"Sit down, Blandish," the doctor said wearily. "You may as well. Perhaps this seems unconventional, but I'll take the responsibility for it. I assure you the delay no longer matters. At any rate, I'm afraid we'll have to do it my way."

"Your way!"

"In order to understand the murder, the motives that led up to it, in order to be prepared, you need to understand the woman who deserved to die. The whole story's there—in the complicated, complex and ruthless character of Valerie Maple. The murder itself is quite simple."

"Simple!"

"Believe me, yes. Valerie Maple laid out a perfect crime, and the perfect crime turned back on her. Hers was the thinking, the plotting and the planning. Never did a victim provide more assistance to her executioner, which is what this killer was. I don't suppose Valerie Maple realized, until the very end, that she had made her own death essential."

Sitting there in the doctor's study, listening to his somber voice, I saw how essential was the death of Valerie Maple to the happiness and well-being of us all. Every one of us had been involved in varying degrees because of her determination to commit a perfect crime; every one of us had suffered at her hands. The evil forces that she had set in motion seemed to rise before me; the dark structure she had carefully and tediously built up stood forth in all its naked ugliness. Valerie Maple had invented Hannah; she had arranged to insure a woman who did not exist, first by blackmailing Ned Havens, and then by threatening Selby to disgrace the family through his uncle; she had produced a skeleton to burn in an incendiary fire also arranged by herself.

"She only overlooked one thing." A curious look that was close to satisfaction crossed the doctor's face. "She overlooked the fact that the perfection of her creation was a danger to the author. She had invented two women. If Valerie Maple died as Hannah, there was an excellent chance that Hannah's 'missing' employer would receive the blame, and that the killer would escape. Believe me there would have been justice in the situation, had it worked out that way. There was justice in the blind and burning hatred that destroyed this double woman. The person who killed Valerie Maple, killed her in a fit of dreadful rage and frenzy, was the one who had cause to hate her the most."

It was at that moment that we heard the shot from Blake House. A distant shot, but clear, distinct and sharp, as only a gunshot can be. And following the shot, a wild and agonized scream came clearly, too.

Before the scream was ended, Al had wrenched open the study door and was racing down the hall and out into the night, with the rest of us pouring after him. Only Dr. Traphaven remained behind, probably because he knew in advance what we would find. He must have known since the telephone call, when he had been asked for an hour of delay. The telephone call had come from Blake House.

I shall never forget the sight that met our eyes when we burst into the library there. Frank was sitting on Selby's worn old leather sofa, with an almost peaceful smile on his face. A thin stream of blood was trickling down his forehead, and the "borrowed" gun was in his hand. Sarah crouched on her knees beside him, no longer screaming. With a handkerchief she was trying futilely to assuage the mortal wound.

"But why? Why? Why?" I can still hear Al's horrified and uncomprehending question. "Why should it have been Frank who killed Valerie Maple? He didn't even know her."

I can still hear Sarah's answer. "He knew her better than any of us, and hated her more. Don't you understand? Oh, of course you don't, but Dr. Traphaven understands. Frank's name is Maple, too. Valerie Maple was his stepmother."

"His stepmother!"

"Frank was the little boy," said Sarah, with the tears streaming from her eyes, "who escaped her poison years ago. His father and his little half-sisters died but Frank lived on. He lived on but in the end, even after she was dead, his stepmother killed him."

Chapter Thirty-three:
THE END OF THE STORY

A week passed before Sarah was able to talk to us, and fill in the remaining details of the story that had begun with the greed and devouring vanity of a vicious woman, and ended in pain and tragedy. On that last evening, Frank, perceiving that his own exposure was inevitable, had telephoned from Blake House to Dr. Traphaven. He had then confessed both to his true identity and to the crime, and in return had asked for and been granted an hour of time. During that hour, while all of us were seated in the study next door, Frank had walked up and down Selby's library and talked to Sarah. He had told Sarah everything, not to justify himself because he felt wholly justified in his own act, but rather to explain what needed no explaining—that he had never meant to implicate any one of us.

Indeed Frank's deepest motive in the murder, a motive that went beyond his bitter personal hatred, was the salvation of our family. Put in its simplest form, Frank had wanted to save us from the menace represented by his stepmother. His personal safety had been secondary, an afterthought. From the beginning, from the moment it had occurred to Frank Phipps Maple that he might throw the blame for Hannah's murder on her "missing" employer, he had placed small hopes in carrying out his part of the illusion.

The single set of fingerprints in the house on Copston Road had been a constant threat. Frank had been able to wipe the telltale prints from the tea things, and for a while we had been misled by the apparent absence of Valerie Maple's fingerprints from her own dwelling. Once Hannah's identity was questioned, however, once her fingerprints were sent west, the truth inevitably came out.

Valerie Maple's fingerprints were on file at the Illinois prison, and fingerprints do not lie.

Frank hadn't known that anyone was interested in Hannah Wilson's fingerprints or that a photostat of them had already been mailed, until the moment he slipped behind the glassed-in cabinet. But then he overheard the call that Dr. Traphaven made to the prison warden. When the doctor requested that the photostat of Hannah's fingerprints be compared immediately with those of Valerie Maple, the listening man had known that he was lost.

It was then that Frank had borrowed the gun from Dr. Traphaven's collection.

"There was no chance after that," Sarah said. "When Dr. Traphaven discovered that Hannah and Valerie Maple were the same, he knew everything. It would have been easy to find out who Frank really was. In point of fact, the doctor guessed. Frank was the only one among us without visible connections or relatives. When Frank telephoned, Dr. Traphaven was waiting for a report from a Chicago orphanage."

"Orphanage?"

"When his stepmother went to prison, Frank had no one left. He—he was shipped off to an orphanage. Out of mercy those people changed his name to protect him from the other children."

When he left the orphanage, came east and single-handedly built up a successful business, Frank Phipps had no reason to resume the notorious name of Maple, or to acknowledge relationship with the stepmother that he hated. I saw that clearly. But it seemed strange to me that with the world so large, Frank should have run across our family, that Al should have become his partner.

"Frank sought out Al deliberately, Jane. We'd suffered through Valerie Maple too, and in the beginning I think he must have wanted to make up for it. And then"—Sarah's firm voice broke—"we began to take the place of the family that he'd lost long ago. Frank could not foresee of course that his stepmother would show up here in Merristone."

Sarah got to her feet and walked blindly to the window. We were gathered in Aunt Mildred's kitchen that winter afternoon, and there were only five of us. Selby and Ruth, joyful in their own release from travail, stayed away. Belton was not invited. But Al and I were there, and Ned Havens sat in Aunt Mildred's favorite rocker, wrapped in her best blankets. Aunt Mildred had changed that week, and for the better. She made no effort to press her daughter's confidence.

At last Sarah turned around. In her eyes still lay the shadow of that last horrible interview, when she had heard from Frank's own lips why and how he had killed his stepmother.

"Despite my background and my heritage," Frank had said to her, with inexpressible bitterness, "I soon found out I wasn't clever enough to commit a successful murder, even with the plan all set up for me. So many things went wrong. I made so many, many mistakes. Some from ignorance of what the situation really was, and some because I didn't share my stepmother's gifts at plotting."

It was of these errors and mistakes that Sarah told us. When a veiled, flamboyant stranger had first settled in Merristone, Frank had actually supposed that Valerie Maple was living somewhere in the Middle West. For years, after the collapse of her brief theatrical career, his stepmother had haunted him. He could hardly move in to a neighborhood before she turned up, demanding money. His relief was great when she informed him she was leaving New York City, so she could spend her declining years "out in Illinois." After that, for many months, he had heard nothing.

On the September day that the four of us walking down Copston Road had encountered the Merristone Enigma, and her famous cats, Frank had learned for the first time with dismay and shock that Valerie Maple had not traveled to Illinois, but was residing in our village. He had gone immediately to the house on Copston Road and requested an explanation. His stepmother had met him with the same story she had given to Ned Havens; she was wearied of her past and of her life, and longed for peace and a new existence. Illinois had too many tragic memories. Frank had little reason to believe her. Curiously enough, we Blakes had lulled his suspicions, caused him to put reluctant credence in the tale. All of us, Selby included, described a woman who was a virtual recluse, a woman whom none of us had even met. A woman who was so shy and retiring, so reticent of society, that she even sent her maid to do the shopping.

"Frank believed in Hannah too," Sarah said. "He believed in a Hannah that he hadn't seen. But then Frank saw Hannah with Selby in New York. And again he recognized his stepmother."

Frank still had no idea of why Valerie Maple was masquerading as two separate women, or why the "maid" had come to New York with Selby, but he didn't need to guess that the purpose behind the double masquerade was evil. That much he knew. When he brought Sarah to Merristone on the fatal Friday and dropped her at Selby's office, Frank drove his car down Copston Road in a fury of anger and suspicion. He parked at a little distance from the Moran cottage, approached on foot, and slipped through the back door to confront his stepmother.

And then, when he turned off the blaring radio, he heard Al and me talking in the living room.

"Frank nearly went insane at that," said Sarah. "When you started toward the kitchen, Janey, he nearly stayed and faced it out. But—but then he didn't. He jumped into Hannah's car and drove away, and when he came back five minutes later he'd missed his chance. Valerie

Maple was already gone. And he didn't know where she'd gone, or why."

So Frank had picked up his own car again and driven to Aunt Mildred's, arriving barely in advance of Al and me, and only because we'd made the trip on foot. I remembered how we'd found him that winter evening, walking restlessly up and down among the family portraits. Frank had seemed nervous and disturbed, but neither Al nor I had dreamed of the storm of hatred and suspicion that was gathering in his brain. Neither of us dreamed he was turning over feverish, footless plans to locate his stepmother, and demand the truth of her. In the end no plan at all was necessary.

When Frank started back downtown for Sarah, and once again drove along the winding twists of Copston Road, lights were shining from the building site. There were no curtains at the windows. Frank had glanced inside. He saw a woman seated on a backless chair, pulled up before a crude, rough table. It was Valerie Maple in the masquerade of Hannah Wilson.

"She still had a chance to live," Sarah said. "She could have put Frank off maybe, told another of those lies of hers. I think she must have been afraid of him at first, because she'd tried very hard not to see him. But when Frank came storming into the dining room, when she realized she was caught, she changed. She decided to brazen the situation out. She sat there, and looked up at him, looked him straight in the eye, and then she told him—"

"The truth," whispered Al. "By God, she told him everything herself. Why she'd settled in Merristone, what she'd done and what she proposed to do that very night. I can almost hear her boasting of her own cunning, glorying in it; she still held the trump cards...."

"So she thought," said Sarah. "Anyhow, she defied Frank to interfere, laughed at him when he began to plead with her. If he dared upset the insurance fraud, she promised to create a scandal that Merristone would never forget. Her own reputation didn't matter; she had none to lose. But how about my father and Selby? How about Frank himself? After all, she reminded him, a good many people would be interested to learn that Frank Phipps was hiding his own connection with a convicted murderess."

It was then that Frank saw Selby's cane lying on the plaster table. Sarah did not describe the brief and terrible scene that followed. It wasn't necessary to tell us that Frank had been too blind with rage and hatred when he seized the cane to identify the weapon in his hand, or even to remember that he was in the dining room of our cottage.

When realization came, when Frank saw his stepmother lying dead, when he recognized the splintered stick and became aware of his surroundings, he had felt no grief but only horror lest all of us should share in the consequences of his crime, and suffer from it. At that moment he would have gone straight to Sheriff Blandish, had it been a matter of himself alone. But we Blakes were already hopelessly involved. The victim herself had seen to that. If Frank confessed to the murder of his stepmother, revealed that she had died at his hands while masquerading as her own maid, the authorities would demand the whole story. Nothing could be withheld.

Thus began the first of Frank's blundering efforts to follow in the footsteps of his stepmother, and to playact and deceive. He had attempted to move the body from the cottage, only to be interrupted by Selby's arrival. It was as he fled from the cottage, as he hurled the spoiled and broken cane into the nearest snowbank intending to return for it later, that he perceived the only chance to save us all. If he could successfully reverse Valerie Maple's own plot, he might make the authorities believe that Hannah's employer had committed the murder and run away.

When Frank resumed the journey that had been interrupted by murder, when he drove on to the village and picked up Sarah and brought her back to Aunt Mildred's, his mind was quite made up. It was not until he sat down with us to that wretched dinner that he had been struck by a fatal flaw in his own reasoning. If the authorities accepted the reality of Veronica Moran, if they believed she had run away, they would immediately inquire into her costume. The clothes she had worn at tea that afternoon, the bright crimson draperies and floating veils, the switch of dyed black hair, all those things were lying scattered about the master bedroom. Hanging in the adjacent closet, complete and intact, was the remainder of her wardrobe.

"Frank had to get those clothes," said Sarah in a faltering voice, "before the Moran cottage was investigated by the police. When we decided to visit the building site, he was desperate. Unless we were delayed there, the whole plan went to pieces. So Frank—"

Again she didn't need to tell us that in his desperation Frank had thrown away the car keys, watched his opportunity and run across the field to the Moran cottage. She didn't need to say that he had entered the cottage burdened with Selby's cane, or to mention his panic and despair when Al and Ruth and I made our own completely unanticipated visit. By the narrowest of margins, his arms full of the floating draperies and veils, he had managed to retreat as far as the porch and take refuge behind the garment rack.

But Ruth had glimpsed the cane, and ventured forth to investigate. Too much was at stake, too much had already been risked, to lose the gamble then. All Frank knew as he crouched behind the frail shield of the garment rack and heard slow, approaching footsteps, was that he faced instant discovery. He hadn't even known that Ruth was the other person on the porch, until he struck her. Had he known, I am convinced Frank would have given up the struggle and that our mystery would have been solved then and there. But it would also have been solved had we realized the significance of Ruth's insistence that she had smelled real perfume, felt real draperies brush her face.

Anxious only to forget that part of the story, I spoke in awkward haste, spoke for all of us. "But look, Sarah. Why did Frank tear up the master bedroom, make such a mess of it? Was that just meant to be confusing?"

"Only partly, Janey. Frank tied Gog and Magog in the closet to draw attention to the *one* costume that was missing. He wanted the police to be convinced that the 'missing woman' was dressed in the crimson. Still, the cats weren't supposed to be too noticeable, and so—"

"But he went through the desk."

Her face sobered. "Valerie Maple had hung on to personal things. There wasn't time to examine it, see if there was anything pointing to the insurance fraud, or to Selby or my father. Frank simply swept up the lot, took everything that might be dangerous. He destroyed most of the stuff, but of course he—he used those circulars."

I started to ask why, and then I realized why Frank had wanted the circulars to be discovered, why he had been so anxious that he had rattled the latch of our bedroom door to draw us to the spot where he had planted them. By disclosing the fact that Veronica Moran was an impostor, by leading us to Valerie Maple's past, he gave the "missing" woman substance, made her real. He showed her as a woman capable of a brutal murder.

More important, by focusing all our interest upon Valerie Maple, Frank had hoped to distract the attention of the police from Hannah. Here he had succeeded too well. Sheriff Blandish had obligingly lost interest in Hannah, but he had searched for Valerie Maple to the point where her escape became incredible. So incredible that everybody began to believe that she, too, had been murdered.

And most people believed that Selby had killed both the maid and the mistress.

Frank had one hope left, and again it was an adaptation of the earlier plot. He knew where his mother had secreted the harp case and the skeleton, the piles of dried old shingles, because she had told him. If he could set fire to the Moran cottage, burn it to the ground and if human bones were discovered in the ashes, it was conceivable the police would believe that Valerie Maple had mysteriously returned home and committed a dramatic form of suicide.

Or they might be baffled to the point where they abandoned the investigation.

"It was Frank's last faint hope," Sarah said, "and—and like all his other hopes and plans, it failed too."

All of my own questions had been answered. Ned Havens stirred and sighed, and I knew he was thinking how strange and sad it was that throughout Sarah's father and Sarah's sweetheart had worked at cross purposes, neither one aware until the very end of the other's presence in the village.

Aunt Mildred rose to begin preparation for the evening meal. But it seemed she had a question left.

"Where did that woman hide the harp case?" she asked. "The police looked and looked and looked."

At that Sarah managed a wan smile. "You've forgotten, Mama. There was one place Sheriff Blandish wasn't allowed to look. Quite close to the Moran cottage. All the time the police were searching, the harp case was hidden in Harriet's woods."

"Well, I never!" cried Aunt Mildred. "And Harriet never once suspected! If that isn't Harriet Strings all over! Too busy tending to other people's business to pay very much to her own."

As though by signal, and certainly by instinct, two pairs of eyes flashed together. Ned Havens and his daughter looked at each other. When Uncle Ned threw off his blankets, and rose to throw a protecting arm around Sarah, I felt my own eyes fill with foolish tears. Sarah had lost a sweetheart who would never have become her husband—I now understood that, feeling as he did about his dreadful youth, Frank would always have remained a bachelor—but in losing her sweetheart, she had gained a father.

I walked out of the kitchen. Al followed. As husbands sometimes do, he misunderstood the tears.

"If you're worrying about our house, Janey dear," he said and drew me close, "about our ever living here, well you mustn't. Belton can sell out to the soonest comer. I'll tell him tomorrow."

"Indeed you won't," I said, through my own tears. "Frank wouldn't want that, and I don't either. Merristone is our home. We'll move into our house the minute Belton and Mr. Thirkle get it finished."

Well, those remarks were exchanged in the last week of January. It is now the middle of May. I've just had a note from Belton promising that our house will be definitely finished and, ready for occupancy the first day of June.

Directly I received the note, I sat down and telephoned my favorite seed house. I started to inquire into the price of roses, thought a bit, and eventually ordered two dozen hardy chrysanthemum plants!

THE END

www.ingramcontent.com/pod-product-compliance
Lightning Source LLC
Chambersburg PA
CBHW050327160726
48002CB00001B/210